Since it was founded in 1969, the Booker Prize has established itself as Britain's foremost literary award. Each October, for one dramatic night, the judges assemble at the Guildhall, London, to present their choice of best novel of the year. The list of winners – often challenging and controversial at the time – reads like a rollcall of great modern fiction.

From the beginning Jonathan Cape dominated the shortlist. It has won the prize no fewer than five times – more than any other publishing house. Now, to celebrate the Booker's twenty-fifth anniversary, Cape is proud to republish its five winners, *The Conservationist, Saville, Midnight's Children, Hotel du Lac* and *The Famished Road*, in a special anniversary edition. Each one is an enduring classic of fine writing and imagination.

THE FAMISHED ROAD

Azaro is a spirit child who is born only to live for a short while before returning to the idyllic world of his spirit companions. Now he has chosen to stay in the world of the living. This is his story.

'Ben Okri's beautifully written and moving novel combines fantasy and the vision of a child, the supernatural and the here-and-now to convey Nigerian peasant life in a changing world. It is the most ambitious as well as one of the most fully realised of this year's novels. It brings a distinctively black African way of writing and seeing things into the mainstream of European fiction'.

Jeremy Treglowan

'One of the truly great post-war novels.'
Harry Eyres, *The Times*

Ben Okri was born in Nigeria. His books have won several awards, including the Commonwealth Writers' Prize, the *Paris Review* Aga Khan prize for fiction, and the prestigious Premio Letterario Internazionale Chianti Ruffino-Antico Fattore. He lives in London.

by the same author

fiction

FLOWERS AND SHADOWS
THE LANDSCAPES WITHIN
INCIDENTS AT THE SHRINE
STARS OF THE NEW CURFEW
SONGS OF ENCHANTMENT

poetry

AN AFRICAN ELEGY

THE
FAMISHED ROAD

BEN OKRI

JONATHAN CAPE
LONDON

First published in this edition in 1993

1 3 5 7 9 10 8 6 4 2

© Ben Okri 1991

Ben Okri has asserted his right
under the Copyright, Designs and Patents Act 1988
to be identified as the author of this work

First published in the United Kingdom in this edition in 1993 by
Jonathan Cape
Random House, 20 Vauxhall Bridge Road, London SWIV 2SA

Random House Australia (Pty) Limited
20 Alfred Street, Milsons Point, Sydney,
New South Wales 2061, Australia

Random House New Zealand Limited
18 Poland Road, Glenfield,
Auckland 10, New Zealand

Random House South Africa (Pty) Limited
PO Box 337, Bergvlei, South Africa

Random House UK Limited Reg. No. 954009

A CIP catalogue record for this book
is available from the British Library

ISBN 0–224–03827–3

Printed and bound in Great Britain by
Mackays of Chatham PLC, Chatham, Kent

To Grace Okri, my mother and friend;
and to Rosemary Clunie

ACKNOWLEDGEMENTS

To Wole Soyinka and the Arts Council of Great Britain, for 1984;
To Harriet Sergeant and an unknown benefactor, for 1986;
And to David Godwin, for faith.

SECTION ONE

Book One

ONE

IN THE BEGINNING there was a river. The river became a road and the road branched out to the whole world. And because the road was once a river it was always hungry.

In that land of beginnings spirits mingled with the unborn. We could assume numerous forms. Many of us were birds. We knew no boundaries. There was much feasting, playing, and sorrowing. We feasted much because of the beautiful terrors of eternity. We played much because we were free. And we sorrowed much because there were always those amongst us who had just returned from the world of the Living. They had returned inconsolable for all the love they had left behind, all the suffering they hadn't redeemed, all that they hadn't understood, and for all that they had barely begun to learn before they were drawn back to the land of origins.

There was not one amongst us who looked forward to being born. We disliked the rigours of existence, the unfulfilled longings, the enshrined injustices of the world, the labyrinths of love, the ignorance of parents, the fact of dying, and the amazing indifference of the Living in the midst of the simple beauties of the universe. We feared the heartlessness of human beings, all of whom are born blind, few of whom ever learn to see.

Our king was a wonderful personage who sometimes appeared in the form of a great cat. He had a red beard and eyes of greenish sapphire. He had been born uncountable times and was a legend in all worlds, known by a hundred different names. It never mattered into what circumstances he was born. He always lived the most extraordinary of lives. One could pore over the great invisible books of lifetimes and recognise his genius through the recorded and unrecorded ages. Sometimes a man, sometimes a woman, he wrought incomparable achievements from every life. If there is anything common to all of his lives, the essence of his genius, it might well be the love of

3

transformation, and the transformation of love into higher realities.

With our spirit companions, the ones with whom we had a special affinity, we were happy most of the time because we floated on the aquamarine air of love. We played with the fauns, the fairies, and the beautiful beings. Tender sibyls, benign sprites, and the serene presences of our ancestors were always with us, bathing us in the radiance of their diverse rainbows. There are many reasons why babies cry when they are born, and one of them is the sudden separation from the world of pure dreams, where all things are made of enchantment, and where there is no suffering.

The happier we were, the closer was our birth. As we approached another incarnation we made pacts that we would return to the spirit world at the first opportunity. We made these vows in fields of intense flowers and in the sweet-tasting moonlight of that world. Those of us who made such vows were known among the Living as abiku, spirit-children. Not all people recognised us. We were the ones who kept coming and going, unwilling to come to terms with life. We had the ability to will our deaths. Our pacts were binding.

Those who broke their pacts were assailed by hallucinations and haunted by their companions. They would only find consolation when they returned to the world of the Unborn, the place of fountains, where their loved ones would be waiting for them silently.

Those of us who lingered in the world, seduced by the annunciation of wonderful events, went through life with beautiful and fated eyes, carrying within us the music of a lovely and tragic mythology. Our mouths utter obscure prophecies. Our minds are invaded by images of the future. We are the strange ones, with half of our beings always in the spirit world.

We were often recognised and our flesh marked with razor incisions. When we were born again to the same parents the marks, lingering on our new flesh, branded our souls in advance. Then the world would spin a web of fate around our lives. Those of us who died while still children tried to erase these marks, by making beauty spots or interesting discolorations of them. If we didn't succeed, and were recognised, we were greeted with howls of dread, and the weeping of mothers.

In not wanting to stay, we caused much pain to mothers. Their pain grew heavier with each return. Their anguish became for us an

4

added spiritual weight which quickens the cycle of rebirth. Each new birth was agony for us too, each shock of the raw world. Our cyclical rebellion made us resented by other spirits and ancestors. Disliked in the spirit world and branded amongst the Living, our unwillingness to stay affected all kinds of balances.

With passionate ritual offerings, our parents always tried to induce us to live. They also tried to get us to reveal where we had hidden the spirit tokens that bound us to the other world. We disdained the offerings and kept our tokens a fierce secret. And we remained indifferent to the long joyless parturition of mothers.

We longed for an early homecoming, to play by the river, in the grasslands, and in the magic caves. We longed to meditate on sunlight and precious stones, and to be joyful in the eternal dew of the spirit. To be born is to come into the world weighed down with strange gifts of the soul, with enigmas and an inextinguishable sense of exile. So it was with me.

How many times had I come and gone through the dreaded gateway? How many times had I been born and died young? And how often to the same parents? I had no idea. So much of the dust of living was in me. But this time, somewhere in the interspace between the spirit world and the Living, I chose to stay. This meant breaking my pact and outwitting my companions. It wasn't because of the sacrifices, the burnt offerings of oils and yams and palm-nuts, or the blandishments, the short-lived promises of special treatment, or even because of the grief I had caused. It wasn't because of my horror of recognition either. Apart from a mark on my palm I had managed to avoid being discovered. It may simply have been that I had grown tired of coming and going. It is terrible to forever remain in-between. It may also have been that I wanted to taste of this world, to feel it, suffer it, know it, to love it, to make a valuable contribution to it, and to have that sublime mood of eternity in me as I live the life to come. But I sometimes think it was a face that made me want to stay. I wanted to make happy the bruised face of the woman who would become my mother.

When the time arrived for the ceremonies of birth to begin, the fields at the crossroads were brilliant with lovely presences and iridescent beings. Our king led us to the first peak of the seven mountains. He spoke to us for a long time in silence. His cryptic words took flame in us. He loved speeches. With great severity, his sapphire eyes glowing, he said to me:

'You are a mischievous one. You will cause no end of trouble. You have to travel many roads before you find the river of your destiny. This life of yours will be full of riddles. You will be protected and you will never be alone.'

We all went down to the great valley. It was an immemorial day of festivals. Wondrous spirits danced around us to the music of gods, uttering golden chants and lapis lazuli incantations to protect our souls across the interspaces and to prepare us for our first contact with blood and earth. Each one of us made the passage alone. Alone, we had to survive the crossing – survive the flames and the sea, the emergence into illusions. The exile had begun.

These are the myths of beginnings. These are stories and moods deep in those who are seeded in rich lands, who still believe in mysteries.

I was born not just because I had conceived a notion to stay, but because in between my coming and going the great cycles of time had finally tightened around my neck. I prayed for laughter, a life without hunger. I was answered with paradoxes. It remains an enigma how it came to be that I was born smiling.

TWO

ONE OF THE reasons I didn't want to be born became clear to me after I had come into the world. I was still very young when in a daze I saw Dad swallowed up by a hole in the road. Another time I saw Mum dangling from the branches of a blue tree. I was seven years old when I dreamt that my hands were covered with the yellow blood of a stranger. I had no idea whether these images belonged to this life, or to a previous one, or to one that was yet to come, or even if they were merely the host of images that invades the minds of all children.

When I was very young I had a clear memory of my life stretching to other lives. There were no distinctions. Sometimes I seemed to be living several lives at once. One lifetime flowed into the others and all of them flowed into my childhood.

As a child I felt I weighed my mother down. In turn I felt weighed down by the inscrutability of life. Being born was a shock from which I never recovered. Often, by night or day, voices spoke to me. I came to realise that they were the voices of my spirit companions.

'What are you doing here?' one of them would ask.

'Living,' I would reply.

'Living for what?'

'I don't know.'

'Why don't you know? Haven't you seen what lies ahead of you?'

'No.'

Then they showed me images which I couldn't understand. They showed me a prison, a woman covered with golden boils, a long road, pitiless sunlight, a flood, an earthquake, death.

'Come back to us,' they said. 'We miss you by the river. You have deserted us. If you don't come back we will make your life unbearable.'

I would start shouting, daring them to do their worst. On one of these occasions Mum came into the room and stood watching me. When I noticed her I became silent. Her eyes were bright. She came over, hit me on the head, and said:

'Who are you talking to?'

'No one,' I replied.

She gave me a long stare. I don't remember how old I was at the time. Afterwards my spirit companions took great delight getting me into trouble. I often found myself oscillating between both worlds. One day I was playing on the sand when they called me from across the road with the voice of my mother. As I went towards the voice a car almost ran me over. Another day they enticed me with sweet songs towards a gutter. I fell in and no one noticed and it was only by good fortune that a bicyclist saw me thrashing about in the filthy water and saved me from drowning.

I was ill afterwards and spent most of the time in the other world trying to reason with my spirit companions, trying to get them to leave me alone. What I didn't know was that the longer they kept me there, the more certain they were making my death. It was only much later, when I tried to get back into my body and couldn't, that I realised they had managed to shut me out of my life. I cried for a long time into the silver void till our great king interceded for me and reopened the gates of my body.

When I woke up I found myself in a coffin. My parents had given me up for dead. They had commenced the burial proceedings when they heard my fierce weeping. Because of my miraculous recovery they named me a second time and threw a party which they couldn't afford. They named me Lazaro. But as I became the subject of much jest, and as many were uneasy with the connection between Lazaro and Lazarus, Mum shortened my name to Azaro.

I learnt afterwards that I had lingered between not dying and not living for two weeks. I learnt that I exhausted the energy and finances of my parents. I also learnt that a herbalist had been summoned. He confessed to not being able to do anything about my condition, but after casting his cowries, and deciphering their signs, he said:

'This is a child who didn't want to be born, but who will fight with death.'

He added that, if I recovered, my parents should immediately perform a ceremony that would sever my connections with the spirit world. He was the first to call me by that name which spreads horror amongst mothers. He told them that I had hidden my special tokens of spirit identity on this earth and till they were found I would go

8

on falling ill and that it was almost certain that I would die before the age of twenty-one.

When I recovered, however, my parents had already spent too much money on me. They were in debt. And my father, who was rather fed up with all the trouble I brought, had grown somewhat sceptical of the pronouncements and certitudes of herbalists. If you listen to everything they say, he told Mum, you will have to perform absurd sacrifices every time you step outside your door. He was also suspicious of their penchant for advocating costly ceremonies, the way quack doctors keep multiplying the ramifications of ailments in order to make you spend fortunes on their medicines.

Neither Mum nor Dad could afford another ceremony. And anyway they did not really want to believe that I was a spirit-child. And so time passed and the ceremony was never performed. I was happy. I didn't want it performed. I didn't want to entirely lose contact with that other world of light and rainbows and possibilities. I had buried my secrets early. I buried them in moonlight, the air alive with white moths. I buried my magic stones, my mirror, my special promises, my golden threads, objects of identity that connected me to the world of spirits. I buried them all in a secret place, which I promptly forgot.

In the early years Mum was quite proud of me.

'You are a child of miracles,' she would say. 'Many powers are on your side.'

For as long as my cord to other worlds remained intact, for as long as my objects were not found, this might continue to be true.

As a child I could read people's minds. I could foretell their futures. Accidents happened in places I had just left. One night I was standing in the street with Mum when a voice said:

'Cross over.'

I tugged Mum across the street and a few moments later an articulated lorry plunged into the house we had been standing in front of and killed an entire family.

On another night I was asleep when the great king stared down at me. I woke up, ran out of the room, and up the road. My parents came after me. They were dragging me back when we discovered that the compound was burning. On that night our lives changed.

The road woke up. Men and women, all in wrappers, sleep-marks on their faces, blackened lamps in their hands, crowded

9

outside. There was no electricity in our area. The lamps, held above the heads, illuminated the strange-eyed moths, casting such a spectral glow over the disembodied faces that I felt I was again among spirits. One world contains glimpses of others.

It was a night of fires. An owl flew low over the burning compound. The air was full of cries. The tenants rushed back and forth with buckets of water from the nearest well. Gradually, the flames died down. Whole families stayed out in the night, huddled amongst the ragged ends of their clothes and mattresses. There was much wailing for lost property. No one had died.

When it was so dark that one couldn't see the far corners of the sky and the forest lacked all definition, the landlord turned up and immediately started ranting. He threw himself on the ground. Rolling and thrashing, he unleashed a violent torrent of curses on us. He screamed that we had deliberately set his compound on fire to avoid paying the recently increased rent.

'How am I going to get the money to rebuild the house?' he wailed, working himself into a deaf fury.

'All of you must pay for the damages!' he screeched.

No one paid him any attention. Our main priority was to find new accommodations. We gathered our possessions and made preparations to move.

'Everyone must stay here!' the landlord said, screaming in the dark.

He hurried away and returned an hour later with three policemen. They fell on us and flogged us with whips and cracked our skulls with batons. We fought them back. We beat them with sticks and ropes. We tore their colonial uniforms and sent them packing. They came back with reinforcements. Dad lured two of them down a side street and gave them a severe thrashing. More came at him. He was such a dervish of fury that it took six policemen to subdue him and bundle him off to the police station.

The reinforcements meanwhile lashed out at everything in sight, unleashing mayhem in a drunken fever. When they had finished fifteen men, three children, four women, two goats and a dog lay wounded along the battleground of our area. That was how the riot started.

Deep in the night it started to rain and it poured down steadily while the ghetto-dwellers raged. The rain didn't last long but it turned the tracks into mud. It watered our fury. Chanting ancient war-songs, brandishing pikes and machetes, gangs materialised in the darkness. They stamped through the mud. At the main road, they fell on cars and buses. They attacked police vehicles. They looted shops. Then everyone began looting, burning, and overturning things. Mum, carrying me, was driven on by the frantic crowd. Along the main road she put me down in order to tighten her wrapper, in full preparation for the worst, when a caterwauling mass of people came pounding towards us. They ran right between us. They separated me from my mother.

I wandered through the violent terrain, listening to the laughter of mischievous spirits. There was a crescent moon in the sky, darkness over the houses, broken bottles and splintered wood on the road. I wandered barefoot. Fires sprouted over rubbish heaps, men were dragged out of cars, thick smoke billowed from houses. Stumbling along, looking for Mum, I found myself in a dark street. There was a solitary candle burning on a stand near an abandoned house. I heard a deep chanting that made the street tremble. Shadows stormed past, giving off a stench of sweat and rage. Drums vibrated in the air. A cat cried out as if it had been thrown on to a fire. Then a gigantic Masquerade burst out of the road, with plumes of smoke billowing from its head. I gave a frightened cry and hid behind a stall. The Masquerade was terrifying and fiery, its funereal roar filled the street with an ancient silence. I watched it in horror. I watched it by its shadow of a great tree burning, as it danced in the empty street.

Then the darkness filled with its attendants. They were stout men with glistening faces. They held on to the luminous ropes attached to the towering figure. Dancing wildly, it dragged them towards the rioting. When it strode past, sundering the air, I crept out of my hiding place. Swirling with hallucinations, I started back towards the main road. Then suddenly several women, smelling of bitter herbs, appeared out of the darkness. They bore down on me, and swooped me up into the bristling night.

THREE

THE WOMEN BOUNDED down the streets. One had a
black sack, another wore glasses, a third wore boots. No one touched
them or even seemed to notice them. They ran through the disturbance
as if they were shadows or visitors from another realm. I didn't utter a
sound.

It was only when they stopped at a crossroad and placed shining
white eggs on the ground, that I noticed they all wore white smocks.
Their faces were veiled. The veils had holes through which I could
barely see their eyes. After they had made their offering at the crossroad they bounded on through the streets, past scenes of rioting, and
into the forest. They ran through pitch darkness, through silence and
mists, and into another reality in which the gigantic Masquerade
was riding a white horse. The horse had jagged teeth and its eyes
were diamond bright. There was a piercing cry in the air. When
the Masquerade and the white horse vanished, I noticed that the
forest swarmed with unearthly beings. It was like an overcrowded
marketplace. Many of them had red lights in their eyes, wisps of
saffron smoke came out of their ears, and gentle green fires burned
on their heads. Some were tall, others were short; some were wide,
others were thin. They moved slowly. They were so numerous that
they interpenetrated one another. The women ran through these
beings without any fear.

We passed gangs of men who were carrying home their loot.
We passed a woman who sat at the foot of a tree, bleeding from
the side of her head. The women took her with them. I listened to
her groans of agony till we stopped at the edge of a river, where
there was a canoe waiting. Before I could do anything the women
bundled me in, clambered on, and rowed us across to an island that
wasn't far away. They rowed in complete serenity as I tried to resist.
When I began to rock the canoe, they pressed me down with their
rough feet and smothered me with their capacious smocks.

We arrived at the island and the woman with glasses lifted me out of the canoe, and led me to a hut. It was really a bathroom. She made me wash. When she had dried me with a coarse towel, she smeared me all over with oils. She led me to the shrinehouse and spread me out on a mat. I tried not to sleep that night and tried not to move either, for even in the darkness all the statues seemed to be alive. The images seemed to breathe, to be watching my every movement, to be listening to my thoughts.

In the morning I found myself in an empty room. I got up and before I could get to the door, the women came in. They had powerful eyes. They were completely silent and they stared at me imploringly, as if it were in my power to save their lives.

With a gentleness that surprised me, they led me to a lovely house and laid out many choice dishes before me. They gathered round and watched as I ate. When I had finished they dressed me in a spotless robe of material so soft and white that I felt I had been wrapped in a cloud. They touched me tenderly and left the room. I went out of the house and wandered round the island in a white enchantment.

The wind blew spells over the sea. The soft white sand teemed with riddles. I went past the shrinehouse and gazed out over the waves. On my way back I came upon the goddess of the island. She was an image with a beautiful face and eyes of marble that glittered in the sun. All around her feet were metal gongs, kola nuts, kaoline, feathers of eagles and peacocks, bones of animals and bones too big to belong to animals. In a complete circle round her were white eggs on black saucers. Her mighty and wondrous pregnancy faced the sea.

At night the eyes of the goddess shone like moonstones. The sea-wind, streaming through her raffia hair, produced a haunting melody. At night I heard her piercing, ecstatic cries. I slipped out. Her magnificent pregnancy was so startling against the immense sea that she could have been giving birth to a god or to a new world.

I was asleep in the shrinehouse, among the sentient figures, when the noise of gongs woke me up. I looked out of the door and saw the women, all in white, doing an enchanted dance round their goddess. I was watching them, in the dark, when something moved behind me. Silently, from amongst the images, a cat came towards me. It sat at my feet, gazing at me with jewelled eyes. I stroked its fur. A voice said:

'Are you a fool?'

I spun round. Apart from the watchful statues, I saw no one. I stroked the cat again. The voice said:

13

'Why hasn't the goddess given birth yet?'

'I don't know,' I replied, without moving.

'Because she hasn't found a child to give birth to. If you're not careful you will be born a second time tonight.'

When it occurred to me that sometimes I could understand the language of animals, I woke from my enchantment, into the full awareness of my danger. Then I heard low groans. In another corner of the room, hidden in the darkness, her foot twitching in dreams of flight, I discovered the woman who had been wounded during the riots. I shook her awake. She opened her dazed eyes at me.

'My son,' she said.

'They are going to do something to me,' I said.

She stared at me impassively.

'My mother will not like it,' I added.

She began weeping. She wouldn't stop. She too had lost a son during the rioting.

'Let's escape,' I suggested.

She stopped weeping. She got up slowly. We crept out of the shrinehouse, towards the canoe. We were rowing across the water when a strangled cry rose from the shrinehouse and gathered volume all over the island. The wind whipped the cries round the raffia hair of the goddess. Waves lashed the canoe. We rowed with great desperation over the turbulent waters. We were half-way across when the women abandoned their ritual and came after us.

Her face bruised, her eyes droopy in the moonlight, the wounded woman rowed like a hero. But the effort was too much for her and as our canoe was driven ashore, she collapsed altogether. I tried to revive her with salt water, but she only groaned in profound resignation.

'My son, my son,' was all she said.

There was nothing I could do. The canoes furiously approached the shore. I muttered a prayer for her and ran and didn't stop till I had completely escaped from that cult of silent women.

FOUR

THAT NIGHT I slept under a lorry. In the morning I wandered up and down the streets of the city. Houses were big, vehicles thundered everywhere, and people stared at me. I became aware of my hunger when I came to a marketplace and saw the bean cakes, ripe fruits and dried fishes, and smelt the fried plantain. I went from stall to stall, staring at the traders. Many of them drove me away. But at a provision stall a man with a severe face regarded me and said:

'Are you hungry?'

I nodded. He gave me a loaf of bread. He had only four fingers, with a thumb missing. I thanked him and roamed the market till I found a barrel on which I sat down and ate.

I watched crowds of people pour into the marketplace. I watched the chaotic movements and the wild exchanges and the load-carriers staggering under sacks. It seemed as if the whole world was there. I saw people of all shapes and sizes, mountainous women with faces of iroko, midgets with faces of stone, reedy women with twins strapped to their backs, thick-set men with bulging shoulder muscles. After a while I felt a sort of vertigo just looking at anything that moved. Stray dogs, chickens flapping in cages, goats with listless eyes, hurt me to look at them. I shut my eyes and when I opened them again I saw people who walked backwards, a dwarf who got about on two fingers, men upside-down with baskets of fish on their feet, women who had breasts on their backs, babies strapped to their chests, and beautiful children with three arms. I saw a girl amongst them who had eyes at the side of her face, bangles of blue copper round her neck, and who was more lovely than forest flowers. I was so afraid that I got down from the barrel and started to move away when the girl pointed and cried:

'That boy can see us!'

They turned in my direction. I looked away immediately and hurried away from the swelling marketplace, towards the street.

They followed me. One of the men had red wings on his feet and a girl had fish-gills round her neck. I could hear their nasal whisperings. They stayed close to me to find out if I really could see them. And when I refused to see them, when I concentrated on the piles of red peppers wrinkled by the sun, they crowded me and blocked my way. I went right through them as if they weren't there. I stared hard at the crabs clawing the edges of flower-patterned basins. After a while they left me alone. That was the first time I realised it wasn't just humans who came to the marketplaces of the world. Spirits and other beings come there too. They buy and sell, browse and investigate. They wander amongst the fruits of the earth and sea.

I wound my way to another part of the market. I didn't stare at the people who floated above the ground or those with the burden of bulbous heads and blond hair, but I became curious about where they had come from. I took to following those that were departing from the market and were heading home because they had done all their buying or selling, or had gotten tired of observing the interesting man-made artefacts of the world. I followed them across streets, narrow paths, and isolated tracks. All the time I pretended not to see them.

When they got to a wide clearing in the forest they said their bizarre farewells and went their different ways. Many of them were quite fearful to look at. Many were quite cute. A good number of them were somewhat ugly, but after a while even their ugliness became normal. I chose to follow a baby spirit with the face of a squirrel, who dragged a great sack. Its companions conversed amongst themselves, laughing in throatless undertones as they went along. One had yellow webbed feet, another the tail of a tiny crocodile, and the most interesting had the eyes of a dolphin.

The clearing was the beginning of an expressway. Building companies had levelled the trees. In places the earth was red. We passed a tree that had been felled. Red liquid dripped from its stump as if the tree had been a murdered giant whose blood wouldn't stop flowing. The baby spirits went to the edge of the clearing where there was a gash in the earth. As I stared into the gash I heard a sharp noise, as of something sundering, and I shut my eyes in horror, and when I opened them I found myself somewhere else. The spirits had disappeared. I began shouting. My voice reverberated in the murky air. After a while I noticed a giant turtle beside me. It lifted up a lazy head, stared at me as if I had disturbed its sleep, and said:

'Why are you shouting?'

16

'I'm lost.'

'What does that mean?'

'I don't know where I am.'

'You are in the under-road.'

'Where is that?'

'The stomach of the road.'

'Does the road have a stomach?'

'Does the sea have a mouth?'

'I don't know.'

'That's your business.'

'I want to go home.'

'I don't know where your home is,' the turtle said, 'so I can't help you.'

Then it lumbered away. I lay down on the white earth of that land and cried myself to sleep. When I woke up I found myself in a pit from which sand was excavated for the building of the road. I climbed out and fled through the forest.

Hugging what was left of my bread, I went down the streets. At a junction I asked a food-seller for water. She gave me some in a blue cup. I ate of the bread and drank slowly of the water. There was a man standing near me. I noticed him because of his smell. He wore a dirty, tattered shirt. His hair was reddish. Flies were noisy around his ears. His private parts showed through his underpants. His legs were covered in sores. The flies around his face made him look as if he had four eyes. I stared at him out of curiosity. He made a violent motion, scattering the flies, and I noticed that his two eyes rolled around as if in an extraordinary effort to see themselves. I became aware of him staring at me too and I finished the water, wrapped up the bread, and hurried off. I didn't look back, but I became certain that he was following me. I could hear the peculiar dialogue of the flies around his ears. I could smell his insanity.

When I walked faster he quickened his steps, ranting. I went through a compound, came out at the housefront, and found him there, waiting. He pursued me, raving in grotesque languages. I tore across the road, through the market, and hid behind a lorry. He dogged my shadow. I felt him as a terrible presence from whom I couldn't escape. In desperation I shot across another road. The hooting of a monster hulk of a lorry scared me and I dropped the loaf of bread and dashed over, my heart wildly fluttering in my chest. When I was safely across I looked back and saw the man in the middle of the road. He had snatched up my loaf of bread and was eating it, polythene wrapping and all. Cars screeched all around him. I carried on running for fear that he might suddenly remember he had been pursuing me.

After a while I got to a familiar street. I had broken the spell of the man's obsession with my shadow. In the heated air of my bewilderment, I tried to understand what was familiar about the area. There were sweet voices of children in the air. I smelt rose blossoms from the garbage. The gutter gave off an aroma of incense. The houses were covered with dust. And yet in the night spaces white birds flew over trees. I kept expecting to recognise something. And when the spaces in the street began to expand, as if sunlight were being released from the objects, transfiguring the area into an expanse of sacred fields, I realised with a shock that it was the strangeness which was so familiar. And then, with my breath quickening, and with moonlight breaking out on the street, I recognised the voices of the children that sang in an intense blue chorus all around me. They were the twilight voices of my spirit companions, luring me to the world of dreams, away from this world where no one cared about me, enticing me to a world where I would never be lost.

The moonlight of their voices became too multiple and too sweet for me to bear. I felt myself breaking out into another space. Everywhere I looked the spirits invaded me with their manifestations. The smell of flowers overpowered me. The songs wounded me with their relentless beauty. Seared by the agony of their melodies, I stumbled across a road and I suddenly saw them all, spirits in full bloom on a field of rainbows, bathing in the ecstasy of an everlasting love. Something sharp tore through my brain. I collapsed on the flowering tarmac, with lorries thundering around me.

FIVE

I WAS TAKEN to a police station. Afterwards I was carried to a hospital where my wounds were treated. When I was discharged a police officer volunteered to look after me till my parents had been found. He was a hulk of a man with a big forehead and hairy nostrils. He drove me to his home in a white car. His wife was lean and tall. She reminded me of the island women and had a complexion like the evening. She made me bathe and dressed me in her son's clothes. We ate a wonderful dish of stew flavoured with shrimps and meat. The rice had a faint aroma of cinnamon. The fried plantain smelt of wild herbs. The fried chicken tasted of delicious spells.

The living room where we ate was very spacious and comfortable. The carpets were thick, and there were framed diplomas on the blue walls. Above a painting of Jesus with his large visible heart, arms outstretched, was the legend:

CHRIST IS THE UNSEEN GUEST IN EVERY HOUSE

There were pictures of the police officer, his wife, and a handsome boy who had sad eyes. The boy looked at me while I ate. After a while I began to see with the boy's eyes and the house resolved about me and I knew that he was dead and I lost my appetite and didn't eat any more.

After dinner the woman showed me to my room. I was frightened to have a whole room to myself. When she shut the door behind her, I realised that it was her son's room. His toys, his school texts, and even his shoes had been neatly preserved. Photographs of him at play hung on the walls. That night I couldn't sleep. There were inhuman footsteps all over the house. In the backyard a cat wailed. And later, in the dark, someone whose complexion was of the night came into the room and kept touching the photographs and rattling the toys. I couldn't see who it was, but when they left I heard the soft tinkling of bells. It was only when dawn broke that I got any sleep.

I stayed in the policeman's house for several days. His wife's eyes were always large with unfinished weeping. I gathered from their nocturnal whisperings that their son had died in a road accident. She treated me well most of the time. She made me lovely bean cakes and vegetable dishes. After a bath she would comb my hair and oil my face. She sang to me while she swept the sitting room or washed the clothes. I sometimes helped her with the cleaning. We dusted the centre table and the glass cabinet with its crystal elephants and tortoises and ceramic plates. We also polished the big mask on the wall. She always dressed me in her son's finest clothes. I only became scared of her when she started calling me by his name.

The noises in the house got worse the following night. I heard someone wandering around as if they were imprisoned. The glass cabinet shifted. The faint bells tinkled. Birds broke into song near my window. In the morning the police officer gave me some pocket money. His wife spoke gently to me, served me food, and watched me eat. In the afternoon the house was silent. The woman wasn't in. All the doors were locked. I slept on a sofa in the living room and woke up with the feeling that I wasn't alone in the house. I was hungry. I felt dizzy. As I wandered about the house looking for an open door, a curious presence entered into me. I couldn't shake it out. It roamed around inside me and said things to me which I couldn't understand. It wasn't long before I felt myself entirely occupied by an unhappy spirit.

I did everything I could to drive the spirit out of me. I kicked and thrashed and screamed. I ran against the walls. After a while I saw myself on the floor, bleeding from the mouth. Something rose out of me and began talking to the room. The woman was standing over me. The spirit that had come out of me was talking to her, but she couldn't hear.

The woman carried me to my room. When I woke up in the evening I felt very ill. I had no idea who I was and even my thoughts seemed to belong to someone else. The disconsolate spirit had left empty places inside me. I slept through the evening, the night, and got up the next afternoon. I hadn't eaten for two days. I had no appetite. With no desire to do anything, I drifted on the white waves of exhaustion.

That night, while I lay on the bed, the door opened. The police officer, his wife, and a herbalist came into the room. I pretended to be asleep. The herbalist had a luminous machete. They talked about me in whispers. After a while they left. Beside my bed there was a bowl of rice and chicken, which I devoured. After I had eaten, and felt a little better, I began to plot my escape.

I listened to all the sounds of the house. There were voices everywhere. I heard the air whispering, the walls talking, the chair complaining, the floor pacing, the insects gossiping. Darkness filled the room. Figures moved about in the darkness. I saw yellow beings stirring, white forms floating, blue shadows flying about the ceiling. But when I heard people talking everything around me became silent and still. I waited. Then I stole out towards the sitting room to listen.

SIX

THERE WAS SILENCE. A hurricane lantern burned low on the dining table, its bluish light creating shadows everywhere. Lower down, seven figures were seated round the centre table. A moth circled them. The eighth figure stood without moving. Soon I made him out to be the police officer. He was in charge of the proceedings.

The longer I looked, the clearer the murky atmosphere became. There were eight glasses on the centre table, dazzling where the bluish light touched them. I made out a half calabash, tilting with its liquid contents. Next to the calabash was a white saucer with lobes of kola-nut and fingers of kaoline. And next to the saucer was the image of a little feathered goddess.

With a deep chanting that altered the air in the room, the police officer made the figures rise. The faint lights showed them up to be policemen in uniforms. They took up the chanting in low tones. Then they stretched out their hands and linked them across the table. When the men sat back down, the officer remained standing.

The flies buzzed. The officer waved the fetish in the air. It had emerald snakelike eyes which glittered in the muted lights. The officer said something and the first of the seven figures got up. He became a man with small eyes and a thin moustache. He sweated nervously along the nose. Trembling slightly, he held the image. Then in a tone of sudden vehemence, he swore an oath of allegiance. The moth circled his head. He swore that under the terrible gaze of the goddess, and under the threat of death, he was honest about the money he had collected, and which he was now presenting.

The seated figures broke into a frightening chant. When they stopped, the first man, sweating intensely in the hot room, broke off a bit of kaoline, chewed some, and marked his forehead with the rest. In a tremulous voice he said that if he had betrayed his oath in any way he should be run over by a lorry. He made a guttural sound. He consecrated his statement by drinking of the potion in the calabash. He brought out the money he had collected, and placed it on the table. Then he sat back into the semi-darkness, and became a figure again.

The police officer counted the money with infinite patience. He grunted, stared at the first man, gave him his share, put some under the saucer, and kept the rest. The ritual was repeated with all the men. The moth circled them the whole time. The second man swore his oath, presented his money briskly, and sat. The third man was huge – broad, big-bellied, with a piercing voice, and dull eyes which roved over the room. The fourth was fat, good-humoured, and he made a joke or two, which was received in stern silence. He completed his oath by brandishing a red knife. With discernible reluctance, he presented his money. The fifth man was smallish and had a grating voice. His oath was an interminable improvisation on the theme of his honesty. Swearing to innumerable gods, uttering the names of secret shrines, he shouted that the deities should kill his only son if he was lying. The police officer flinched. The fifth man sat down.

The sixth man was thin, tall, and dignified. He didn't sweat. The moth didn't circle him as he enacted his ritual, and the lamp brightened perceptibly when he ended his chant. When the next figure rose a noise sounded behind me, and I hid. Nothing happened. I went back to watching the scene, fascinated that the moth had alighted on the forehead of the seventh man. All through his oath, sweating furiously, he did nothing to get rid of it. He swore his allegiance in an intense mood. And while he was drinking of the potion, swearing his eternal honesty, a photograph of the police officer's son crashed to the floor. The glass didn't break in the frame. The hurricane lamp flickered, grew in illumination, and I watched the moth beating its wings against the hot glass. The other figures stared silently at the seventh man. In an unshaken voice, he went on with his oath, while placing his money on the table. Then suddenly, without completing his oath, he put on his cap, and left the house.

The ceremony proceeded as if nothing odd had taken place. The men drank heavily, talked in whispers, improvised songs, and danced vigorously. When the meeting ended, they put on their caps, made their fraternal greetings, and stumbled out of the house in drunken merriment.

I went back to my room. I waited for the last of them to leave. And then I waited for silence. When the silence came I crept out

23

to the sitting room. The police officer was sprawled in an armchair, his shirt soaked through with sweat. There was a fleck of foam at the corner of his mouth. A fly alighted on his lower lip, wringing its spindly arms, drinking of his sleep.

The room stank of sweat and khaki, blood and feathers, ash and fear. The moth had made of itself a burnt offering. Blood had stained the table. Bundles of notes showed from the shirt pocket of the police officer's uniform. The feathered goddess was now on a nail above the door, directly opposite the picture of Christ and the legend.

The police officer snored. I tiptoed past him, opened the front door quietly, and stepped out into the night. I began to move away when my legs brushed against something hairy. Managing to hold back my scream, I found myself staring into the luminous eyes of a white dog. The dog regarded me for a long time as though it were in two minds whether to raise an alarm. I made a friendly sign, went back into the house and, creeping past the sleeping form of the police officer, slid into my room.

I stayed in bed and didn't sleep. I tried to interpret all the noises of the house. I heard voices in the wall saying that a victim was awaiting its sacrifice. In the morning the police officer told his wife to keep the doors locked at all times. In the afternoon she went out. She stayed a long time. When she returned I heard her in the kitchen. After a while she brought a plate of beans and fried plantain and left it outside my door. I took it in but didn't eat. My hunger got so great that I became dizzy. Throughout the afternoon and evening I suffered the tormenting mockery of my spirit companions. When I couldn't bear my hunger any more I brought out the plate and was about to eat when a bad smell wafted up from the food. I found a newspaper, poured the food between its pages, hid the wrapping, and left the empty plate outside the door.

That night, in the dark, with my eyes pressed tight, and with all the fury of my empty stomach, I summoned up the image of my mother. When I saw her very clearly, I spoke to her, begging her to come and save me. After I had spoken to her I fell asleep, certain that she had heard me.

SEVEN

I HEARD SOMETHING rattling the roof. It had started to rain. The wind beat against a window. I got out of bed, crazed with hunger. I sat on the floor, huddled in the dark, and when there was a knock I didn't even move. The door opened and a giant figure said:

'Come and eat with us.'

Mesmerised by hunger, I followed the man to the dining table. I sat down morosely and stared at the flies singing over the food. The police officer's wife filled my plate with generous quantities of pounded yam, choice selections of goat meat, and soup rich in vegetables. The food smelt wonderful and the steam from the bowl occupied the room with its tomato and oregano seasonings. My hunger made the world seem bluish. For the first time I understood the atmosphere of the house, I understood why the spirit had entered me. When I blinked I saw ghosts around the police officer and his wife. They were all over the room. The ghosts were tall and silent and some had weak beards. An incubus with white wings hovered near the window. I blinked again and saw a spirit with eight fingers and a single twinkling eye. Another, in a policeman's uniform, had an amputated foot. He ate of the food with bloodstained hands a moment before the officer did. A ghost, existing as only a pair of milk-white legs, balanced on the head of the woman. A homunculus which looked like a yellow plant danced on the food. I must have been staring at them in astonishment for the officer suddenly said:

'What are you staring at?'

I shook my head. Then I noticed that in a corner, across from where they ate with such innocent relish, sitting forlorn and abandoned, was the ghost of their son. He had lost both his arms, one side of his face was squashed, and both his eyes had burst. He had bluish wings. He was the saddest ghost in the house.

'Nothing,' I said.

They looked at one another, and then at me. I couldn't bring

25

myself to eat after seeing the ghosts play with the food with their bloodied hands. I sat and stared at the flies.

When they had finished eating they got up from the table. The man went to the armchair and his wife brought him a large bottle of Guinness, which he drank with both feet on a stool. His wife joined him. I listened to the ticking of the grandfather clock in the silent house. The ghosts gathered round the man and wife and stared at them in silent amazement. The spirit with the twinkling eye drank the froth of the Guinness a moment before the officer did. The officer drank contentedly. When his wife got up to fetch a soft drink for herself, the ghost with milk-white legs went with her. When the officer went to the toilet the spirit in uniform accompanied him. And when they were sitting peacefully the ghosts stood in front of them so close that their faces almost touched. The ghosts were silent, and did nothing.

The grandfather clock chimed. I realised that the ghosts and spirits were in the house because the officer had somehow been responsible for their deaths. I hurried to my room, shut the door and lay in the dark, staring at the ceiling. When the clock stopped chiming, an orange light suddenly shot through my brain and the darkness became faintly illuminated and I saw the disconsolate ghost of the boy in a corner of the room. After a while it got up and floated towards me and stared down with its burst eyes and lay just above me, its wings stirring the air. I felt oppressed. I couldn't breathe and couldn't move. It was impossible to sleep and when I managed to shut my eyes I had the horrible feeling that a heavy form was pressing down on me, compacting itself into my body. I couldn't scream and I struggled in vain. The walls in the house began to whisper about the seventh man and of how he had been run over by a lorry while directing traffic.

As the form pressed itself into me, it began to rain outside and I became calm. It rained steadily. The wind kept rattling the corrugated roof and driving in water through gaps in the window frame. It got cold. I turned and faced the wall. When I realised I could move I got up and sat on the bed. The ghost of the boy was up on the ceiling, like a perpetual bluish haze. Thunder growled above the house and lightning cracked. The rain poured down and the wind, faintly howling, banged away at the window. Lightning struck again. It seemed intent on the house. The whole place, the window and the room, lit up in a candent flash. After a while I smelt smoke drifting in from under the door.

The smoke filled the room and I began to cough and when I ran out I was barely able to see. The smoke was very thick and when I made it to the kitchen, coughing and smarting in the eyes, I discovered that the place was on fire. I banged on the doors and the officer came out, his stomach sagging, his eyes red.

'There's fire in the kitchen,' I cried.

As we fought the fire with buckets of water, the ghosts stood around watching us. The woman kept weeping. The man cursed. The rain intensified. The kitchen became thoroughly wet. Rain poured in under the sitting room door and soaked the carpet. The wind broke a window and slugs and hairy caterpillars were blown in. Little snails appeared on the walls. Thunder clapped outside. Inside, the ghost of the boy wandered around the house, wandered right through his parents, without recognising them, and without being affected by their distress.

After we had successfully fought the fire and mopped the soaking floor, everyone went back to bed. I heard them tossing and whispering all night. I didn't sleep. In the early hours of the morning, before dawn had broken, and when night was beginning to change mood, there were urgent knocks on the door. The door shook and the banging became so wild and erratic it seemed as if the wind and thunder wanted to be let in. I hurried out of my room, towards the door, but the man got there before me. I moved closer. There was a woman standing in the doorway, her hair bedraggled and wet, her eyes distracted, her neck strung, her feet bare. The rain poured down on her mercilessly. There were dead cockroaches about her feet. I saw a rope round her neck, connecting her to the sky. The rope transformed into a thread of lightning. For a moment I thought I had known her in another life or in the world of spirits. I pushed past the officer. I stood on the threshold. Then, with light in my head, and hunger in my voice, I cried:

'Mother!'

At first she didn't move. She didn't seem to recognise me. She stared at me with empty eyes. After a short silence she suddenly dropped all the things she had been carrying, and embraced me, without uttering a sound. Then she lifted me up into the air and held me tightly to her warm, wet body.

EIGHT

I WAS AWOKEN by voices in the dark. I was on Mum's shoulder and I saw faces of women in the rain, faces lit up by lightning flash. They crowded us, arms outstretched, eyes warm. We were surrounded on all sides. The women touched me and looked at me as if I were a wonderful thing that had fallen from the sky. They fondled my hair, rubbed my skin, and felt my bones as if, in being lost and found, I belonged to all of them. I had brought with me a new hope. They too became reasons for staying on this earth, to sometimes taste the joys of homecoming.

Mum put me down. My legs were weak. Everything looked strange. Our new compound looked very odd indeed. I walked on shaky feet, staggering, and Mum took my hand and steadied me. Then she led me to a room, opened the front door and, pointing, said:

'Your father is waiting for you.'

There was a man asleep on the chair. I didn't recognise him. He had a bandage round his head and his left arm was in a dirty sling. He was unshaven and his bare chest heaved as he snored. The room was very small. It was full of the mood of his sleep, of hunger, and despair, sleepless nights and the gloom of candle smoke. On the centre table, in front of him, there was a half-empty bottle of ogogoro, an ashtray, and a packet of cigarettes. There was a mosquito coil on the table as well and its acrid smoke filled the air. The man sleeping on the chair was like a giant in fairy tales. His big feet were on the table. He slept very deeply, frightening me with the great movements of his chest.

When lightning flashed outside, and the downpour increased, the man woke up, a stern look in his eyes. Then his eyes changed. They became big and bloodshot. Bewildered, he gazed around the room as if he had woken up into an alien world. Then he saw me in the doorway. For a long moment he stayed like that, caught in an enchantment, his arms stretched out. Jumping up suddenly and with such energy that he sent the chair flying from underneath him, he rushed towards me. I ran round the table. He pursued me, but I ran the other way, keeping the table between us. I had no idea why I was running away from him or why he was running after me. When I found an opportunity I fled screaming towards the door, out of the room, but he caught me in the passage, under the torrential rain. Hollering, he kept throwing me up in the air, filling me with dread. And when he held me to him firmly, so that I was overwhelmed with his great bristling energies and his quivering heart, I burst out crying without knowing why.

When the rain stopped, Mum stripped the dead boy's clothes off me and later burned them with kerosine and herbal fluids. The clothes burned for longer than expected. Her eyes bright with superstitions, she kept feeding the yellow and black flames with kerosine. When the clothes burned down to curlicues of ash she gathered them into a newspaper and went out in the dark towards the forest.

On her return she seized my hand, pushed me to the bathroom which had millipedes on the walls, and made me bathe from a bucket of specially treated water. I had to use a brown soap which produced little foam. As I struggled to wash myself, Mum stayed outside the squalid bathroom, and told me all that had happened since the night of the riots. The way she told it filled me with wonder about her.

That night, when the crowds separated us, the unleashed Masquerade had pursued women across streets because they were not supposed to see its terrifying presence. She looked for me in every corner, under every car, had shouted my name where houses were burning. And when she went back home, hoping I might be there waiting, she learned that Dad too had disappeared.

'In one night,' she said, 'I lost my only child and my husband.'

She stayed up the whole night, outside the burnt compound, with all our possessions scattered about the street. In the morning the tenants moved to new compounds, to different ghettos. Mum managed to distribute our property among relations. Then she went to all the hospitals and police stations she could find. She walked the whole city, inconsolable in her loss. And when she was about to succumb to despair, in a last effort she went to a police station in the centre of the city and was told that Dad was there, imprisoned for taking part in the riots. She managed to see him. He had been beaten by the police and there was an ugly cut on his forehead, bruises on his face, and his arm hung beside him like a diseased appendage. The next day, after much begging and some bribery, Dad was freed. He went to work that day and found that he had been sacked. During that time Mum had succeeded in finding a room for us to rent. She had also found a way to pay a month's rent in advance. Dad came to his new home bad-tempered and in a violent mood. He fell ill that night, muttering about insane soldiers who had killed white men in wars across the seas.

Mum was frantic over my disappearance. Her friends suggested consulting a herbalist. At first she was doubtful; but after she had tried everything and failed, gone to police stations and hospitals, and been unable to find me, she relented. She was taken to a herbalist. There was a mound of broken glass in front of her hut. Mum had hardly stepped in when the herbalist, a fierce-looking woman with one eye that glittered more than the other, told her from the shadows that she knew the purpose of Mum's visit.

'Go away,' she shouted in a cracked voice, 'bring me a white cockerel, a bottle of gin, feathers of a dove, and three pieces of chalk. Then I will help you.'

When Mum returned with the items the woman, attired in a severe black smock, consulted her cowries. She made offerings to her goddess who sat in a corner of the room, brooding in the dark with shining sunglasses. Then she told Mum to leave. She wanted to sleep on her divination. Mum came back the next morning and without any preamble the herbalist told her that the fee would be very expensive because the case was very difficult.

'Your son is trapped in a house of ghosts,' she said.

Mum was so terrified that she left instantly, gathered all the money she had saved from her trading, took some off Dad, and borrowed the rest. The herbalist went on to tell her that I was being held by a man and a woman who either wanted to keep me as their own child or sacrifice me for money, and that I was surrounded with such powerful spells that if Mum didn't act quickly I would be lost to her for ever. Mum paid the fee and sat in the dark, listening as the strange-eyed herbalist embarked on the most extravagant conjurations she had ever witnessed. The herbalist wrestled with the powers of the house, trying to break the spells surrounding me. After five hours, during which Mum sat rigid with fear, the woman emerged from her secret chambers and said:

'I have broken all the spells except one. That one is too powerful for me. Only lightning can break that spell.'

Mum sat confused. The herbalist gave her instructions. Mum went home, her heart heavy.

That night she was lamenting her condition, blaming herself for having lost the only child she had, a child who had chosen to live, when a distant relation paid a visit. She had heard of Mum's troubles and had come to offer consolation. She brought a few gifts and congratulated Mum on finding me. Dad took it as a good omen. Mum was puzzled. Then it emerged that the relation had seen a picture of me in the newspaper on the day after my accident. That was how Mum traced me to the police station and eventually to the officer's house.

Mum went back to the herbalist, who now gave the final set of instructions. Mum was to go to the house, to be humble, to thank the officer and his wife for keeping me, to take them presents, and to throw the white cockerel into the room so they could transfer their sacrifice from me to the bird. And then she was to run away from the place as fast as her legs could carry her. But before she could do any of this lightning had to first strike the house. Mum had waited in the rain, outside the house, for three hours. She had stood patiently, with thunder growling above her, watching as lightning flashed in different places, over many houses and trees. And she stayed like that, not moving an inch, till lightning struck directly over the house of ghosts where I was held captive.

NINE

AFTER I HAD bathed, after I had eaten, they made me sit in Dad's chair and asked me to tell them my story. I began telling them when the lights changed in the room and mighty hands lifted me up and put me on the bed. I saw Dad smiling beneath his bloodied bandage. Mum shifted the chair and centre table, spread out a mat and slept on the floor. Dad sat on his wooden chair, smoked peacefully, and lit a mosquito coil. I listened to him talking to the silent room, asking riddles that only the dead can answer.

I slept all night and all day. When I woke up it was evening. The room was empty. A kerosine lamp burned steadily on the centre table. When I first opened my eyes on the new world of home everything was different. Large shadows everywhere made the spaces smaller. The floor was rough. Long columns of ants crawled alongside the walls. There were ant-mounds near the cupboard. An earthworm stretched itself past Dad's shoes. Wall-geckos and lizards scurried up and down the walls. At the far corner of the room a washing line was slack with the weight of too many clothes. Mum's objects of trade were all over the place. Her sacks were piled around the cupboard. Blackened pots and crockery and basins were scrambled everywhere. It was as if Mum and Dad had moved in, dumped their possessions wherever there was space, and had never found time to arrange anything. The more I took in the cracks in the walls, the holes in the zinc ceiling, the cobwebs, the smells of earth and garri, the cigarette and mosquito coil smoke, the more it seemed we hadn't moved at all. Everything felt the same. The only difference was that I wasn't used to the sameness.

The light in the room was dull in the evening. Mosquitoes and fireflies had come in. A dying fly buzzed its last song up on the ceiling, among the net of cobwebs. The lamp-light kept fluttering, its black smoke drifted up to the ceiling. The smell of burning wick and kerosine smoke reassured me. I was home. And being at home was very different from being in the comfortable house of the police officer. No spirits plagued me. There were no ghosts in the dark spaces. The poor also belong to one country. Our surroundings were poor. We didn't have a bathroom worth speaking of and the toilet was crude. But in that room, in our new home, I was happy because I could smell the warm presences and the tender energies of my parents everywhere.

Hanging on crooked nails on the walls, there were framed, browning photographs of my parents. In one of the pictures Mum sat sideways on a chair. She had a lot of powder on her face, and she had the coy smile of a village maiden. Dad stood next to her. He had on a baggy pair of trousers, a white shirt, and an askew tie. His coat was much too small for him. He had a powerful, tigerish expression on his face. His strong eyes and his solid jaw dared the camera. He looked the way some boxers do before they become famous. There was another photograph in which I sat between them, small between two guardians. There were smiles of shy sweetness on our faces. As I stared at the photograph in that little room where the lamp produced more black smoke than illumination, I wondered where the sweetness had gone.

I went out searching for Mum and Dad. They weren't in the backyard. In the kitchen women sat in front of a blazing wood fire, sweat dripping from their faces, their fleshy arms and partly bared breasts glistening. I watched them as they fried bean cakes, chicken, and fish, and as they prepared delicious-smelling stews. When they saw me they raised their voices in bright greetings, and I fled. At the housefront Dad was narrating his prison experiences to a rowdy gathering of men. Mum was across the road, haggling with an old woman. Dad got to a point in his narration where he thought it necessary to illustrate a particular action. He leapt up from his chair, bristling with good humour, and began marching up and down, stamping his boots on the earth, swinging his one good arm, dangling his head, shouting war charges in seven languages. It was meant to be an impersonation of the insane soldier who had fought the British wars in Burma. His mind had been unhinged by the blast of detonators, nights spent with corpses and by the superstitious incredulity of having killed so many white men. He had become a man who knew only two things – how to march and how to charge. He marched all day long in prison and he charged all night long in his sleep. The men laughed at Dad's impersonation and Dad laughed so explosively that the bloody patch widened on the bandage round his forehead. No one noticed. I made a sound; Dad turned and saw me. And when he saw me he abruptly stopped laughing. After a long moment he started moving towards me and I ran across the street, towards Mum. Half-way across I saw a bicyclist pedalling furiously at me. Mum screamed, I fell; the bicyclist wobbled, missed my head, and cursed as he sped away. Mum rushed over, picked me up, took me back to the housefront, and gave me to Dad to look after.

'Why do you keep running away from me, eh?' Dad asked, with sadness.

I said nothing. I stared at the faces of the compound men, big faces stamped with hardship and humour. The night slowly descended on us and the kerosine lamps came alight, one by one, along the street.

That evening Dad became the guardian giant who led me into the discoveries of our new world. We were surrounded by a great forest. There were thick bushes and low trees between the houses. The bushes were resonant with the trilling of birds and crickets. Dad led us down a narrow path. We passed women with bundles of firewood on their heads, buckling along and talking in strange languages. We passed young girls returning from distant streams, with buckets of water balanced on their heads.

'Do you see all this?' Dad said, waving his good arm to indicate the forest and the bushes.

'Yes,' I replied.

'It's bush now, isn't it?'

'Yes.'

'But sooner than you think there won't be one tree standing. There will be no forest left at all. And there will be wretched houses all over the place. This is where the poor people will live.'

I looked around again in amazement; for I couldn't see how the solid forest could become so different. Dad chuckled. Then he was silent. He put his hand on my head and, with the voice of a sad giant, he said:

'This is where you too will live. Many things will happen to us here. If I ever have to go away, if I ever disappear now or in the future, remember that my spirit will always be there to protect you.'

Dad's voice quivered. When he was silent again, I started crying. He lifted me with his powerful arm and carried me on the rock of his shoulder. He made no attempt to console me. When I had

34

stopped crying, he chuckled mysteriously. We stopped at the first palm-wine bar we came across.

He ordered a gourd of palm-wine and kept teasing the woman who served him and who kept topping off my tiny glass. When Dad drank from his half calabash, I drank from my glass. It made Dad happy. He said:

'Learn to drink, my son. A man must be able to hold his drink because drunkenness is sometimes necessary in this difficult life.'

I sat beside him on the wooden bench, drinking as he drank, taking in the smells of the bar, its odours of stale wine, peppersoup, and fish-sacks. Flies were exultant everywhere. While talking, the clientele kept waving them off from their faces. At a corner of the bar, on a far bench, in the half light of the lanterns, a man sat with his back against the wall, his head flopped in drunkenness as he dozed. Dad ordered another gourd of wine, his face glistening with delight. He exchanged jokes and anecdotes with the clientele, who were all perfect strangers. Then he began a game of draughts.

At first he played without seriousness, joking all the while. He played a game in this spirit and won. He played another and lost. He joked less the more he lost. His voice grew more aggressive and he hit my head with his sharp elbows without noticing. The two men became so obsessed with their game that they began to accuse one another of cheating. Their fists waved threateningly over the draughtboard. Their voices became heated. The onlookers, who had placed bets on the players, were even more passionate than those who were playing. Dad, losing steadily, abused his opponent virulently; his opponent replied with incredible vehemence. I got worried. Dad placed an absurd bet on himself and his opponent doubled it. Things suddenly got very tense in the bar and Dad drank heavily, sweating. He ordered two more gourds of wine. It got so tense that when the onlookers said anything they were pounced upon. It took long anxious moments to quell the furious exchanges. Dad increased the bet and his head started bleeding again. His opponent, a huge man with a small head, kept staring at Dad with such contempt that I wanted to bite his fingers. He turned to me with his small drunken eyes and said:

'Your father doesn't know how to play.'

'Shut up,' I snapped.

There was a startled silence.

'What did you say?' he asked incredulously.

'Nothing.'

Dad said:

'Leave my son alone. Play the game. Use your brains, not your mouth.'

His opponent, consumed with indignation, said:

'You mean to tell me that you allow that small boy – whose mother's liquid hasn't yet dried on his head – to abuse me!'

'Play, my friend,' Dad said coolly.

'We don't bring up children like that where I come from,' the man said, glowering at me.

'My friend, play your game.'

The man got so angry at Dad's indifference that his concentration was entirely thrown off balance. He kept fuming at me, swearing in many languages. Dad beat him steadily, drinking less the closer victory seemed. And then with a devastating flourish he won the set of games, and swept his opponent's hard-earned money into his pocket. His opponent, in an extreme fit of bad-temper, drank down the entire contents of his gourd of palm-wine, rained insults on us, complained bitterly about the contemporary bad breeding of children, and staggered out into the encroaching darkness.

It turned out that he had left without paying for his drinks and his peppersoup. The madame of the establishment ran after him and we heard them squabbling. Dad finished off his gourd with perfect serenity. He was very pleased with himself and his face shone with profound satisfaction. When I had finished the wine in my tiny glass, he paid the madame's assistant, and we left.

Outside a crowd had gathered. The bad-tempered loser refused to pay the madame for the simple reason that I had told him to shut up.

'I won't pay till you tell that boy to apologise to me,' he shouted.

'That is not my business,' she bellowed back. 'All I want is my money!'

'The boy insulted me in your bar,' he replied.

The woman stopped listening. When we went past the crowd we saw that she was dragging him about, yanking him around by the pants. He kept trying to free himself from her masterful grip on his trousers, a grip which encompassed his private parts. He tried to prise her fingers apart and when that failed he took to hitting her hands, screaming insults at everyone. Then, suddenly, to our astonishment, the woman lifted him up by the pants and threw him to the ground. The crowd yelled. The man flailed, got up, shouted and huffed. Then he pounced on her, lashing at her face. Dad started towards him, but his rescue attempt was cut short. The madame grabbed the bad loser's crotch and he screamed so loud that the crowd fell silent. Then, with a practised grunt, she lifted him on her shoulders, turned him round once, showing his mightiness to the sky, and dumped him savagely on the hard earth. He stayed unconscious for a while, his mouth open. She then proceeded to turn him upside-down, emptying out all the money in his pockets. She took what was owed her, stripped him of his trousers, went into the bar, came back out with a filthy gourd, and drenched him with stale palm-wine.

He recovered instantly. When he saw the fullness of his public disgrace, he screamed in disbelief, and fled towards the forest, his underpants dripping with the shame of stale wine. We never saw him again. The crowd was so amazed at the woman's performance that everyone stared at her with their mouths wide open. The woman went back into her bar and cleared the tables as if nothing had happened. Then, as we looked on, she broke the draughtboard in half and threw it outside. When she looked up and saw the crowd staring at her in mesmerised silence she strode towards us. In a loud voice, hands on hips, she said:

'Do you want to drink or do you want to look?'

The crowd, awoken from the spell, broke up into numerous voices. Some went into the bar, to drink of her myth. Others went back to their different areas, taking with them the embellished stories of the most sensational drama they had witnessed for a long time. The woman served her new clientele with superb nonchalance. That evening was the beginning of her fame. Everyone talked about her in low voices. Her legend, which would sprout a thousand hallucinations, had been born in our midst – born of stories and rumours which, in time, would become some of the most extravagant realities of our lives.

TEN

WHEN WE PARTED from the crowd that was busily generating her myth, Dad led us through the bushpaths and into the forest. I walked in a drunken haze beside him. We passed a tree whose lower branches were covered with yellow dresses. A black cat followed us from a distance. It was dark in the forest till we got to a clearing. In the middle of the clearing a solitary wooden pole had been stuck into the earth. The pole had burst into flower. Little buds had grown out along its length and some of the buds had opened into the beginnings of branches. Dad said:

'This is what you must be like. Grow wherever life puts you down.'

I stared at the flowering pole. Then, touching my head affectionately, Dad told me to stay there and wait for him. He went off and I listened to his footsteps recede into the forest.

A yellow wind stirred the leaves. Branches cracked. An animal cried out. The black cat, eyes aglow, ran past me in the direction Dad had gone. It looked back at me once. I waited. Noises accumulated in the forest. An owl flew over my head and watched me from a branch. I heard footsteps approaching and I could have sworn that they belonged to a heavy man, but when I looked I saw an antelope. It came up to me, stopped near the pole, and stared at me. Then it came closer and licked my feet. When a branch cracked amongst the trees, the antelope started and ran off. I waited, motionless. It began to drizzle. Water flowed down the invisible paths of the forest and collected at my feet. Again, I heard converging footsteps all around me. Then I saw something move. The air swelled. A woman stepped out of a tree and limped towards me. Her head hung loosely on her neck. She stared at me from her shapeless face and she walked with her body leaning in one direction. She was deformed in a way I couldn't define. She had on a white robe. Her eyes were dark and small. When she got quite close to me she stopped and started laughing. I didn't move. The wind startled the branches. The water at my feet made me shiver. The woman, laughing rather dementedly, walked round me. Her face was twisted and her eyes shone in the darkening lights. When she was in front of me again, she slowly stretched her hands out towards my neck. At the same moment, the owl, uttering its nocturnal cry, flew from the branch and swooped past, circling us twice. It made another cry and soared upwards. A crack sounded, like a tree splitting, and I saw the owl falling, as though it had been shot in the mid-air of a dream. It landed on the earth and struggled, wings flapping feebly. Then it turned into a little pool of yellow water and evaporated into the air.

The woman stopped laughing. Instead of reaching for my neck with her rough hands, she grabbed the flowering pole and began pulling it out of the earth, a satanic expression on her face. She wrenched the pole, and she had to keep pulling because it had developed strong roots. When she had successfully wrenched out the pole along with its deep roots, she turned and dragged it behind her.

As I watched her limping away I noticed, among the roots, a glistening black snake covered with earth. The snake wound its way up the pole, towards the woman's hands, as she dragged it with her deeper into the forest. After a while I didn't see her any more. Then I heard a sharp cry. Then silence. I did not move. It had begun to grow very dark. A millipede climbed up my leg and I did not disturb it. I saw the black cat again. It came towards me, slunk past, and ran off in the direction we had originally come from. Not long afterwards I saw Dad emerging from the forest with a great sack on his shoulder. He looked exhausted, as if he had been wrestling with demons. When he got to where I was standing he said:

'Did you move?'

'No.'

'Good.'

I reached down and flicked the millipede off my leg.

'Did you see anything happen?'

'A woman came out of a tree. An owl fell down and turned to air. Water gathered at my feet.'

'Excellent,' he said. 'Let's go home.'

We set off. I didn't see the black cat anywhere. I asked Dad:

'Why did the woman tear the pole out of the earth?'

'What pole?'

'The one that was there.'

'Where?'

'There.'

'There wasn't a pole there,' he said.

I didn't speak for a while. Then I said:

'A snake came out of its roots and bit her.'

'That's good. Life is full of riddles that only the dead can answer,' was Dad's reply.

We went home in silence. We went down numerous paths. A dog limped in front and then it stopped to stare at us. Blood dripped from the sack on Dad's shoulder. Blood had widened and dried on the bandage on his forehead.

'What did you catch?' I asked.

'A wild boar.'

'Why are you bleeding?'

'The trap caught the boar and it didn't die. It was still struggling when I got there. I had to kill it with my hands. It kicked my head.'

I walked behind him in silence, listening to the forest noises and to the sound of his breathing. The journey home seemed longer than the journey out. When we came to the palm-wine bar the madame was nailing up her signboard. I couldn't read its legend in the dark. She regarded us as we passed. Dad saluted her. She didn't reply.

When we got to our new home the children ran out to meet us. The men came to help Dad with the sack, but he didn't want any help. The women talked excitedly. Our door was open. Folding chairs had been arranged all around the tiny space. The centre table was loaded with drinks. There was a bowl of kola-nuts and kaoline on the floor. There was the potent aroma of fresh stew in the air. The room was empty. Dad went to the backyard and we found Mum in the kitchen. She was fanning the wood fire, tears running down her face, a mighty pot on the grate. When she saw us she came out and held Dad tight and picked me up. Dad put the sack down on the kitchen floor. He looked at me for a moment, and said:

'I have kept my promise.'

Then he went out of the kitchen, to the room, came back with towel and soap, fetched water from the well, and had a long bath. I stayed with Mum in the kitchen, coughing when she coughed. The water boiled in the pot. Women of the compound came and helped her with getting the boar out of the sack. They poured boiling water on its skin, loosening its hair. They shaved it. Five men helped them butcher the fierce-looking animal. They decapitated it, cut it to pieces and gutted out its monstrous intestines. Then the women began the cooking of the wild animal that Dad had caught in the forest.

When the meat was cooking, on another fire a great pan was sizzling with oil. The whole compound smelt of aromatic stew, peppers, onions, wild earthy herbs, and frying bushmeat. When everyone could be seen salivating in anticipation, Mum made me go and bathe. I wore a new set of clothes. Visitors and compound-dwellers came one by one to our room. They took their seats. Mum combed my hair and gave me a parting. Dad also had a parting. Mum bathed. In the bathroom she dressed up in her fine clothes. She did her hair and made up her face in the passage.

Soon our little room was crowded with all kinds of people. Many of them were from our compound, one or two were from our previous habitation, a few of them were total strangers, and a lot of them were children. It was hot in the room and everyone sweated. All the chairs were filled and all the floor space taken. A woman struck up a song. A man struck up a more vigorous song. The children looked on. Mum came in with a plate of alligator pepper seeds, a saucer of cigarettes, and breadfruit. And then we heard a flourish outside.

It was Dad. He was at the doorway with an empty bottle in one hand, a spoon in the other. He was beating a tune out of glass. He wore a black French suit and had a fresh change of bandages. An eagle's feather stuck out from the back of his head. He looked happy and a little drunk. He came in, beating his metallic tune on glass, dancing and singing to the music of his own invention. The crowd laughed, cheering in appreciation. Everyone began to chatter. Voices rose in volume. Jokes passed across the sweating faces. I felt a stranger amidst the celebration of my homecoming.

Then to our delight a woman appeared at the door, sounding a heraldic song. Mum came in with three women, carrying a great steaming pot of stew. Behind her were three more women, bearing basins of jollof rice, yams, beans, eba, and fried plantains. Children brought in paper plates and plastic cutlery. The aroma of the marvellous cooking overpowered the room. Everyone straightened. Faces were bright with aroused appetites. There wasn't a single throat that didn't betray the best hopes for a feast of abundant cooking in which all anticipation would be fully rewarded.

ELEVEN

THE FOOD WAS brought in and covered in a corner.
Everyone talked to disguise the flood of their salivation. The oldest
man in the compound stood up and called for silence. The jokes,
chatter, invented nicknames, and robust arguments peppered the air,
increasing the heat of the room. The call for silence was repeated. It too
became a cause of much jesting. Dad had to raise his voice and threaten
the crowd with his good arm before the noise became controllable.

The old man made a libation at both posts of the door and prayed
for us and thanked the ancestors that I had been found and asked that
I never be lost again. When he finished his prayer he launched into a
long rambling speech in which he welcomed us to the compound as
new tenants, in which he aimed a few well turned barbs at real and
imaginary enemies, and in which he released a torrent of proverbs and
saws and anecdotes that fell like stones to the depths of our hunger.
The longer his speech went on, the more depressed the faces became.
His proverbs made us more famished, edgy and irritable. When the
old man had satisfied his hunger for speech-making, Dad replied to
his good wishes. He expressed gratitude for our general safety and
good health, and prayed for all those present. The old man broke the
kola-nut. He gave a lobe to Dad, who chewed off a bit and passed
it on, prayer-laden, to Mum and then to me.

The drinks were distributed to the crowd. There were large
quantities of ogogoro and palm-wine for the men, stout for the
women, soft drinks for the children. While the drinks were being
poured and handed over expectant faces sweating with thirst, one
of the men struck up a song, and a woman said:

'The only time men start to sing is when food is ready.'

The women burst out laughing and the man's song was drowned
in mockery. The women began a lovely song of their own, in village
choir voices; but Dad, ever mischievous, picked up the empty bottle
and tapped away at it with a spoon and spoiled the rhythm of the

women. Then everyone fell to singing their different songs and for a moment there was no discord amongst the many voices.

The feast became a little rowdy. The room was too small to hold the vast number of people squashed into every available space and even the walls creaked in protest. Clothes fell down from nails and lines. Dad's boots passed from hand to hand, precipitating many jokes, and were eventually thrown out of the window. The room was so hot that everyone sweated furiously. The heat made everyone look older. The children cried, intensifying the edginess and hunger. But the drink loosened tongues, and a hundred arguments and conversations steamed the air. The women asked Mum how she had found me. Mum told them things she hadn't told me, but she kept quiet about the herbalist. The gathering began vying with loud voices, offering variations of similar stories they had heard about. A woman told of a wizard who had hidden a child in a green bottle. Another woman, who had been taking a noticeable interest in Dad, told of how her sister was found floating on a stream, her head crowned in sacrificial beads.

'That's a lie!' Mum said suddenly, to everyone's astonishment. 'You never told us you had a sister . . .'

Dad interrupted, picking up his bottle and spoon, creating a modest din. He got up and sang and danced. The men sang along with him the popular high-life tune which mocked the eternal rivalries among women. Dad got carried away with his own song and tried to organise everyone into dancing. There was no space in which to move and Dad, fairly drunk by now, became abusive to anyone who wasn't responsive. At first it was a general sort of abuse. But when he got specific with one of the men, disruption set in. The man stormed out and a delegation had to be sent to beg him back. He came back, but before he resumed his floor space, he made sure of his vengeance.

'Is it this wretched room you're so proud of?' he said loudly to Dad. 'Big man, small brains!'

Dad smiled sheepishly. Then Mum rounded on him, asking him to be more polite to his guests, and she got so worked up in her inexplicable rage that she too stormed out, leaving the crowd somewhat confused. No one was sent out after her. Embarrassed by the silence, Dad invited everyone to pour themselves more drinks and he proposed a toast to his wife. But the drinks had run out, and Dad had no money left, and we all sat staring at our empty bottles. In the brief silence Mum returned, bringing relatives we hadn't seen for a long time, and the gathering cheered her return; and Dad, inspired by

43

the cheering, hurried out of the room (ignoring Mum's protestations that we should celebrate within our means), went to the shop across the street, and came back with cartons of beer.

The feast got rowdier. The men kept calling for more drinks. The old man, quite drunk, began a stream of contradictory proverbs. A man with a thick beard complained about how the smell of the food was making him lean. Amidst all the voices, the anticipations which had topped themselves, the long patient waiting which in the end satisfies its own hunger, the food was served. Plates of rice and bushmeat passed before gluttonous faces but, because the crowd was so big, and the numbers vastly outstripped Mum's calculations, everyone had much less food than suggested by the size of the boar. People had talked themselves into such a hunger that the food barely went round. Like the miracle of multiplying fishes in reverse, the food diminished before it got to the guests. The rice was swiftly consumed, the boar disappeared into the capacious stomachs of the ravenous gathering, the stew dried out in the pots, and people stared at their plates in drunken puzzlement. The bearded man grumbled that the meat he had eaten was so small that it had made him hungrier. Discontentment spread; the smell of the food, sumptuous and throat-tickling, lingered in the air, reminding us of the betrayed promise of an abundant feast. Amid the discontentment, Dad tried hard to please everyone. He made jokes, told riddles, fell into impersonations. He danced, and made music with his bottle. Meanwhile people ate, spat their bones on the floor, spilt their drinks, and wiped their hands on our curtains. Dad plied the gathering with drinks, borrowing heavily, sweating in bizarre exultation. The bearded man, substituting drunkenness for hunger, drank so much that when he attempted to dramatise his first encounter with a white woman he staggered and fell on his chair, breaking its back. Another man ran outside, threw up in the passage, and came back looking like a lizard. Dad, who was more than pleasantly drunk, held forth about the violence he would have unleashed if he had gone to the police officer's place to get me. Mum found the perfect moment for revenge.

'Why didn't you go, eh?' she said cuttingly, 'Because you were too drunk!'

There was another embarrassed silence. Dad, slightly cross-eyed with drunkenness, looked round at everyone. Then he displayed his arm in the sling. And then, for no apparent reason, almost as if he were snatching riddles out of the air, he said:

'When I die, no one will see my body.'

44

The silence became profound. Mum burst into tears and rushed out of the room. Two women went after her. Dad, entering a grim mood, drank intensely, and then suddenly began to sing beautifully. For the first time I heard deep notes of sadness in his powerful voice. Still singing he bent over, lifted me up, and held me to him. His eyes were a little bloodshot. He gave me his glass to drink from and after two gulps I became quite drunk myself. Dad put me down on the chair, went outside, and returned with Mum in his arms. Mum's eyes were wet. Dad held her and they danced together and the gathering, touched by the reconciliation, sang for them.

While the room quivered with jagged drumming on the table, syncopated rhythms of voices, the bottle-music, and general revelry, the photographer from across the road turned up, wearing a white hat. His name was Jeremiah. He had a wiry beard, and everyone seemed to know him. He became the instant butt of jokes. Some mocked his bad timing at missing the tastiest boar that ever ran amok in the forests. Others urged him to take off his white hat and get drunk as swiftly as possible. And the women wanted to know why he hadn't brought his camera. He went back out and soon returned with his camera and everyone abandoned the dancing and organised themselves for a group photograph. The men fought for the most visible positions. The old man, claiming right of seniority, posed in front of everyone. The women went out to brighten themselves and came back to disrupt the photographer's arrangement. Mum picked me up and posed with Dad next to the old man. The photographer gave many instructions as he set up his camera. He went back and forth, making us contort our heads. He made Dad twist his legs, made Mum hold her neck at an awkward angle, and made me fix a quite insane smile on my face. After much fussing, the photographer proceeded to embark on his own set of dramatic poses. He crouched, stood on tiptoes, knelt, climbed on a chair, and even seemed to imitate an eagle in flight. He drank generously from a bottle of beer. Swaying, leaning backwards, his eyes shining, he made us say:

'Sheeze.'

While we played around with the word, fishing humour out of its strangeness, he took the first picture. When the camera flashed, followed by an odd explosion, ghosts emerged from the light and melted, stunned, at his feet. I screamed. The crowd laughed. The photographer took five pictures in all and the ghosts kept falling at his feet, dazed by the flash. When he went to his studio to drop off his camera, the ghosts followed him. When he came back they weren't

45

with him. He joined the boisterous merriment and got wonderfully drunk.

Not long afterwards the landlord turned up. The crowd cheered him. Mum had to rustle up some food. Dad had to buy more drinks on credit. I was fussed over and thrown up in the air till my ribs ached and I was prayed for all over again. The photographer had to go back and get his camera.

After much prancing and mystery-making, as if he were a magician, the photographer lifted up his camera. He was surrounded by little ghosts and spirits. They had climbed on one another to take a closer look at the instrument. They were so fascinated by the camera that they climbed on him and hung on his arms and stood on his head. He was very drunk and he cheerfully took three pictures of the landlord with his flywhisk. When he had finished he couldn't be bothered to go all the way back to his studio so he hung the camera on a nail. The spirits and the children gathered round it, pointing and talking in amazed voices.

The men who were drunk began a furious argument. Some of the women took their children to bed. The men were in the full flow of their loud voices when the curtain parted, a hush descended, and the madame from the bar stepped in. The landlord, on seeing her, made a frightened sound. Everyone stared at her in drunken silence. The spirits left the camera and surrounded the woman. They stayed at a distance. The woman smiled and waved a benevolent greeting to all of us. Dad got up, welcomed her warmly, found her a seat, and proceeded to tell everyone about the fantastic beginnings of her myth. Everyone knew the story already and they stared at her as at an august, if unpredictable, guest. Mum rustled up some food for her. Dad sent off for more drinks on credit, but it wasn't necessary for she had brought five gourds of palm-wine to help celebrate my homecoming. When the ogogoro Dad sent for arrived she took the bottle, stood up abruptly, sending waves of silence everywhere by the sheer force of her legend and her bulk. She held my hand and said:

'Is this the boy we are celebrating?'

'Yes,' the crowd said.

'Is this the boy who was lost and found?'

'Yes!'

Then she turned. With her big eyes gazing at me steadily, she said:

'The road will never swallow you. The river of your destiny will always overcome evil. May you understand your fate. Suffering will never destroy you, but will make you stronger. Success will never confuse you or scatter your spirit, but will make you fly higher into the good sunlight. Your life will always surprise you.'

Her prayer was so wonderful that everyone was silent afterwards. They stared at her in amazement. Then Dad, recovering from the shock of the words, said:

'AMEN!'

The gathering repeated it. The woman, still standing, made a libation, a short communal prayer, then she drank half the bottle of ogogoro in a single, sustained gulp, her great breasts quivering in the hot room. When she had finished she sat down, her fleshy face coming out in sweat. The spirits encompassed her, talking about her in astonished voices.

She didn't stay very long. And when, too soon for everyone's liking (for they wanted to decode her mystery), she got up and said she had to return to her bar, we all tried to persuade her to stay. But she was beyond persuading. Dad thanked her for coming. Mum thanked her for the prayers and the wine. As she went to the door, swaying like a great ship, she stopped, looked hard at me, and said:

'You have a strange son. I like him.' Then to me she added: 'Come and visit me one of these days, eh?'

'I will,' I said.

When she left the room the spirits went with her. That night we found out her name. She was known as Madame Koto.

TWELVE

AFTER ALL THE revelry, the feast ended with men asleep on their chairs, children sprawled on the floor, bottles everywhere and bones on the window-sill. The photographer snored with his nose close to Dad's rescued boots, and the landlord drooled with flies around his ears. I was sitting against a wall, weaving in and out of sleep, surrounded by the confusion of human bodies, when I heard those sweet voices singing again. My spirit companions, their voices seductive beyond endurance, sang to me, asking me to honour my pact, to not be deceived by the forgetful celebrations of men, and to return to the land where feasting knows no end. They urged me on with their angelic voices and I found myself floating over the bodies of drunken men, and out into the night. I walked on the wings of beautiful songs, down the street, without the faintest notion of where the voices were leading me. I floated down the bushpaths and came to a well that was covered with a broad plank. On the plank, there was a big stone. I tried to move the stone, but couldn't. I floated round and round our area. My feet ached. I stopped and saw my toes bleeding. I did not panic. I felt no pain. Soon I was at the edge of the great forest whose darkness is a god. I was about to enter the darkness when I saw the black cat, its eyes glowing like luminous stones. Then footsteps converged on me. I turned, and ran into the massive figure of Madame Koto.

She caught me, lifted me up to her heavy breasts, and took me back home in silence. Mum had been looking for me everywhere. When she saw us she rushed over, carried me across the men asleep in their chairs, the children dozing against the walls, and laid me on the bed. Madame Koto lit a stick of incense, shut the window, and went outside with Mum.

I heard Madame Koto telling her how she had found me. I listened to the men snoring. I heard Mum thanking Madame Koto. My spirit companions were weeping. I slept and woke up when I heard a noise at the door. Someone came in with a lamp. I saw the lamp, and its illumination, but I didn't see who was bearing it across the room. There was darkness behind the lamp. Darkness put the lamp on the table. The curtain fluttered. I lay still and waited. Nothing happened for a while. When I woke up, the lamp was gone. In its place there was a candle on a saucer. I saw Dad moving from one sleeping figure to another, waking them up, urging them to go home. The men were so drunk that they didn't want to move. The children had to be carried out in their sleeping positions. When Dad came round to the photographer and touched him on the shoulder the poor man jumped up and said:

'Where's the riot? Where's my camera?'

Dad laughed. The photographer shook his head, groped for his camera among Dad's shoes, couldn't find it, and cried out. He eventually found the camera in the empty pot of stew, amongst the bones of the boar. He snatched it out, cleaned it with his shirt, and staggered off to his studio.

When the landlord was woken up he jerked his head, looked around suspiciously, and said:

'Where's my rent?'

Then he climbed into bed and put his arm round me, as if I were a woman. Dad dragged him out into the passage and left him to his devices. In the room the bearded man woke up and wondered if the feast had begun yet and asked why he hadn't been served any boar's meat. One of the children started crying. When Dad came back into the room the bearded man asked for some beer. Dad drove him out. It was only after they had gone that we saw the debris of the feast. Our clothes were scattered everywhere. Two chairs were broken. Glasses had been shattered on the floor and it was a wonder that no one had cut themselves. Someone had vomited half out of the window and half in. The place stank of the children who had wet themselves in their sleep.

Mosquitoes whined. Dad lit a coil. Mum swept the floor, arranged the clothes, cleared out the plates, cutlery, and bones. Then she disinfected the room. Dad sat on his chair, drinking and smoking quietly. Mum spread out the mat. Then she blew out the candle and went to sleep.

Dad sat alone in the dark. Every now and again he said:

'We have kept our promise.'

The only points of light were the mosquito coil, its smoke spiralling to the ceiling, and his cigarette. In a way I came to think of Dad as a cigarette smoked alone in the dark.

I watched him that night as if he were a fabled being. Sometimes he got up and paced the room, perfectly avoiding Mum's sleeping form, his cigarette vanishing and reappearing. I watched him go back and forth. As I watched him, the darkness expanded. I saw Dad's cigarette at one end of the room and heard him pacing at the other end. It seemed he had become separate from his action. Then I saw multiples of him smoking at different corners of the room. I shut my eyes. When I opened them it was morning and Dad was in his chair, asleep. I turned over. I heard him creaking his joints. When I turned round again, Mum was up, the mat was gone, the room was clean, the mosquito coil was just an aluminium stand and a spiral of ash on the centre table, and Dad was no longer asleep in his chair.

THIRTEEN

I LEARNT THAT Dad had gone out early to look for a job. Mum was exhausted from the search, the feast, all the walking, the worrying and the cooking. That morning she brought out her little table of provisions to the housefront. She sat on a stool, with me beside her, and dispiritedly crooned out her wares. The dust blew into our eyes. The sun was merciless on our flesh. We didn't sell a single item.

In the afternoon, the people that Dad had borrowed from to buy drinks came to collect their money. They threatened to seize Mum's goods. They hung around till evening. Mum begged them to wait for Dad to get back, but they wouldn't listen. What annoyed Mum the most was the fact that the creditors were people from our compound, who were at the feast, who had gotten drunk on our wine and had thrown up on our window-sill. The loudest amongst them was actually responsible for breaking the back of the chair and destroying two glasses. Another of our creditors, as we learned later, was Madame Koto. She was the only one who did not come to drag for her money. But the others hung around Mum's stall and spoiled her prospects of business.

By the evening Mum had begun to cough. Her eyes were inflamed from all the dust and whenever she stood up she staggered. When she went to the backyard she weaved about a little as if her failure to attract customers and shake off the creditors had made her drunk. Then I noticed, when she returned, that her eyes had gone strange. Every once in a while, after crooning despairingly to the indifferent potential customers of the world, her eyes would roll round in their sockets. As the evening wore on, when the winds changed, and a chill insinuated itself into the passing of the sun, Mum began to quiver on her stool, her teeth chattering. She went on stubbornly trying to sell her provisions, quivering under the bad wind, her face taut, her nose sweating, her eyes a little distracted. The other compound women who noticed the change told her to rest, but she didn't move. We

51

sat there, with our wares on the table, in the dark, covered in dust.

When Mum finally packed up her table, the evening had deep-ened, and the wind had begun to whistle in the tall trees. Trembling, determined, and silent, she washed all our clothes in the backyard. She cleaned the room, made a fresh pot of stew, and pounded yam for Dad's dinner. And then, battered by exhaustion, she went to sleep. But the creditors allowed her no rest. In a renewed effort, they kept turning up outside our room, whispering about the money we owed them, exaggerating the amounts to each new gossip-monger, and knocking on our door. When Mum reached the limit of her tolerance she shouted at them. They vowed loudly never to sell anything on credit again. They went on demanding their money till night fell.

We began to worry about Dad. It got darker and darker, the night birds began their songs, and still he hadn't returned. When we had exhausted ourselves with worry, when Mum was asleep on the bed, and I was dozing on the floor, Dad stamped into the room, bringing angry shadows with him. His bad temper stank from his alcoholic breath. He lit a candle, saw Mum asleep on the bed, and burst into rage.

'I have been everywhere in the world, looking for a job to feed us, and you are asleep? Wicked woman that you are!'

Dad fumed and shouted for thirty minutes, without listening, without using his eyes. Mum got out of bed, trembling violently, and went to the kitchen.

'Mum is not well,' I said.

'There's nothing wrong with her, she's just wicked, that's all.'

'She's not well,' I said again.

He didn't hear me. Mum came in with his tray of food. The plates clattered because of her trembling, which she tried to control. Dad, in his fury, didn't look up at her. He ate noisily and with a mighty appetite. He didn't even give me pieces of fish or invite me to join him as he often did. After he had finished eating every single morsel on the plates, his mood calmed, and he told us about how he had walked the entire city, under the blistering heat-waves, looking for a job, and had found none. During the silence which followed, Mum told him about the creditors, and Dad found fresh reasons to be angry. He threatened that he was going to beat them up for harassing Mum. He said he would scatter their teeth all over the forest. He said he would beat them so thoroughly that they would become old men overnight.

'I will feed their brains to the wind!' he shouted.

Mum expended a great deal of energy trying to dissuade him from such violent measures. But a demon of anger had got into Dad and he fumed and cursed all through the night. He smoked cigarette after cigarette, creaking his joints, striding up and down, filling the room with his restless temper. He grumbled about how much he had helped people and how they had always let him down, about all the creditors who came to our feast, polished off our boar's meat and beer, and turned round to harass Mum at the first opportunity. He complained bitterly about how people ate off him and then stabbed him in the back. I had heard these complaints all my life. His cigarette burned angrily as he dredged up a fresh variation. Mum would wake up suddenly. His blistering tirade was aimed at everything. I fell asleep with Dad cursing the treachery of the world way into my dreams.

When I woke up, Mum was sweating and quivering on the bed. Dad had bought malaria medicines and bitter roots which were marinated in yellow alcohol. Mum's teeth chattered, her eyes were at odd angles, and Dad sat beside her, his bad arm folded, the blood dried on his bandaged head. He applied warm compresses to her face and forehead. I got up and greeted Mum, but she could barely speak. She held me tightly to her hot body and I began to tremble myself. She held me so tightly that my teeth chattered as well and soon I felt myself being invaded by her fever. My eyeballs became hot. Dad, noticing what was happening to me, snatched me from Mum's frightened embrace, and made me drink of the bitter dongoyaro, as a precaution. Then he ordered me to go and bathe. I cleaned my teeth and bathed and when I got back, Dad had prepared some food. We sat and ate together from the same bowl, while Mum heaved in her illness on the bed.

We had finished eating, and Dad was preparing to go out, when the creditors came one after the other, as if they had planned it. They knocked on the door, came in, said something vaguely nice about me, expressed their profuse sympathies for Mum, praying that she should recover soon. They asked if Dad's wounds had improved, didn't wait for a reply, and then they left. Minutes later, with the air of people who had forgotten something of less than vital importance, they came back again, one after the other, and reminded Dad of how much he owed them, how they didn't usually lend money or give credits, and how this was a special case, and how hard things were at the shop, and so on. They ended by expressing their sympathies again to Mum, and left.

Their sly and hypocritical manner got Dad very enraged. He paced the room, boiling in fury. Then, suddenly, unable to contain himself any longer, he stormed out of the room. I followed him. He went to the backyard and we saw all the creditors huddled together, talking in low business tones as though they were about to form a limited liability company. Dad went amongst them, scattering the meeting. They tried to run to their different rooms but Dad called them back, each by his particular name, and he insulted them for fifteen incandescent minutes. They bore his insults in silence. When he had finished with them, turning with his unique dismissive flourish and storming back to our room, everyone was aware that we had just made ourselves three new enemies in the compound. As Dad left, the creditors regrouped and talked more intensely than before. They were like demented conspirators.

When I got back to the room, Dad had dressed up in his black French suit. He offered libations to his ancestors, and prayed for Mum's recovery. Then he wore his only pair of boots, which gave the room a poignant smell of leather, old socks, and footsweat. As he went out of the door Mum woke up from her sleep, screaming. She wouldn't stop and Dad held her and gave her more dongoyaro and she twisted around on the bed and then, just as suddenly, she became still, with tears running down her face and collecting in her ears. Dad stayed with her a while and watched her tossing in her sleep. When her sleep had become a little more regular, Dad told me not to leave her side, and to take care of her, that he had to go and find some money, and would be back soon. He went out with his head hung low, as if for the first time acknowledging the blows from above.

I sat on Dad's chair and watched over Mum. I watched her sleeping face till my eyes began to throb. Then suddenly Mum got up, her upper body stiff, her eyes unfocused, and she began to speak in an unfamiliar language. She stood up and went around the room, clearing things, straightening the table, folding the clothes, brushing Dad's shoes, fidgeting amongst the pots and basins, speaking in this unnatural language all the while.

'Mother!' I cried.

She neither heard nor saw me. She picked up blackened pots and pans with dented bottoms and went out of the room. I followed her, tugging at her, till one layer of her wrapper came off in my hands. She

54

went to the kitchen. Still muttering in a new-found tongue, her eyes blank, she started a fire in the grate and began to cook an imaginary pot of stew. She did everything mechanically, her body acting without her mind, as if she were in a dream. When the firewood blazed she placed an empty pot on the grate and sat on a stool and stared at the pot till it started to give off an acrid smell of burning metal.

'Mum!' I cried again.

She turned towards me, looked right through me, got up, went out of the kitchen, and collapsed beside the well. I screamed and women rushed to us and carried her to our room. She lay on the bed, breathing heavily, and the women stood around, casting deep shadows, hands to their breasts, heads low, standing in silence, as if in the presence of a corpse.

I sat on Dad's chair and watched over her. Women left and returned with confusing medications in green jars and dark bottles, and they administered conflicting treatments, and made her drink strange potions, drugs, oils, and distillates. Mum slept, breathing hoarsely, and the women left. I watched over her till my stomach ached and my eyelids became heavy. Then I woke up with a start. Mum's breathing had changed. I listened. I watched. Then I noticed that her breathing had become almost inaudible. The room changed, voices sang in my head, a lizard clambered on to the bed and ran over Mum's arm, and then everything seemed to stop. For a moment it seemed my own breathing had ceased altogether. I drew a breath and a spider fell from the ceiling. I drew another and I fell off the chair. I got up and sat again and then it became clear that it was Mum who had stopped breathing. Flies played around her mouth. She didn't stir. Then as I watched, as I listened, a sharp pain went through my ears, colours and masks appeared in my eyes, and then as I held my breath I saw a blue mist rising from Mum's form. I heard a child crying. The lizard scuttled past my feet. I woke Mum up and still she didn't stir. I called her and she didn't move. The blue mist grew thicker over her like steam from a boiling cauldron of water, and it collected and became more defined, and I grew really scared when the mist changed colours rapidly, becoming green, then yellow, turning red, bursting into a golden glow, and back to blue again. When I was sure I wasn't imagining the mist, when it turned reddish silver, radiant in the darkness of the room, I couldn't bear it any longer. When she didn't move, didn't breathe, I ran all the way to Madame Koto's bar to tell her that my mother was dying.

The bar was shut. At the backyard Madame Koto, wearing blue

wrappers and a red blouse and a filthy head-tie, was struggling with a huge chicken.

'Madame Koto!' I called.

She glared at me, striking me dumb, and the chicken flew out of her hands. She pursued it into the bushes, grabbed it firmly, gave me a sour look, and said:

'Your father owes me money.'

Then she forgot about my presence altogether. The chicken fought in her hands and she grabbed its thickly feathered neck. Twisting her mouth, she held the chicken's body down with her foot, and sliced its throat with jagged motions of her long knife. The chicken's blood burst out from the gash, staining the air, splattering my face, deepening the red of her blouse. The blood poured into a hole she had dug in the earth and the chicken fought, its comb rising and falling, its mouth opening and shutting in its final spasms, and when it died its eyes were open. They stared at me. Then Madame Koto washed the knife, sweat dribbling down her face and breasts. She regarded me with big eyes as if she were going to swallow me. I was crying.

'Because of a chicken?' she said, sucking her teeth.

She reached for a kettle of boiling water. I held on to her blouse, pulling her, my mouth wet, unable to speak. She pushed me away and I fell backwards on the ground and I stayed there, kicking the air, and eventually I said:

'My mother is dying.'

'How do you know?' she asked, eyeing me.

'Smoke is coming from her.'

'Smoke?'

'Red smoke,' I said.

She got up immediately, washed her hands, and started to hurry towards our compound. But at the barfront she stopped and said:

'Go and boil some water. I'm coming.'

I was confused. She went to her room, came out with a handful of herbs, stamped around the bushes, tearing off leaves from plants. Then she fetched a coarse sponge, dark green soap, a black metal container, looked round, saw me, and said:

'Go! Boil water! I'm coming.'

I rushed home, started a fire in the kitchen, and boiled water in the pan that Mum had burnt. Madame Koto arrived soon afterwards. She washed and boiled the leaves. We went to the room. Mum was still on the bed. The mist above her had almost vanished. Madame Koto

56

tried to put leaves in her mouth, but they merely stayed on her lips. Then she poured a distillate in a cup, added black oils and ogogoro, held Mum's head up and tried to get her to drink. Mum choked and Madame Koto called her name with such violence it sounded like a whip. She went on whipping Mum with her name, calling back her spirit, in a very peculiar birdlike voice.

After a long time Mum opened her eyes and stared at Madame Koto. Then at me. She stared at us utterly without comprehension. Her eyes stayed open, unmoving, blank. Grief threw me to the floor and I thrashed about and wailed because I thought Mum had died. Then, from a great distance, I heard Mum speak, and I fell silent. In a very feeble voice, she said:

'I saw my son in the land of death. Azaro?'

'Yes?'

'What were you doing there?'

'I'm here, Mum,' I said.

She stared beyond me. Madame Koto gave her more of the herbal mixture to drink. Then she made her drink some peppersoup, and got her to sit up straight. Then she told me to talk to Mum, to keep talking to her; and as I spoke to Mum about whatever came to mind the mist above her changed colour and slowly disappeared.

'The smoke is going!' I cried.

Madame Koto opened the door and the window. Light and air filled the room and Mum fell asleep in her sitting position, her head flopped forward. We stretched her out. I listened to her rough breathing. After a while Madame Koto said we should let her rest. She went back to her bar and to the chicken she was about to cook for food. I stayed outside our room, and kept listening. I watched the children playing as I listened.

When Mum called my name three times I hurried in and sat on the bed. Her face was covered in sweat. The room smelt of illness. There was a little foam on her lips and sweat on her forehead. Her lips quivered. She could scarcely speak.

'My son,' she said, 'I saw you walking on your head. You were walking away from me. I pursued you but you ran very fast. And you were laughing at me, my son.'

'I'm not laughing at you, Mum.'

'When I caught you,' she continued, 'I saw you had no eyes and no mouth, and you had little legs on your head. There was a white rope round you and it went up to the sky. I pulled the rope and it pulled me. I couldn't cut it. And then the rope jumped from your

57

feet to my neck. The rope pulled me up to the sky and I passed the moon and a red cloud shut my eyes.'

'Mum, your eyes are not shut.'

'It was because of you that the white rope jumped to my neck. What were you doing walking upside-down?'

'I don't know.'

'How did you get little legs on your head?'

'I don't know, Mum.'

'Go and fetch me some water, my son. I am thirsty.'

I ran out and fetched water in a clean cup and when I got back she was fast asleep. Her breathing was much gentler.

Early in the evening the compound women came to see how Mum was doing. She sat up and received them. They prayed for her recovery. They left and Madame Koto came with a bowl of food and another of peppersoup. Mum didn't want to eat, she was so weak, but we pressed her. I washed the plates and took them back to Madame Koto's bar. Then afterwards the creditors came to ask for Dad under the pretext that they had come to wish Mum well. When Mum saw them she got very upset and shouted at them, accusing them of poisoning her.

I came in and saw Mum staggering and throwing things at them. She was very lean, and she swayed, and threw shoes at the creditors. I joined in the attack. They retreated. When they were outside they cursed us and encouraged their children to throw things at us and one of them threw a stone which hit Mum on the head and she collapsed at my feet and a tragic wail rose collectively from the women of the compound. The creditors fled. The women carried Mum into the room. She came to as they crossed the threshold. Her eyes were hard and when she lay on the bed she had a strange little smile on her mouth as if she finally understood something that had always eluded her.

The smile stayed on her mouth all evening. I listened to the flies. The sounds of the evening intensified. The flies played on Mum's smile and she made no attempt to wave them away. I waved them off and Mum looked at me expressionlessly. I sat on the bed and watched the night creep into the room through the open window.

It was quite late when a sound at the door woke us up. I was curled up in a corner of the bed and Mum's eyes were wide open. I looked up at the door and saw Dad standing there like a tall ghost, his eyes bright, his sling gone. He was like a giant who was lost. He didn't move for a long moment. Then he lit a candle, shut the window and the door, and when he sat down a thick cloud of white dust billowed out from the seat of his trousers. His hair was white. His eyelashes were white. His hair was dishevelled. He had a bewildered expression on his face that frightened me. He stank of cement, dried fish, garri, and white dust. He sat silently for a long time, without moving. When he did move his joints creaked. His bad arm hung loosely by his side. His bandage had gone and the wound was covered in white dust. Then suddenly, out of the silence of the slow burning candle, he said:

'How's your mother?'

'She nearly died today. Madame Koto helped us.'

He breathed deeply and shut his eyes. He was silent and still for a while and I thought he had fallen asleep. Mum's eyes were open and devoid of expression.

'Is there any food?'

'No.'

Dad was silent again. Then, wearing his bathroom slippers, taking his towel and soap, he went to bathe. He came back clean and handsome, with all the white dust and the cement smells gone. But his eyes were heavy and he still looked bewildered and he still frightened me. He rubbed himself with oil, combed his hair, and lit a mosquito coil. We moved the centre table and spread the mat. The room stank of his boots and his clothes. He sat on the chair and I lay on the mat, a pillow beneath my head. He smoked into the night.

'So what happened today?' he asked after a while.

I wanted to tell him about the creditors and Mum, but I felt a certain weariness about him which made the night heavy, and so I said:

'Mum nearly died.'

He released a long sigh. Then he got up, looked down at Mum, placed his palm on her forehead, and shut her eyes. He went back to the chair and smoked some more and I could measure the sadness of his thoughts by the way he dragged on the cigarette and the way he sighed while exhaling.

I watched the bright point of his cigarette in the dark and it eventually lulled me into Madame Koto's bar. Dad was there. The bar had moved deep into the forest and all her customers were animals and birds. I sat on a bench which was really the back of a goat and I drank off the back of a bull. A massive chicken without feathers strode into the bar, sat next to me, and ordered palm-wine and peppersoup. Madame Koto didn't want to serve the chicken, but Dad said:

'Serve him!'

Madame Koto went out and fetched a great broom and she chased the chicken round the bar, lashing its head. Dad laughed. The chicken laughed. Madame Koto tripped, fell, and got up. She whacked the chicken on the head, and missed. The chicken ran out of the bar, destroying the door frame, and laughed deep into the forest. I looked round and saw Dad asleep on the chair, his head bent forward, snoring. I woke him up and he leapt with a start and fell off the chair. When he got up he said a leopard with glass teeth had been pursuing him in his dreams. He lay down beside me on the mat. With his smell in my nostrils, he made me worried and unhappy. He was restless beside me and his bones kept creaking. He kept sighing and muttering words to his ancestors and I found myself again in Madame Koto's bar deep in the forest. Dad wasn't there. The customers this time were all invisible and I saw the air drinking palm-wine. Madame Koto sat on a chair made of chicken feathers. Dad began to snore. He snored so hard that the long wooden broom in the corner began to sweep the bar, spreading white dust everywhere. Madame Koto commanded the broom to be still but Dad went on snoring and the broom took on a will of its own and attacked the cobwebs and swept the tables and when it attempted to sweep Madame Koto out of her own establishment she lost her temper. Then I saw her fighting with the long broom. The broom hit her on the head. I laughed. Dad stopped snoring. She grabbed the broom, threw it over her shoulder, and smashed it on the floor, breaking its neck. The handle of the broom began to bleed. With blood on her face, Madame Koto turned to me, who was dreaming her, and said:

'You laughed at me? You're next!'

She started towards me with a demonic expression, and I cried out. Dad put his arm round me and said:

'Go to sleep, my son. Nothing will harm you.'

After a long silence, as if answering an important question which the night and his parents and his hopes had put to him, he said:

'I have been carrying the world on my head today.'

Soon afterwards he fell asleep. He slept like a giant.

FOURTEEN

DAD WAS PRAYING over Mum's body. There was a herbalist in the room. He looked very fierce and wise and stank of old leaves. He chewed on a root and his teeth were brown. He sprinkled the room with liquid from a half-calabash. There were candles on both sides of Mum's body. She lay on the mat, breathing gently. Her eyelids shone with antimony. The corpse of a bat lay by her face. Razor incisions had been made on her shoulders and I watched the blood turn black as the herbalist smeared the cut with ash. The herbalist made her sit up and drink from a bowl of bitter liquid. Mum contorted her face. The herbalist began whipping the air, driving out unwanted spirits with his charmed flywhisk. The air crackled with their cries. When he had sealed our spaces with gnomic spells, he made Mum sit up again. Under our intense gaze, he bit Mum's shoulder and pulled out a long needle and three cowries from her flesh. He went outside and buried them in the earth.

When he had finished with his treatment Mum fell asleep, looking more peaceful than before. The herbalist and Dad haggled about money. Dad's voice was strained and he kept pleading for the charges to be a little lower. The herbalist wouldn't budge. Dad said it was all he had. The herbalist wouldn't relent. Dad sighed, paid, and they sat talking. I hated the herbalist for taking so much money off Dad, and I cursed him. They talked as if they were friends and I hated him even more for pretending to be our friend. When he got up to leave he seemed to notice me for the first time. He stared hard at me and gave me a pound, which I gave to Dad. I took back my curse, and he left. I sat on Dad's legs and we watched Mum sleeping soundly on the bed.

Late in the afternoon Dad said he was thirsty. We went to the bar. Madame Koto's establishment was empty except for the flies. I heard her singing in the backyard. Dad called her but she didn't hear. We both called her, banging on the table, and still she couldn't hear us. We were banging away at the table, calling her name, when the front door swung open and a black wind came in and circled us and disappeared into an earthenware pot of water.

'Did you see that, Dad?' I asked.

'What?'

'The black wind.'

'No.'

Madame Koto came in, her hair a mess, her hands covered in animal gore.

'So it's you two. I'm coming.'

She went back out and minutes later was back, her hands clean, her hair in place.

'What do you want to drink?'

Dad ordered the usual palm-wine and bushmeat peppersoup. When the wine was served the flies thickened around us. A wall-gecko watched us as we drank.

'Look at that wall-gecko, Dad.'

'Don't mind it,' he said without looking. 'It's our friend, watching over us.'

The peppersoup was hotter than usual and I kept blowing to cool its fire.

'Drink some water,' Madame Koto said.

'No, I don't want water.'

'Why not?'

'The black wind went into it.'

'What wind?'

'Don't mind him,' Dad said.

She eyed me suspiciously.

'You have a strange son,' she said, and sat across from us at the table.

'And a good wife,' Dad added. 'I heard what you did. Thank you.'

She ignored Dad's gratitude. With her big eyes fixed on me, she said:

'About this money you're owing me . . .'

'Me?' I said.

'Not you. Your father.'

'Yes?'

'I'm not like the other people.'

'What other people?'

'The people you owe and who . . .'

She stopped, looked at Dad, and then at me.

'I will forget the money if you let your son come and sit in my bar now and again.'

Dad looked at me.

'Why?' he asked.

'Because he has good luck.'

'What good luck? He has given us nothing but trouble.'

'That's because he is your son.'

'I can't agree. He is going to school.'

'I don't want to go to school,' I said.

'Shut up.'

Madame Koto stared at Dad, her eyes brighter.

'I will pay for him to go to school.'

'I can pay for my own son,' Dad replied proudly.

'All right. I will forget the money. Just let him come and sit here for ten minutes every three days or so. That's all.'

'Do you want to turn him into a drunkard?'

'His father is not a drunkard.'

Dad looked at me. He looked at me with new eyes. The wall-gecko hadn't moved. It watched us the whole time.

'I will discuss it with his mother.'

'Good.'

'But these people I owe money, what about them?'

'What about them?'

'You were going to tell me something.'

'Didn't your son tell you?'

'What?'

'That they threw stones at your wife?'

'Who? Who threw stones?'

Madame Koto got up and fetched some more palm-wine.

'I can't tell you.'

Dad turned to me, and he looked so fierce that before he asked me anything I told him who the people were and what had happened. He downed half a glass of palm-wine in one gulp, rubbed the spillings all over his sweating face, and stormed out of the bar without paying.

By the time we got to our compound Dad had managed to whip himself up into a fantastic rage. We ran into one of the creditors who was just coming out of the toilet. Dad went straight up to him and without saying a single word he feinted with a right jab at the fellow's face and punched him in the stomach. The creditor bent

63

over, grunting, and Dad grabbed him round the waist and threw him, back first, on the ground. When Dad straightened, dusting his hands, he saw another creditor, whose son had stoned Mum on the head. The second creditor had witnessed the efficiency of Dad's fury and had started to run. Dad chased after him, caught him, tripped him, helped him up, lifted the poor fellow on his shoulders, showed him to the sky, and tossed him on to a patch of mud.

The first creditor, who had quickly recovered from his fall, came running towards us swinging high a burning firewood. Dad was delighted. He ducked the arc of the firewood, smashed the fellow in the stomach again and confused him with repeated left jabs to his face. Then with a cry that amazed everyone he floored the creditor with a right cross.

The second creditor, covered in mud, came at Dad, swearing in three languages. Dad practised his right jabs on his nose till he began to bleed and then polished him off with a left hook. People had gathered. The second creditor was a motionless heap on the floor and the wives and relations of the fallen man crowded Dad. He kept hitting at the men, lashing out with both hands in wild swings, intent on entirely separating their heads from their bodies. The men were scared and in their fear they walked into Dad's swinging punches. He knocked out three of them with his bad arm alone. The crowd was mesmerised by his prowess.

'Boxer! Boxer!' they chanted.

The wives of the creditors pounced on Dad and scratched his face and went for his crotch and I heard him cry out. He managed to push them away. Then he ran. The women and children pursued Dad, who fled both from their rage and from his own fear of hurting them. When they couldn't catch Dad they turned their anger on me and I fled screaming to Madame Koto's place and hid behind the earthenware pot. The women and relatives shouted outside. They were too afraid of Madame Koto's reputation to come in and disrupt her establishment. She heard their noises from the backyard and I saw her securing her wrapper tightly round her waist, in complete readiness for battle, as she strode towards them, shouting:

'Yes, what do you people want? WINE OR WAR?'

The pack of them scattered at Madame Koto's terrifying advance. When they had retreated completely, I came out from behind the earthenware pot. Madame Koto smiled at me. Then she poured me a tumbler of palm-wine. I drank with the flies and, later, Dad, dodging among the shadows of the bushes, came and joined me on the bench.

We drank till it was evening. When I got to my third tumbler of wine I noticed that the wall-gecko was still staring at us. It had a red stripe on its head. It never nodded and its eyes were like tiny beads of sapphire. When anyone else looked at the wall-gecko, it ran on.

'What are you looking at?' Dad asked.

'Nothing,' I said.

When it got dark Dad sent me to the compound to see if Mum was still asleep. I was reluctant to go. He gave me a good piece of bushmeat and filled my little tumbler with wine and I drank it all down and he said:

'Be the true son of your father.'

I smiled drunkenly and went out of the bar. The bushpaths were quiet. Then I heard a cock crowing and the lively insects and the night birds clearing their voices for their chorus of nightsongs. I swayed and the world turned and everything became silent again. I passed a tree with a blue cloth dangling from a branch and I was about to take the cloth when a dog barked at me. I wasn't scared. I felt, for some reason, that I knew the dog from somewhere. When the dog saw that I wasn't afraid it backed away and trotted off into the forest and I followed its stiffened tail. Then I remembered Mum and continued with my journey to the compound. It was a perfectly straightforward path from Madame Koto's bar to our house but the dog had confused me and all the paths had fractured. I followed one path and it led me into the forest. I followed it back and I arrived at a place I had never seen in my life before. All the houses were gigantic, the trees were small, the sky low, the air golden.

I tried to get out of this place, but I didn't know how. I took the path back to the forest but it led me deeper into that land. I stopped and it was quiet and I didn't even hear the flies buzzing or the insects thrilling or birds twittering. The heat was different. Then I noticed that nothing in that strange place cast a shadow. The light of the red sun went right through everything. There was no wind. The air was still and cool. When I began walking again I didn't hear my own footsteps. After a while I wasn't afraid. In a way everything became familiar to me and I went on along the fractured paths. I walked for a long time. Then I saw a man coming towards me. He had white stripes on his face. His eyes were green. But when I looked at him properly something about him changed and I saw that his legs were unnaturally hairy and that his face was upside down on his neck. The features of his face were all scrambled

65

up. His eyes were on his cheeks, his mouth was on his forehead, his chin was full of hair and his head was bald except for his beard, and I couldn't make out his ears. I had to bend my head and twist my thinking to make sense of his features. I couldn't understand how I had perceived him as normal the first time I saw him. He went past me without saying a word. The eyes at the back of his head watched me cautiously.

I took another path to avoid him, but further down I saw him approaching. I went on trying to get away from him. It seemed we were caught in an invisible labyrinth. Each time I encountered him he seemed more intent on me. When I came to a grove of blue trees, I hid behind one of them. Inside the tree I heard loud and passionate voices as if from an important meeting. I took a path and to my shock I saw myself approaching. I stopped and the other person who was me said:

'What are you doing here?'

'Me?'

'Yes.'

'What about you?'

'What about me?'

'What are you doing here?'

'Why do you ask?'

'Because I want to know.'

'I am on a message.'

'What message?'

'To you.'

'To me?'

'Yes.'

'What is the message?'

'I was sent to tell you to go home.'

'That's what I am trying to do.'

'Are you sure?'

'Yes, of course. Anyway, who sent you?'

'Who do you think?'

'I don't know.'

'Our king.'

'What king?'

'The great king.'

'Where is he?'

'What sort of question is that?'

There was a pause. I looked hard at the riddle who stood before me. He stared hard at me too.

'You look like me,' I said.

'It's *you* who looks like *me*,' he replied.

Then as a suspicion of who he was began to dawn on me, he said:

'Take that path there and you will be all right.'

I looked where he was pointing and I saw the dog I had followed earlier. When I looked back at the other person who was me, he had gone. I followed the dog. We went down the path for some time. There were blue strips of cloth on the trees. The path narrowed, became tiny, and I felt I was walking on a wall. I had been keeping my eyes on the path, making sure I didn't deviate from it, and I didn't notice when we broke out of the forest. When I looked up I saw Madame Koto, resplendent in yellow, dressed as if for a party.

'Where have you been?'

'I don't know,' I said.

She shook her head in mild exasperation and carried on to her destination. When she left I couldn't find the dog anywhere, and I went on home.

It had grown very dark. I got to our compound, hurried to our room, and found no one in. Mum wasn't on the bed. The room was neat. The corners smelt of disinfectant. I left the room and wandered down the passages. No one seemed to be around. Then in the last room I heard all the concentrated noises of the compound, crowded into a single place. There was a lot of shouting. Dad's voice kept rising above the din. When I looked into the room through a crack in the door, I saw the whole compound there, gathered in a boisterous meeting. There were no drinks on the table. On one side of the room there were the creditors and their relations. The two that Dad had beaten up were shouting at the back. One of them had a machete, the other a club. Between them and the centre table were the men and women of the compound. On the other side of the room were Mum and Dad and lots of children and the photographer, who was busy taking pictures. The landlord was the arbitrator. Every time the flash went the landlord stiffened into a pose. Dad was quiet and Mum looked well. One of the creditors said:

'If you're so strong why not become a boxer!'

'I will,' Dad replied.

The other creditor said:

'Why don't you join the army, use your muscles, and get killed. It's only here that you are strong.'

The landlord held up his hand to command silence. The flash

went. He stiffened. The creditors shouted about their money and their wounds. They sounded like children. Dad smiled. The landlord, amid flashes, gave his verdict. He fined Dad ten pounds, a hefty fine indeed. The creditors were jubilant. The landlord said Dad should pay his debts and the fine in one week or move out of the compound. Then, with the jubilant voices claiming the air, he went on to additionally fine Dad a bottle of ogogoro for the purposes of communal reconciliation. Dad said he had no money and that he would have to buy it on credit. The women of the compound laughed. The camera flashed. The landlord, in a moment of unusual magnanimity, offered to buy the ogogoro of reconciliation. The compound people cheered his wisdom. I sneaked away from the door, went to the housefront, and played with the other children on the sand.

Not long afterwards I heard the compound voices emerge into the passage. I went to the backyard, washed my face and feet, and went to the room. Mum was bustling around as if she hadn't been ill. Her face was a little flushed and her eyes were bright. Recovery had charged her spirit and regenerated her face. Dad sat on a chair, smoking. He looked happy. Food was spread out on the table. The wound on Dad's head had healed, his bad hand no longer dangled.

'Where have you been?' he asked.

Mum rushed to me and held me to her and I breathed in her body smells. It felt as if I had been away for days, as if I had wandered off into a phase of forgetfulness.

'My son!' Mum cried, her eyes unusually brilliant.

Dad put out his cigarette and said:

'You missed the compound meeting. They fined me. I got tired of waiting for you, so I came home. Your mother is well now. The gods have answered our prayers.'

I held on to Mum. Dad continued:

'Sit down and eat. From tomorrow, up till the time you begin school, you will go to Madame Koto's bar. You will stay there a few minutes every day, eh.'

I nodded. I washed my hands. We ate together and Dad kept plying me with choice bits of crayfish and chicken, while Mum carefully took out the bones from the spiky freshfish and fed me juicy morsels. The room was bright with their radiance. I felt strange. I had missed the important moment which had transformed the lights in our world.

We finished eating and I took the plates to the backyard and washed them. On my way back I passed one of the creditors that Dad had beaten up. His face was bruised, ferocious, and cowardly. When he went past he gave me a secretive knock on the head. When I got to our room my eyes were watering. Mum and Dad were sitting together on the bed. Mum looked at me and said:

'Look, our son is crying with happiness.'

I smiled and the pain eased. I cleared the centre table, spread the mat, and stretched out. Dad went to his chair. The candle burned low and Mum lit another one. I watched the mystery of the flame. Mum arranged her provisions in a basin.

'I'm going to start trading again,' she said.

Dad smiled.

'My wife is a serious businesswoman,' he said.

Then he looked at me.

'People think I will make a good boxer. A man across the street saw me when I beat up the creditors. He said he would introduce me to some trainers and managers. A good trainer. Free of charge.'

He laughed. He punched the air and rocked backwards.

'I will be a great boxer. People say there is money in boxing.'

He hit out at the air again. He began to punch the candle flame, putting it out with each perfect execution, and relighting it.

'I fight fire and become fire. Anyone who fights me fights the sun.'

He laughed again. I kept on watching the mystery of the flame. Mum made a weary sound. I looked and saw she wasn't happy about Dad becoming a boxer. She was counting her small change. She said:

'Your father used to box and wrestle in the village. They used to call him Black Tyger. He beat up all the young men. One day, before a fight, he punched a big hole in the wall of his father's enemy.'

Dad laughed out loud. Mum continued.

'The enemy put a curse on him. Then people went around saying that if your father fought again, he would be beaten. They said he would go mad for one week. Your father stopped fighting. The villagers gave his title to someone else. But his supporters kept coming to get him to fight and win back his title as champion of the village. They all bet heavily on him. At first your father refused and then out of pride he accepted. The man, a small man, threw your father in the last round. Your father lost.'

'But I didn't go mad for one week. That was all village talk.'

'But you came to the city.'

69

'Yes, I came to the city.'

They both fell silent. It seemed, almost, as if they had come to hell. Mum finished counting her small change and sat on the bed. Dad sighed.

'I haven't seen my father in five years,' he said.

Suddenly a rat began chewing away at something beneath the cupboard. A big fly started up, as if it had just awoken from a long sleep, and buzzed about the room. A moth rose from Dad's boots and circled the candle flame in a descending spiral. Dad lit a cigarette and smoked meditatively. The noise of the rat increased and other rats joined in the chewing. Mum's face twitched. Dad said:

'Your grandfather is completely blind now. He is the head-priest of our shrine, Priest of the God of Roads. Anyone who wants a special sacrifice for their journeys, undertakings, births, funerals, whatever, goes to him. All human beings travel the same road.'

He paused. Then continued:

'I was supposed to succeed him as priest but the elders of the village said: "Your son is a fighter. How can a fighter be the Priest of Roads? The god has chosen a successor outside your family. But who knows the future?" Your grandfather was very disappointed about this. He is blind now and he wears dark glasses and wanders through the village and the world without any walking stick or any help. Our old people are very powerful in spirit. They have all kinds of powers.'

His voice was very sad.

'We are forgetting these powers. Now, all the power that people have is selfishness, money, and politics.'

The rats went on eating. The moth came too close to the candle flame, singed its wings, and fell into the wax. The smoke from its burnt wings was dense and didn't rise high and the moth writhed in the wax and caught fire. I blew out the two flames, took the moth from the wax, and lit the candle again. Dad said:

'The only power poor people have is their hunger.'

Mum said:

'Those rats!'

She stretched her limbs on the bed. Dad finished with his cigarette. I got out my pillow and cover-cloth. Dad blew out the candle and I listened to the rats eating and the fly buzzing in the darkness. Dad got into bed. The springs creaked. The rats went on chewing and Dad, in the darkness, said:

'Azaro, rats can be our friends. They can sometimes tell what is happening in the world. They are our spies. Listen to them, Azaro, and tomorrow tell me what the rats are saying.'

I listened to the rats. One of them had teeth of yellow diamonds. They didn't seem to be saying anything and soon I heard the bed-springs creaking in their particular rhythm of other nights. The movement of the bed overcame the noise of the rats. I slept and woke up and heard Mum sighing differently and the bed shook and humped shapes wandered about in the darkness and I slept again.

I woke suddenly and the bed still moved and soon I didn't notice the musical creaking of the springs for I could hear beneath those sounds the shrill intensity of the rats. Just before I fell asleep again I stopped hearing the bed altogether because I suddenly realised that if I tried hard enough I could understand the language of rats. They were saying, as they ate their way through Mum's sack of garri, that the world is tougher than fire or steel. I didn't understand what they meant and I dozed off trying to get them to explain it to me. But they couldn't understand me because, unlike us, they speak only one language.

Book Two

ONE

THE WORLD IS full of riddles that only the dead can answer. When I began to go to Madame Koto's place I understood why the spirits were curious about her. I went to her bar in the afternoons after school. She was often in the backyard. She was often digging the earth, planting a secret, or taking one out. One day I hid and watched her and saw her plant round white stones in the earth. I did not know their significance or even if they had any.

Sometimes when I came in from school she would be in the bushes in the backyard and as soon as she heard me she would shout:

'Sit down! Sit down and attract customers! Draw them here!'

I would sit and swot flies. The palm-wine everywhere made the flies so plentiful that sometimes when I inhaled I was sure I breathed them in as well. I would sit in the empty bar, near the earthenware pot, and would watch passers-by through the curtain strips. At first when I sat there alone no one came to drink and it seemed as if I was bringing more bad luck than good.

In the afternoons the bar was empty. One or two people who had no jobs would come in and haggle over the price of a glass of palm-wine. The moment someone came into the bar Madame Koto treated them respectfully. What she hated was people standing outside uncertain. She preferred them to go away rather than come in. She was very decided in this respect.

Women sometimes came by in the afternoons. They were mostly hawkers of sun-bleached goods. They talked about their children or their husbands or about the forthcoming elections and about the thugs and violence, the people of different parties killed in skirmishes deep in the country. The women always came with bundles on their heads. They often looked both sad and robust, or spirited and lean. Many of them were hawkers on their way to the market or just stopping to get some shade and some respite from the dusty ghetto paths. They talked in high-pitched voices and congregated round Madame Koto in the backyard as she sat on a stool preparing the evening's peppersoup.

When the women came by they always teased me, saying:

'There's the boy who would marry my daughter. Look at him, he's being trained in the ways of women.'

They all had children strapped to their backs. The ways of women: I learned a lot about what was happening in the country through them. I learned about the talk of Independence, about how the white men treated us, about political parties and tribal divisions. I would sit in the bar, on a bench, with my feet never touching the floor, and would listen to their stories of lurid sexual scandals as sleep touched my eyes with the noon-day heat. It was always hot and the flies and wall-geckos, the gnats and midges, were always active.

The women would talk for a while. Madame Koto would buy a thing or two from them, and they would set out on the hot roads, touching me or smiling as they went.

Sometimes Madame Koto would vanish altogether and leave me in the empty bar. Customers would come in and I would stare at them and they at me.

'Any palm-wine?'

'Yes.'

'Serve us, then.'

I wouldn't move.

'You don't want to serve us?'

I wouldn't speak.

'Where is your madame?'

'I don't know.'

They would wander off to the backyard and come back and sit for a while.

'What is your name?'

I wouldn't tell them. They would leave disgusted and I wouldn't see them again for a long time afterwards. When Madame Koto returned and I told her about the customers she spoke harshly to me.

'Why didn't you come and call me?'

'Where?'

'In my room.'

'Where?'

'Come.'

She showed it to me. That was when I realised she had a room in the compound. Her room was near the toilet. She never let me in, and the door was always locked. I also learnt that in the afternoons she often went to the market to buy ingredients for her evening's cooking, finding the right herbs for her flavoured peppersoup. Sometimes she bought ground tobacco and rolled it around in her mouth all afternoon long.

One afternoon I was sitting in my customary position when the earthenware pot began to rattle. I put my hands on it and it stopped. I took my hands off and it rattled. I went to the backyard, looking around for some sort of explanation. When I came back I saw, standing in the doorway, three of the strangest-looking men. They were unusually tall and very black. Their eyes were almond-shaped, they had small noses, their arms were quite short, and the smiles on their faces never altered. They spoke among themselves in nasal voices that sounded as if they had no chests. I couldn't understand what they said. They refused to move from the doorway. They looked around the bar, inspecting it, studying the place, each facing a separate direction, as if their different heads connected a central intelligence.

Their eyes were deep and dull and confusing. I could not be sure at any given moment if they were looking at me or at the ceiling. I indicated the benches. They shook their heads simultaneously. They just stood there, completely blocking out the light from the door. I looked at their short arms, limp at their sides, and my head nearly fell off in fright when I discovered that all of them without exception had six fingers on each hand. Then I noticed that they were barefoot and their toes were inturned like those of certain animals. They radiated a potent and frightening dignity. I got down from the bench and ran to Madame Koto's room and shouted that she had three strange customers. She bustled out towards the bar, tightening her wrapper round her, spitting out the ground tobacco in her mouth. When I got there she was outside. I looked around. The flies and wall-geckos had gone. A black cat peeped at me from the backyard door. I went after it and it leapt over the wall of the compound. I went to the barfront and couldn't find Madame Koto. I went into the bar and she was wiping the table tops with a wet rag, saying:

'I didn't see anybody. Call me only when customers arrive, you hear?'

I didn't nod or say anything.

✣

After Mum recovered from her illness she became sadder and leaner and more sober. Each morning when she woke up from sleep she went around the room as if something had knocked her out the night before and she could not place what it had been. Dad took to going to bed late and waking early. When I got up in the mornings he had gone off to look for jobs. Mum would potter about the room, muttering to herself about rats and poverty.

On some mornings I woke to the commotion of Mum thrashing the cupboard with a broom. She lashed at the cupboard, whipped underneath it, flogged her basins of provisions and sacks of garri as if they had personally offended her. Sometimes cockchafers scattered everywhere under her lashing and they clambered on to my face and I would jump up. Mum, oblivious, wreaking vengeance, would carry on lashing them. She would sweep their corpses on to a pan, dump the broom, go out to dispose of the cockchafers, and we would settle down to eat. She always gave me some bread to take to school and she always walked me as far as the junction and then carried on, basin balanced on her head, through the streets, crooning out her provisions.

For a while Dad disappeared from my life. I woke up and he wouldn't be there. I went to sleep and he wouldn't have returned. He worked very hard and when I saw him on Sundays he seemed to be in agony. His back always hurt and in the evenings me and Mum had to walk on him to ease the pain. His back was very strong and ridged and I could never balance on it. When Mum trod on him his spine creaked and we took to rubbing him with a foul-smelling ointment we got from an itinerant herbalist. Dad worked hard carrying heavy loads at the garage and marketplaces and he earned very little money. Out of what he earned he paid the creditors, who came to our room every evening to remind us that they were still alive. And out of what was left we could barely manage to pay the rent and eat. After some days of not seeing Dad I asked Mum what had happened to him.

'He's working for our food,' she said.

It was night. Children played in the passage. Inside, we had no light because we couldn't afford a candle. Mum moved about in the darkness in uncomplaining silence. She kicked something and cursed and sat down and I lit a match and saw blood pouring out of the big toe of her right foot.

'The right foot is supposed to be lucky,' she said.

The blood dripped to the floor and I said:

78

'Shall I boil water?'

She said nothing. The match burnt down to my fingers. Her blood became the colour of the darkness. I couldn't hear her breath, couldn't see her. And before I could light another match she got up and limped to the backyard. When she came back she had washed the cut and I asked her what she had put on it.

'Poverty,' she said.

I lit another match and studied the toe.

'Don't waste the matches,' she said sharply.

The cut still bled through the black stuff she had covered it with.

'Ash,' she said.

The light went out. We didn't move. The rats began to chew and the cockchafers began to stir in the cupboard.

'Time for you to sleep,' she said.

I didn't move. I wanted to stay awake till Dad returned. It grew late and dark. After a while I heard Mum say:

'I'm going to warm the food.'

We hadn't eaten since the morning. We had been going to sleep on empty stomachs for days.

'I'm coming with you.'

'Go to sleep or a ghost will grab you.'

'Let it try.'

She moved in the dark and I heard her at the door. Light came in and Mum went out. I sat in the darkness, listening. I tried to get up but something held me down. I tried to move but the darkness had become a resistant force. I lowered myself to the floor and crawled around on my hands and knees. Something crawled up my arm. I made to get up, frightened, and hit my head against the sharp edge of the centre table and I stayed like that till the darkness stopped dancing. Then I searched for Dad's chair and sat down. I could see the outline of things. I stayed there till Mum came back in.

'You're still up?'

'Yes.'

'Go to sleep.'

'I'm hungry.'

She was silent. Then after a while she said:

'Wait for your father. We will all share his food.'

I thanked her. She found me in the darkness and held my head to her and I heard her crying gently and then she said, in a lighter voice:

'Let me tell you the story about the stomach.'

'Tell me a story,' I said, expectantly.

She went back to the bed. I couldn't see her. The rats ate and the cockchafers fretted. She began.

'Powerful people eat very little,' she said.

'Why?'

'Because they are powerful. There was once a great medicine man in my village who would fly to the moon at night and then would walk across the mighty ocean to visit spirits in the country of white people . . .'

'Why?'

'Because he went to attend an important meeting concerning the future of the whole world. And to be able to attend the meeting he must do something great. So he flew to the moon and to many planets. After he had done that he went to the country of white people and before they allowed him in they asked him one question.'

'What?'

'They said: "Mr Medicine Man from the village of Otu, what did you eat before you went to the moon?" '

'And what did he say?'

'A cricket.'

'Only a cricket?'

'Yes, a small roasted cricket.'

We were silent for a while. I pondered the story with my feet not touching the floor.

'Is that the story of the stomach?'

'No,' Mum said in the darkness.

We were silent again. Then Mum began, saying:

'Once upon a time . . .'

I sat back in Dad's chair and folded up my feet.

'. . . there was a man without a stomach. Every year he used to worship at a great shrine. One day he met a stomach without a body. The stomach said: "I have been looking for you. What are you doing without me?" And then the stomach jumped on the man and became part of him. The man carried on with his journey to the shrine. But before he got there he became very hungry. The stomach said: "Feed me." "I will not," said the man. "When I didn't have you I travelled far, was never hungry, was always happy and contented, and I was strong. You can either leave me now or be quiet." . . .'

Somewhere around that point in the story I fell through the back of the chair and I flew on the back of a cricket and I was the man without a stomach, heading for a feast on the moon.

And then I found my eyes open and there was a candle lit on the table. Dad was standing above me, swaying. He looked both crushed and stunned.

'My brain has been pressed down, my son,' he said.

I quickly got down from his chair. He paced up and down the room, holding his head. And then he sat down heavily and was still.

'I found the candle at the market,' he said, and fell asleep.

Mum laid out his food and woke him up. He blinked.

'I have been carrying the most terrible loads in my dreams,' he groaned.

'You should eat,' Mum said.

We had gathered round the table. Dad didn't move. His face was lit by the candle. All the tendons on his neck showed up thick and tense. His face glistened, and veins throbbed on his temples. He surprised us by suddenly speaking:

'They have begun to spoil everything with politics,' he said in a ghostly and exhausted voice. 'Now they want to know who you will vote for before they let you carry their load.'

He paused. His eyes were bloodshot.

'If you want to vote for the party that supports the poor, they give you the heaviest load. I am not much better than a donkey.'

'Eat, you're tired,' Mum said.

Dad shut his eyes and began mumbling something which I took to be a prayer. He didn't open his eyes for a long time. And it was only when he began to snore that we knew he had fallen asleep again. Mum didn't want to disturb him a second time so we ate half the food and saved the rest for him to eat in the morning. We ate more quietly than the rats did.

Before I woke up in the morning Dad had gone and all I had of him were the smells of his boots, of mud, of cigarettes, the mosquito coil, and his sweat. The mood of the room was infected with his exhaustion.

We had cut down our food. That morning we had pap and bread. Mum went off to the market, went hawking her boxes of matches, sweets, cigarettes and odds and ends down the roads on a quite empty stomach. She looked much leaner and her blouse hung from her and the straps fell over her shoulders as if she had shrunk in her clothes.

As I walked behind her to the junction where we parted I felt very unhappy about the thinness of her voice amongst the noises of the ghetto. As she went off on her arduous journeys she seemed so frail that the slightest wind threatened to blow her away into the molten sky. Before she went she gave me a piece of bread, and told me to behave myself at school. I followed her a short way. She was barefoot. It pained me to see her stumble on the rubbish and stones of the paths. It seemed very harsh not to be able to go hawking with her, not to be able to protect her feet, and help her sell off all her provisions. I followed her and then she turned, saw me, and waved me on to school. I slowed down, turned back, and watched her disappear into the expanding ghetto.

TWO

WHEN I WENT to Madame Koto's bar after school, the place was empty. I was hungry. Sitting near the earthenware pot, I kept telling myself that I didn't have a stomach. I slept and woke up. Flies had come into the bar. I went to Madame Koto's room to ask for food and was about to knock when I heard her chanting. I heard the ringing of a bell. I was about to go back to the bar when two women of the compound saw me and said:

'What are you doing?'

I said nothing. They held me and I shouted. Madame Koto came out. She had antimony on one side of her face, kaoline on the other, and her mouth was full of the juice of ground tobacco. The women looked at her, then at one another, and hurried on.

'Why didn't you knock?' she asked, her mouth dripping with the tobacco.

'You were busy.'

'Go to the bar.'

'I'm hungry.'

'How can you be hungry with that small stomach?'

Then she went back to her room. The bells started up. I went to the bar and the flies played around my nose. It got very humid and I couldn't breathe and my hunger got unbearable. I went out of the bar and wandered along the paths. It was excruciatingly hot. Trees shimmered in the sun. The shadows were dense. Insects sizzled among the bushes. A lizard half crossed my way and then it stopped, turned towards me, and nodded. A bell rang. Its jangling noise scared me and I jumped out of the path, into the bushes, and a huge man with a wide mouth rode past on a little bicycle. He gave an insane laugh as he shot past. I stayed in the bushes and only came running out when I felt my legs burning with stings. I had trodden on an army of ants. I got them off me and was about to return to the bar when I noticed that the poor lizard was dead in the middle of the

83

path. The bicycle had ridden over it and it had died with its head caught in an exaggerated nod. The ants marched towards it and I picked up the lizard by the tail and took it with me towards the bar, intent on giving it a good burial.

Outside the bar there was a man standing barefoot in the heat. He had on only a pair of sad-looking underpants. His hair was rough and covered in a red liquid and bits of rubbish. He had a big sore on his back and a small one on his ear. Flies swarmed around him and he kept twitching. Every now and then he broke into a titter. I tried to go round him but he kept cutting off my path.

'Madame Koto!' I called.

The man came towards me. He had one eye higher than the other. His mouth looked like a festering wound. He twitched, stamped, laughed, and suddenly ran into the bar. I went after him, carrying the dead lizard as if it were a protective fetish. I found him crouched behind the earthenware pot. He snarled at me.

'Madame Koto!' I called again.

The madman tittered, baring his red teeth, and then he rushed at me. I threw the dead lizard in his face. He laughed, screamed, and fell on the benches, tittering in demented delight. He got up, walked in every direction, oblivious of objects, knocking over the long wooden tables and the benches. He came after me. I ran in circles. He scuttled round the floor like a monstrous quickened crab. With the exhilarated animation of a child, he discovered the dead lizard and began playing with it. He sat on an upturned table, his eyes making contradictory journeys round their sockets. Then he began to eat the lizard.

'MADAME KOTO!' I screamed, with the full volume of my horror.

She came rushing in, holding a new broom. She saw the confusion in her bar, saw the madman eating the lizard, twitching and tittering, and she pounced on him, hitting him with the head of the long broom, as if he were a cow or a goat. The madman didn't move. He ate with a weird serenity. Madame Koto knocked the lizard from his hands. Then, tying her wrapper tighter round her waist, she went for his neck with her big hands.

He turned his head towards me, his eyes bulging. White foam frothed from the sides of his mouth. Then, with a sudden burst of energy, and a cry uttered at white heat, he tossed Madame Koto off him, stood up straight like an awakened beast, and charged at everything. He fought and clawed the air, uttering his weird cry.

Then he changed. He brought out his gigantic prick, and pissed in every direction. Madame Koto hit his prick with her broom. He pissed on her. She rushed out and came back with a burning firewood. She burned his feet and he did a galloping dance and jumped around and tore out of the bar and ran tittering towards the forest.

Madame Koto looked around her wrecked bar. She looked at the burning firewood in her hand and then she stared at me.

'What sort of child are you?' she asked.

I began to pick up the benches.

'Maybe you bring only bad luck,' she said. 'Since you have been coming my old customers have gone and there are no new ones.'

'I'm hungry,' I said.

'Attract customers, draw them here, and then you will have food,' she said, going to the backyard.

Later she took the benches and tables outside and scrubbed them with a special soap. She swept the bar and washed the place with a concentrated disinfectant. She brought the tables and benches back in when the sun had dried them and then went to have the bath she always had before the evening's customers arrived.

When she finished bathing she came to the bar with a bowl of peppersoup and yam. She slammed it down and said:

'Since you're so hungry you better finish it.'

I thanked her and she went back out. I washed a spoon and settled down to eat. The soup was very hot and I drank a lot of water. The yam was soft and sweet. There were pieces of meat and offal in the soup and I had almost eaten them all before I realised that one of the pieces was actually a chicken's head. The pepper burned in my brain and I was convinced that the chicken's head was eyeing me. Madame Koto came in carrying a fetish glistening with palm oil. She dragged a bench under the front door, climbed on it, and hung the fetish on a nail above the door. I noticed for the first time that she had a little beard.

'I don't like chicken's head,' I told her.

'Eat it. It's good for your brain. It makes you clever, and if you eat the eyes you will be able to see in the dark.'

I didn't eat it. She came down, dragged the bench back to its position, and stood in front of me.

'Eat it!' she said.

'I'm not hungry any more.'

Madame Koto regarded me. She had rubbed pungent oils on her skin. She looked radiant and powerful. The oils smelt badly and I think they were one of the reasons why the spirits were interested in her.

'So you won't eat it?'

I knew she would become angry and would never give me food in future if I didn't eat it; so, reluctantly, and hating every moment of it, I did. I cracked the chicken's head with my teeth. I broke its beak. I swallowed down its red comb. I scraped off the thin layer of flesh on its crown.

'What about the eyes?'

I sucked out the eyes and chewed them and spat them out on the floor.

'Pick them up!'

I picked up the eyes, cleared the table, and went to wash the plates. When I got back she had set down a glass of her best palm-wine for me. I sat in a corner, near the earthenware pot, and drank peacefully.

'That's how to be a man,' she said.

The palm-wine got to me fairly quickly and I dozed sitting upright. I woke up when some rowdy customers came in. They smelt of raw meat and animal blood.

'Palm-wine!' one of them shouted.

Flies congregated round the new customers. Madame Koto brought them a great gourd of wine. They drank the lot very quickly and the evening's heat increased their smells. They got rowdier. They argued furiously amongst themselves about politics. Madame Koto tried to calm them down but they ignored her altogether. They argued with passionate ferocity in an incomprehensible language and the fiercer they got the more they stank. One of them whipped out a knife. The other two fell on him. In the confusion they scattered the table and benches, broke the gourd and glasses, and managed to disarm the man. When they had put the knife away one of them cried:

'More palm-wine!'

Madame Koto went out and fetched her broom. They saw the violence on her face.

'No more palm-wine!' she said. 'And pay for what you've broken.'

They paid without any complaints and went out arguing as vigorously as they had been doing.

I went back to my corner and finished my glass of palm-wine. Madame Koto poured me some more. The aroma of her rich-scented peppersoup floated in from the backyard. The evening wore on and customers drifted in. Odd customers. A man came in who was solidly drunk already. He kept cursing and swearing.

'Look at that toad,' he said about me. 'Look at that fat woman with a beard,' he said about Madame Koto.

Then he rushed outside, came back, and asked for a gourd of palm-wine. When he was served he drank quietly, occasionally perking up to abuse everything. He abused the lizards, flies, the bench, and the ceiling. Then he fell quiet again and drank peacefully.

Another customer came in who was so totally cross-eyed that I began to feel cross-eyed myself from staring at him.

'What are you looking at?' he demanded angrily.

'Your eyes,' I said.

'Why? Haven't you got eyes of your own?'

'Yes, but I can't see them.'

He came over and knocked me on the head. I kicked him on the shin-bone. He knocked me again, harder, and I rushed out and grabbed Madame Koto's broom and came back in and hit him on the head with it. He cried out. He backed off. I hit him again. The drunken man began to curse. He abused cross-eyed people, abused brooms, swore at children, and became quiet. Madame Koto came in and seized the broom from me. I sat down.

'Serve me palm-wine,' the cross-eyed man said. 'And warn that boy of yours. He has been insulting my eyes.'

'What's wrong with your eyes?' Madame Koto asked, staring intensely at him.

He didn't reply and he sat down into a moody silence. After he had been served, he drank a great quantity in one go, looked at me, found me staring at him, and then he turned away, trying to hide his eyes from me.

'Serve me peppersoup!' he shouted.

Madame Koto served him and he devoured the meat and drank the soup very fast.

'Tell that boy not to stare at me,' he said.

'Why?'

He drank some more palm-wine and peered over his shoulder at me. His eyes interested me. One of them was green. Looking at the green eye had a strange effect on me.

'I will give you money if you look somewhere else,' he said.

'How much?'

Trying to hide his face, he came over and emptied all his spare change on the table. I pocketed it and watched him go back to his seat. He kept checking up on me. I had taken my eyes off him but it was hard to look anywhere else after the experience of seeing him. His eyes, in their strangeness, were magnetic. I kept my eyes off him and looked around the bar and noticed green patches on the floor. I couldn't understand where they came from. I drank some more palm-wine. The alarming realisation that the green patches were the stains of the madman's piss was beginning to dawn on me when the lights changed in the bar and the drunken man cursed and from the floor there rose a host of green spirits. They rose up and they grew till their heads touched the ceiling and then they shrank till they were no taller than the average chicken. They were all cross-eyed. They milled around the areas of the madman's piss and they stamped and made swarming noises. Everywhere I looked I saw cross-eyed spirits. I cried out and the drunken man abused the moon and Madame Koto came and took me outside and gave me some water and alligator pepper to chew on.

'You should go home now,' she said.

I was silent.

'Have some fresh air. Then go.'

I stayed outside a while. The moon was out in the sky. It was big, clear, and white. It was white, then it became silver, and I saw things moving on its face and I couldn't stop staring because it was so beautiful and so low in the dark blue sky. I watched it for a long time and sweet voices stirred in my ears and Madame Koto came out and said:

'What are you doing?'

She looked up, saw the moon, and said:

'Why are you looking at the moon? Haven't you seen a moon before?'

'Not like this one.'

'Come in, take your things, and go home. It's getting late.'

I pulled myself away from the moon and went back into the bar with her. The bar was full of the oddest people. There was a man in the corner who said loudly that he had just come back from Hitler's war. No one believed him.

'Hitler died years ago,' someone said.

'I killed him,' said the loud man.

'How?'

'I used a special juju. I blew pepper into his eyes and his moustache stood up and I killed him with this knife.'

88

He whisked out a knife, brandished it, and no one seemed concerned. In another corner a man kept tossing his head. Another man snorted. There was a younger man next to the drunk. He had a bright scar down his face. The drunk cursed and stopped and cursed again. The green cross-eyed spirits mingled with the clientele and one of the spirits climbed the wall like a new kind of lizard and studied Madame Koto's fetish.

It was a very odd night. The bar saw its most unusual congregation of the weird, the drunk, the mad, the wounded, and the wonderful. Madame Koto weaved her way through them all with the greatest serenity. She seemed fully protected and entirely fearless. I think she made a lot of money that night because as I was leaving she did something rare. She smiled at me. She was happy and graceful amidst all the bustle. She gave me a piece of uncooked yam and I took the expanding paths back home to Mum.

THREE

OUR ROOM WAS crowded. Mum was back early. She looked sun-eaten and tired. Sitting disdainfully on Dad's chair, with his feet on the table, was the landlord. Sitting on the bed, standing round the room, were the creditors and their relations. They looked angry and helpless. Everyone was silent when I came in. I went over to Mum. She put her arms round me and said:

'You all have to be patient.'

'How can we be patient?' said one of the creditors.

The others nodded vigorously.

'Patience will kill us. We have to eat and trade.'

'True.'

'But we have paid most of the money,' Mum said.

'But not all.'

'And not in one week,' added the landlord.

'Patience doesn't kill.'

'Nonsense,' said a creditor. 'Patience is killing my son. You think I will pay the native doctor patience?'

The landlord laughed and brought out a kola-nut from his voluminous robe. He ate it alone. I watched his lips turn reddish. Mum was silent and as the landlord munched away on his kola-nut the rats started chewing.

I looked round at the creditors as if their presence had robbed me of food. I said nothing.

'Look at his big stomach,' the landlord said of me, chuckling.

'Leave my son alone.'

'All we want is our money,' one of the creditors said, staring at me.

'I don't have your money,' I said.

'This boy is worse than his father.'

Mum stood up suddenly.

'If you have come to insult us leave our room,' she said.

She shut the door and the window. It became dark in the

room and Mum refused to light the candle. Every now and again the landlord lit a match and looked at everyone. The rats ate louder and Mum launched into a song of lamentation. The creditors didn't move. The landlord went on chewing.

When Mum stopped singing the silence became deeper. We remained in the silence and the gloom till there was a knock on the door.

'Who is it?'

'The photographer.'

'What do you want?'

'The photographs are ready.'

'So what?'

'Don't you want to see them?'

The landlord got up and opened the door. He stayed in the doorway, looking at the pictures with the help of the photographer's torch. Then he came into the room. The photographer trailed behind him, a camera on his shoulder.

'They are good,' the landlord said, passing the torch and the pictures round.

The creditors became animated and talked about images of the celebration, how so-and-so looked drunk, how that person's eyes were shut like a rogue's. Then the landlord said, as the photographs came back to him:

'Why is Madame Koto's face like that?'

Madame Koto's face was smudged. She looked like a washed-out monster, a cross between a misbegotten animal and a wood carving.

'She's a witch,' one of the creditors said.

'She's not,' I said.

'Shut up,' said Mum.

When I looked closer at the pictures we all seemed strange. The pictures were grained, there were dots over our faces, smudges everywhere. Dad looked as if he had a patch over one eye, Mum was blurred in both eyes, the children were like squirrels, and I resembled a rabbit. We all looked like celebrating refugees. We were cramped, and hungry, and our smiles were fixed. The room appeared to be constructed out of garbage and together we seemed a people who had never known happiness. Those of us that smiled had our faces contorted into grimaces, like people who had been defeated but who smile when a camera is trained on them.

The photographer was very pleased with the results and quoted prices for copies. One of the creditors said he would get his copy when Dad paid up. The landlord said:

'I look like a chief.'

'Thief,' I said.

Mum knocked me on the head.

'Your son looks like a goat,' the landlord said.

The creditors laughed. Mum said:

'We want to sleep now. Everyone should leave.'

'Is that how you talk to your landlord?'

'Okay, everyone should stay,' Mum said. 'Azaro, prepare your bed.'

I got up in the dark, moved the centre table, and unrolled my mat. I lay down. The creditors' feet were all around my head. The landlord went on chewing. After a brief silence one of the creditors said:

'All right, if I can't get my money now, I'm going to seize something.'

He got up from the bed, lifted the centre table, and went to the door.

'Goodnight, landlord,' he said, and left.

Mum didn't move. Another creditor, asking the landlord to light a match for him, took Dad's boots. The third one said:

'I won't take anything but I will keep coming back.'

The photographer said:

'I will come tomorrow.'

The landlord said:

'Tell your husband I want to see him.'

Then they all left. Mum got out of bed and warmed some food for Dad. When she finished she counted the money she had made that day. She put some aside for buying provisions and some towards the rent. The candle was low and as it burned towards the end its poor illumination showed up Mum's bony face, her hardening eyes, and the veins on her neck.

'I saw a mad boy today. They tied him to a chair and his mother was crying.'

'What happened to him?'

'How should I know?'

We were quiet.

'How is Madame Koto?'

'She's fine.'

'Does she ask about me?'

'No.'

'What does she do all the time?'

'She stays in her room. Today she had a lot of strange customers. She put up a juju on the wall. A madman came into the bar and ate a lizard and pissed everywhere.'

'If it's like that you must stop going there.'

'I don't want to.'

'Why not?'

'I don't want to.'

'How was school?'

'I don't like school.'

'You must like school. If your father had gone to school we wouldn't be suffering so much. Learn all you can learn. This is a new age. Independence is coming. Only those who go to school can eat good food. Otherwise, you will end up carrying loads like your father.'

We were silent again.

'You must be careful of Madame Koto.'

'Why?'

'People have been saying things about her. We don't know where she comes from. And that juju of hers, who made it?'

'I don't know.'

'Don't touch it.'

'I won't touch it. But what do they say about her?'

'You're a small boy. You won't understand.'

'Tell me.'

'Go to sleep.'

'Did she kill someone?'

'Go to sleep.'

We fell silent and Mum put away her basin of provisions and her money. She hadn't made much and the sourness of her face told me she was wondering whether walking the streets of the world, day after boiling day, crooning out her provisions till her voice was hoarse, was worth the little she earned at the end of it all. She sighed and I knew that in spite of everything she would carry on hawking. Her sigh was full of despair, but at the bottom of her lungs, at the depth of her breath's expulsion, there was also hope, waiting like sleep at the end of even the most torrid day.

As I drifted in the corridors of sleep, I heard a great loud voice singing from the gateway of the compound. The voice was rough and drunken. Another voice cried:

'Black Tyger!'

Dad kicked open the door and staggered into the room like a dreaded announcement. Mum jumped up and hurriedly lit a reserve candle. Her brightened face was tinged with uncertainty. Dad stood in the doorway like a drunken giant. His shoulders were hunched. He held a bottle of ogogoro in one hand. Both of his trouser legs were covered in mud up to the knees. He had on only one shoe. The room stank of drunkenness and mud. His neck creaked. Twisting his mouth, blinking as if reality were blinding him, he said, very loudly:

'I am going to join the army!'

And then he collapsed into a heap on the floor. We rushed over to help him up. He revived quickly, saw us struggling over him, and shoved us away. I was sent flying to the corner where his shoes used to be. Mum tumbled on to the bed. He staggered up, weaved, snatched up his bottle of ogogoro, took a deep drink, and said:

'How is my family?'

'We are well,' replied Mum.

'Good. Now I have some money. We can pay off the bastard creditors. We can pay off everybody. And then I will shoot them.'

He made an exaggerated imitation of a machine-gun.

'Aren't you hungry?' asked Mum.

'I fell into mud,' said Dad. 'I was coming down the road, drinking, singing, and then the road said to me: "Watch yourself." So I abused the road. Then it turned into a river, and I swam. It changed into fire and I sweated. It transformed into a tiger, and I killed it with one blow. And then it shrunk into a big rat and I shouted at it and it ran, like the creditors. And then it dissolved into mud, and I lost my shoe. If I had money I would be a great man.'

We stared at him in fear and confusion. He weaved a bit, stretched his back, and staggered towards his chair. He did not sit down but stood regarding the chair as if it were an enemy.

'You're looking at me, chair,' he said. 'You don't want me to sit on you, eh, because I fell in mud, isn't that correct?'

The chair said nothing.

'I'm talking to you, chair. Are you better than my bed? I talk to you and you move. What do you think you are, eh?'

The chair pondered the question for too long, so Dad kicked it – with his shoeless foot. He cried out, and looked at the chair again.

'Sit on the bed,' Mum said.

Dad looked at her venomously. Then he turned back to the chair.

'Be Still!' he said, with great authority.

The chair was still.

'That's better. Now I'm going to sit on you, whether I'm covered in mud or even in gold, you hear? And if you move, I will beat you up.'

He paused.

'They don't call me Black Tyger for nothing.'

Then he sat down heavily and the chair creaked so loudly that for a moment I thought it would disintegrate under his drunkenness. The chair wobbled and for some reason Dad wobbled with it and then he got up and grabbed it and flung it against the window. The chair clattered on the floor and the window flew open. Mosquitoes and midges invaded us and lizards scurried up the walls and rats scattered from underneath the cupboard and ran confused about the room. Dad went wild, grabbing at the chair, and lashing at the rats. He pursued them everywhere and banged his head against the cupboard. A rat fled towards the door and he chased it, dumping the chair, stamping, making machine-gun noises.

He stayed outside for a while and Mum picked up the chair and put it upright in its customary position. After a long while, Dad came back in with someone else's wrapper round his waist. He had bathed, and water dripped from his hair and he looked like a deranged boxer. His trousers were over his shoulder. Dad came in quietly, his eyes bright, and he looked at us furtively as though we might be angry with him. He drank some water and attempted to shut the window, but it wouldn't shut. He tried again. He raised a fist against it and sat slowly into the chair. He got up suddenly, ducking his head, throwing combination punches. Then he struggled into a pair of khaki trousers. His chest was bare and he was sweating already and his body glistened.

Dad looked very powerful. His shoulders were big and moulded like rock-shapes. His neck was thick. I had never noticed that his jaws were so square and his forehead so large. His nose was bigger than I remembered and he had a bristly growth of beard. His muscles rippled impressively. His transformation surprised me.

He was very restless and he kept moving, kept throwing left and right hooks in the air. He was oblivious of us. We watched him intently. He looked rough and wild. Eventually he sat down again and shut his eyes. Then he jerked his head up, and looked around.

The candle-light made his face fierce. To the ceiling he said:

'I carried loads today till I thought my neck and my back and my soul would break. Then I threw down the load and said: "Never again!" But I earned nothing, and I have a family to feed, and I carried the load and said: "There must be another way of earning money," and I thought, "I will join the army," and then later I saw Aku, our relative, and I borrowed some money from him.'

He was silent again and he shut his eyes.

'How is Aku?'

'Fine.'

'And his wife?'

'Well.'

'Did you see their children?'

'No.'

Then Dad raised his feet, to rest them as usual on the centre table. His feet hung in the air.

'What happened to the table?' he asked, opening his eyes, his feet still in the air. 'It was here when I came in.'

He dropped his feet and began to look for the centre table. He looked around the room, under the bed, behind the cupboard. He went outside and came back in again. We were silent.

'Where is the table?'

We said nothing. He glared at me and then at Mum as if we had been playing tricks on him.

'Where is it? Did it walk away? Did you people hide it? Did you sell it to buy food? Was it stolen? What happened to it, eh?'

He got agitated. His muscles rippled restlessly on his chest, his jaws worked furiously. Our silence angered him even further and Mum was forced to tell him what had happened. Then Dad truly went wild. He growled like an enraged lion, drew himself up to his fullest titanic height, stormed out of the room, and began raging down the passage so loudly that it seemed as though thunder had descended amongst us.

He woke up the whole compound with his fury. He banged on the doors of the creditors and strode up and down the passage demanding back his property that the creditors had stolen from him. The children woke up and began crying. Lights came on in the rooms and one by one people appeared at their doors with startled expressions on their faces. Some of the men had machetes and one man had a dane gun. The women went around saying:

'What has happened?'

Their husbands called them back harshly. Dad went on raging, accusing the creditors of robbing him of his entire property. One of them came out and said:

'I didn't take anything. I said I would wait for you to get back.'

'Who stole my furniture, then?'

The creditor stuttered and said:

'I didn't take anything.'

Dad counted out some money, gave it to him, and went on mounting his towering campaign against the other two.

'They are hiding now behind their wives' wrappers and yet in broad daylight they THREATENED my WIFE and SON and STOLE ALL MY THINGS! They are RATS COWARDS THIEVES AND ROGUES. Let them come out and DENY it!'

When the compound people understood what was going on they went back to their rooms. The lights went out one by one. Only the two eldest tenants came out to try and settle matters. Dad didn't listen to them and went on shouting. One or two men, hidden in the darkness of their rooms, said:

'It's Black Tyger. He's drunk.'

'Yes, I'm drunk,' Dad said loudly. 'But it doesn't stop me cursing the armed robbers.'

He went on to demand that the creditors return his furniture to his room immediately or he would break down their doors and burn down the house.

'He's mad,' someone said.

'Yes, I'm mad! I am a mad Tyger and I will burn everything down if those armed robbers don't return my things NOW!'

The two elders made another attempt at conciliation. Then they tried to hold him down. Dad tossed them off and went on raging like a dangerous animal.

Somewhere in the compound a husband and wife began quarrelling. After a while a door opened and one of the creditors came out timidly, carrying the centre table. With his head hung low, he crept to our room and Dad's voice raged over him in utter scorn. The creditor dropped the centre table outside our door and was creeping back to his room when Dad blocked his way and said:

'Is that where you found it, eh, you thief!'

'I'm not a thief. You owe me money.'

'Is that where you found it?'

The creditor turned back and picked up the table. I was about to open the door for him but Dad shouted:

'Don't open the door for that COWARD!'

So the creditor dropped the table, opened the door, went in with the table, and came out again.

'What about my money?' he asked in a low voice, as he passed Dad.

There was a brief silence. Then Dad threw his money on the floor.

'There's your money, coward.'

The creditor looked from the money on the floor to Dad who towered over him. Then he bent down and picked up the money.

'Money will kill you,' Dad said. 'You drank of my beer, ate of my food, and because of a small amount of money you behave like a rat?'

The creditor scurried off to his room and locked his door. The noise of him quarrelling with his wife continued. After some time their lights went out.

Dad stood sheepishly in the middle of the passage, a little diminished for lack of confrontation. He was returning to our room when the other creditor came creeping out with the pair of boots.

'You too!' Dad cried, resuming his charged state. 'So you stole my boots!'

The third creditor ran to our room, dropped the boots, and came out. Dad stood in front of him, feet solidly planted. There was silence. The cocks crowed. Then Dad threw his money on the floor, and the third creditor picked it up without any fuss and hurried back to his room and locked his door.

Dad stood, feet planted solidly on the floor, waiting for further provocation. He had started moving when a woman from the room of the third creditor said:

'If you're so powerful, why don't you join the army!'

'If I join the army,' said Dad, whirling round, 'your husband will be the first person I will shoot.'

I trembled.

No one else ventured to say anything. Dad waited for someone to speak. The wind swept harder through the passage. The mosquitoes fell on him. The silence deepened and the darkness became indistinguishable from the different rooms. A child started crying. Someone smacked it and it cried even louder. Other babies woke and cried and then one by one the crying ceased and the compound fell asleep. Dad came back in.

He sat on his chair. His boots stood in their proper place except that the third creditor had mischievously displayed his socks so that the holes were visible. The centre table was slightly out of place and

I put it in its proper position. Dad rested his feet on the table. Then he lit a cigarette.

Mum had been sitting on the bed, her face stony, her eyes deep, her hands on her head as though she were witnessing the beginnings of a tragedy.

Dad's feet stank and I noticed that his one shoe was falling apart.

'No food?' he asked, in a gentle voice.

Mum passed his food. Dad washed his hands, beckoned us to join him, and ate. I didn't feel hungry any more and neither did Mum. Dad ate alone. He had a wonderful appetite and when he finished there were only cracked bones left on the plates. Then my hunger returned and I regretted not eating with him.

Mum cleared the plates. I cleared the table and spread out my mat. Dad lit another cigarette and a mosquito coil and sat still. He went on smoking and it was only when I was falling asleep that I noticed one of the chair's feet was broken. Dad slept on the three-legged chair and I watched his jaw lower and his face relax. He was awoken by his sudden fall. I showed no sign of having noticed. He got up, grumbling. He blew out the candle and climbed into bed beside Mum.

The next morning no one spoke to us in the compound. Dad went off to work early and suffered nothing of the whisperings that followed us everywhere or the silence that greeted us when we went to the backyard. Mum bore it all very well. She said her greetings to people when she passed them and her face remained impassive when they didn't reply. She bore it all as if she were used to that treatment all her life. It was harder on me though. The children stared at me with sour faces and made it clear they didn't want my company. The compound people became united in their dislike of us.

We were eating some pap and bread in the room when Mum said:

'From today I will start at the market. One woman allowed me to rent her stall. I will not go hawking very much any more.'

I was pleased at the news. Mum fondled my hair.

'Now, go to school and afterwards stay at Madame Koto's place till I come for you, eh?'

'Yes, Mother.'

'I will be locking the door and taking the key so that no one will be able to do anything strange to us when we are away.'

I nodded. But as we prepared to leave the room there was a knock on our door. Mum opened it and found the landlord standing outside.

'Tell your husband', he said, without the slightest formality, 'that if he repeats what he did last night I will throw him out. I don't care if he is called Black Cricket. I myself am a lion. If necessary I will send my boys to beat him up. If he gives me any more trouble, if he borrows money from anybody in this compound again, if he threatens to burn down my house, he better go and find himself another landlord, you hear?'

Mum didn't say anything. Her face was stony. The landlord went down the passage and we saw him go into the room of the second creditor. He emerged shortly afterwards with two of the creditors. The landlord, surrounded by the women and children of the compound, relieved himself of a lengthy speech about the difficulty of building houses, about tenants more terrible than Dad that he had destroyed, and about how powerful he was.

'If anybody gives me any trouble,' he said, waving a fetish around, 'I will show them that trouble is my secret name. Tyger or no Tyger, this is my compound. I did not steal the money to build it!'

And then he bustled out of the compound, with the women and children trailing behind him.

Mum waited in the room for some time before she hurried out, with her tray of provisions on her head. I went out with her. She locked the door and without waiting to escort me to the junction, she shot off in the opposite direction to the one the landlord had taken. She did not call out her wares and I watched her as she disappeared from view.

Without any pocket money, or any slice of bread, I lingered. I did not feel like going to school. I was late already and knew I would be publicly punished, whipped in front of everyone, and made to kneel out in the sun. I went to the housefront instead. The compound women came out with chairs and plaited their hair and gossiped. It was from them that I first heard the rumours about Madame Koto. The women talked quite crisply about our association with her. They talked and kept eyeing me maliciously. They said of Madame Koto that she had buried three husbands and seven children and that she was a witch who ate her babies when they were still in her womb. They said she was the real reason why the children in the area didn't grow, why they were always ill, why the men never got promotions, and why the women in the area suffered miscarriages. They said she was a bewitcher of husbands and a seducer of young boys and a poisoner of children. They said she had a charmed beard and that she plucked one hair out every day and dropped it into the palm-wine she sold and into the peppersoup she made so that the men would spend all their money in her bar and not care about their starving families. They said she made men go insane at night and that she belonged to a secret society that flies about in the air when the moon is out. I got tired of hearing what they had to say and I decided that being punished at school was infinitely better.

FOUR

WHEN I GOT to Madame Koto's bar early that evening the place was shut. I knocked but no one opened. I waited for a while. A man with one leg and a pair of crutches made from flowering branches came up to me.

'Is it shut? Has she closed down?' he asked.

'I don't know.'

'Shame,' he replied.

He had sand on his hair. His face was twisted as though he had witnessed great evil. The stump of his amputated leg was covered with a filthy cloth. He looked up at the signboard, spat, and hobbled away. I went to the backyard. There was a fire blazing. Madame Koto's cauldron of peppersoup bubbled away. Its steam looked like tormented genies. Further on, hidden by the bushes, was Madame Koto's massive form. At first I thought she was doing something quite private, so I looked away. But when I looked again she had straightened and was inspecting the white beads which she dug into the ground at night and unearthed in the day. She emerged from the bushes with a cutlass in one hand, the white beads in the other.

'What are you staring at?' she asked gruffly, hiding the beads.

'Nothing.'

She hurried away to her room.

When I saw her next she was wearing the white beads round her neck. She came to the fire and threw some ingredients into the cauldron. The soup made a curious hiss, almost of protestation. It bubbled turbulently within the cauldron. Then it foamed and spilled over, nearly putting out the fire. Madame Koto said to the soup:

'Be quiet!'

The fire blazed. And to my astonishment the soup became calm, as if it had never been boiling.

'The bar is shut,' I said.

'Yes.'

'What happened?'

She didn't say anything. The soup was turbulent again. It swelled into green foam, its bubbles a little monstrous and glutinous, and when they burst a powerful fragrance came over the air.

'What did you put in the soup?'

'Demons,' she said, glancing at me.

'To attract customers?'

She glanced at me again, her eyes bright with curiosity.

'What gave you that idea?'

'No one.'

'So why did you ask?'

'I just asked.'

'Don't ask too many questions, you hear?'

I nodded.

'Are you hungry?'

I was, but I said:

'No.'

She smiled in a manner that didn't make her less fearsome and said:

'Look after the soup. I'm coming.'

But she went. She shuffled towards her room and as soon as she had gone the cauldron hissed and the soup overflowed.

'Be quiet,' I said.

The soup gathered into a tremendous wave of foam and rushed over the sides. Before I could do anything it completely put out the fire, poured over the wood, and became little green rivulets on the sand.

'Madame Koto! The fire has gone out!' I called.

She came over, looked at the fire, saw the soup streaking the sand like batik dyeing, and said:

'What did you do to it?'

'Nothing.'

She bent over and got the fire going again, blowing at the embers. I stared at the soft folds of flesh on her neck. She stood up.

'Don't touch it,' she said, and was about to return to her room when we heard commotion from the barfront.

Two men, one fat, with a bandaged neck, the other stout, leaning on a blue walking stick, were banging away at the bar door.

'Madame, aren't you open? We want some palm-wine and your famous peppersoup.'

'Not yet open,' she said. 'Come back later.'

They looked disappointed and they grumbled about how some people were not serious about business. But they left.

'Troublemakers,' she said, and went off to have her usual bath before the evening customers began to arrive.

I watched over the soup. I got very hot from the heat of the fire and the infernal sun. I got bored with the soup. It boiled away quite unremarkably. It no longer bubbled and seemed to have given up its demons. Occasionally an impatient customer turned up and rattled the door and I had to go and tell them that the bar hadn't opened yet. They all seemed parched and their tongues hung out as they regarded me. After a while, when I felt sure the soup could take care of itself, I wandered down the paths to ease my own restlessness.

Steadily, over days and months, the paths had been widening. Bushes were being burnt, tall grasses cleared, tree stumps uprooted. The area was changing. Places that were thick with bush and low trees were now becoming open spaces of soft river-sand. In the distance I could hear the sounds of dredging, of engines, of road builders, forest clearers, and workmen chanting as they strained their muscles. Each day the area seemed different. Houses appeared where parts of the forest had been. Places where children used to play and hide were now full of sandpiles and rutted with house foundations. There were signboards on trees. The world was changing and I went on wandering as if everything would always be the same.

It took longer to get far into the forest. It seemed that the trees, feeling that they were losing the argument with human beings, had simply walked deeper into the forest. The deeper in I went, the more I noticed the difference. The grounds were covered in white sand. Piles of brick and cement were everywhere. Further on, by the paths, there were patches of dried excrement. The smell compounded the dryness of the air. I stood under a withering bamboo tree and a cat appeared in front of me. It looked up, and went into the forest. I followed it till we got to a clearing covered in leaves and rubber seeds. It was very cool and it smelt like the body of a great mother. Insects sizzled and birds piped all around. An antelope ran past with her little ones. I lay down and slept. I hadn't been sleeping long when I heard my name ringing through the trees. I remembered Madame Koto and ran back to the bar. When I got to the backyard the fire was smouldering, the cauldron had been removed from the grate and was on the floor. Madame Koto came out of her room and I said:

'I thought you were bathing.'

'Bathing? How can I? Where have you been?'
'Playing.'
'Where?'
'Along the paths. I thought you were ...'
'... bathing. Come!'
I followed her. She opened the back door of the bar. The light flooded in. Lizards scattered from the tables. A slick gecko inched up the wall. The bar was a mess. It was almost unrecognisable. There was vomit on the floor; benches were scattered and upturned; tables were in unusual positions; fish and chicken bones were all over the floor; spilt palm-wine stank, covered in flies; and columns of ants had formed along the walls. The place looked wrecked. It had the air of a ransacked and deserted marketplace.
'What happened?'
'Troublesome customers,' was all she said.
We set to work clearing the place. I swept the floor and brushed out all the ants. We moved the tables. She poured sand on the vomit and swept it out to the front. We rearranged the benches. I sprinkled water on the floor and swept again. The areas of the madman's piss were still greenish. The cross-eyed spirits had gone. As we moved the tables Madame Koto farted. I was startled by the sudden voluminous noise. Her face showed no sign that I had noticed. She sprinkled disinfectant over the vomit-stains and then she opened the front door for air to come through. Then she went to have her bath.
The wind didn't really come through the bar. It was stuffy and smelt of Madame Koto's fart. I went outside for a while and when I came back in the smell had cleared. I sat in my corner while Madame Koto struggled with the gourds and calabashes outside. Some of her women friends came to see her on their way back from hawking.
'My daughter's husband!' they said to me as they passed through the bar, with basins on their heads.
In the backyard they talked about politics, about the thugs of politicians and how businessmen and chiefs sprayed money at parties and celebrations. Madame Koto fed them and they prayed for her prosperity and they left, their voices low and sweet as they chatted away down the street.

As the evening wore on the bar stayed empty. No one came; I slept; and I was woken up by a lizard that had dropped from the wall. I got up and saw a man sitting at a table. He had a swollen eye and his lower lip was unnaturally thick. He spoke in a heavy, slow voice, as if he found words too bulky to roll over his big lip.

'Is that how you treat customers?' he asked.

I called for Madame Koto. She came in and the man said:

'Have my friends come yet?'

'What friends?'

'My friends.'

'No one has come yet. You want some palm-wine?'

'I will only drink when my friends arrive. They have all the money.'

'I will serve you,' said Madame Koto, 'and when they come you can pay me.'

'I will wait,' insisted the man.

Madame Koto went out. The man sat perfectly still. Then he shut his good eye. His bloated eye stayed open. Soon he was asleep and began to snore. I had been looking at him intently for a while when I became aware that the bar was filling up. I looked round and saw no one except the man. But the bar was full of drunken and argumentative voices, laughter, vitriolic abuses, and the unrestrained merriment of hard-drinking men. I went and told Madame Koto about it.

'Rubbish!' she said, following me.

When we got into the bar the voices had materialised and the place was quite full.

'Plenty of people,' she said, eyeing me.

I was surprised; but when I sat down my surprise turned to bewilderment. The people in the bar were stranger than any I had seen before. The group that sat round the man with the bloated eye looked alike. Their eyes were all swollen and their lips were big and bruised. At first I thought they were all boxers. Then I noticed that two of them had only one hand each and the original man had only three fingers. He wore rings on all the fingers. They talked loudly but their voices were disproportionately more powerful than the movements of their mouths.

Across from them sat two men, dressed identically in agbada of fish-printed material. They both wore skullcaps and very dark glasses. I was convinced that they were both blind; but they talked and gesticulated as though they had perfect sight. On another table there was a man who sat alone. He had no thumbs and his head, amazingly contorted like certain tubers of yam, was altogether bald. He wore a wristwatch that ticked loudly and when he yawned I saw that he had no teeth at all, in spite of looking quite young.

106

There was a woman next to him, whose skin was more indigo than dark-brown. She kept adjusting her shoulders and did not smile or speak.

Madame Koto came round to serve them.

'These are my friends,' the original man with the bloated eye said.

'Where do you all come from?' Madame Koto asked.

'Here. This country, this city. Here we live, here we die.'

Just as he finished speaking, two albino men came in. They were freckled, their eyes were green, and they were quite beautiful. Their eyes kept shutting and opening, wobbling from side to side, as if they couldn't stand the light. The rest of the company cheered them as they came in. They smiled and took their seats opposite the toothless young man.

'What do you want to drink?'

'Palm-wine, naturally, and your famous peppersoup,' said the original man.

Madame Koto went out to serve them. While she was out a very tall man and woman came in. Their legs were very long. The rest of their bodies were quite short. They had small heads and eyes that were so tiny that it was only when they came near me that I could perceive their pin-point brightness. They came over, stood perfectly straight for a moment, and then, like bizarre actors, they leant over to me, keeping their legs and top halves straight, and said, in voices that could only have come from children:

'We want some peppersoup, please.'

I ran out and told Madame Koto.

'Leave me alone, I'm coming!' she said.

I went back in. The tall couple had seated themselves at my table. They sat straight and their knees were awkward underneath the table and I noticed that they had the longest necks I had yet seen on any human being.

'Are you politicians?' I asked.

'What?' asked the man, in his child's voice.

'Politicians.'

'What is that?'

'You're not politicians,' I said, closing the conversation.

They kept glancing at me and I found their faces very disconcerting. I tried to sit there without noticing them when the woman brought out a feather from her wrapper and offered it to me.

'No, thank you,' I said.

She smiled and put it back. Madame Koto came in with the

107

gourds of palm-wine and voices erupted in weird jubilation. I fetched glasses and cups and distributed them round. When I gave the cups to the men with dark glasses they grabbed my hand and said:

'What's your name?'

'Why?'

'We like you. We want to take you with us.'

'Where?'

'Wherever.'

'No.'

'Yes.'

I tried to wrench my hand free but their grips were very strong and their bony fingers bit into my flesh.

'No.'

'Yes.'

I pulled again but my flesh bruised and began to bleed. I screamed, but the voices in the room were so loud they cut off my screaming. I kicked, missed, and hurt my toes on the foot of the table. Then I scratched one of them in the face, and snatched off his glasses. Both of his eyes were totally white. They could have been made of milk. They were white and blank and unmoving, as if they had been stuck there, malformed, in the empty sockets.

I opened my mouth to shout, but the man laughed so powerfully and his mouth was so black that I froze in my attempt. I couldn't move. I felt transfixed, as if I were suffering a living rigor mortis. Then a searing pain went up my spine, ended in my brain, and I woke up to find myself in my usual corner, with the tall, small-eyed couple staring at me. Everyone else was drinking. Steaming bowls of peppersoup were in front of all the customers. They drank steadily and talked in curious voices.

The two albino men kept twisting and jerking as if their bodies were uncomfortable. They were silent. The toothless man was also silent. They all kept looking at me. More customers came into the bar. There was a man with a head like that of a camel, a woman with a terrible hip deformation, another man with white hair, and a midget. The woman had a large sack on her back, which she gave to the albinos. The albinos unfurled the sack, shook it out, sending dust clouds into the air. They glanced at me furtively, and hid the sack under the table.

The four people who had come in looked for places to sit and then crowded my table. I had to get up for them. I fetched a little stool and sat near the earthenware pot and watched the bar become overcrowded.

Amidst all this Madame Koto was radiant with her necklace of white beads. As the evening progressed she got darker, more dignified, while the clientele got rowdier. She was untouched by it all, even when the men teased her. The original man with the big eye, which got more bloated as he drank, as if his eye were a stomach all to itself, said:

'Madame, come and sit on my lap.'

'Let's see if you can carry your wine first, before you carry me,' she replied, with great dignity.

'This madame is too proud,' said another man in the identical group.

'Proud and strong,' she said.

'Come and sit with me, let's talk about marriage,' said the man whose head was like a tuber of yam.

'Marry yourself.'

'So you don't think I am man enough?' asked the original man, waving his three fingers for more wine.

'No,' she said.

The bar rocked with the oddest sounds of ironic laughter. The men with dark glasses laughed very hard and banged away at the table.

'Maybe that boy is her husband,' said one of them, taking off his glasses and polishing them.

His white eyes didn't move. They were so birdlike, so ghostly, that I couldn't tell what or where they were looking at.

'That's my son,' she said.

'Is that so?'

'Yes.'

'Will you sell him to us?'

The bar suddenly became very quiet. Madame Koto stared at the two men with dark glasses. All the other customers watched her carefully. Then she turned to me, a curious gleam in her eyes.

'Why?'

'So we can take him with us.'

'To where?'

'Many places.'

'For how much?'

'As much as you want.'

'You have plenty of money?'

'Too much.'

The silence in the bar was incredible. Then the midget laughed. He laughed like a goat. The tall man with small eyes laughed as well. He sounded like a hyena.

'Name your price, Madame.'

Madame Koto looked at the customers as if seeing them for the first time.

'Any more palm-wine for anybody?'

'Palm-wine!' they cried in unison.

'And peppersoup!'

And they all burst out laughing and resumed their vociferous conversations as if nothing had happened.

Madame Koto served them and they drank and ate and kept asking for more. They drank a great deal and didn't get drunk. They sat, all of them, drinking and talking as if the wine were water. It was only the two men in dark glasses who got drunk. They kept polishing their glasses. One of them even brought out an eye and polished it and blew on it and dipped it into his palm-wine and pushed it back into his red eye-socket. Then he put his glasses back on. They chewed and swallowed their chicken bones. They ate and drank so much that Madame Koto began to despair. She had run out of wine and food and the night hadn't even properly set in. As she bustled up and down, starting a new fire, making hurried arrangements for more palm-wine, the midget came up to me. Smiling very expansively, he said:

'Take this. You might need it.'

It was a little pen-knife. I put it in my pocket and forgot all about it. Then he went to the backyard. I heard him urinating in the bushes. He came back, smiling, and left without a word, and without paying. I told Madame Koto about it and she said:

'What midget?'

I went back to the bar. I sat down. The tall man said:

'Come with me.'

'To where?'

'I will take you round the world. On foot. I make all my journeys on foot. Like a camel.'

'No.'

'If you don't come with me I will take you by force.'

'You can't.'

He smiled. The woman smiled as well. I decided they were more drunk than I had thought and ignored them.

The bar was so full of people that there were no seats left. Some of them sat on the floor. I was nudged off my stool. The smells in the bar became terrible and strange, the smells of corpses and rain and oregano, of mangoes and rotting meat, of incense and goats' hair. And then, suddenly, I found I could no longer understand what anybody was saying. They all spoke as if they had known one another for a long time. They spoke in alien languages and occasionally pointed at Madame Koto's fetish. It seemed to amuse them. Then they glanced at me, made calculations with their fingers, laughed, drank, became solemn, and looked at me again.

Madame Koto came in and announced that her supply of food and wine was finished. She demanded that they pay up and leave her bar. A great chorus of disappointment rose from the clientele.

'Pay and go,' Madame Koto said. 'Pay up and go. I am closing up for the night.'

No one paid her much attention. Her temper rising, she stormed out of the bar. The voices grew rowdier, wilder. Previously I had heard the voices before the people had materialised. Now, I heard the voices but, as I looked round, the customers were vanishing. I shut my eyes in disbelief. When I opened them the bar was completely empty, and completely noisy, except for the two albinos and a beautiful woman whom I hadn't noticed before. On the far table were the two pairs of dark glasses. The original man with the bloated eye, the group that looked like him, the tall couple, the two white-eyed men, were all gone. The bar was silent and everything was still and the wind whistled faintly on the ceiling, as if a hurricane had passed and hadn't been noticed.

'Where is everyone?' I asked the albinos.

The beautiful woman smiled at me. The albinos twisted, shrugged, stood up, and spread out the sack. The woman distracted me with her smile. And then the albinos sprang at me and covered me with the sack. I struggled and fought, but they expertly bundled me in and tied up the sack as if I were an animal. And as I resisted, kicking, I heard the noises of the world, the voices of all the different people who had been in the bar. They talked in their inhuman languages in leisurely animation, as if they were merely setting out on a pilgrimage to a distant land. Overcome with fear, unable to move, surrounded by darkness and the death-smells of the sack, I cried:

'Politicians! Politicians are taking me away!'

My voice was very faint, as if I were shouting in a dream. Even if I had cried out with the voice of thunder, no one would have heard me.

They took me down many roads, rough-handling me in the sack. They swung me round, they changed me from one shoulder to another, and the sack kept tightening about me. I heard the noises of lorries and cars, the tumultuous sounds of a marketplace. All the time I fought and struggled like a trapped animal. The more I strained for freedom, the more they tightened the sack, till I had no room to struggle. My feet were around my head and my neck was twisted to breaking point. I couldn't breathe and I fought the panic that washed over me in waves. The blankness of death came upon me. I shut my eyes. It was no different when I opened them. At one point I fell into a strange sleep in which the figure of a king resplendent in gold appeared to me and vanished. My spirit companions began singing in my ears, rejoicing in my captivity and in the fact that I would soon be joining them. I could not shut out their singing and I'm not sure which was worse: being bundled away by unknown people to an unknown destination or hearing my spirit companions orchestrate my passage through torment with their sweet and excruciating voices.

When I had fought and my energy was exhausted and I couldn't do anything, I called to our great king, and I said:

'I do not want to die.'

I had hardly finished when the figure of the king appeared to me again and dissolved into the face of the midget. By now I had ceased to hear any sounds outside, except for the rushing of waves, the hissing of water, and the keening of birds. Suddenly, I remembered the pen-knife the midget had given me and began another struggle to find it. I searched my pockets. I searched the sack, and couldn't find it. My fear became unbearable. Then a quietness came over me. I gave up. I accepted my destiny.

Water poured into the sack. I became convinced that I was being taken to an underwater kingdom, where they say certain spirits reside. As I tried to keep the water out of my mouth, I felt something metallic like a frozen fish banging against my head. It was the pen-knife. I wasted no time in cutting my way out. The sack material was very tough but the water had softened it a little and it took some time to cut my way out and when I did the outside world was black like the bottom of a well. I fell out into the water with a splash.

'The boy has escaped!' a voice cried.

It was very dark, the river could have been the night, and the water was bitingly cold. I stayed under without moving. And then very gently I swam back to the shore, serene in my element.

I struggled through the bulrushes and the tiger-lilies of the marsh, over twisted mangrove roots and flickering eels, and when I gained the soft silt-sand I went on running till I got to a main road. It was very dark; I was hungry, wet, lost; and I heard voices all around me, the twittering, vicious voices of my spirit companions wailing in disappointment. I ran till the road became a river of voices, every tree, car, and face talking at me, cats crossing my path, people with odd night faces staring at me knowingly. At crossroads people glared and seemed to float towards me menacingly. I fled all through the night.

The road was endless. One road led to a thousand others, which in turn fed into paths, which fed into dirt tracks, which became streets, which ended in avenues and cul-de-sacs. All around, a new world was being erected amidst the old. Skyscrapers stood high and inscrutable beside huts and zinc abodes. Bridges were being built; flyovers, half-finished, were like passageways into the air, or like future visions of a time when cars would be able to fly. Roads, half-constructed, were crowded with heavy machinery. Here and there nightwatchmen slept under the stars with dull lamps as their only earthly illumination. The moon was round and big and it seemed bright with the face of an awesome king. I was comforted by its presence. I walked on with a terrible hunger for a destination, for Mum's face, and Dad's smells. I walked past the kerosine lamps of the somnolent street-traders.

'Small boy, where are you going at this time?' they often asked me.

But I replied to no one. I wandered till my bare feet broke into blisters. And then, as I walked about in the darkness of being lost, I saw a disembodied light ahead of me, a tiny moon the shape of a man's head. I followed the light. And it led me on longer journeys. And when I got to an area I vaguely recognised, my feet gave up on me and I collapsed at the roadside. I crawled to the nearest tree and curled myself up between its great roots which were above the ground and I fell asleep under the safety of the waning moon. The mosquitoes tormented me. The ants bit into my flesh and their stings persisted. But I slept through it all, and dreamt about a panther.

When I awoke the moon was still in the sky, like a ghost unwilling to disappear under the force of daylight. It was dawn. A few people were standing over me, with puzzlement on their faces.

'He's not dead!' one of them cried.

I got up quickly; they came towards me with arms outstretched; I fled from them. I ran through the quickening dawn, with the sun riding the sky. The air heated, the sand warmed underfoot; and women of the new African churches, who wore white smocks and rang bells, cried out to the sleeping world to awake and repent. I passed prophets emerging from the forest with dew and leaves in their hair, cobwebs meshing their beards, their eyes demented with visions. I passed sorcerers with machetes that crackled with flames in the morning light, making sacrifices at dawn of red cocks, who poured gnomic chants on the untrodden roads. I also passed workers who had woken early and with sleepy faces made their ways through the mist, pierced by the sun, to the garages and bus-stops.

My feet were fresh on the paths. Dew wet my ankles. Hunger dried my lips. News-vendors roused the dawn with their horns, announcing to the awakening world the scandals of the latest political violence. The industrious women of the city, who carried basins of peppered aromatic foods on their heads, tempted the appetite of the world with their sweet voices. The worms of the road ate into the soles of my feet.

I came to another familiar place; the passionate chants of the muezzin roused the Muslim world to prayer. I had turned a corner, and had gone up a path that became a track, when three men in blue smocks rushed at me. I tore into the bushes, ran amongst the trees, and cried out into the echoing forest. Birds scattered from branches and pods fell from the treetops. I shook off the men, but I went on running, for the world seemed populated with people intent on me for one obscure reason or another.

While running through the forest paths I stepped on an enamel plate of sacrifices to the road. The plate was rich with the offerings of fried yams, fish, stewed snails, palm oil, rice and kola-nuts. Shell fragments and little pins stuck in the soles of my feet. I started to bleed. I was so hungry that I ate what I could of the offerings to the road and afterwards my stomach swelled and visions of road-spirits, hungry and annoyed, weaved in my brain. I went on bleeding and a black cat with golden eyes followed the trail of my blood. My head boiled with hallucinations. I walked on broken glass, on the hot sand of bushpaths, on hot new tarmac.

The roads seemed to me then to have a cruel and infinite imagination. All the roads multiplied, reproducing themselves, subdividing themselves, turning in on themselves, like snakes, tails in their mouths, twisting themselves into labyrinths. The road was the worst hallucination of them all, leading towards home and then away from it, without end, with too many signs, and no directions. The road became my torment, my aimless pilgrimage, and I found myself merely walking to discover where all the roads lead to, where they end.

And then I came to a place where I thought the roads terminated. An iroko tree had been felled across it. The tree was mighty, its trunk gnarled and rough like the faces of ancient warriors. It looked like a great soul dead at the road's end. Beyond, the road sheered into a deep pit. Across, on the other side, were sand-carrying lorries. Strange sounds lisped in the tree trunk, voices echoed in its hollows. I sat on a branch of the tree to ease my feet. And then, while the road-spirits raged in me, I saw a two-legged dog emerge from the forest. It stopped and regarded me, whimpering frequently. I was so amazed to see the dog standing on only two legs that I forgot my hunger and pain. It had a left forefoot and a right hindfoot and it stood, wobbling, as though on invisible crutches. The dog stared at me. And with a heavy, inconsolable sadness it turned and limped away. In my astonishment at seeing it walk I followed it as it limped on curiously.

The two-legged dog led me through the forest. It was a lean dog, with intense eyes and a sensitive tail and flea-ridden ears. I wanted to get rid of the fleas but I restrained myself and followed it at a distance, till I came to a clearing. I recognised the clearing at once. The dog limped on deeper into the forest. I watched it go and it stopped only once to look at me. I waved, but the dog did not understand my gesture. It went on limping, a solitary and heroic dog, surviving with only two legs and a sad face.

I carried on home. At the edge of the forest I saw Madame Koto with a plate of chicken and yam in her hands. The white beads weren't round her neck. She stopped at the roadside, looked in all directions to make sure no one was about, and proceeded with her passionate supplications. I watched her secret fervour. When she had finished with her praying and chanting, she lit a candle and put it on the plate. She placed a finger of kaoline and some cowries beside the candle. Then she straightened, undid her kerchief, looked in all directions, and hurried away. I passed her road offering. I scurried past her barfront. I ran home.

FIVE

Dad was sitting on his three-legged chair, smoking a cigarette. There were plates of uneaten food on the table. Mum was in the bed. The window was open and the light that came in increased the unhappiness in the room. Mum rushed at me and threw her arms round me, as if to protect me from punishment. She made me sit on the bed and began weeping. Dad didn't move.

'Where have you been?' he asked, in a dangerous voice.

It was clear that neither of them had slept that night. There were circles of sleeplessness round Dad's eyes. Mum looked as though she had lost weight overnight.

'Where have you been?'

'I was lost.'

'How did you get lost?'

'I played and got lost.'

'How?'

'I don't know.'

'What about Madame Koto?'

'I don't know.'

'She came looking for you last night.'

I said nothing.

'You didn't tell her where you were going.'

'I can't remember.'

'Have you eaten?' Mum asked.

'Don't ask him such questions,' Dad said, loudly. 'First he must tell me where he has been.'

'Let him sleep.'

'That's how you women spoil your children.'

'Let him rest, then he will talk.'

'If he doesn't talk he won't rest. He has prevented my going to work. I want to know what he has been doing.'

'Azaro, tell your father where you've been.'

'I got lost.'

'Where?' Dad's voice rose.

He sat up straight. His chair wobbled.

'I don't know.'

'You are a wicked child,' he said, reaching for the cane he had beside him, which I hadn't noticed.

He came at me; Mum stood between us; Dad shoved her away and grabbed my neck with his powerful hand and bent me over and flogged me. I didn't cry out. He whipped me and I kicked him and escaped from his grip and he followed me and whipped my legs and my back and my neck. I ran round the room, knocking things over in my flight, and Dad went on caning me. Mum tried to hold him, to restrain his fury, but Dad went on whipping me and he flogged her too and Mum screamed. I hadn't uttered a sound and Dad was so enraged that he went on thrashing me harder and harder till I ran out of the room, into the compound. He bounded after me but I fled out to the housefront and up the street and I stopped only when I was a good distance away. Dad gave up chasing me, but he stood threatening me with the cane. I stayed where I was. He called me. I didn't move.

'Come here now, you vicious child!'

I still didn't move. Dad got very angry because he couldn't get his big hands on me.

'Come here now, or you won't eat!'

I didn't care about food or sleep or anything. He suddenly made a sprint for me and I ran towards Madame Koto's place and he caught me just before I got there. He grabbed me by the back of my shorts and lifted me up and whipped me and dragged me home. He was so frightening in his fury that I screamed as if he were a spirit that was abducting me to some unknown destination. When he dragged me into the room he tossed me on the bed and thrashed me till sweat poured down his chest. When he was satisfied that he had whipped the wanderlust out of me he threw down the pulped cane and went to have a bath.

I came out all over in heavy welts. I groaned on the bed, swearing a terrible spirit-child's vengeance. Mum sat beside me. When Dad returned from the bathroom he was still angry.

'You are a problem to me,' he said. 'A problem child. When I think of all the things I could have done – if it wasn't for you.'

He started towards me again, but Mum interposed firmly and said:

'Haven't you flogged him enough?'

'No. I want to thrash him so thoroughly that next time he will think of us before he gets lost again.'

'He's had enough. His feet are bleeding.'

'So what? If I were a severe father I would put pepper on his wounds to teach him an everlasting lesson.'

Dad sounded more furious than ever; but Mum stood firm, determined that no more beating should be visited on me. Grumbling, complaining about his lot, about how I held him back, how much of a better child he had been to his parents, Dad put on his drab khaki work-clothes. Mum tried to get me to eat. I didn't want to eat while Dad was around. I had been crying in a steady monotone.

'If you don't shut up now,' he thundered, reaching for a boot, 'I will thrash you with this!'

'Yes, and kill him,' Mum said.

I went on with my steady monotonous weeping. Further punishment couldn't make me feel worse than I already did. He dressed in a bad temper. When he was finished he picked up the cane and came over to me and said:

'If you move from this room today or tomorrow you might as well stay lost, because when I finish with you . . .'

He deliberately didn't complete his sentence, for greater effect. Then he brought the cane down lightly on my head, and stormed out of the room. I was relieved to see him go.

Mum was silent. She waited a while before she said:

'Do you see the trouble you've caused, eh?'

I thought she was going to berate me as well. I braced myself for her onslaught. But she got up and went out and I fell asleep. She woke me up. She had brought in a basin of warm herbal water. She made me soak my feet. Then with a candle-heated needle she expertly plucked out the roadworms that had eaten into the soles of my feet. But before that she made them wriggle with hot palm-oil. Then she disinfected my cuts. She pressed herbal juices on my welts. With strips of cloth she tore from one of her wrappers, she bandaged mashed leaves against the soles of my feet. The leaves stung me for a long time. She went and got rid of the needle and the water in the basin. I climbed into bed. She made me get out again to eat. I ate ravenously and she watched me with tears gathering in her eyes. When I had eaten I climbed back into bed. She gathered her provisions and as my eyes shut, she said:

'Stay in and lock the door. Don't go anywhere. Don't open the door unless it's me or your father, you hear?'

I barely nodded. With her tray on her head, she went out into the compound, out into the world; I locked the door and fell asleep in the unhappiness of the room.

Dad had no need to worry about me going out. I slept through the whole day. In several entangled dreams I fought with the three-legged chair that was trying to abduct me. And when I woke it was only because Mum had returned. I woke up feeling as if an alien spirit had crept into my body during my sleep. I tried to conquer the abnormal queasiness and heaviness of body, but my head seemed larger, full of spaces, and my feet began to swell. It was only that night, when I saw Mum split up into two identical people, when Dad's fiendish smile broke into multiples of severity, when my eyeballs became hot, and my body shook, and great blasting waves of heat poured through my nerves, that I realised I had come down with a fever.

'The boy has got malaria,' Mum said.

'If it's only malaria, we're lucky,' Dad growled.

'Leave him alone.'

'Why should I? Did I send him to go and walk about all day and all night? Did you send him? All we told him to do was stay at Madame Koto's bar. We didn't tell him to go and walk about and catch some road-fever.'

'Leave him alone. Can't you see that he is shaking?'

'So what? Am I shaking him? He probably went and walked on all the bad things they wash on the roads. All those witches and wizards, native doctors, sorcerers, who wash off bad things from their customers and pour them on the road, who wash diseases and bad destinies on the streets. He probably walked on them and they entered him. Look at his eyes.'

'They have grown big!'

'He looks like a ghost, a mask.'

'Leave him.'

'If he wasn't ill, I would thrash him again.'

Then to me, he said:

'Do you think of us, eh? How we sweat to feed you, to pay the rent, to buy clothes, eh? All day, like a mule, I carry loads. My head is breaking, my brain is shrinking, all just so that I can feed you, eh?'

Dad went on like that through the night. I trembled and my head was shot with heat and hallucinations. Dad's head became very big, his eyes bulbous, his mouth wide. Mum looked lean, bony, and long. They became giant shadows in my fever. They towered above me on the bed and when they spoke about me it seemed they were talking about a ghost, or about someone who wasn't there. For I wasn't there in the room. I was deep in the country of road-fevers.

All the sounds of the compound were magnified through the night. I couldn't eat, I kept throwing up, and all I could keep down was water. Mum kept vigil over me with a candle, Dad with a cigarette. Shadows wandered around the room. I felt I was retreating from the world of things and people. Late at night Mum made some peppersoup. It was hot and spiced with bitter herbs. It made me feel a little better. Then she poured me a half-tumbler of ogogoro which had turned yellow with marinating roots.

'Dongoyaro,' Mum said, insisting that I drink it all down in one gulp.

'If you don't, I flog you,' Dad threatened.

I drank it all down in one and was shaken to the foundations of my stomach with its infernal bitterness. Bile rushed to my mouth; it was so bitter that I shook in disgust. Mum gave me a cube of sugar, which didn't sweeten my mouth one bit. And all through my sleep, all the way to the next morning, my mouth was still bitter.

'The bitterness drives away the malaria,' Mum said, tucking me into bed.

'Bitterness is what the boy needs,' Dad said, his voice heavy.

He was still angry with me for keeping them up all night, for making them suffer so much worry; and now he could not forgive me because I was ill and had cheated him of a target for his annoyance. Protected from his rage by my fever, I slept that night wracked with bad dreams and road-spirits.

Saturday morning, three days later, I was still ill. My mouth and eyes were dry and I kept hearing birds twittering in my ears. Mum was clattering among the basins and cleaning up the room. Dad wasn't in; Mum said he had gone to work at the garage. Towards noon Jeremiah came round with photographs of the party. Mum told him he'd have to come back. He grumbled about how expensive it was taking pictures of poor people, but he left without creating a scene.

It became very hot in the room. The air coming in from the

window brought flies and gnats, but it didn't cool anything. I sweated profusely on the bed till I was lying on a pool of dampness. My body hurt all over and the soles of my feet itched and a headache expanded my brain. I watched Mum cleaning the room in a haze of dust and dryness. She looked the picture of forebearance. She said:

'You must listen to your father and be careful how you walk on the road.'

'Yes, Mum.'

'The road swallows people and sometimes at night you can hear them calling for help, begging to be freed from inside its stomach.'

'Yes, Mum.'

She cleaned out the cupboard and prepared my food. I ate little. She made me get out of bed and bathe. With the daylight hurting my eyes, with the noises of the compound jangling my nerves, and the stares of the other tenants increasing my sense of multiplication, I went to the backyard. Mum had prepared warm herbal water.

'Bathe of it properly,' she said, 'or I will do it for you.'

It was cold when I took off my clothes. But the water was hot and the soap smelt good. I was led back to the room feeling new. Mum rubbed me over with herbal oil.

'Time for your dongoyaro,' she said.

I could have fainted at the anticipation of its bitterness.

'If you don't drink it all down I won't allow you go out today.'

I drank it all down. Later I marvelled that my urine was the deep yellow colour of its bitterness.

The afternoon brought the bustling noises of the compound people scrubbing their roomfronts. I heard them chattering, either going out on Saturday outings or being visited by friends or relations. Mum got me to dress up in my fine clothes which I wore only at Christmas. She parted my hair and touched my face with powder, which I sweated off. And then Madame Koto came to see us.

She looked very dignified in her white magic beads and her elaborate wrappers and her massive blouse. She was dressed as if she were going to see wealthy relations.

'Azaro, what happened to you?'

'I was lost.'

'You just disappeared.'

'We should tie up his feet,' Mum said. 'He walks too much.'

Madame Koto laughed and brought out a bowl steaming with goat-meat peppersoup.

'Are there demons in it?' I asked.

She gave me a severe stare, smiled at Mum, and said:

'It's full of meat and fish.'

It tasted better than the soup she served her customers. I drank it all down and ate all the meat and fish and my stomach bulged.

'You didn't finish the one I made you,' Mum said.

'I did.'

Madame Koto packed the bowl back into her bag.

'Get strong quick, and come and sit in the bar, eh,' she said, heading for the door.

Mum escorted her out. I could hear them talking. They left the roomfront and I couldn't hear them any more.

Mum was gone for a long time. The soles of my feet began to itch. Then as I lay there, moving in and out of sleep, in and out of dreams, loud new voices crackled from the street. The voices were so magnified that I wondered what sort of human beings produced them. I couldn't hear what they said. I felt I was imagining them, that they were another manifestation of the spirits. The compound children ran up and down the passage, talking excitedly. I heard the men and women talking in animated tones as if some fantastic new spectacle had appeared in our street, a bazaar, a public masquerade, a troupe of magicians, with contortionists and fire-eaters. The crackling voices drew closer and sounded from the rooftops of all the houses. The compound appeared empty, everyone had gone out to see what was going on, and I could hear a baby crying in its temporary abandonment.

Overcome with curiosity, I got out of bed. The crack of an iron ruler shot through my head and ended between my eyes. The room swayed. The crackling voice outside spoke from an elevated stationary position. Darkness formed round my eyes and then cleared. I made for the door. The passage was empty. All the compound people were gathered at the housefront. All the housefronts of the street were crowded with people. And everyone was staring at the spectacle of an open-backed van with a megaphone. A man in resplendent white agbada was talking with great gestures. It was the first time I had heard such amplification of voice.

The inhabitants of the street crowded round the van, hunger on their faces. Their children were in tattered clothes, had big stomachs, and were barefoot.

'What is it?' someone asked.

'Politicians.'

'They want votes.'

'They want our money.'

'They have come to tax us.'

'I saw them when I went hawking. They keep giving reasons why we should vote for them.'

'They only remember us when they want our votes.'

The man in the van spoke for himself.

'VOTE FOR US. WE ARE THE PARTY OF THE RICH, FRIENDS OF THE POOR . . .'

'The poor have no friends,' someone in the crowd said.

'Only rats.'

'IF YOU VOTE FOR US . . .'

'. . . we are finished,' someone added.

'. . . WE WILL FEED YOUR CHILDREN . . .'

'. . . lies.'

'. . . AND WE WILL BRING YOU GOOD ROADS . . .'

'. . . which the rain will turn into gutters!'

'. . . AND WE WILL BRING ELECTRICITY . . .'

'. . . so you can see better how to rob us!'

'. . . AND WE WILL BUILD SCHOOLS . . .'

'. . . to teach illiteracy!'

'. . . AND HOSPITALS. WE WILL MAKE YOU RICH LIKE US. THERE IS PLENTY FOR EVERYBODY. PLENTY OF FOOD. PLENTY OF POWER. VOTE FOR UNITY AND POWER!'

By this time the mocking voices were silent.

'AND TO PROVE TO YOU THAT WE ARE NOT EMPTY WORDS BRING YOUR CHILDREN TO US. WE ARE GIVING AWAY FREE MILK! YES, FREE MILK FROM US, COURTESY OF OUR GREAT PARTY!'

On and on they went, crackling abundant promises on the air, launching future visions of extravagant prosperity, till they broke down the walls of our scepticism. The compound people abandoned their doubts and poured over to the van. Feeling the road sway, with the magnified voice quivering in my ears, I went with them. I was surprised to see our landlord on the back of the van. His face glistened with the smile of the powerful and he had on a lace agbada. There were stacks of powdered milk on the back of the van and men with bristling muscles, bare-chested, ripped open the sacks and dished out the milk with yellow bowls to the women who had rushed over with containers. The landlord, like a magician in a triumphant moment, handed out bowls of milk to the great surging mass of people. All around me the throng had become rowdy; the crowd converged round the van, arms outstretched, and the rush for free milk broke into a frenetic cacophony. The crowd shook the van, voices clashed in the air, children cried out under the crush, hands clawed at the sacks, and the frenzy became so alarming that the man at the megaphone began shouting:

'DON'T RUSH. WE HAVE ENOUGH FREE MILK FOR THE WHOLE COUNTRY . . .'

His pleading only made things worse; people surged round with basins, had them filled, rushed to their homes, and returned with greater vigour. Soon the whole street, in a frightening tide of buckets and basins, of clanging pots, and rancorous voices, rocked the van. The landlord looked sick with fright. Sweat broke out on his face and he struggled to take off his agbada, but it got caught in the outstretched clawing hands of all the struggling hungry people. The more he tried to get it off, the more entangled it became in all the hands. It was as though his clothes too had become an extension of his party's promises, a free gift to everyone. On the other side of the van I saw Madame Koto engaged in negotiations with the man at the megaphone, pointing vigorously in the direction of her bar. All around her the crowd hustled. The women's kerchiefs were torn off, shirts were ripped apart, milk spilt everywhere and powdered the faces of the women and children. With their sweating, milk-powdered faces they looked like starving spirits. The crowd surged, voices swelling, and the driver started the van's engine. The hunger of the crowd wreaked itself on the van; the handers-out of milk began to shout; the driver got worried; the landlord's agbada had been torn off him by the crowd. He battled to get it back, clinging on to its edges in desperation, pleading. But the crowd, with confused clawing motions, raking the milk sacks from under the feet of thugs, dragged the landlord's agbada with them. He clung on stubbornly and they dragged him along with his garment, out of the van, till only his feet were left showing, kicking vainly at the air. One of the thugs stopped dishing out the milk and held on to the landlord's feet, to keep him in, but lost the battle against the confused fury of motions, and the landlord disappeared into the great welter of bodies. His agbada was passed from hand to hand, above the crowd; and soon so many hands grasped at the lace garment that it tore into several pieces in the air and patches of its blue cloth flew this way and that like the feathers of a plucked parrot.

When the landlord next emerged his hair was covered in mud and someone spilt milk on him and he looked like a travesty of an Egungun and when he tried to get back on the van his fellow party men wouldn't let him because they didn't recognise him. He shouted his indignation and the thugs, abandoning their activity, set on him, bundled him off, and threw him to the ground, a good distance from the van. The intrepid photographer appeared with his camera and took pictures of the miserable landlord and the surging crowd. The landlord got up in a great fury, shook his fists, swore at the party and, covered in mud and dried milk, his clothes in tatters, his pants all twisted, he stormed away down the street, a solitary figure of wretched defiance. The photographer went on taking pictures. The men on the van posed in between doling out milk, smiling in weird fixity at the camera, while the crowd jostled. I saw three tough-looking men suddenly snatch sacks of milk from the van; I saw them run off down the street, pursued by the party thugs. Children were squashed by the jostling. A man fainted. Women cried out. A girl was prodded in the eye. Someone else, elbowed in the mouth, spat blood into the air. The photographer flashed his camera at a woman with a swollen eye, a basin of milk on her head. I saw a man running out from the crowd's vanguard, with deep scratches bleeding down his face. The windows of the van were smashed in the mêlée. Blood mixed with milk on the earth. I heard Mum screaming. I fought my way in the direction of her cry. I saw Madame Koto leaving the scene of confusion with utmost dignity, her beads gleaming in the sun. I searched for Mum in the crowding, in the heated sweat and hungry violence of the swelling multitude. Elbows crashed on my head and someone's fist cracked my nose, drawing blood. I fought my way back out, stumbling over feet of solid bone and rough legs. The van suddenly started moving. It knocked over a man and dragged with it a hundred surging bodies. The crowd poured after the van as if in a holy crusade. The thugs on the back of the van, resorting to a diversionary tactic, tore open a hidden sack and began throwing pennies and silver pieces in the air. The coins landed on our heads, we caught them with our faces, were sometimes blinded by their force as we surged, and we scrambled for them, forgetting the milk, while the van drove away, crackling its announcements, its party promises, and the venue of the party's next great public spectacle. The children ran after the van, while the rest of the crowd, caught in the spiral of its own fever, scrambled for coins.

The photographer chased the van, endlessly taking pictures of the thugs flexing their muscles, while party leaflets sailed in the air above us, words we would never read. And when the van had disappeared from our street, when the amplified voice faded into the depths of the area, we recovered slowly from our fever. The road was full of spilt milk and party leaflets. Children searched the dust for hidden coins. Mum emerged from a group of women, her face bruised, powdered milk on her hair, her blouse torn.

'I won't vote for them,' said the woman with the swollen eye.

Mum saw me and came after me, transferring her annoyance, and shouted:

'Go back to bed!'

I hurried across the street. Everything swayed. A party leaflet stuck to my foot. Powdered milk tickled my nostrils. The heat grew in my ears. A headache hammered away between my eyes. I lingered at the compound-front, listening to voices comparing their experience, arguing about politics. And when I saw Mum crossing the road, I hurried off into the room. Mum brought in her basin of free milk, with a look of exhausted triumph on her face. She placed the basin on the cupboard, as if the effort she had put into acquiring it had somehow made it quite special. Then she went to have a bath. The compound people converged in the passage and got into heated discussions about which of the two main parties was the best, which had more money, which was the friend of the poor, which had the better promises, and they went on like that, tirelessly, till the night fell slowly over the spectacle of the day.

It was quite dark when Dad returned. He looked sober and exhausted. He looked miserable and moved listlessly and his face hung down as if he would burst into tears any moment. He complained about his head, his back, his legs. He grumbled about the political thugs who were giving him trouble at the garage.

'I nearly killed one of them today,' he said, with a raving expression in his eyes.

Then his voice changed.

'Too much load. My back is breaking. I must find another job. Join the army. Be a nightsoil man. But this load is getting too much for me.'

There was a brief silence. Then Mum told him about the great event of the day and showed him the milk. She seemed quite proud of having put up a good fight to obtain a basinful against all the competition.

'Now we can have milk in our pap,' she said.

'Not me,' I said.

'You think their milk is too good for you, eh?'

Dad tasted the milk and wrinkled his face.

'Rotten milk,' he said. 'Bad milk.'

And then he fell asleep in the chair, overcome with exhaustion. He had not bathed, nor had he eaten, and he stank of dried mud, cement, crayfish, and garri sacks. Mum stayed up for a while to see if he would wake; but Dad slept on, grinding his teeth, snoring. And so Mum stretched out on the mat, blew out the candle, and soon began to snore herself.

I stayed awake for a while. I was still feverish and the darkness quivered with figures moving about blindly. Just before I fell asleep I heard a noise on the cupboard and as I looked I saw something growing out of the milk. It grew very tall and white and resolved itself into a ghostly agbada. There was no one in the agbada and it took off from the powdered milk and flew around the room. Then the garment, all white, folded itself, compacted, and settled into the form of a bright indigo dragonfly. It buzzed its wings round the room and disappeared into the impenetrable darkness of a corner. My headache grew more severe. The milk and its peculiar nightgrowths were my singular memories of that Saturday when politics made its first public appearance in our lives.

SIX

SUNDAY BROUGHT US the secret faces of politics.

Dad's relations came to visit. They came with their children, all of them stiff and shy in the good clothes they rarely wore. We didn't have enough chairs for them and Mum had to swallow her pride and borrow chairs from our neighbours. The compound was aflame with politics. Our relations came to visit, but they also came to criticise. They attacked Dad for not visiting them, for not attending the meetings of our townspeople, for not contributing to wedding presents, funeral arrangements, and endless financial engagements. Dad responded badly to their criticisms. He blamed them for not helping him, for not being visible during his times of crisis; and their recriminations flew back and forth, developed into terrible arguments, with everyone shouting at the top of their voices, till they all seemed more like implacable enemies than like members of an extended family.

They seemed so much against one another that I felt ashamed being in the room, witnessing it all. The wives and children of our relations avoided looking at me and then I suspected that they hated us as much as we avoided their company. After a long period of shouting one of our relations tried to change the subject by bringing up politics and the coming elections. It was the most unfortunate change of subject. Another great altercation started and burned vehemently in the small room. Dad, who supported the Party for the Poor, quivered during the argument, unable to contain his rage; our relation, who supported the Party of the Rich, was very calm, almost disdainful. He had more money than Dad and lived in a part of the city that already had electricity.

The room vibrated with their differences and at times it seemed they would fall on one another and fight out the battle of ascendancies. But Mum came in with a tray of food and drinks. Dad sent for some ogogoro and kola-nuts and made a libation, praying for

128

harmony in the extended arms of the family. Our relations ate in silence. After they had eaten, they drank in silence. Conversation had been exhausted. When the silence got too oppressive the wives of our relations went out into the passage with Mum and I heard them laughing while the men sat in the room, embarrassed by their differences.

The afternoon intensified with the heat. Voices in the compound grew louder; children played in the passage; neighbours quarrelled; our relations said they were going; Dad didn't disguise his relief. One of the wives gave me a penny and called me a bad boy for not visiting them. Dad saw his relations off. He was away a long time. When he got back he was in quite a storm of bad temper. He raged against all relations, against all the relatives who had more money than him. He cursed their selfishness, and swore that they only came to visit to make themselves feel better in comparison with our condition. He worked himself into a tremendous verbal campaign against the Party of the Rich and in the height of his denunciation his eyes fell on the basin of powdered milk. He snatched it from the top of the cupboard and stormed out. I heard Mum pleading with him not to throw the milk away and then I heard her sigh. Dad came back with an empty basin and a wicked gleam in his eyes.

Mum sulked and Dad held her close and danced with her; she tried to push him away, but Dad clung to her, and soon she was hitting him affectionately on the back. I turned over on the bed. The fever had been retreating from me and I felt better with each hour. I heard them dancing, heard Mum's weakening protestations, and heard Dad suggest that they go visiting. Mum liked the idea. Dad went and bathed and when he got back Mum went. It took Mum a long time to get ready and while she powdered her face and arranged the elaborate ornamented folds of her head-gear and dug out her necklaces and bangles, her wrappers and white shoes, and plaited her hair hurriedly in the mirror, Dad was already asleep on his three-legged chair. The room was very hot and patches of sweat appeared on Dad's French suit, his only decent clothes. And when Mum was ready she was entirely transformed. All the tiredness, the overwork, the boniness of her face, the worry expressions on her forehead, had gone. Her face sparkled with freshness, lipstick, and eyeshadow. Her skin-tone had been softened with foundation and rouge. And I saw in Mum something of the innocent beauty that must have made the village air lustrous when Dad first set eyes on her. She looked radiant and every movement scented the room with her cheap perfume. The sweat ran down her powdered face and her eyes were bright with excitement. She touched Dad and he woke up with a start, his eyes bloodshot and bulging, his jacket armpits wet through with sweat.

'You women take so long,' Dad said.

'We may be poor, but we're not ugly,' Mum said.

Dad woke into a good mood. He rubbed his eyes, downed a short of ogogoro, forebade my going out, hooked his arm under Mum's and, in a picture of wedded bliss, stepped out into the world.

I waited till they had gone. Then I got up, poured myself some ogogoro, downed it, and went to the passage to watch the bustling Sunday afternoon life of the compound.

As the afternoon passed on into the evening the children crying in the compound began to cough. Men and women queued up outside the toilet, and everyone complained of stomach trouble. The women doubled-up and sat miserably on stools outside their rooms. A man heaved and threw-up beside the well. Women screamed that they had been poisoned and said they had crabs clawing around in their intestines. Children seared the evening with the livid heat of their weeping. Then the refrain of vomiting began.

The compound people without exception looked sick and when they passed me they glared at me as though I were in some way responsible for the mass illness. All the jollity and good feeling of Sunday gave way to groans, to cries of incomprehension, and demands for a witch-doctor's investigation. This went on all evening. The compound became a place of vomiting; tenants vomited at the housefront, along the passage, in the toilet, outside the bathroom, and the sound itself seemed to become catching. The children, unable to hold anything down, were rushed to the toilet. They were treated with castor oil, to neutralise whatever poisons they had ingested. But nothing worked. I sat outside and watched it all in amazement. Then one of the creditors' wives went past me, stiffened, turned to me, her eyes opening wide, and, in a groan that sounded like a curse, released a flood of undigested beans and rice and bile all over my Sunday clothes. She disappeared into the backyard. I washed off her vomit and went to the housefront and filled my pockets with stones. I stopped when I saw Mum and Dad returning from their outing and ran back to the room. Dad was high-spirited and drunk. Mum's face was flushed in sweat and love, her eyes bright, her radiance beautiful.

'What were you doing outside?'

I told him what had happened.

'What were you going to do?'

'Stone her.'

'Go and stone her!' he said.

I went out and threw stones at their door and missed and broke one of their windows.

The creditor came out, looking desperately sick.

'Are you mad?' he asked, wielding a machete.

'Your wife vomited on me,' I said.

The creditor burst out laughing and then he froze and rushed to the backyard.

'Everyone must have eaten something bad,' Dad said.

And then Mum told how mystified she had been at seeing people sick everywhere, at the endemic vomiting along paths and housefronts. The friends they went to visit had been ill the whole time. It seemed a plague had come upon us, insinuated itself into our intestines.

'The whole world is sick, but my family is well,' Dad said, proudly. 'That's how God reveals the just. By their fruits we shall know them. We are a strong family.'

He went on in this vein, singing lustily, till the dragonfly awoke in the room and soared violently to the ceiling and kept crashing against the walls in drunken flight.

'That insect looks like my relative,' Dad said, laughing.

'It came from the milk.'

'What?'

'The insect.'

'When?'

'Last night. Everyone was asleep. Then the insect flew out of the milk.'

'The milk!' Dad cried, in a moment's comprehension.

He rushed out into the compound, shouting:

'THE MILK! IT'S THE MILK!'

Mum picked up a slipper and stalked the dragonfly and stunned it against the wall and smashed it so hard it became an obscene greenish smear. With a look of supreme indifference, she flicked down the bulbous bits of the dragonfly and swept it out into the passage. After she had washed off the smear with a rag, she went to the creditor's room. She demanded that they clear their vomit from our roomfront and wash my stained clothes. In the meantime Dad was banging on doors, rousing everyone, overcome by the exhilaration of his drunken discovery, shouting:

'They have poisoned us with the milk!'

Dad's statement became a cry of understanding that was carried from one mouth to another, almost a rallying call, till the words gained ascendance over the ugly noises of vomiting. The women got out their containers and basins of the politicians' milk and emptied them on the street. The heaps of rotten milk grew. Other compounds also had their heaps and as I looked along the street I saw the pilings of powdered milk like mirror-images in front of stalls. The inhabitants of the area gathered and held a long public meeting about the rotten milk of politics.

The photographer hobbled about, from housefront to housefront, holding his stomach, his face wretched and pale. Bravely, he took pictures of the milk-heaps and vomit outside the houses, and got the women and children to pose round them. He took shots of sick children, men in contorted forms of agony, women in attitudes of hungry outrage.

The meeting went on for hours. The street was angry and someone suggested burning down the local offices of the rich people's party. They were angry but they were also helpless and they couldn't decide on the best course of action. They talked, could find no solutions, and as night fell they dispersed to their rooms, hobbling, wracked by spasms, exhausted of anything to vomit.

The compound became a little friendlier towards us that night. Everyone thanked Dad for his rallying cry, for finding the cause of the malaise. The creditor's wife cleared her undigested ill-feeling from our roomfront, and the creditor himself did not ask us to pay for his broken window. All through the night children went on weeping. But the refrain of vomiting lessened, as if knowing the problem had somehow reduced the condition. The toilet was unusable.

Dad made libations to his ancestors long into the night. He prayed for many things, so many that I lost track of the details, and it occurred to me that his ancestors might also be confused by them. We went to sleep in fine spirits, bonded by prayer, and glad that we had survived what became known as The Day of the Politicians' Milk. That night I slept on the mat. As darkness passed into dreams I heard them again on the bed, moving gently with the music of the springs. The movements stopped. And then a voice, out of the darkness, said:

'I wonder if the rats are awake.'

SEVEN

THE NEXT TIME I went to Madame Koto's bar the place was full of big blue flies. The smell of animal skin and sweat and fresh turned earth assailed me. It was hot and stuffy, crowded with total strangers. All of them looked as freakish as the people who were there the last time.

The difference was that there had been a grotesque interchange among the clientele. There was an albino, but he was tall and had a head like a tuber of yam. The man who was bulbous in one eye was white and blank like a polished moonstone in the other. The two men who were sinister in dark glasses now had white hair and curious hip deformations. The youth who had no teeth was now a woman. I recognised them all beneath their transformed appearances. There were others I hadn't seen before. One of them looked like a lizard with small, fixed green eyes. And amongst these strange people were others who seemed normal, who had stopped off on their way home from their jobs for an evening's drink. The place was so crowded that I had to struggle through the tight-jammed bodies, all of them raucous, all of them singing, passing abuses and bad jokes across the bar. I heard voices that were unearthly, languages that were nasal and alien, laughter that could only have come from dead tree trunks at night or from hollow graves. I began to feel ill again just pushing my way through their bodies which smelt bloodless and looked pale.

The mutant customers made the bar feel entirely different. They conferred on everything a dull yellow light. The bar itself gave the impression that it had been transported from its familiar environs of our area to somewhere under the road, under the sea, to a dimly remembered and unwanted landscape. Their laughter made the lights lurid. Their merged voices made me twitch. And the toothless woman, breaking suddenly into a high-pitched squeal of pleasure, unleashed on me a surprising rush of fear.

133

I managed to make my way to my position near the earthenware pot. All the seats were taken, and two midgets shared a stool, drinking serenely. I did not recognise either of them, but they both smiled at me. The toothless woman turned towards me, staring hard, and then, very slowly, pulled out something from beneath the table. I watched, fascinated by her magician's gesture. When she had pulled it out completely, I saw that it was a sack. I screamed and tried to get out of the door, but every available space was packed. The crowd jostled me, blocking my way, as though they were deliberately trying to prevent my escape, while not seeming to do so. I shouted and a deep-throated laughter drowned my voice. I pushed and the harder I tried the more completely I was surrounded.

Then I realised that more people were pouring in from the doorway, materialising, it seemed, from the night air. The clientele kept multiplying, filling out the spaces. They stood over me, giant figures with hair that fell off in clumps on my face. Their multiplication frightened me. The woman with no teeth became two. The midgets became four. The two men with dark glasses and white hair became three. The man with a bulbous eye acquired a double, and the double had a bulbous eye on the other side of his face. I calmed down. I had no weapon against their multiplication. The noise lowered. Everything quivered. I moved slowly, as if under water, towards the edge of a bench. I sat down. The people who surrounded me kept glancing in my direction every now and again, as if discreetly trying to make sure I was still in the bar. I became aware of being watched by everyone, even when they were not looking at me. I became convinced that they all had hidden and invisible eyes at the sides and the backs of their heads. And it was only when I looked up at one of the men who was so tall his head seemed to almost touch the cobweb-infested rafters that I knew the purity of fear.

The man had a wide mouth, prominent nostrils that flared unnaturally when he breathed, and two big disproportionate ears. And to my horror he had no eyes. I screamed very loud and I kicked the man's shin and he leant over to me and opened his mouth wide as if he were going to swallow me. Then he stayed like that, in apparent contemplation. I found myself staring into the horror of his mouth. It was very dark and ugly and at the back of his mouth there was a single luminous disc, like a flattened moonstone, and I was horrified to see the disc blinking. Then I realised I was staring at an eye. I drew back in my shock and the eye elongated towards me and then moved around like a bright marble stuck in his throat. I spat at the eye and struggled away from him, kicking and raving. The man made a cawing sound and leant over again, his mouth open, and he looked for me, but I had made it across the room.

I felt a moment's relief; but when I saw the people surrounding me I struggled to escape again. Some of them were tall eyeless women. And next to me sat the three men in dark glasses. All three of them turned their heads in my direction. One of them took off his glasses and instead of the blank white eyes I had expected he had normal ones.

'What's wrong with you?' he asked.

'Nothing.'

'Why did you spit into that man's mouth?'

'The boy is insane,' said another of the three.

'Unbalanced,' said the first.

'Drunk,' said the second.

'Hold him!' said the third.

'Yes, grab him before he spits at us.'

I edged away, keeping an eye on them. As I watched them, they began to transform, breaking out of their moulds. Their shoulders seemed momentarily hunchbacked. Their eyes blazed through their glasses and their teeth resembled fangs. I edged away, slowly, and found another corner, and stared intently at everyone. The clientele kept changing, becoming something other. What they were underneath kept emerging under the fleeting transparency of their skins. After a while I thought my eyes were playing elaborate tricks on me, or that my fever was invading me in strange ways, and I shut my eyes. When I opened them the tall women with no eyes had disappeared. I ran out of the bar and took the long way round to the backyard.

Madame Koto was sitting on a stool, holding her head. Occasionally she made a vomiting sound, and groaned. She didn't have her white beads. She looked like a compressed rhinoceros on the stool. I touched her and she started.

'Oh, it's you!' she said.

Her face was sunken. She looked quite ill.

'What happened to you?'

She gave me a sour look, made a desperate vomiting motion, held her stomach, and said:

'It was the milk.'

'You drank it?'

135

'Of course,' she barked.

'We didn't.'

She said nothing. She fell into another futile spasm of vomiting. She looked dreadful.

'What about the people in the bar?'

'What about them?'

'They were the ones who carried me away.'

'When?'

'The last time I was here.'

'Nonsense!'

'True!'

'Where did they carry you to?'

'To the river.'

'Which river?'

'I don't know. But they are witches and wizards.'

'How do you know? Are you one yourself?'

'Look at them.'

'They are just troublemakers. They have finished all my pepper-soup. And I am not well enough to deal with them.'

'What shall I do?'

'I don't know. Do what you like, but leave me alone, or I will vomit on you.'

She sounded so malicious in her bad temper that I believed she would do it. I went back to the bar and stayed at the door. I listened to the loud sinuous voices, I watched them as they laughed and banged the tables, and then I made an instant discovery. I realised for the first time that many of the customers were not human beings. Their deformations were too staggering and they seemed unaffected by their blindness and their eyelessness, their hunched backs and toothless mouths. Their expressions and movements were at odds with their bodies. They seemed a confused assortment of different human parts. It occurred to me that they were spirits who had borrowed bits of human beings to partake of human reality. They say spirits do that sometimes. They do it because they get tired of being just spirits. They want to taste human things, pain, drunkenness, laughter, and sex. Sometimes they do it to spread mischief and sometimes to seduce grown-ups or abduct children into their realm. The moment I saw them as spirits, drinking palm-wine without getting drunk, confused about the natural configuration of the human body, everything made sense. And then I became certain that Madame Koto's fetish had somehow been attracting them. I was confirmed in this notion by the fact that they seemed to cluster most thickly beneath the fetish. I knew what I had to do. I went outside and said to Madame Koto:

'Your bar is full of spirits.'

'LEAVE ME ALONE!' she shouted.

I left her alone and went round to the front and searched for a branch that was forked at the end. I went down the widening paths and found sticks, but they were either not long enough or strong enough. I got to the edge of the forest and heard trees groaning as they crashed down on their neighbours. I listened to trees being felled deep in the forest and heard the steady rhythms of axes on hard, living wood. The silence magnified the rhythms. I found a branch which seemed perfect. I broke off the long wood of the forked ends, lacerated myself on the splinters and bled. I took the stick back with me to the bar.

At the backyard Madame Koto was still on the stool, looking like a rhinoceros whose horn has been cut off. She held her head and uttered a low wailing sound. I went into the bar through the front door. The disguised spirits were now completely uproarious. They had overrun the place in an orgy of merriment, jumping up and down, dancing to non-existent melodies, fighting, singing unfamiliar songs in harsh languages. The man with the bulbous eye was playing with his other detachable one. A man who had removed his arm from its socket was hitting the toothless woman on the head with it. The spirits were drunk with their borrowed humanity and frolicked in their grotesque merriment.

I climbed on a bench and prodded the fetish with the stick. I had lifted it off the nail and was bringing it down when one of the spirits saw me from the other end of the bar and gave a piercing cry. I got down hastily. The fetish fell from the stick. There was a terrible silence in the bar. And then the disguised spirit who had shouted, pointed at me, and in a voice of command, cried:

'SEIZE THAT BOY!'

I snatched the fetish from the floor, feeling its potencies burning into my palm, and fought madly past the borrowed legs of the spirits, and gained the doorway. I stumbled and fell at the barfront. For a moment I couldn't find the fetish. I searched around furiously while the commotion in the bar spilled outside. I eventually found the fetish under the bushes, where it seemed to have crawled, like a crab. I caught it just as Madame Koto responded to the clamour. She saw me and shouted:

'Azaro, are you mad? Bring that thing back!'

In her heavy milk-contorted gait, she bounded after me. She wasn't the only one. The spirits were after me as well, and one of them held his detached arm in the air like a misbegotten club. I fled down the paths. Their heavy footsteps sounded behind me and they shouted my name:

'Azaro! Azaro!'

The whole area rang with my name. So fearfully did the spirits call it out that the lights changed and yellow clouds materialised beside me. It seemed I had entered another realm. Like animals who have discovered speech, they screamed my name, each in a different voice. I ran behind huts, hid behind sandheaps, but they were able to smell me out. The dogs barked my name, odd-looking goats blocked my path, and chickens flew out of the bushes in front of me. The trees rebounded the vowels of my name and I felt everything was in conspiracy with the spirits to betray my hiding-places. Nothing seemed safe for me; not the rutted foundations of houses, where I was set upon by strange insects, nor the circular well, in which I considered hiding, but from which my name echoed, nor the anthill, behind which red soldier ants deployed their malignant forces. So I made for the forest; I passed Madame Koto's sacrifice to the road; the plate was intact, but the food and ritual objects had gone. I went and lay down behind the great fallen tree, where I had seen the two-legged dog. But I feared I might roll over into the pit and, unable to get out, become part of the new road. So I ran deeper into the forest.

The spirits were all over the place. They gave every tree a voice. I saw a rusted machete on the ground and picked it up. The man with the bloated eye pounced on me and I smashed his arm with the machete and he did not utter a sound, nor did he bleed. I dug the fetish into his bad eye and he let me go, blinded by Madame Koto's powers. I ran on till I was lost. I was not sure any more why I was running. I stopped. I wandered amongst the silent, listening trees. I no longer heard the footsteps of the spirits. But from afar I could still hear them calling my name. Their voices were feeble on the wind.

It was rapidly getting dark. The wind blew hard through the trees. Trees groaned, branches cracked, and the wind among the leaves sounded like a distant waterfall. Pods exploded from on high and one of them fell on my head, like a mighty knock, and I dropped to the ground. In the silence and darkness that came over me I found myself riding the invisible horse of the night. I rode through the trees.

All around me were silent figures in great masks. All around me were ancestral statues. Wherever I rode I saw immemorial monoliths with solemn faces and beaded lapis lazuli eyes. The monoliths were of gold, self-luminating in the darkness. One of the statues moved and turned into Madame Koto. Her golden wrapper fluttering about her, she climbed on to a caparisoned horse of the night and commanded the other statues and monoliths to follow her. The figures in great masks moved. The statues moved. They climbed their horses, and rode after me.

I rode furiously and arrived at a place where all the winds of the world converged. The winds blew the army of statues one by one off their horses and they broke into golden fragments. Only Madame Koto, an implacable warrior, stayed on her horse and thudded after me. Just before she fell on me, it began to rain. The water, pouring down, gradually effaced her, beginning with her raised arm and her grim sword. Her arm dissolved into an indigo liquid and poured down her face; and her face dissolved slowly, as if the rain were an acid that ate away flesh and steel. Then her hair fell off and her head became reduced; and then her head rolled off into a ball of red waters and her shoulders melted and eventually her great massive bulk disappeared and all that remained were her two big fierce eyes which throbbed on the ground and stared at me. And then the horse neighed and lifted its front hooves in the air and turned and galloped away, bursting her two eyes with its hind feet. Then it too disappeared, amid infernal sounds, into the effulgent winds.

I found myself wandering under the downpour. The fetish was still in my hand. I wandered in the relentless rain, till I found the clearing. I was weary. The fetish seemed to have grown heavier and its leaden weight frightened me. I threw the fetish into the middle of the clearing, away from any trees. Then I decided to bury it, just in case the spirits or Madame Koto accidentally found it. I dug a hole with a stick. Water filled the hole. I didn't mind. I stuck the fetish into the hole and covered it over with wet earth and then I stuck branches and sticks around the hole to remind me where I had buried the fetish. Then I made my way back to the edge of the forest and stayed under the eaves of a hut till the rain softened.

I was cold. My teeth rattled. The hand with which I had held the fetish was dyed indigo. The skin of the palm peeled away in wet flakes as though the fetish had eaten my flesh. The rain softened, drizzling, and I made my way home cautiously. Dogs howled in the dark. The wind blew strongly and lifted off the roof of a bungalow and knocked it over to the adjoining compound. The tenants wailed in the horrible voices of those who have been judged and damned, as if God had ripped off the cover of their lives and exposed them to a merciless infinity. They screamed in terrible desolation like Adam and Eve being sent out of the Garden of Eden for ever. It was a sad night, with the children crying and the rain pouring over their possessions. There was nothing I could do to help and I went on home, listening to thunder rumbling from its distant homestead, and lightning crackling its multiple candent fingers over the great trees.

Everything held menace for me. The barking of dogs was like the gnashing of vengeful spirits. Branches cracking sounded as if they were about to spring on me. And even the clothes and garments flapping on washing lines seemed so like Madame Koto, dissolved from the world of flesh, threatening to wreak eternal havoc on me for the loss of her fetish. I went a long and complicated route to avoid going past her barfront. And when I got home Dad was on his three-legged chair, smoking a cigarette; the mosquito coil was on the table; the broken window had been mended; and fresh sweet cooking warmed the room with its aroma. Mum came in with a tray of food and said:

'You're just on time.'

Dad looked at me, laughed, and said:

'So the rain beat you?'

I nodded, shivering.

'Dry yourself,' Mum said.

I went and had a quick wash and dried myself with Dad's towel. I came back in and sat on the half-spread mat. I ate with Mum and Dad from the same bowls. The candle-light illuminated our faces. After I ate, I curled up on the mat, planting my secrets in my silence, and slept as if nothing unusual had happened.

EIGHT

I DID NOT go back to Madame Koto's place for a while. I feared her anger. I feared her customers. And so after school I avoided going past her barfront. I would come home and find the door locked. I would sit outside our room and wait for Mum, who often returned late from hawking and the market.

The compound was quiet in the afternoons. The sunlight fell heavily on all things and made it difficult for sounds to travel and made the air somnolent. At the compound-front women who had done all their housework dozed on the cement platform. The heaps of powdered milk, beaten by the rain, spread their poisonous whiteness along the runnels of the widening paths. Dogs slept with one eye open, their tails pestered by flies. Little children played listlessly on the sand. Older children who had returned from school changed their uniforms and came out, their faces dark with sunlight and dust except where the sweat ran down. Their mothers sent them on errands. Transfixed by the sunlight, I listened to the music of distant radios and the muezzin's rousing call to prayer.

Across the street the photographer bustled about with his camera, undeterred by the sleep-making sunlight, looking for interesting subjects. Sometimes he hung up the photographs he had washed in the glass cabinet outside his studio. We often went over to look at the wedding pictures of people who were complete strangers to us. He pinned up some of the pictures of the celebration of my homecoming. Beside them were the lurid photographs of the chaos unleashed when the politicians came round with their rotten milk. The rest of the cabinet was taken up with images of defiant women, milk heaps, street inhabitants pouring away the milk against a grainy backdrop of poverty. He was very proud of the photographs and when we gathered too close to the cabinet he would rush over and drive us away, saying:

'Don't touch the cabinet or you will spoil the photographs!'

The more he drove us away the more we gathered. The cabinet outside the studio became our first public gallery. Every afternoon, after school had ended, we went there to see what new subjects he had on display, what new funerals, what parades, how the thugs were harassing the women traders at the marketplaces, what newborn baby he had captured crying at the world. He was our first local newspaper as well.

It was the children who first showed interest in his photographs. Then the adults, on their way to work in the morning, began to stop to see what new images the industrious photographer had on display. They also stopped in the evenings when they returned. He always surprised us and began to play up to our expectations. He became very popular with the children. Whenever we saw him coming down the street with his camera we never failed to cheer him. He would smile, pretend to take pictures of us, and would disappear into the secret chambers of his studio. After a while we forgot his name and he became known to us simply as 'the photographer'.

In the afternoons, after being driven away from his glass cabinet, I often played with the other children. We had a whole universe in which to play. We played along the maze of streets and expanding paths, around huts and houses, in building sites, and in the forests. When I got tired and hungry I would ask the photographer for food. Sometimes he would complain that I was disturbing him, but mostly he would give me a piece of bread, saying:

'Your father hasn't paid for his pictures yet.'

On another day, with a glint in his eyes, in a tone of conspiracy, he said:

'Worry your father for me. I will give you a shilling if he pays for his pictures.'

He went on pestering me like that, asking if I had in turn been pestering Dad. He then threatened never to feed me again or speak to me till the pictures had been paid for. One day I saw him looking hungry and miserable and when I asked him what was wrong he snarled at me, snatched up the tripods of his camera and, screaming that no one ever paid for their photographs, pursued me down the street. He was quite fierce that day. His hunger and bitterness made him ugly, and I avoided him for a while.

His hunger got worse. In the mornings he no longer bothered to change the photographs in the glass cabinet. He no longer bothered to surprise us. The old images turned brown and sad and curled up at the edges under the bleaching force of the sunlight. In the nights

142

we heard him raving, abusing everyone for not paying up, shouting that it was people like us who drove honest men to crime and corruption. His clothes became shabby and his beard turned wiry and brown. But even his hunger couldn't extinguish his spirit and in the afternoons he still went up and down the place, taking pictures with demented eyes and in a constancy of bad temper.

The children stopped gathering round his cabinet. We invented new games and played football. One afternoon, while playing, we kicked the ball too hard into an unintended goal, smashing the photographer's cabinet. He came out, waving a machete, his eyes mad, his movements listless, his tongue coated with white sediments. He trembled in the sunlight, feeble and ill. He came to the cabinet, looked at the destruction we had wrought, and said:

'Don't touch the cabinet! I kill anyone who touches it!'

And so the football remained in the cabinet with the smashed glass and the browning photographs. The adults who went past shook their heads in bewilderment at this strange new form of photographic montage. The football was still in the cabinet when it rained. Water flooded the images. Insects bred in the cabinet and curious forms of mould and fungi grew on the innocent subjects of his industry and we all felt sad that the photographer had lost interest in his craft. He wasted away in his tiny room, trembling in the grip of an abnormal fever, and when we saw him he was always covered in a filthy black cloth.

I felt so sad about his pictures that I began to pester Dad, who always got into a temper whenever the subject was raised. So I pestered Mum, but she got bonier the more I pestered her; and so I stopped, and forgot the sadness altogether. And in the afternoons, because I couldn't go to Madame Koto's bar, nor look at the pictures in the broken glass cabinet, my feet started to itch again, and I resumed wandering the roads of the world.

Sometimes I played in the forest. My favourite place was the clearing. In the afternoons the forest wasn't frightening, though I often heard strange drums and singing and trees groaning before they fell. I heard the axes and drills in the distances. And every day the forest thinned a little. The trees I got to know so well were cut down and only their stumps, dripping sap, remained.

I wandered through the forest, collecting rusted padlocks, green bird-eggs, abandoned necklaces, and ritual dolls. Sometimes I watched the men felling trees and sometimes the companies building roads. I made some money running errands for the workers, errands to young girls who rebuffed their advances and to married women who were secretive and full of riddles in their replies, errands to buy cooked food and soft drinks. With the pennies they gave me I bought bread and fried coconut chips and iced water for myself. And then I saved some of the money and offered it to the photographer for our pictures. But when he saw how much I offered he burst into a feverish temper, and chased me out, thinking that I was mocking him.

The days were always long except when I played or wandered. The streets were long and convoluted. It took me hours to get lost and many more to find my way back again. I began to enjoy getting lost. In my wanderings I left our area altogether, with its jumbled profusion of shacks and huts and bungalows, and followed the route of the buses that took workers to the city centre. At the roadsides, women roasted corn. In palm-wine bars and eating-houses, men swallowed fist-sized dollops of eba, gesticulating furiously, arguing about politics. At a barber's shop, I watched a man being shaved bald. Next to the barber's shop there was a pool office. A man, wearing a blue French suit, his arms round a beautiful woman, came out; I started towards him. He didn't recognise me. When he got into a car, with the woman, both smiling on that hot day, and when they drove off, it occurred to me that I had seen the future incarnation of my father's better self, his successful double.

I went on walking till I got to the garage. Activity bustled everywhere. There were lorries and transport vehicles and buses reversing, conductors rhythmically chanting their destinations, commuters clambering on, drivers shouting insults at one another, bicyclists tinkling their bells. Traders cried out their wares, buyers haggled loudly, and no one seemed to be still.

There was no stillness anywhere and I went on walking and saw a lot of men carrying loads, carrying monstrous sacks, as if they were damned, or as if they were working out an abysmal slavery. They staggered under the absurd weight of salt bags, cement bags, garri sacks. The weights crushed their heads, compressed their necks, and the veins of their faces were swollen to bursting point. Their expressions were so contorted that they seemed almost inhuman. I watched them buckling under the weights, watched them become knock-kneed, as they ran, with foaming sweat pouring down their bodies. Their trousers were all soaked through and one of the men, rushing past me, farted uncontrollably, wobbling under the horrible load.

Further on I came to the lorries that brought the bags of garri from distant regions of the country. The carriers of loads were lined up at the open backs of the lorries awaiting their turns, with rolled cloths on their heads. I watched the men being loaded, watched them stumble off through the chaos. Each man bore his load differently. Two men at the back of the trucks would lift the bags on to the heads of the load-carriers. Some of the carriers flinched before the shadow of the bags, some recoiled before the loads had even been lifted, and a few invariably seemed to rise towards the load, anticipating its weight, neutralising their pain, before the terrible moment. But there was one among them who was different. He was huge, had bulbous muscles, a toweringly ugly face, and was cross-eyed, I suspected, from the accumulation of too much weight. He was the giant of the garage. They lifted a bag on his head. He made inscrutable noises and flapped his hand.

'More! More!' he said.

They lifted a second bag on his head and his neck virtually disappeared and his mighty feet sank into the muddy street.

'He's mad!' said one of the load-carriers behind him.

'He's drunk!' said another.

He turned towards them, his mouth twisted, his face contorted, and shouted, in a strangled voice:

'Your father is mad! Your mother is drunk!'

Then he turned to the two men at the back of the truck and gesticulated again. He flapped his hand so violently it seemed he was trying to attack them. They drew back in horror.

'MORE! MORE!' he cried.

'That's enough,' said one of the two men.

'Do you think we are politicians?' said the other.

His gestures became more furious.

'He's not mad,' said the carrier behind him. 'He's poor, that's all.'

'MORE! MORE!' the giant squealed.

'Look, go! That's enough even for you.'

'MORE! MORE!' he said, his voice disappearing.

They lifted one more sack on his head and an extraordinary sound came from his buttocks; his head vanished altogether; the sound continued, unstoppable; and he staggered one way and then another. Those waiting to be loaded fled from behind him. He wobbled in all directions, banging into stalls, toppling tables of fresh fish and neat piles of oranges, staggering into traders' wares, trampling on basins of snails. Women screamed at him, pulling at his

145

trousers. He went on staggering, balancing the weights, slipping and miraculously regaining his footage, grunting and swearing, uttering the words 'MORE! MORE!' under his breath, and when he went past me I noticed that his crossed eyes were almost normal under the crush, and his muscles trembled uncontrollably, and he groaned so deeply, and he gave off such an unearthly smell of sweat and oppression that I suddenly burst into tears.

People had gathered all around. People had stopped what they were doing, just to see if this man who wasn't really a giant could manage all that weight. They watched the spectacle of that squat, thick-set man, and it was the only moment I saw people in stillness. And when the man, wobbling and weaving, got to where he was supposed to be relieved of the bags, the unloaders weren't there. He turned, calling for them; they came running out of a bukka, and arrived too late; for he suddenly threw down the three mountainous bags all at once; one of them spilled open; and he stood perfectly still for a moment, blinking, while people all around cheered him and sang out his nicknames; and then he fell in slow motion on to the sacks and did not stir till he had been dragged to the roadside and revived with a bucket of water and a tumbler full of palm-wine.

After a while he got up, his knees knocking, and went back to the truck and took to carrying only two bags. People still kept watching him, to see if he would do something extraordinary with the bags. But the only thing he did, after a few trips, was go into a bukka, put away a great bowl of pounded yam, swallowing handfuls that would have choked a bull. The spectators who left, resuming their busy lives, missed seeing him perform an impromptu fandango with the madame of the bukka and then run off without paying, the madame hot on his heels waving a frying pan.

The garage was the most confusing place I'd ever seen: people shouting everywhere, lorries revving, truck-pullers yelling, music blaring from new record shops and drinking houses, cars screeching, women screaming at pickpockets, and men fighting over who would carry the suitcases of travellers. Across the road a woman was whipping a madman with a broom. Behind me a thief was caught and set upon by traders. There were boys all over the place, roaming around with hungry and cunning eyes. Outside a run-down shed the old bicycle-repairer sat on a chair, smoking a cigarette, surveying the whole confusion. A bus had broken down and people were pushing it. A woman, fat and rich-looking in expensive lace, was ordering a lot of men around. She looked very powerful and had an expression of distilled scorn on her face as she commanded the men to take her baggage from the boot of a taxi. There was so much to see, so much to listen to, with clashing sounds and voices pulling the attention this way and that, with everything happening in frantic simultaneity, that it was impossible to walk straight. I kept bumping into people, stumbling into potholes of mud, tripping over the rubbish that was soggy on the ground. I would be watching one thing, a girl washing a baby's bottom at the roadside, when a car horn would blast noisily behind me, startling the life out of me. Or I would be wary of the cars behind me, driving by so close that it seemed they were slowly and deliberately trying to run me over, when someone would shout:

'Get out of my way, you rat!'

I would jump out of the way and a truck-puller, dragging behind him the entire contents of a modest household, or a load-carrier, straining under a monstrous weight of yams, would storm past. I became dizzy, hungry, and confused. No one paid much attention to anyone else. On one side of the street a man would suddenly bolt off with a trader's tinbox of money. On the other side a woman would be arguing with a customer about the price of breadfruit, while her child was crawling under a stationary lorry. I was going towards the lorry to get the child out when a great cry started all around me. The woman had just realised that her child was missing. The cry was so piercing that other women instantly gathered around, holding their breasts and agitating the air with their hands. The lorry driver started his engine, the child screamed, the women rushed towards me, shoved me out of the way, and some of them went under the lorry, while others pounced on the driver and harassed him for parking his ugly vehicle in front of their stalls. The driver didn't stand for it and insulted them back and a frightening din of abuse ensued, the women getting so involved that they forgot the child they were concerned about in the first place. I was by now quite obliterated with mud and dirt and I went on further, looking for a water-pump.

I couldn't find one and I came to a place where men were offloading cement bags from the back of a trailer. Again there was a multitude of load-carriers, their faces obscured by cement-dust, with cement on their sweating eyebrows and on their hair. I wondered how they managed to comb it in the mornings. Some of the load-carriers were boys a little taller than me. I watched the boys buckling under the cement bags, staggering off, dumping them down, coming back, till their supervisor called for a break, and they all went and sat around the outdoor table of a bukka and washed their hands and sweated into their food, eating voraciously.

When they resumed work again I noticed that amongst them was an old man, his son, and his grandchildren, who could not have been much older than me. Among the grandchildren was one who had just started carrying loads that day. He kept crying about his neck and his back and he cried all through the carrying but his father wouldn't let him stop and drove him on with his tongue, saying he must learn to be a man, and that there were boys younger than him who were a pride to their families, and at that moment he pointed at me. Fearing that the supervisor might notice me as well and take it into his head to order me to break my neck carrying cement bags, I hurried on, searching for a water-pump, till I came to another lorry where men were offloading bags of salt. And I was staring at the strange number plate of the lorry when I heard the protestations of a familiar voice.

I heard the voice briefly and I sought the face. And then I saw Dad amongst the load-carriers. He looked completely different. His hair was white and his face was mask-like with engrained cement. He was almost naked except for a very disgusting pair of tattered shorts which I had never seen before. They loaded two bags of salt on his head and he cried 'GOD, SAVE ME!' and he wobbled and the bag on top fell back into the lorry. The men loading him insulted his ancestry, wounding me, and Dad kept blinking as the sweat and salt poured into his eyes. The men loading him shouted about how he had been giving them a lot of trouble and behaving like a woman and if he couldn't carry mere bags of salt he should crawl back into his wife's bed. Dad was still staggering, like a boxer under the onslaught of too many blows, when the loaders dumped the second bag on his head for the second time. For a moment Dad stood perfectly still. Then he wobbled. His muscles twitched erratically. The bags were very huge and compact, like boulders of rock, and salt poured out of one of them on to Dad's shoulder.

'MOVE! MOVE ON!' said one of the loaders.

'OR YOU WANT ANOTHER BAG, EH?' said the other.

For a moment I thought Dad was going to succumb to the dare and be forced deeper into the earth by the sheer weight of bags that could have been pillars of stone. And I couldn't bear the thought of it and in a voice so thin in the midst of the chaos all around, I cried:

'Dad! No!'

148

Several eyes turned towards me. Dad swung many ways, trying to locate the source of the cry, and when he faced my direction he stopped. His face kept twitching and his neck muscles kept palpitating, as if he was suffering a cramp. One of the loaders said:

'MOVE ON, MAN!'

And as the salt poured on his shoulder, tears streamed from his eyes, and there was shame on his face as he staggered right past me, almost crushing me with his mighty buckling feet. He appeared not to have seen me and he struggled on, trying to bear the load with dignity, weaving in the compensating direction of the load's gravity. He weaved uncontrollably, women and children scattering before his advance as if he were an insane animal. Sweat poured down his back and I followed him at a distance, grieving for the cuts and wounds on his arms. As he was turning a corner he tripped, regained his balance, wobbled, and then slid on the mud and rubbish on the road, and fell. The salt bags dropped slowly from his head, and I thought, shutting my eyes and screaming, that they would crush him. But when I opened my eyes I saw the bags in the mud. One of them had rolled over the gutter. Dad stayed on the ground, covered in mud, not moving, as if dead, while his blood trickled from his back and mixed with the rubbish of the earth. And then the supervisor came running towards him, shouting; and a truck-pusher went past him, growling; and Dad suddenly got up, rolling and sliding on the mud, losing grip and standing again, and then he ran in two directions before shooting across the road. A lorry almost knocked him over, but he went on running, and I could see him fleeing into the labyrinth of stalls, ducking under the eaves of kiosks, till he disappeared into the confusion of the garage market, with people tearing after him because they thought he was a thief. I didn't stay and I didn't want a water-pump any more. I half-ran, half-walked the distance home. And I was unhappy. My wanderings had at last betrayed me, because for the first time in my life I had seen one of the secret sources of my father's misery.

NINE

WHEN I GOT home I sat outside and didn't play with any of the children. I felt very wretched and didn't notice the daylight pass into evening. Mosquitoes and fireflies appeared. Lamps were lit inside rooms. The men of the compound talked about politics, about the Party of the Poor. They too had come with loudhailers and leaflets and had promised a lot of things and had won considerable support because they said they would never poison the people.

It was dark when Mum returned. She looked haggard and sunblackened. She shuffled into the room, dropped her tray of provisions, fell on the bed, lay there unmoving, and was instantly asleep. I warmed the food and swept the room. When she woke up, she looked better. She sat down and ate. After eating she lay on the bed and I sat on Dad's chair, watching the door. She was silent. I told her I had seen Dad; she started to work up a temper about my having begun wandering again, but she was too tired to sustain it. She lay there, grumbling in an ancient monotone about how hard life was, and I listened intently, for I had begun to understand something of what she meant. We stayed up till very late, in complete silence, waiting for Dad to return.

'What did your father say when you saw him?' she asked eventually.

'Nothing.'

'How can he say nothing?'

'He said nothing.'

'You didn't see him.'

'I did.'

'Where?'

'At the garage.'

We went on waiting. We stayed up, dozing fitfully, till dawn faintly lighted up the sky. Mum became very agitated.

'What has happened to him?' she asked me.

'I don't know,' I said.

She began to weep.

'Are you sure you saw him?'

'Yes.'

'Was he well? Did he talk to you? What did he say? I pray nothing has happened to him. What will I do if something bad has happened? How will I live? Who will take care of you?'

She went on like that, talking, asking questions, muttering, breaking down into sobs, till I fell asleep on the chair. When the cocks cracked the egg of dawn with their cries, Mum got out of bed, washed her face, and prepared to go and search for Dad in the police stations and hospitals of the world. She had just put food out for me, when Dad appeared at the door. He looked terrible. He looked like an anguished ghost, a forlorn spirit. His eyes were red, his face white and drawn, cement and yam powder all over his brow, his beard wild. He looked unwashed and I knew instantly that he had been roving the streets all night. He avoided my eyes and Mum rushed to him and flung her arms round his neck. He flinched and Mum said:

'Where have you been, my husband? We were so worried . . .'

'Don't ask me any questions,' Dad growled, pushing Mum away from him.

He went and sat on the bed, staining it with dried mud. He blinked rapidly. Mum fussed over him, trying to anticipate his needs. She hurried out and prepared food. He didn't touch it. She boiled water for him to bathe with. He didn't move. She touched him tenderly and Dad exploded:

'Don't trouble me, woman! Don't bother me!'

'I don't want to . . .'

'Leave me alone! Can't a man do what he wants without a woman troubling him? I have a right to do what I want! So what if I stayed out last night! You think I have been doing nothing? I've been thinking, you hear, thinking! So don't trouble me as if I've been with another woman . . .'

'I didn't say you have been with . . .'

At that exact moment Dad leapt up into a tidal rage and scattered the plates of food and tossed away the centre table and grabbed the bedclothes and hurled them across the room. They landed on me, covering my face. I stayed like that with the bedclothes over my head while Dad raged. Mum cried out and then stifled the cry. I heard Dad hitting her. I looked and Dad was slapping her on the head, kicking

151

the table, shaking Mum, pushing her, muscling her around, and her arms flailed, and then she submitted herself to his anger, and I got up and rushed at him, and he shoved me aside and I fell on his boots and hurt my bottom and I stayed there without moving. And then, quite suddenly, Dad stopped hitting her. He stopped in the middle of a slapping motion, which changed into an embrace. He held her tight while she sobbed, shaking. Dad also shook, and he led her to the bed and held her, and they stayed like that, unmoving, embracing awkwardly, for a long time. Outside I could hear the cocks crowing. The compound people were preparing for work. Children cried. The female prophet of the new churches chanted for the world to repent. The muezzin pierced the dawn with calls to prayer. Dad kept saying:

'Forgive me, my wife, forgive me.'

And Mum, sobbing, shaking, also kept saying, as if it were a litany: 'My husband, I was only worried, forgive me . . .'

I got up and crept out of the room and went to the housefront. I slept on the cement platform till Mum came to wake me. When I went back into the room Dad was asleep on the bed, his mouth open, his nose flaring and softening, an agonised expression on his wrinkled forehead.

I lay on the mat and didn't go to school that day. Mum lay with Dad on the bed till the afternoon and then she went off to the market. When I awoke, Dad was still asleep. He slept with his suffering still on his face.

That evening the van of bad politics returned. The women, children, and jobless men of the area went up and down the place as if something terrible were going to happen. The street became crowded. I went across to the photographer's studio and saw the van of the politicians who had poisoned us. They blared passionate speeches through their loudhailer. We listened in silence to the politicians of bad milk. We listened as they blamed the other party for the milk. We listened as they maintained, with ferocious conviction, that it was their rivals, the Party of the Poor, who had been impersonating them, pretending to be them.

'THEY WERE RESPONSIBLE FOR THE MILK, NOT US. THEY WANT TO DISCREDIT US,' the loudhailers cried.

We found their statement very strange because at the back of the van were the very same people who had come round the first time. We recognised them all. Now they came with bags of garri, but with twice the number of thugs. They had whips and clubs among the garri bags and they seemed prepared for charity and war at the same time.

'WE ARE YOUR FRIENDS. WE WILL BRING YOU ELEC-TRICITY AND BAD ROADS, NOT GOOD MILK, I MEAN GOOD ROADS, NOT BAD MILK,' the politicians maintained, with great vigour.

People massed round the vehicle. The photographer darted around with his camera. He wasn't taking pictures, but he seemed to have awoken completely from his hunger and his fever. The thugs handed out pans of garri but no one came forward to receive any. The people massed silently round the van. It was as if a message was being passed along. There was something ominous in their silence.

'TRUST US! TRUST OUR LEADER! TRUST OUR GARRI! OUR PARTY BELIEVES IN SHARING THE NATIONAL GARRI AND . . .'

'LIES!' someone cried from the crowd.

'THIEVES!' said another.

'POISONERS!'

'MURDERERS!'

The four voices broke the stranglehold of the loudspeaker. The politician who had been launching into his litany of promises lost control and stammered. The loudspeaker gave off a high-pitched screeching noise. The people increased round the van. They were silent again and they followed the van silently as it moved, women with hungry resentful faces, men with thunderous brows. The thugs jumped down from the back of the van. One of them said:

'WHO CALLED US THIEVES?'

No one answered. The thug's eyes fell on the photographer. His camera made him conspicuous. As the thug moved towards the photographer the politician cried, through the agency of the loudhailer:

'WE ARE YOUR FRIENDS!'

Then he repeated the words, with other entreaties, in his language, appealing to local sentiments. At that same moment the thug punched the photographer, whose nose started to bleed. No one moved. The thug lifted his great fist again and the photographer ducked into the crowd, screaming, and the men went on offering pans of garri, and the politician went on with his claims, and suddenly a stone smashed the van's window and undammed the fury of angry bodies. Several hands clawed at the van; someone cracked the politician on the head and he screamed into the loudspeaker. The driver started the vehicle;

it jerked forward and knocked a woman over. The photographer recorded the moment. The woman howled and the men hurled stones, breaking the side windows and shattering the windscreen. The crowd surged to the front of the van, preventing it from moving. The thugs jumped down and whipped people, the photographer frenziedly took pictures, and the people went on stoning the side windows till they gave completely and then they threw rocks at the men handing out garri. The men shouted, blood appeared on their faces; the politician appealed for calm; someone in the crowd cried:

'Stone them!'

Another said:

'BURN THE VAN!'

The thugs went on whipping till a fierce crowd of men surged over them. When the thugs reappeared they were almost naked. The women, with a special vengeance, cracked firewood and planks on their heads. And a smallish woman, whose three children were still suffering the worst effects of the poisoning, was seen rushing from her house, shouting:

'I'm going to pour boiling water on them! CLEAR THE WAY-O!'

And people cleared a way for her and she emptied the basin of boiling water on to the thugs who were hiding at the back of the van; they screamed and scattered everywhere, tripping over their garri bags, falling over the furious bodies, and when they hit the ground the crowd lashed at them with whips and sticks and when they ran the crowd pursued and stoned them. The thugs ran, pleading, but no one listened, and they were stoned till they were bloody all over. They fled into the mudflats and the marshes and a contingent of people followed them. The thugs waded thigh-deep in marsh and brackish waters and disappeared into the wild forests; the contingent returned with the news, their anger unabated.

Only the driver was left in the van. The violence had so stimulated the people that we set about punishing the vehicle, kicking and denting its bodywork, hitting its tin and aluminium construct with metal rods and firewood, and the van did not scream, and so chanting and cursing, we gathered and heaved all our energies together and lifted it and tipped it on its side and, with the tentative agility of a cockroach, the driver clambered out and managed the distinction of being the only one to escape without a beating, for as soon as he got out he fled down the street towards Madame Koto's bar, where he was offered invincible asylum.

The van stayed overturned. Through the night people went on

sporadically wreaking their impotent vengeance on the van. They went on even when we heard that a truckload of policemen were on their way, armed with guns and batons. By the time the policemen arrived the impotent rage had turned sulphurous; burning brands had been stuck into the petrol tank and the night exploded into yellow incandescence at the same moment that the policemen, barking orders, blowing whistles, jumped down from their trucks. They stood around watching helplessly as the van burst into flames and thunder. They questioned a few people but everyone had just arrived, just been awoken from sleep, no one had seen or heard anything, and the police took in five suspects. They couldn't do anything about the flaming van, which cracked the air in a final spasmic explosion. All night the van smouldered and the fire brigade did not come to put out the flames. And it was only when the police were pulling away that we saw the faces of those taken in for questioning. The photographer was one of them. He had managed to get rid of the evidence that was his camera. He looked stony-eyed and brave. He waved at us as they dragged him away.

The burnt van stayed in the street for a long time. At night shadows came and scavenged the engine. One morning we woke to find that it had been uprighted and moved as though the night had been attempting to drive it away. The children of the area found in it a temporary new plaything. We learned how to drive it, wrenching around its steering wheel, taking long journeys across great wastes of fantasies.

Rain poured on the burnt van, the sun and the dust bleached its paint, and after a while all the big flaking letters of the party's insignia were obliterated, and nothing was left to identify the vehicle, or to rescue it from forgetfulness. It wasn't long before it vanished from the street, not because it was no longer there, diminishing with each day's sunglare, but because we had stopped noticing it altogether.

The photographer was released three days after he was taken away. He said he had been tortured in prison. He was louder and more fearless than before. Prison seemed to have changed him and he went around with a strange new air of myth about him, as if he had conceived heroic roles for himself during the short time he had been away. When he arrived the street gathered outside his room to give him a hero's welcome. He told us stories of his imprisonment and of how he had survived fiendish methods of torture inflicted on him to get out the names of collaborators, planners of riots, destabilisers of the Imperial Government, and enemies of the party. He made us dizzy with his stories. People brought him food, palm-wine, ogogoro, kola-nuts, kaoline, and he could have selected quite a few wives from the admiring female faces of that evening if he had not already permanently entered new mythic perceptions of himself that excluded such rash decisions. I hung around outside the photographer's studio, listening as the adults talked in solemn tones and as they drank long into the night of his triumphant return. Even Dad went over to pay his respects.

The next day woke us up to a great excitement. Everywhere people were talking in animated tones. Everywhere people who had been content to listen to the news of the country only in the form of rumours were now to be seen scrutinising the same page of the newspaper, as if overnight newsprint had been given a new importance. It was only when I got back from school that I understood the excitement. For the first time in our lives we as a people had appeared in the newspapers. We were heroes in our own drama, heroes of our own protest. There were pictures of us, men and women and children, standing helplessly round heaps of the politicians' milk. There were pictures of us raging, attacking the van, rioting against the cheap methods of politicians, humiliating the thugs of politics, burning their lies. The photographer's pictures had been given great prominence on the pages of the newspaper and it was even possible to recognise our squashed and poverty-ridden faces on the grainy newsprint. There were news stories about the bad milk and an editorial about our rage. We were astonished that something we did with such absence of planning, something that we had done in such a small corner of the great globe, could gain such prominence. Many of us spent the evening identifying ourselves amongst the welter of rough faces.

Mum was clearly recognisable among the faces. Ten million people would see her face and never meet her in their lives. She was carrying a basin of rotten milk; and the dreadful newsprint distorted her beauty into something wretched and weird; but when she returned from the market in the evening people crowded into our rooms and talked about her fame, how she could use it to sell off her provisions, about the thugs, who had sworn terrible reprisals, and about the landlord, who was furious that his own tenants had partaken in the attack on his beloved Party.

Most of us were delighted to see ourselves on the front pages of a national newspaper; but nothing amazed us as much as seeing a special picture of the photographer himself, with his name in print. We pointed at his name over and over again and went round to his room to congratulate him. He was very high-spirited that evening and he went from place to place, followed by a swelling tide of wondering mortals, talking about national events in intimate terms. He came to our compound and was toasted in every room and he laughed loudly and drank merrily. Neither his new fame, nor the alcohol made him fail to remind us that we still owed him money for our photographs.

When Dad returned from work and learned of Mum's picture in the papers he was both a little proud and a little jealous of her. He said she looked like a starving witch-doctor. But that didn't stop him from cutting out the page of the paper and sticking it to the wall. Every now and again, while smoking a cigarette, he would look at the picture and say:

'Your mother is getting famous.'

The photographer eventually made it to our room and Dad sent me to buy some drinks. When I got back the photographer was staggering about the place, quite drunk, diving behind the chair, shooting an imaginary camera, acting the part of thugs and politicians, while Mum and Dad fell about in laughter. He was very drunk and he kept wobbling on Dad's chair and saying:

'I am an International Photographer.'

He went on to tell us how many commissions he had received since he became famous. People who had gone to congratulate him now wanted him to photograph them in their huts, their shacks, their crowded rooms, their filthy backyards, along with their extended families, in the hope that he would publish their images on the pages of the newspapers. The photographer got very drunk indeed and fell off Dad's chair. We made him sit up straight. He would be talking and then he would doze off, his mouth still open. He would suddenly wake up and with amazing precision continue his speech exactly where he left off.

He sat there, back against the wall, the window over his head. With his lean face, his excitable eyes, his bony forehead, his sharp jaws, and his energetic gestures, he seemed as if he belonged in the room, as if he were a member of our hungry and defiant family.

One moment he was talking and the next moment I didn't hear him any more. His mouth moved, but his words were silent. The candle flickered on the table. I was confused by the phenomenon.

'Prepare food for the International Photographer,' Dad said, with great warmth.

I went with Mum to the backyard. We prepared eba and stew for everyone. When we got back to the room the photographer was fast asleep on the floor. We woke him up and he carried on with a conversation whose beginning eluded us. He ate with us, declined any more drinks, thanked and prayed for us and, wobbling at the door, he made a statement which touched us.

'You are my favourite family in the compound,' he said.

Then he staggered out into the night. Me and Dad walked him to his door. Dad shook hands with him and we came back. Dad was silent, but he looked proud and tall and he didn't stoop under the memory of all those weights. When we passed the burnt van Dad paused and studied its form in the darkness. Then he touched me on the head, urging me on, and said:

'Trouble always happens after celebration. Trouble is coming to our area.'

TEN

AFTER SCHOOL THE next day, I came home and found strange people around the van. Our landlord was among them. He kept waving his arms furiously, pointing at all the houses along the street. The other men looked very suspicious and wore dark glasses. We watched them for a while. They went round the van, talking intensely about it; they touched the van, poked it, looked round at the street, then, nodding, they went towards Madame Koto's bar, looking back in severe scrutiny at the van as they went. When they had gone a few of the street's people went and gathered round the van and studied it and prodded it as if by doing this they would find out what the men's interest was all about.

That same afternoon three men in French suits turned up at the photographer's place. He wasn't in and they stood in front of his glass cabinet, staring at the new pictures he had stuck up. The men stared at the pictures with great interest and they aroused our curiosity and we were impatient for the men to leave. But the three men stayed.

They were dressed identically, wore dark sunglasses, and kept looking nervously at the surrounding houses. They waited for the photographer for a long time and with great patience. They stood in front of the cabinet, without moving, while the sun changed the position of their shadows. The photographer's co-tenants became curious about the three men and sent children to ask them if they wanted to buy soft drinks or food. They didn't; and so two women, with children on their backs, went over to them and asked a lot of questions and got quite heated and made gestures which started people gathering and the three men became embarrassed and went for a walk. They walked up the street and I followed them. They went to Madame Koto's bar and ordered a glass of palm-wine each.

I went back to the photographer's compound and sat near the glass cabinet. After a while I saw him coming, weighed down by

159

his new myth and his camera and his tripod stand. I ran over to
tell him that three men had been waiting for him.

'For me? Why?' he asked, turning back in the direction he
had just come from.

'I don't know, but your compound people gave them trouble.'

'What did they look like? Are they policemen?'

'I don't know. They were tall and wore glasses.'

'Dark glasses?'

'Very dark. I couldn't see their eyes.'

He started walking in a hurry. He went towards the main road.
I tried to keep up with him. I held on to his hand.

'Leave me alone.'

'What are you going to do?' I asked.

'Run.'

'Where?'

'Away.'

'What about the men?'

'What men?'

'The men in dark glasses.'

'Let them wait. When they have gone, I will come back.'

Then he broke into a run, looking furtively in all directions, as
if he had suddenly realised that he was surrounded by visible and
invisible enemies. He ran in a zigzag along the street. He ducked and
dashed under the eaves. He wound his way in and out of compounds,
crouching low, his tripod bobbing behind him, till he disappeared.

I went back to our compound and sat outside and watched the
photographer's house. The three men didn't reappear. After a while
I went to look at the new pictures in the cabinet. They showed thugs
beating up market women. They showed the leader of the Party of
Bad Milk from odd angles that made his face seem bloated, his eyes
bulbous, his mouth greedy. He had pictures of politicians being
stoned at a rally, he caught their panic, their cowardice, and their
humiliation. He also had photographs of beautiful girls and a choir
of boys and a native doctor standing in front of a wretched-looking
shrine.

I looked at the pictures a long time and I got tired and the
sun was pitiless on my brain, burning through my hair and skull
and turning my thoughts into a yellow heat. I went and sat outside
our door and I didn't know what else to do; so I set out to look for
Mum at the marketplace.

As I walked down our street, under the persistence of the yellow sun, with everything naked, the children bare, the old men with exhausted veins pumping on dried-up foreheads, I was frightened by the feeling that there was no escape from the hard things of this world. Everywhere there was the crudity of wounds, the stark huts, the rusted zinc abodes, the rubbish in the streets, children in rags, the little girls naked on the sand playing with crushed tin-cans, the little boys jumping about uncircumcised, making machine-gun noises, the air vibrating with poisonous heat and evaporating water from the filthy gutters. The sun bared the reality of our lives and everything was so harsh it was a mystery that we could understand and care for one another or for anything at all.

I passed a house where a woman was screaming. People were gathered outside her room. I thought thugs were beating her up and I went there and learned that she was giving birth and that she had been in labour for three days and three nights. I asked so many questions that the gathered adults finally noticed I was a child and drove me away. I went on with my wanderings, not knowing where I was headed, except that I had conceived the desire to see Mum. Every female hawker I saw I thought was her. There were so many hawkers, and all of them selling identical things, that I wondered just how Mum sold anything at all in this world of relentless dust and sunlight.

I walked for a long time, the street burning my soles, my throat dry, my head sizzling, till I reached the market. There were stalls of goods everywhere. And filling the air were the smells and aromas of the marketplace, the rotting vegetables, the fresh fruits, the raw meat, roasted meat, stinking fish, the feathers of wild birds and stuffed parrots, the wafting odours of roasted corn and fresh-dyed cloth, cow dung and sahelian perfume, and pepper-bursts which heated the eyeballs and tickled the nostrils. And just as there were many smells, so there were many voices, loud and clashing voices which were indistinguishable from the unholy fecundity of objects. Women with trays of big juicy tomatoes, basins of garri, or corn, or melon seeds, women who sold trinkets and plastic buckets and dyed cloth, men who sold coral charms and wooden combs and turtle-doves and string vests and cotton trousers and slippers, women who sold mosquito coils and magic love mirrors and hurricane lamps and tobacco leaves, with stalls of patterned cloths next to those of fresh-fish traders, jostled everywhere, filled the roadside, sprawled in fantastic confusion. There was much bickering in the air and rent-collectors hassled the women and cart-pullers shouted for people to get out of their way and mallams with goats on leashes prayed on white mats, nodding under the sun, stringing their beads. The floor of the market was soggy with mud and decomposing food and the children ran around mostly naked. The women wore faded wrappers and dirty blouses; their faces were like Mum's in her suffering and their voices were both sweet and harsh, sweet when attracting customers, harsh when haggling. I went about the market confused by many voices that could have been Mum's, many faces that could have been hers, and I saw that her tiredness and sacrifice were not hers alone but were suffered by all women, all women of the marketplace.

At an intersection of paths there was a fight raging. Men were shouting, stalls were overturned, dogs barking, sticks whizzing through the air, fish stinking, flies buzzing. There were so many flies I was amazed that I didn't breathe them in. I circled round the fight; I went from stall to stall, my head barely reaching the heights of displayed goods. I often found myself staring into the dead eyes of fishes, into basins where great crabs and giant lobsters were entangled in their mass of claws, in buckets where hammer-headed fishes and eels whipped their tails against the aluminium. I searched for Mum till my eyes hurt with too much looking and my head spun with too much exertion. Then, suddenly, with the sun burning itself into evening, with so many people around, everyone active, everything moving, I was overcome with a strange panic. I couldn't see a single familiar face in that jostling universe. And then just as suddenly, in flashes of lightness and dark, I began to see Mum everywhere. I saw her writhing in the basin of eels. I saw her amongst the turtles in the plastic buckets. I saw her among the amulets of the sellers of charms. I saw her all over the market, under strange eaves, in the wind that spread the woodsmoke and the rice-chaffs; I felt her everywhere, but I couldn't break the riddle of the market's labyrinths where one path opened into a thousand faces, all of them different, most of them hungry in different ways.

I saw women counting their money and tying it at the ends of their wrappers. Children, abandoned temporarily, cried on the floor, under the stalls. I walked round and round the market spaces, unable to go any deeper, unable to find my way out, unable to go on because my feet hurt, and unable to stop because of the perpetually moving crowds who pushed me on or shoved me aside or trampled me or shouted at me and I was confused by everything and I sat under a stall of snails and wept without any tears.

Then time changed. Darkness slowly swallowed the day. I came out from under the stall and struggled through the crowd till I arrived at another stall where an old man sold all kinds of roots and herbs. He was an old man with the youthful eyes of a dove and white hair on his head, a white moustache and an ash-coloured patch of straight beard. His stall was the quietest place in the whole market. He sat alone on a bench. He called no one to buy his wares and no one came. Behind him, dangling from multicoloured ropes and threads were yellow roots, blue roots, pink tubers, the skull of a monkey, the feathers of a parrot, the dried heads of hooded vultures and ibises, the fierce paws of a lion, the wings of an eagle, and a mirror that changed colour with the lights. His stall was quite clean; behind the ropes and threads and bizarre items was a tarpaulin tent, stained with mud. If he was a herbalist, he must have been a learned and highly selective one, for before I reached him a man in an immaculate white suit approached him, nodded, and they both went inside. They stayed in for a while.

I stared in wonder at the items on his table, the rusted stems of gum trees, red leaves dried in the sun which smelt of distant journeys, carved roots that resembled the crude shapes of human beings, strangely angled bones, the beryl-coloured seeds of rare medicinal plants, transparent seashells, dried flame-lilies, berries and aniseeds and the green pimples of peacocks, dazzling blobs like the eyes of cats that refuse to dry in the sun, crushed cane-brakes and broken rings from the depths of the sea, and a hundred other oddities, all scattered on a dirty blue cloth. I sat on the old man's chair and waited. And while I waited I listened to the whooping noises behind me in the tent. The noise kept changing into the spectral sound that only spirits can make. Then it changed to the noise of a thick rope being whipped round fast. Then into the sound of mermaids sifting the white winds through their long hair on golden river banks. Then came a scream that was not a scream of terror; it stayed sharp; then it resolved itself into laughter. The man in the immaculate white suit came out sweating, with a little blue sack over his shoulder. The old man also came out. He wasn't sweating. He regarded me.

'I'm looking for my mother,' I said.
'Who is your mother?'
'A trader in this market.'
'Do I know her?'
'I don't know.'
'Why are you looking for her?'
'Because she is my mother.'

The old man sat down. I stood.

'Where did you lose her?'

'At home.'

'Are you a message?'

'I don't know.'

'Did she send you on a message?'

'No.'

'Did spirits send you to me?'

'I don't know.'

'Does she know you are here?'

'No.'

'Does she know where you are?'

'I don't think so.'

The old man stared at me with his strange eyes. He picked up a root and turned it over in his hands. Then he bit a little from it and chewed, thinking. He offered me the root. I took it but did not bite into it. He studied me.

'So does anybody know you are here?'

'No.'

He smiled and his youthful eyes became clouded, their colour changed. For a moment he reminded me of a hooded bird.

'So why did you come to me?'

'I don't know.'

He picked up another root. It was shaped like a child with a big head. He bit off the head of the child, spat it out, and bit at its arm, and chewed.

'What is your name?'

'Lazarus.'

'What?'

'Azaro.'

He looked at me again, as if I were some sort of sign.

'Are you clever at school?'

'I'm looking for my mother.'

'Does your mother teach you things?'

'Yes.'

'Like what?'

'How to fly to the moon on the back of a cricket.'

The old man's expression didn't change.

'Do you have brothers and sisters?'

'Only in heaven.'

He studied me, touching his beard. He looked round the turbulent marketplace. He got up, went into his tent, and came back with a cracked enamel plate of yam and beans. I was hungry. Forgetting Mum's warning about strangers, I devoured the food. It was delicious. The old man watched me with a gleam in his eyes. He kept muttering low incantations under his breath. I thanked him for the food and he said:

'How are you feeling?'

'Full up.'

'Good.'

He took the plate in and came out with a plastic cup of water. The water tasted like it came from a deep well. It was sweet and smelt faintly of rust and the strange roots on his table. I drank the water and felt thirstier than before.

'How are you feeling now?'

I was about to speak when it occurred to me that the world had become dimmer. A faint spell of evening had settled on my eyes. I felt curiously light and inside me there were wide open spaces. I tried to move. But my spirit felt lighter than my body. My spirit moved, my body stayed still. And when I thought I had moved a considerable distance I found that I was actually at the beginning of the movement. Then I felt everything turning round and round, slowly at first, like a circling wind that was itself the evening settling; and then things went faster and dimmer and the old man's face grew abnormally large and then it grew so small I could hardly make out his eyes. And then from a great distance I heard him say:

'Lie down, my son.'

Then, with the sound of feathers beating behind him, he left in a hurry, dissolving into a bright wind.

The sounds of the marketplace took on a new quality. A million footfalls magnified on the earth. Voices of every kind rose in massive waves and distilled into whispers. From afar, I heard the muezzin calling. I felt it was calling me, but I could not move. Bells and angelic choirs sounded close to my ears and then would melt away. I watched a fight start across from where I was sitting. The two women flew at one another and when they were dragged apart their wrappers drifted in the air like monstrous feathers. They pounced on one another again, in great rage and velocity, and bits of their wigs and kerchiefs and blouses floated around them in slow motion. I was fascinated by their fury. I was about to move closer when a voice, which seemed to come from nowhere, and which was not the voice of a spirit, said:

'Where is the old man?'
'Gone.'
'Where?'
'He ran away.'
'From what?'
'From me.'
'Why?'
'Because I am looking for my mother.'
Pause.
'Where did he run to?'
'Into the wind.'
'What direction?'
'I don't know.'
'Who is your mother?'
'My mother is in the market.'
'How do you know that your mother is the market?'
'I didn't say she was the market.'
'What did you say?'
'She's a trader in the market.'
'Why are you looking for her?'
'I don't know.'
'What is your name?'

I answered the question, but obviously my answer hadn't been heard, because the question was asked three times, each time fainter than the last. The wind blew my answers away and my head hit the hardness of silence and the world went dark. From the moon, which was suddenly above me, close to me, and which had the luminous face of the great king of the spirit world, I heard other voices, full of darkness, which said:

'Look at him.'
'He is looking for his mother.'
'She has big eyes all over the market.'
'People pay her to shut her eyes.'
'Her eyes never shut.'
'They see everything.'
'They see all our money.'
'They eat all our money.'
'Our power.'
'Our dreams.'
'Our sleep.'
'Our children.'

'They say her son flies to the moon.'
'That's why he has big eyes.'
'Look at him.'

The voices continued, turning on themselves, as in a numinous ritual. The moon lowered over me. My face became the moon and I stared, one-eyed, into the darkness of the marketplace. And then, with the moon's light inside me, filling the wide open spaces, I felt myself being lifted up by the darkness, pushed on by invisible hands. And the voices followed me, voices without bodies.

'Maybe he's not well.'
'Maybe he is mad.'
'Strange things are happening to us.'
'To our children.'
'They say he is looking for the spirit of Independence.'
'They say he is looking for himself.'
'For his own spirit.'
'Which he lost when the white man came.'
'They say he is looking for his mother.'
'But his mother is not looking for him.'
'They say she has gone to the moon.'
'Which moon? There are many moons.'
'The moon of Independence.'
'So he is looking for her moon?'
'Yes.'
'Strange things are happening.'
'The world is turning upside down.'
'And madness is coming.'
'And hunger is coming, like a dog with twelve heads.'
'And confusion is coming.'
'And war.'
'And blood will grow in the eyes of men.'
'And a whole generation will squander the richness of this earth.'
'Let us go.'
'Look at him.'
'Maybe what is to come is already driving him mad.'
'Maybe he is not well.'

And then the voices drifted away on the air. A bright wind blew over me. The lightness in me found a weight. The invisible hands became my own. Darkness settled over the market as though it had risen from the earth. Everywhere lamps were lit. Spirits of the dead moved through the dense smells and the solid darkness.

167

And then suddenly the confusing paths became clear. My feet were solid on the earth. I followed the bright wind that made the paths clearer. It led me in a spiral through the riddle of the market, to the centre, where there was a well. I looked into the well and saw that there was no water in it. There was only the moon. It was white and perfectly round and still. There were no buckets round the well and the soil around it was dry and I concluded that no one could fetch water from the moon at the bottom of the well and I began to climb down into the well because it seemed the best place to lie down and to rest in a deep unmoving whiteness. But then a woman grabbed the back of my shorts and lifted me up and threw me down and shouted:

'Get away from here!'

I followed the waning brightness of the path and came to a place where white chickens fluttered and crackled noisily in large bamboo cages. The whole place stank profoundly of the chickens and I watched them fussing and beating their wings, banging into one another, unable to fly, unable to escape the cage. Soon their fluttering, their entrapment, became everything and the turbulence of the market seemed to be happening in a big black cage. Further on, deeper into the night, I saw three men in dark glasses pushing over a woman's flimsy stall of provisions. They threw her things on the floor and she patiently picked them up again. She cleaned the soiled goods with her wrapper and put them back on the table. The men tipped over the table. The woman cried for help, cried out her innocence, but the marketplace shuffled on, went on with its chaos, its arguing, its shouting and disagreeing, and no single voice, unless it were louder than all the voices put together, could make the market listen. The woman abandoned her pleas. She straightened her table, and picked up her provisions. The men waited calmly till she had finished and tipped the table over again. I went closer. One of the men said:

'If you don't belong to our party you don't belong to this space in the market.'

'Where will I find another space?'

'Good question,' said one of the men.

'Leave. Go. We don't want people like you.'

'You're not one of us.'

'Everyone else in this part of the market is one of us.'

'If you treat people like this why should I want to be one of you, eh?' the woman asked.

'Good question.'

'True.'

'So go.'

'Leave.'

'We don't want you here.'

'But what have I done? I pay my dues. I pay the rent for this space, nobody has ever complained about me . . .'

Two of the men lifted up her table and began carrying it away, blocking the path. The woman, screaming like a wounded animal, jumped on the men, tearing at their hair, scratching their faces, clawing off their glasses. One of the men shouted that he couldn't see. The two other men held the woman and hurled her to the ground. One of the men kicked her and she did not scream. A thick crowd had gathered because of the blocked path. Enraged voices filled the air. The woman got up and ran among the stalls and after a moment reappeared with a machete which she held with awkward and fearful determination in both hands. And, uttering her murderous cries, she hacked at the men, who fled in different directions. The man with his glasses clawed off went on screaming that he had been blinded and he lashed out, flailing, and the woman rushed at him and raised the machete high above his neck and let out a strangled grunt and a great unified voice gathered and broke from the crowd and they surged round her and for a moment all I saw was the machete lifted high above the shadowy heads. Women began clearing their stalls. One of them said:

'This Independence has brought only trouble.'

And the moon left me and everything became dark and I found myself briefly in a world inhabited by spirits, with voices jabbering ceaselessly. The commotion settled around me and the old man with the ash-coloured beard was saying to the woman:

'Pack your things and go for the night. You almost killed someone. You were lucky we stopped you. Go home to your husband and child. Those people will be back. Don't come to the market for some time. You are a brave and foolish woman.'

The woman said nothing. With a stony face of rugged sweetness, she packed her provisions into her basin. She stopped now and again to wipe her nose and her eyes with her wrapper. All around women were offering advice. She was half-covered in mud. It was difficult to tell what part of her hair was mud and what part wasn't. When she had finished packing she lifted her basin on to her head and, standing tall, walked through the crowd. The old man disappeared amongst the masses. The moon left me completely and I saw the woman's face in the lamplights. And when the night stopped turning I saw Mum in the woman I hadn't recognised. I went after her and held her feet and she pushed me off, forging on in her defiance. And I held on to her wrapper and cried:

'Mother!'

She looked down, quickly dropped her basin to the floor, and embraced me for a long moment. Then she held me away and with stony watery eyes said:

'What are you doing here?'

'I was looking for you.'

'Go home!' she commanded.

I pushed through the crowd and could hear her sobbing behind me. She stayed behind me till we cleared the market. As we left I saw the old man at another stall, with the moon in his eyes, watching me with a subtle smile. When we got to the main road Mum dropped her basin and picked me up and tied me to her back with the wrapper and lifted the basin on to her head.

'You are growing,' she said, as we carried on home.

'Not everything grows in this place. But at least you, my son, are growing,' she said, as we made the journey through the streets.

There were lamps burning along the roadsides. There were voices everywhere. There were movements and voices everywhere. I planted my secrets in my silence.

ELEVEN

WHEN WE GOT home it was already very dark and Dad was back. He sat in his chair, smoking a cigarette, brooding. He did not look up when we came in. I was very tired and Mum was worse and when she set down her basin on the cupboard she went over to Dad and asked how the day had been. Dad didn't say anything. He smoked in silence. After Mum had asked him the same question three times, with increasing tenderness, she straightened and was making for the door, mud on one side of her face like a hidden identity, when Dad exploded and banged his fist on the centre table.

'Where have you been?' he growled.

Mum froze.

'And why are you so late?'

'I was at the market.'

'Doing what?'

'Trading.'

'What market? What trade? This is how you women behave when you get into the newspapers. I have been sitting here, starving, and there is no food in the house. A man breaks his back for you all and you can't prepare food for me when I come home! This is why people have been advising me to stop you trading in that market. You women start a little trade and then begin to follow bad circles of women and get strange ideas in your head and neglect your family and leave me here starving with only cigarettes for food! Will a cigarette feed me?' Dad shouted in his angriest voice, his hands lashing out everywhere.

'I'm sorry, my husband, let me go and . . .'

'You're sorry? Will sorrow feed me? Do you know what kind of a terrible goat and donkey's day I have had, eh? You should go and carry bags of cement one day to know what sort of an animal's life I have!'

Dad went on shouting. He frightened us. He made the room unbearably small with his rage. He would not listen to anything and he did not notice anything and he went on about his vicious day. He went on about how idiots had been ordering him around and thugs bossing everyone and that he was a hero and how he felt like giving up this whole life.

'What about me?' Mum said.

'So what about you?'

'You think I don't feel like giving up, eh?'

'Give up!' Dad screamed. 'Go on, go on, give up, and let your son starve and wander everywhere like a beggar or an orphan!'

'Let me go and make food,' Mum said in a conciliatory tone.

'I'm not hungry any more. Go and make food for yourself.'

Mum started towards the kitchen and Dad pounced on her and grabbed her neck and pressed her face against the mattress. Mum didn't resist or fight back and Dad pushed her head sideways, towering over her so I couldn't see her face, and then went back to his chair.

'Leave Mum alone,' I said.

'Shut up! And where have you been anyway?' Dad asked, glaring at me.

I didn't answer. I scurried out of the room. Soon Mum came out and we went to the backyard. We made some eba and warmed the stew.

'Men are fools,' was all Mum said as we sat in the kitchen, staring into the fire.

When we finished cooking we served the food. We all ate silently. Dad was particularly ravenous. He finished his eba and asked for more. Mum left in the middle of her eating and made some more for him, which he swallowed shamelessly in great dollops. The steaming eba didn't seem to affect his hands or his throat. When he had polished off his second helping he sat back and rubbed his stomach contentedly.

'I do a man's work and eat a man's food,' he said, smiling.

We didn't smile with him.

He sent me off to buy some ogogoro and cigarettes. As he drank and smoked his temper visibly waned. He tried to joke with us and we didn't respond at all.

'So what kept you?' he asked Mother.

'Nothing.'

'Nothing?'

'Nothing,' she said, not looking at him.

He looked worried and asked me what kept us.

'Nothing,' I said.

'Nothing?'

'Yes.'

'Then what is that mud doing on your mother's face?'

'Nothing,' I said.

He looked at both of us as if we were conspiring against him. He went on asking us and we went on refusing to tell him. He sought a temper but, having eaten and feeling contented, he could not whip one up. Mum was silent, deep in her solitude, and her face was impassive. It showed no pain, no unhappiness, but it showed no joy or contentment either. Dad pleaded for us to tell him what had kept us.

'Did anyone threaten you?'

'No.'

'Did they steal your things?'

'No.'

'You didn't hear any bad news?'

'Nothing.'

'Did the thugs harass you?'

Mum paused a little before she said:

'Nothing.'

Dad creaked his back and stretched. He was deeply uncomfortable and almost miserable. Mum got up, cleared the table, and went to bathe. When she came back she went straight to bed. Dad sat in his chair, belching, and smoking, suffering the insomnia of one who cannot fathom the mystery of his wife's implacable silence. I spread out my mat and lay watching him for a while. His cigarette became a star.

'There's a full moon out tonight,' he said.

While I watched his silhouette, the moon fell from the sky into the empty spaces of the darkness. I went looking for the moon. I followed great wide paths till I came to a shack near a well. The photographer was hiding behind the well, taking pictures of the stars and constellations. His camera flashed and thugs in dark glasses appeared from the flash and proceeded to beat him up. The camera fell from the photographer's hands. I heard people screaming inside the camera. The thugs jumped on the camera and stamped on it, trying to crush and destroy it. And the people who were inside the camera, who were waiting to become real, and who were trying to get out, began wailing and wouldn't stop.

The photographer snatched up the broken camera. We ran into

the shack and discovered that it had moved over the well. We fell down the well and found ourselves in a hall. The three men in dark glasses were everywhere, constantly multiplying. Dad was smoking a mosquito coil and he looked at me and said:

'What was mud doing on your mother's face?'

One of the thugs in dark glasses heard him and saw us and said: 'She is not one of us.'

The thugs ran after us. Me and the photographer fled into a room and encountered the sedate figure of Madame Koto, dressed in lace with gold trimmings, with a large fan of crocodile skin in her hand. She invited us in, welcomed us, and as we sat three men came and bound us. They shut us in a glass cabinet which would not break. Outside the cabinet chickens fluttered and turned into politicians. The politicians, wearing white robes, flew about the place, talking in strange languages. I stayed there, trapped behind glass, a photograph that Dad stared at, till dawn broke.

TWELVE

A FEW DAYS later I came upon Madame Koto and the three men. They were standing near a tree. They were involved in a passionate argument. Madame Koto looked fat and haggard. She didn't have the white beads round her neck. When she saw me she stopped arguing. She made a movement towards me and a fear I couldn't understand made me run.

'Catch him!' she cried.

The three men started after me, but without much conviction. They soon gave up the chase. I didn't stop till I was near our compound.

I sat on the cement platform. Chickens roamed the street. Two dogs circled one another and when the afternoon seemed at its hottest one of the dogs succeeded in mounting the other. It was only when children gathered around them that it occurred to me that the two dogs were stuck. The dogs couldn't separate themselves and the children laughed. They threw stones at the dogs and the pain forced them to come unstuck and they ran, howling, in opposite directions.

I sat watching the listless motions of the world. The bushes simmered in the heat. Birds settled on our roof. Dust rose from numerous footsteps and became inseparable from the blinding heat. My sweat was dry. The flies came. The wind stirred and turned into little whirlwinds; dust and bits of paper and rubbish spiralled upwards. Children ran round the whirlwinds and only their piercing cries carried, along with the birdsong, over the somnolent air of the world.

Everything blazed in the bright liquid heat. Sounds had their edges softened. Beggars dragged themselves past. Roving cobblers and tailors came around the compounds. Men who sold charms and slippers made in the desert and bamboo artefacts and bright red mats also came round. Then a goatherd led his goats down the street. The goats shat and left their smells in the air, unmoved by the wind. I got bored watching the ordinary events of the world. Flashes from the photographer's glass cabinet called me. I went over and looked at the pictures. They hadn't been changed. I went to the photographer's room. I knocked and no one answered. I knocked again and the door was opened cautiously. The photographer's face appeared at my level. He was crouching and he said, in a voice spiked with fear:

'Go away!'

'Why?'

'Because I don't want people to know I'm in.'

'Why not?'

'Just go!'

'What if I don't go?'

'I will knock your head and you won't sleep for seven days.'

I thought about it.

'Go!' he cried.

'What about the men?'

'What men?'

'The three men?'

'Have you seen them?' he asked in a different voice.

'Yes.'

'Where?'

'They were talking with Madame Koto.'

'That witch! What were they talking about?'

'I don't know.'

'When did you see them?'

'Not long ago.'

He shut the door quickly, locked it, and then opened it again.

'Go!' he said. 'And if you see them again come and tell me immediately.'

'What will you do?'

'Kill them or run.'

He shut the door finally. I stood there for a while. The image of his frightened face lingered in my mind. Then I left his compound and went and sat on our cement platform and kept a steady watch over all movements along the street. The sun made the air and the earth shimmer and as I kept watch I perceived, in the crack of a moment, the recurrence of things unresolved – histories, dreams, a vanished world of great old spirits, wild jungles, tigers with eyes of diamonds roaming the dense foliage. I saw beings who dragged clanking chains behind them, bleeding from their necks. I saw men and women without wings, sitting in rows, soaring through the empty air. And I saw, flying towards me in widening dots from the centre of the sun, birds and horses whose wings spanned half the sky and whose feathers had the candency of rubies. I shut my eyes; my being whirled; my head tumbled into a well; and I only opened my eyes again, to stop the sensation of falling, when I heard the shattering of glass. The noise woke up the afternoon.

Across the street three men were smashing the photographer's glass cabinet with clubs. Then they hurriedly removed the pictures on display. People of the street, awoken by the noise, came to their housefronts. The men, in a flash, had snatched the pictures and had gone into the photographer's compound. The people who came out looked up and down the street and saw nothing unusual. The action had moved to the photographer's room. I rushed across the street.

When I got to the room his door was wide open and the men weren't there. Neither was the photographer. His window was wide open, but it was too high for me to look out of; I ran to the backyard. I saw no one. But I noticed that the backyard led to other backyards. I followed a route past the bucket latrine alive with flies and maggots. The smell was so bad I almost fainted. Another path led to the swamp and marshes and the forest of massive iroko and obeche and mahogany trees. There were deep footprints in the soft soil behind the houses. I followed the footprints, sinking in the mud, till the soft soil shaded into marshes. There was rubbish everywhere. Strange flowers and wild grass and evil-looking fungal growths were profuse over the marshes. Bushes were luxuriant in unexpected places. A wooden footbridge was being constructed to the other side. The footprints merged into many others on the soft soil. Some of them went into the marshes. I looked around, couldn't find anyone, and gave up the search. I went back home, washed the mud off my feet, and resumed watch over the street. Nothing unusual happened.

In the evening Mum returned and was surprised to see me.

'So you stayed home? Good boy. I thought by now you would have wandered to Egypt,' she said.

She was back earlier than usual because she hadn't gone to the market that day. She had gone hawking. Her face was sun-shadowed.

That night I was listening in my childhood hour of darkness. I was listening to Mum's voice and Dad's songs, listening to stories of recurrence told down through generations of defiant mouths. In that hour laced with ancient moonlight, I was listening to tales of inscrutable heroes who turned into hard gods of chaos and thunder – when dread paid us a visit. The night brought the dread. It announced itself through piercing voices from the street, crying out in lamentation at the repetition of an old cycle of ascending powers.

We rushed out into the blue memory of a street crowded with shadows. Wild men were wreaking devastation on windows, wooden doors, and human bodies. We rushed out into the haze, into the smell of burning hair, into the acrid yellow smoke from the barber's shop, into the noises of corrupted ritual chants and caterwauling and machetes giving off electric sparks, crying for medicinal war.

The voices howling for vengeance stampeded the street. The green bodies bristling with antimony sweated animal blood from their naked chests. They were a river of wild jaguars. Their deep earth songs overwhelmed the wind and came from everywhere, from the stars and the broken flowers. They chanted for destruction. Their whooping filled the night. Their sweating bodies flashed in the lamplight. Their murderous utterances washed over our forgetfulness.

It was impossible to tell who they were. Their chants erupted from crowds gathered outside compounds, from people who we thought were familiar, whose shadows changed beside us into a dreaded heat, whose screechings broke into weird bird-cries. Even amongst us people were answering the call of old bloodknots and secret tidal curfews.

In great numbers the thugs and ordinary familiar people alike poured over the road of our vulnerability, wounding the night with axes, rampaging our sleep, rousing the earth, attacking compounds, tearing down doors, destroying rooftops. In the wound of our cries we did not know who our enemies were. From the darkness figures with flaming faces attacked us, descended on us with sticks, stones, whips, and wires. It was some time before we realised that we were in the grip of an act of vengeance, a night reprisal, with the darkness as our antagonist. One by one the lamps were extinguished.

The darkness conquered our voices. A great cry, as of a terrifying commander ordering his troops, sprang into the air. There was the silence of deep rivers. Everything became still. It was as if the night had withdrawn its violence into itself. The wind breathed over the houses and howled gently through the trees. The whisperings of spirits flowed on the wind. The voices of water and slow footsteps floated towards us. It was as if the wind itself were preparing for a final onslaught.

Then the stillness was broken by the panic of the innocent.

There was another cry, not of our antagonists, but of a woman who had seen something wonderful and monstrous. The cry started it all. The innocents turned and with one mind tried to flee back to their rooms. The panic crossed our paths, and collided our bodies in the solid darkness. All over, women wailed for their children. I moved amongst the shadows and ran out into the homeland of darkness, across the street. I thought I was headed for safety. I couldn't see where I was going. Then voices all around me began shouting:

'Kill the photographer!'

'Beat his photographs out of him!'

'Finish him off!'

'Blind him.'

'Blind our enemies!'

'Destroy them!'

'Teach them a lesson.'

'Show them power!'

'Break their fingers.'

'Crack their heads!'

'Crush the photographer.'

'And leave his body in the street.'

'Let the birds eat him!'

'For mocking our party.'

'Our power!'

'Our Leader!'

Their chants intensified. Their footsteps became voices, became one, and then multiplied, like fire. The dead rose under the weight of such footsteps, under such voices, under such intent. I banged my head against something solid, scraped my elbow against the jaws of the dead, clawed my way through jagged rust, and discovered I had reached the safety of the burnt van. I hid in the driver's seat and watched, in that night of blue memories, the drama of the Living that only the Dead can understand.

I couldn't see anything. But from across the street I heard, first in a whisper, then loudly under the spell of grief:

'Azaro! Azaro! Where are you?'

It was Mum.

'Azaro! Azaro!'

Then there was silence. In my childhood hour of darkness, I listened to Mum waiting for my response. But the night and the wind defeated us. From mouth to mouth, from one side of the street to the other, I listened with horror as the wind blew the name.

179

'AZARO! AZARO!'

The wind passed the name on. The name flowed to our part of the street and then towards Madame Koto's bar. The name surrounded me, wavering above the burnt van in a thousand quivering voices, as if God were calling me with the mouths of violent people.

Even the dead played with my name that night.

I listened in my childhood hour as the name eventually flowed towards the photographer's compound and echoed faintly down the passage before passing away into silence. I did not hear Mum's voice afterwards.

As I sat in the car, overcome with fear, I saw the dead rising. I saw them rising at the same moment that the second wave of havoc started with the chants of the antagonists. The dead joined the innocents, mingled with the thugs, merged with the night, and plundered the antagonists with the cries of the wounded. The dead uttered howls of mortal joy and they found the livid night a shrine glistening with fevers. They revelled in that night of mirrors, where bodies shimmered with blood and silver. The dead shook off their rust of living and seized up steel. Their lips quivered with the defiance of the innocents, with the manipulations of politicians and their interchangeable dreams, and with the insanity of thugs who don't even know for which parties they commit their atrocities.

It was a night without memory. It was a night replaying its corrosive recurrence on the road of our lives, on the road which was hungry for great transformations.

The dead, slowly awakening the sleep of the road, were acrobats of violence. They somersaulted with new political dreams amongst men, women, and children. I heard several voices, without fear or beyond it, uttering a new rallying call. Then I heard fighting. I heard the bright howls of resistance, footsteps running into the darkness, flashing steel on solid bodies, chests painted with antimony being beaten down, and women with mortars for pounding yam pounding on shadows. I heard strong men bewildered by the mutinous wind, deep voices crying out the names of hard gods. I realised that the antagonists were being repulsed. The people from the photographer's compound were in the vanguard. The dead were curiously on the side of the innocents. Voices I knew bravely cried:

'Fight them back!'

'Fight for your freedom!'

'Stone them!'

'They poisoned us with milk.'

'And words.'

'And promises.'

'And they want to rule our country!'

'Our lives!'

'And now they attack us!'

'On our own street!'

'Fight them without fear!'

Machetes burst into flame. Chants were reversed in syllables. Spells were broken on the jagged teeth of night. The antagonists attempted a last desperate rally.

'Pour petrol on the house!'

'Burn it down!'

'Burn out the photographer!'

'Burn out Azaro!'

I trembled in the van. Someone hurled a firebrand at the photographer's compound. The dead caught it and ate up the flames. Someone threw another brand in the air. It landed on the van, and spluttered out on the bonnet. Something crawled up my legs. Smoke drifted in from a side window. The van was alive with spiders and worms. I started to get out of the van. I had got my head out of the other window when I heard a great deafening blast from the photographer's compound. After the blast there was a profound silence. The wind whistled over the noise.

And then the shadows, the footsteps, the green bodies, the fierce jaguars, the disaster-mongers, the fire-breathers, the rousers of the dead, and the rampagers of sleep, became fleeing footfalls scattered by the wind and the great detonation. The dark walls of their bodies disintegrated. Their voices were not so menacing any more, but full of fear.

Another gunshot, not aimed in any particular direction, but cracking the air as though a star had exploded over our street, made the escaping stampede of antagonists more desperate. I could hear them falling over one another, running into the terrors of their own making, colliding into their own shadows, into the luminous bodies in the dark. I could hear them screaming the names of their mothers, calling for their wives, wondering who would take care of their children, as the innocents crashed their heads with bottles, as the men of the street rained an insistent beat of clubs on their retreat, and as they fell under the anger of lacerating claws and blunt-edged cutlasses.

New forces had joined the night, converted the night, made it the ally of the innocents. When the tidal force had retreated, the agitation quelled, when the antagonists had started their trucks and taken off at Madame Koto's end of the street – the hosts of the dead descended into the open bleeding mouth of the earth. I saw them from the van. I watched the world dissolving into a delirium of stories. The dead descended into the forgetfulness of our blue memories, with their indigo eyes and their silver glances.

The inhabitants of the street regained the night. Voices were reawakened. Lamps came on one after another. People tentatively gathered at compound-fronts. The only thing that was missing was the photographer to record the events of the night and make them real with his magic instrument. I got out of the van and fled across the street, into the despairing arms of Mother.

In the morning we learned about the wounded, about the woman slashed across the face with a knife, the man whose head was raw with the blunt vengeance of a machete, the people whose noses were cut open with broken bottles, those flagellated with wires, the man who had lost half an ear, the woman whose back was burnt. Against the innocents who were wounded, we heard of the death of an antagonist. We also heard one party claim that the atrocities had been committed by the other.

The energies that went into fighting back exhausted the street. We did not celebrate our resistance. We knew that the troubles were incomplete, that the reprisals had been deferred to another night, when we would have forgotten. The inhabitants of the street, frightened and angry, set up vigilantes. They were armed with knives, clubs, and dane guns. We waited for new forms of iron to fall on us. We waited for a long time. Nothing happened the way we expected. After two weeks, the vigilantes disbanded. We sank back into our usual lives.

The photographer vanished altogether. His room had been wrecked. His door was broken down, his clothes shredded, his mattress slashed, his available pictures and negatives destroyed, and some of his cameras broken up. His landlord, who had no sympathy for heroes, went around looking for him, demanding that his door be repaired.

We feared that the photographer had been murdered. His glass cabinet remained permanently shattered. It looked misbegotten. It became a small representation of what powerful forces in society can do if anyone speaks out against their corruptions. And because the photographer hadn't been there to record what had happened that night, nothing of the events appeared in the newspapers. It was as if the events were never real. They assumed the status of rumour.

At first the street suffered fear. Stall-owners stopped selling things in the evenings. The street seemed darker than usual at night. People became so cautious that no one opened their doors merely because they were knocked on. Those who usually went out drinking, and who returned late, took to getting drunk in their rooms, and singing into the nights.

After a while, when nothing happened, when no reprisals fell on us, it seemed that nothing significant had happened. Some of us began to distrust our memories. We began to think that we had collectively dreamt up the fevers of that night. It wouldn't be the first or the last time. Meanwhile, the river of wild jaguars flowed below the surface of our hungry roads.

On many of those nights, in my childhood hour, Mum told me stories of aquamarine beginnings. Under the white eye of the moon, under the indigo sky, in the golden lights of survival in our little room, I listened to the wisdom of the old songs which Dad rendered in his cracked fighting voice. Mesmerised by the cobalt shadows, the paradoxical ultramarine air, and the silver glances of the dead, I listened to the hard images of joy. I listened also to the songs of work and harvest and the secrets of heroes.

Outside, the wind of recurrence blew gently over the earth.

Book Three

ONE

THE VISITATION OF dread didn't change our lives in any particular way. Mum went on being harassed at the market. When she moved her stall to another part of the market the thugs would turn up, posing as potential customers. They pestered her and tipped over her things and took her goods without paying. Then they would denounce her, making the most outrageous accusations, and those who wanted to buy provisions from her went somewhere else. Mum came home without selling much. She made very little money.

Dad returned earlier each night. He too was increasingly harassed. He was more worn out than ever and his back hurt so much that some mornings he had difficulty standing up straight. Dad became clumsier. His neck ached all the time. He developed sores on his feet. The skin around his shoulders, the back of his ears, his neck, and all along his spine began to peel away. His skin turned a greyish colour because of the salt and cement that spilled on him from the loads he carried.

For a while I ceased in my wanderings. When I got back from school I stayed outside our compound and played in the streets. In the evenings I ran errands for Mum and Dad, who were too fatigued to do anything. I bought candles, mosquito coils, ogogoro. I warmed the food, washed the plates, cleaned the room. I picked herbs for Dad to use in his secret medicines. I went to herbalists for medicines with which to treat Dad's back. We all went to bed early and Dad didn't sit for long hours in his chair.

When the candle burned low, and the rats began to eat, I would put out the light and lie awake in the dark. I would listen to Mum and Dad snoring on the bed. Sometimes when I fell asleep a lighter part of me rose up from my body and floated in the dark. A bright light, which I could not see, but which I could feel, surrounded me. I would be lifted out of my body, would find it difficult to get out through the roof, and would be brought down suddenly by the noise of the rats eating. Then I would sleep soundly.

One night I managed to lift myself out through the roof. I went up at breathtaking speed and stars fell from me. Unable to control my motion, I rose and fell and went in all directions, spinning through incredible peaks and vortexes. Dizzy and turning, swirling and dancing, the darkness seemed infinite, without signs, without markings. I rose without getting to heaven. I soared blissfully and I understood something of the inhuman exultation of flight.

I was beginning to learn how to control my motion that night when something happened and a great flash, which was like a sudden noise, exploded all through me. I seemed to scatter in all directions. I became leaves lashed by the winds of recurrence. I felt myself falling through an unbearable immensity of dark spaces and a sharp diamond agony tugged deep inside my lightness and I tried to re-enter myself but seemed diverted into a tide of total night and I fought and tried to be calm and then I felt myself falling with horrible acceleration into a dark well and just before I hit the bottom I noticed that I was falling into the face of a luminous moon. The whiteness swallowed me and turned to darkness. I burst out screaming. And when I regained myself I heard, for a moment, the rats chewing, my parents snoring, and someone banging relentlessly on the door.

I stayed on the mat for a while without moving. I had a violent headache. Lights spun in my eyes. I felt empty inside. My body felt odd. The knocking continued and interrupted my parents' breathing. Even the rats fell silent. I got up and went to the door and asked:

'Who is it?'

Dad turned on the bed. Mum stopped snoring. The person knocking didn't answer. One of the other tenants from their window, shouted:

'Who is that knocking? If you don't want trouble leave now, you hear?'

The knocks came again, gently, like a code that I was expected to understand. I opened the door. Crouching in front of our low wall, his camera dangling from his shoulder, was the photographer. His frightened eyes glowed in the dark.

'It's me,' he said.

I stared at him for a long time. He didn't move. The neighbour shouted:

'Who is there that wants to die?'

I opened the door wider for the photographer and, still crouching, he came hurriedly into the room. I lit a candle. I saw that he was bleeding from the head. He sat on my mat, blood dripping down his forehead, past his eyes, and soaking his yellow shirt. He breathed heavily and tried to quieten it. His hair was rough, his face bruised, one eye was swollen, his lower lip was puffed and discoloured.

'What happened to you?' I asked.

'A small thing,' he said. 'Nothing that a man cannot bear.'

He sat, then he knelt, his head in his hands. When he looked up his eyes were big and bright, full of fear and wisdom.

'I heard all about what happened in the street. It is happening everywhere. One way or another we will continue to fight for truth. And justice. And we will win.'

His blood was on his hands. He wiped it on his shirt-front. The red on the yellow made me feel ill.

'Believe me,' he added.

It was a while before he spoke again. His eyes were remembering and there was a faint smile on his lips.

'When the three men came the other night I jumped out of the window, ran out into the marshes and stayed there, hiding under the wooden foot-bridge, till the worms began to eat into my feet. I came out from under the bridge. I was afraid. A dog whined at me and followed me wherever I went. A two-legged dog. The wretched animal went on annoying me and whining and people kept staring at me and I didn't know who was an enemy and who wasn't so I kicked the dog. It fell down and didn't get up.'

He paused.

'Then I went to a friend's house. He had a girl-friend with him. I washed my legs and stayed outside. Then I went to look for my relatives.'

He stopped.

The rats continued chewing away at our lives.

'What's that?' he asked, starting.

'Rats.'

'Oh, them,' he said.

He was silent and I thought he had forgotten what he was saying. He blinked and rolled his eyes and groaned. A drop of blood that rolled down his forehead stopped on his cheek. I watched it as he resumed what he was saying.

'I stayed with one or two relatives. I noticed that strange people started watching their houses. I heard about what happened in the street. I owed rent. I needed things for my camera. I thought enough time had passed. And then I found myself coming back home tonight. As I came I hid in dark places and tried to be careful but as I neared my compound two people jumped on me and hit my head with a cutlass and a stick and I fought them and ran into the forest. I stayed there. The mosquitoes bit me. The two-legged dog began to whine in the darkness. I couldn't see it. I became hungry and I heard voices in the trees and then I decided it was time to come home and face the music.'

He paused again. The blood didn't move on his cheek. Then he continued.

'I took another route. This time I didn't hide and I avoided dark places because I wanted our street people to recognise me. As I neared home two people, who had been hiding in the burnt van, jumped out and set on me. I shouted and they gave me as good a beating as they could before they ran. And then I came here, because I didn't feel safe in my room or anywhere else.'

He was silent again. He listened to the rats and wiped his cheek with the back of his hand.

'They must be big rats,' he observed.

'How do you know?'

'You can tell by listening to them.'

I listened.

'They have big teeth, sharp teeth,' he said. 'Did you know that in Egypt rats ate up a whole camel?'

'What is a camel?'

'The only animal that can survive in the desert.'

I marvelled at the idea of such an animal.

'And rats ate it?' I asked.

'Yes.'

'How?'

'With their teeth.'

I listened to the rats.

'Will they eat us?'

'They would have done so by now. But you can't be sure.'

'Of what?'

'Of their hunger.'

I listened again.

'But I know a good poison for killing them. The best. I will bring you some.'

The rats stopped eating.

'They can understand us,' I said.

'Good.'

He stood up.

'This head is hurting me. Lead me to the backyard. I want to wash away all this blood.'

I went out with him. The wind swept hard through the passage. At first it was very dark and I thought the clothes on lines were men in black glasses, but the wind made them flap, and I got used to the darkness. The photographer washed his wounds from a bucket near the well. He groaned in horrible agony. When we got back to the room Dad was awake.

'Who is that?' he asked as I came in.

I lit the candle. The photographer stood at the door with water and blood dripping down his neck. Dad looked at both of us without changing his expression. While the photographer dried his hair on his shirt I told Dad what had happened. I tried not to be loud, but soon Mum woke up. After Mum had learned what was going on she went and warmed some food for the photographer and pressed ointments on his wounds. They all talked deep into the night. They discussed what they could do for him and insisted that he stay till the morning. They decided many other things as well but I don't know what they were because I became drowsy and fell asleep.

When we woke up in the morning the photographer had gone. On the centre table there were the pictures of the celebration of my homecoming.

TWO

IN THE DIABOLICAL heat of that afternoon six illegiti-
mate sons of minor warlords, whom I first thought were minotaurs,
enacted a battle of ascendancies. They fought near the burnt van. No
one came to separate them. They lashed at one another with long sticks,
clubs, and whips. They all looked alike. They were the interchangeable
faces of violence and politics. They were all muscular. They looked like
failed boxers, like the thugs and the bullies and the carriers of loads that
I had seen at the garage. They were hungry and wild. Their chests were
bared. Their faces were awesome. And they fought for hours as if they
were in a dark place, trapped in a nightmare.

Whips cracked. I saw the swift descent of a club; one of the
men fell; three others surged over him. Two others grappled with
the three and a man behind flogged their backs indiscriminately with
a horsewhip. Soon they were all covered in foams of sweat and gore.
Two of the men, fierce antagonists, their deep bronze skins glistening
under the burning orb of sun, detached themselves from the chaos
of bodies and concentrated on one another. The one whipped the
other's back, whipped the taut back till the skin broke into strips
of whitish underflesh and soon turned red. The other bore it and
after a while lifted his own whip and repeated the process on the
other, lashing and flogging, with an absolute silence, utterly devoid
of passion. They were disinterested enemies. They went on lashing
and bearing the whips. Then one of them broke the spell, caught
the other's whip, and they both grappled, fell rolling on the ground,
their backs covered with blood and sand.

One threw the other, kicked his head, and uttered a modest cry of exultation. The one on the floor picked up a stone.
The other rushed at him. The one with the stone pressed it
into the eye of the other, drawing a green sort of blood. The
other didn't cry out. They began punching each other, hitting
one another in a dream-like sequence. The bloodied eye grew

greener and wider. The inhabitants of the street watched the fight, perplexed.

The other four men battled with one another senselessly. They fought on the bonnet of the burnt van. They fought all over the ground. They fought on the glass fragments from the photographer's cabinet, bled, with bits of glass sticking from their backs, but went on fighting as though pain were alien to their flesh. At first it seemed we could make out a pairing; then their entangled combat baffled us, for they fought one another, every which way, without passion, without politics even, their eyes bulging. It became impossible to tell what party they supported, what codes they were fighting for, or what was the purpose of their battle. They fought in the strangest ways, throwing sand into one another's eyes, spitting, offering their faces up for punches, bearing the blows stoically, sometimes being knocked down by them and picking themselves up again and resuming the fray with absolute disinterested ferocity. One of them was kicked in the crotch and he jumped up and fell down, and rolled uncontrollably. When he got back up he kept stamping the ground. And while he tried to sort out his agony another man, who I thought was on his side, came and smashed his head with a brick and he fell down and stretched out like a dead animal.

'They are the madmen of our history,' one of the inhabitants on the street said. 'They are just waiting for a crazy war to come along.'

And then quite suddenly the man who had stretched out like a dead animal began to twitch on the earth. He twitched and kicked and made guttural noises. Then, like a figure in a nightmare, he rose from his death, his upper part stiff, his eyes dull and passionless. When he stood up he released a deep-throated sound of laughter. He brought out something from his back pocket, waved it in the air seven times, pressed it between his hands till he crushed out a flow of red juices, and then hit the chest of an advancing antagonist with his open palm.

The man who had been hit screamed as if he had been branded, and then he fell heavily on the ground and thrashed about in mortal agony. The man with the peculiar weapon repeated his feat with another antagonist, slapping him on the face so hard it sounded like a minor thunderclap. We saw the man's face turn red and the redness began to drip as if it were melting wax. The man turned round and round, shouting and stamping, and fell on his knees, holding his face. And when he stood up again, swaying, we saw his raw underflesh in the shape of a man's palmprint. The skin had dissolved. He wailed like a madman who was being tortured.

The three men now gathered and thoroughly beat up the only man left standing on the other side. They threw him to the ground five times in succession. They jumped on his chest and kicked his head and lifted him up and knocked him around till he collapsed altogether. Then the alliances clarified themselves. The three men picked up their large shirts, waving them like monstrous flags, and went up the street, arms held high, chanting the songs of their ascendancy, the songs of the Party of the Poor, or was it of the Rich. No one could be certain. Then I recognised the new incarnation of their recurrent clashes, the recurrence of ancient antagonisms, secret histories, festering dreams. The three men went their way, dancing up the street, and no one cheered them, no one acknowledged their victory, and no one thought of them as heroes.

The three thugs of the Rich Party – or was it the Poor Party – lay writhing on the ground. The one who had been hit on the chest got up, groaning. The sign of a palm was imprinted on his massive chest as on burnished brass. He went and helped the other two. Like a sad bunch of thieves, like crooks who had been set upon, like a defeated army of rogues, they leaned on one another, wailing, each twisted in the direction of their injury's gravity. They staggered down the street, hobbling away from their vanquishers.

THREE

WHEN THE FIGHTERS left, the air of the street was charged with fear. It was late evening. The sound of a plate breaking, of two people quarrelling, made us suspicious. The heat and the glare restrained the movement of things and I did not wander far from home that day because I feared that all over the world thugs with fire in their brains were pounding one another in a weird delirium of history.

Staying in that day taught me how long a hot afternoon could be, how the heat could slow time down. I sat on the cement platform and listened to the flies. Flying ants were all over the place. Lizards ran up and down walls, sunning themselves, nodding. I went to buy some beans from an itinerant trader of cooked food. She had a constant companionship of flies. And she had the most amazing signs tattooed to the sides of her mouth. When she smiled the signs looked odd, but when she was serious they made her look beautiful. She sold me a few pennies' worth of beans and offered to sell me Kokoro at a discount.

'What is Kokoro?' I asked.

'They are the ants that feed off the beans.'

'Ants?'

'Yes. They are good for you. They make you brilliant and help you grow up fast.'

I bought some fried ants as well and went and sat in the shade. I ate the beans and the ants and drank some water. Then I got drowsy and slept outside our door. The sun burned on me and when Mum got back and woke me up I couldn't see anything for almost a minute. I was quite blind and everything was composed of blue and red and yellow whorls. Mum led me into the room and made me lie down. When I woke it was evening. The blindness had given way to the world's variety of colours. Mum had gone out.

Mum's absence got me worried. I locked the door, hid the key under the threadbare doormat, and went looking for her. I went down the street and encountered our landlord. With a cold gaze and a contemptuous voice he asked if my parents were in.

'No,' I said.

'When will they be back?'

'I don't know.'

'Tell them I am coming to see them tonight about my rent and another matter, you understand?'

I nodded. He hurried towards our compound. I went on. My stomach started to ache and I felt sure the fried ants were crawling around inside. Suddenly a powerful stench invaded the air. Everywhere I turned the stench was there, unbearable, unavoidable. And then I saw the nightsoil man coming towards me. I didn't want to offend him so I didn't move or run. But I held my breath. He staggered and wobbled under the heavy weight. Hooded and masked in a filthy blue cloth, I saw his bulging eyes, and his fierce glare. He grunted, buckling, as he passed me. Feeling the full pressure of airlessness, I ran; and when I breathed I felt very ill. So did everyone else. Before I knew it I was near the bar. And outside, in front of the bar, talking in between covering their noses, were Madame Koto and Mum. I went back home. The smell stayed in the air and even when I shut the door it was still there.

After a while Mum came in. She looked very tired. She said Madame Koto had been asking after me. I told her the landlord's message; she got very agitated.

'The rent? We don't have enough money. When did he say he was coming?'

'Tonight.'

She sat still for a while. Then she went over to her basin of provisions, took out a tin box, and started counting her money. She counted it for a long time, with sweat breaking out on her forehead. When she finished she sat still again for a while. Then she unloosened one end of her wrapper and counted the money she had there. It got quite late. I lit another candle. Mum was quite oblivious of everything. She was still counting her money, calculating how much she needed for a fresh stock of provisions, how much profit she had made, when imperious knocks sounded on our door. Mum jumped up, spilling most of her money on the floor. She picked it up in a hurry and put it away before she said, with sweat on her eyelashes:

'Azaro, see who is knocking.'

I went to the door and opened it and the landlord came

in, pushing me into the room, opening the door wide, as if he wanted the whole world to hear what he had to say. He had three other men with him. They were strangers. They were very big, with well-developed muscles, and the mad eyes of political thugs. They wore matching uniforms and they came into the room and stood, side by side, with legs planted wide, their backs against the wall. They folded their arms and looked at us with the sort of contempt reserved for insects.

The landlord looked round, saw the semi-broken window, and began, explosively, to rage. He was thoroughly incoherent and he only made sense when he calmed down a little and demanded that the window be repaired before his next visit. He moved dramatically up and down the room, reserving, as usual, his loudest voice and his most dramatic gestures for when he was nearest the door. The compound people had gathered outside and some of them were looking in. Waving his hands, whipping the voluminous folds of his agbada this way and that, he turned and said:

'Is your husband not in?'

'No.'

'What about my rent?'

'When he comes back he will give it to you.'

'He didn't leave it?'

'No.'

Striding as if he were on stage, waving his hands angrily, the landlord said:

'Why do I have to come and pester you for my rent, eh? When you wanted the room you came and begged me. Now I have to come and beg you for my rent, eh?'

'Things are hard,' Mum said.

'Things are hard for everybody. All the other tenants have paid. Why are you so different, eh?'

'When my husband returns . . .'

'He starts trouble.'

'It's not so.'

'Your husband is a troublemaker.'

'Not at all.'

'He thinks he is strong.'

For the first time Mum acknowledged the presence of the three muscular men standing with their backs against the wall. She looked at them and they stared back at her without moving.

'My husband is strong, but he is not a troublemaker,' she said finally.

One of the three men laughed.

'Shut up!' the landlord barked.

The man's laughter dwindled into a hollow cackle. The landlord sat on Dad's chair and it wobbled precariously. He sat there, scrutinising us, as if deciding what to do next. Then he brought out a lobe of kola-nut from his pocket and began chewing. We were all silent. The candles twitched; shadows lengthened and shortened in the room. The three men looked gloomy and ghoulish, and the upward illumination, catching their faces, made their cheeks and eyes hollow.

'So when is your husband returning?'

'I don't know.'

The landlord munched his kola-nut.

'Well,' he said, after a reasoned pause, 'the other matter I have come about is simple. I do not like the way my own tenants have behaved towards my party. You people beat me up the other day. What have I done to you, eh?'

At this point he got up and resumed his melodramatic pacing. His hands flailed and his voice got louder at the door as if he were addressing an invisible audience.

'I have told this to all my tenants. Anybody who wants to live in my house, under this roof that I built with my own hands, should vote for my party. Did you hear me?'

Mum did not nod. She stared grimly at the twitching candle.

'It doesn't matter if you answer or not. I have said what I have to say. If you have ears, listen. If you want to be my tenant, when the election comes you will go and vote for my party man.'

He paused.

'It's simple. All you have to do is press ink next to his name. A simple matter. My party will bring good roads and electricity and water supply. And remember this: we have people at the polling station who will be watching you. We will know who you vote for. Whether you vote for our man or not we will win anyway. But if you don't vote for him there will be trouble. You might as well begin to look for another place now and see if you can find another landlord as good as me. Tell this to your husband. I don't have time to come back. And send me my rent latest tomorrow morning. That's all.'

He was now standing behind Dad's chair. He had finished his speech. His back was to us and he seemed to be waiting for a response. There was only silence. And the spitting candle. The three men looked like statues. They looked like dead men. I could barely see the whites of their eyes.

'God knows,' the landlord continued, 'that I want the best for my tenants. But the tenant that doesn't want a good thing should go. There's power and there's power: anyone who looks for my trouble will get enough trouble for life. I am a peaceful man but the person who spoils my peace will find that I am a LION. I am an ELEPHANT. My THUNDER will strike them. And on top of that I will send my boys to beat them up!'

He was now at the window. He put the kola-nut back into his pocket. He brought out a white handkerchief and wiped his face. Then he turned to face Mum directly. We were all concentrating on him. Except Mum. She went on staring into the candle-flame as if she saw in it a new kind of destiny.

The landlord opened his mouth to speak when a gentle wind came into the room and turned into a dark figure, towering but bowed. And with the figure came a reminder of the nightsoil van. The figure was Dad and the landlord slowly shut his mouth.

The three men crowded away from Dad, away from the wall, and regrouped in stances of half-fight next to the cupboard. Suddenly the room seemed cramped and Dad made it worse by shutting the door. The upward illumination of the candle-light caught his face as well, and made him look like a man undergoing a terrible martyrdom. His cheekbones were highlighted, his eyes sunken, and his head was stark. He looked baffled. He stood in front of the door and stared at every one of us, turning to face each one of us directly. His neck seemed stiff. He somehow gave the feeling that he had lost the connection between what he saw and what he understood. He gave the impression that he had been bashed on the head and that his centre had been dislocated. He looked confused, as if he had entered the wrong room and had no idea how to get out again.

'Dad!' I cried.

He looked at me without comprehension. It was only after a while that we became aware of the stench in the room.

Suddenly one of the three men made a noise, as of holding back bile. Then he rushed to the window and spat out. The landlord spat on the floor, stepped on it, and twisted his foot as though he were crushing out a cigarette. Another of the men went behind Dad and opened the door. Moths, midges, and flying ants came in, and mosquitoes whined in the silence. The moth circled the candle and I felt that time had moved backwards and was trapped there.

Dad went towards Mum and sat heavily on the bed. There was shame on his face. Shame, humiliation, and defiance. The landlord, unable to come out with what he had been about to say, moved towards the door. His sense of drama had deserted him. He seemed to have sensed a new kind of menace in Dad. I sensed it too. He said:

'Your wife will tell you what I had to say.'

He hurried out of the room without repeating his demand for the rent. His henchmen ran out behind him, casting their last looks at Dad.

We sat in the room suffused by the bewildering odour. It was as though an unpleasant vent had burst under our floor. We sat without moving, without speaking, till one of the moths got its wings burnt and extinguished the candle. In the darkness I felt for the matches on the table. Then I heard Mum say, with great unhappy tenderness:

'My husband, what has happened to you?'

When I lit the candle Mum's arms were around Dad's neck. She held him tight, her face in his hair. Then, becoming aware of the light, she disentangled herself from him, and unloosened his shoes. Dad did not move. She pulled off his shoes and gave them to me, saying:

'Your father has stepped on something. Go and wash the shoes inside the bathroom. Don't do it by the well.'

I took the shoes and went out. The wind blew through the passage, lifting dust into my eyes. The wind was cool; it smelt of trees and the night, of bushes and aromatic herbs scenting the air. It also smelt of kerosine and candle-smoke, but it did not have the curious odour in our room. At the backyard I borrowed one of the tenants' lamps, fetched some water, got some useless newspaper and bits of wood. I looked at Dad's shoes and there was nothing unusual on them. They did not smell badly, except of sweat and hard-working feet. But I washed the shoes anyway and washed my hands and went back in.

Dad was now sitting on his chair. Mum was asking him if everything was all right. I was certain he hadn't said a word all the time I had been out. Mum looked distressed, as if his secret anguish was eating away at her. When I put the shoes down in the corner, Dad brought an envelope from his pocket and gave it to Mum. She opened it, brought out some pound notes, and looked at him in astonishment. He said:

'It's the rent.'

Mum was so overcome with emotion that she knelt at his feet and held his thighs and said over and over again:

'Thank you, thank you, my brave husband.'

She said it with such proud sadness she made me feel that those who suffer are strangers to this world. Dad did not acknowledge her, nor did he show any sign of emotion, but his face was so strange I was sure he was feeling much more than he was able to express.

After a while Mum made Dad some food. He went and had a long bath. He came back with only his towel round his waist. He sent me to go and buy him a small bottle of Hausa perfume.

I walked a long way up our street, towards the main road, before I came upon a cluster of Hausa night traders who sold Indian incense, beads, perfumes, and charms. I bought a cheap bottle of perfume and ran back. Dad had changed clothes. He applied great quantities of the perfume to himself and thoroughly stank out the room with its crude ingredients. We washed our hands and ate in silence.

After we ate Mum went and soaked Dad's clothes in disinfectant and hid the bucket deep in the backyard. Dad stayed up, sitting in his chair. He did not drink and did not smoke. He was very sober. He looked like he would never recover from the shock of a certain kind of self-knowledge. Mum sat up with him. They were silent for a long time. Then as I fell asleep I heard Mum ask, as though she were prepared to accept the possibility:

'You didn't kill someone, did you?'

I opened my eyes. Dad shook his head. They were both silent. Mum lit a mosquito coil. I shut my eyes again.

Later that night there was a knock on the door. It was the photographer. He sneaked in hurriedly. Dad opened his eyes and said:

'Ah, photographer, it's you.'

'Yes, it's me.'

'Sleep well.'

'And you, sir.'

The photographer lay down with me on the mat. He showed me a little round, transparent bottle. It had a yellow powder inside.

'This,' he said, 'is the most powerful rat poison in the world.

Tomorrow, if I return early, we will finish off those rats once and for all.'

He kept it among his things. I blew out the candle. We floated in the darkness and the dreadful perfume of the heated room.

FOUR

FOR MANY DAYS Dad remained sullen. We got used to the perfume. He offered no explanation. And it was only when he was told of what the landlord had said that he recovered his spirit. He said even if they killed him he wouldn't vote for the landlord's party. He went around the compound saying this. Some of the neighbours nodded when he made his declaration. Mum warned him that the landlord had spies in the compound.

'Let them spy,' Dad said, 'but I won't vote for that useless party.'

'I know, but don't tell them.'

'Why not? Am I a coward?'

'No.'

'Then I must say what I believe.'

'But you heard what the landlord said.'

'Let the landlord drop dead!'

'Lower your voice.'

'Why?'

'Spies.'

'Let the spies drop dead too!'

'I am afraid for us.'

'There is nothing to fear.'

'But I am afraid.'

'What right has the landlord to bully us, to tell us who to vote for, eh? Is he God? Even God can't tell us who to vote for. Don't be afraid. We may be poor, but we are not slaves.'

'Where are we going to find another room?'

'Our destiny will provide.'

And so it continued. Sparked off by his own defiance, Dad began to speak of himself as the only one who would not vote for the landlord's party. All over our area party-supporters became more violent. They went around in groups terrorising everyone. We heard stories of people who were sacked from their jobs because they were on the wrong side of politics. Mum grew afraid of the market and didn't go as regularly as she wanted. Money became short. Mum had to reduce our food.

We saw the photographer only late at night. On some nights I waited for him to knock but he didn't. When I saw him he began to speak of leaving the area. He went on taking his unusual pictures and a few more appeared in the papers. Whenever he was seen people gathered around him. He had become something of a legend. For the period he stayed with us he tried to turn the corner where Dad kept his shoes into a dark-room, with no success, because Mum, paranoid of spiders' webs, kept sweeping and cleaning and exposing light to all dark places.

One night some men came to our compound to ask about the photographer. They claimed to be journalists. They said they'd heard he was staying with tenants in the compound. The tenants denied it, but they began to keep watch. At night we saw strange men leaning against the burnt van, staring at our house. When I told the photographer about it he became scared and we did not see him for many days.

Madame Koto appeared at our room during that period. She appeared out of the air, startling me. Mum was in, but Dad hadn't returned. I was so startled that before I could run she grabbed me and said:

'You are a bad boy.'

'Why?'

'Running away from your elders.'

She gave me some money.

'Why have you been running away from me, eh? What did I do to you?'

'Nothing.'

'Why did you throw away my juju?'

'Nothing.'

Mum laughed. Madame Koto let me go. She sat on the bed, beside Mum. She was as fat as ever, plump as a mighty fruit, but her face had become a little bit more frightening than I remembered. She did not have her white beads round her neck. Her face was darker; her eyes, shaded with eye-pencil, made her look mysterious. The quantity of wrappers round her increased her volume. The two women talked in low tones. I drew closer to listen. Madame Koto gave Mum a packet whose contents I never discovered. Then she turned to me and said:

'I want you to come back. Your mother agrees. Since you stopped coming the bar has been empty.'

'I will discuss it with your father,' Mum added.

They went on talking. I went and played at the housefront. When Madame Koto was leaving she called me.

'I am going now,' she said, 'but tomorrow I want you to come and attract customers to the bar, you hear?'

I nodded.

'I will prepare you special peppersoup with plenty of meat.'

Then she waddled off into the darkness.

Dad returned exhausted that night. Mum did not discuss anything with him. The photographer did not turn up. The rats went on eating.

FIVE

MADAME KOTO'S BAR had changed. She had put up a
new signboard. The signboard had a painting of a large-breasted
mermaid serving drinks and steaming peppersoup. There were multicoloured plastic trailings at the doorway. Swishing aside the curtain
strips, I went in. The door was now blue. It was dark and cool inside.
The benches were shorter. The tables had plastic coverings. As if she
anticipated more trouble and more customers she had begun to install
a counter at the far end of the bar, across from the backyard door.
The walls were cobalt. It felt more peaceful in the bar. I went to the
backyard and saw a little girl washing plates and spoons. She stared at
me suspiciously.

'Where is Madame Koto?'

She didn't reply.

'Can't you talk?'

Still the girl didn't say anything. I went to Madame Koto's room
and knocked. She didn't seem to be in. So I went back into the bar
and sat near the earthenware pot. Flies buzzed in the serenity of
the place. The little girl came in and remained at the threshold of
the door, the curtain strips covering her face. She watched me. She
had a long sad face and big eyes. She had little scarifications on her
cheeks. She was too sad and too passive to be beautiful. She went
on staring at me and I got irritated.

'Why are you looking at me, eh?'

She stayed mute. Then she went to the backyard and carried
on with her washing of plates and cutlery.

Throughout the afternoon no one came to drink and I did not see
Madame Koto. I slept on the bench and woke up suddenly. It was
quiet. There was a kerosine lamp on the table. I felt I had materialised in some underwater kingdom. I searched for the girl and could
not find her. When I got back Madame Koto was in the bar with a
carpenter.

'Where have you been?' she asked, shouting above the carpenter's hammering.

'I went to look for the girl.'

'Which girl?'

'The girl who was washing the plates.'

She stared at me as if I had turned into a fish, or as if I had gone mad.

'What plates?'

'The plates in the backyard.'

She went out and looked and came back shouting.

'Something is wrong with you,' she said.

I went to the backyard and saw the plates and cutlery piled in a heap. They were all unwashed. A cauldron of peppersoup bubbled away on the firegrate near the heap.

'Go and wash the plates,' she bellowed, 'before I get angry with you.'

I was reluctant, but I went. I fetched water from the well, sat on the stool, and washed the plates and cutlery. The fire, heating my face and drying my eyes, made me dizzy with its curiously fragrant woodsmoke. I listened to the carpenter hammering and the firewood crackling. I got very dizzy from breathing in the smoke and from the blast of the heat so that I started to sway and the evening began to turn. The peppersoup spilled over in green bubbles and poured over the firewood and the little girl came and lifted off the hot lid of the cauldron with her bare hands. Then she stirred the soup with a long wooden ladle which had the shape of a human palm at the serving end.

'Get away from here!' I cried.

When she brought out the ladle the serving end was missing. The wooden hand had become part of the soup.

'Look what you've done!' I shouted.

She threw away what was left of the ladle and went off in a sulk. Soon she returned with a long and large bone. She stirred the soup with it and the bone dissolved.

'If you don't go away I will beat you,' I threatened.

She lifted the lid back on the cauldron and crouched near the grate and stared into the fire. She put out her hands, as if to warm them, and then she threw two white cowries into the flames. The firewood cried out, popping and crackling, and a thick indigo smoke filled the air and engulfed the girl and when the smoke cleared I saw her melting. First her outstretched hands melted into the air and then her shoulders and then her body. Her head remained on the ground and her big sad eyes went on staring at me impassively till she dissolved altogether. I screamed and everything went white. I fell towards the fire. When I came round I was on the floor, my back on the ground. My shirt was soaked. Madame Koto stood above me.

'What's wrong with you, eh?'

'I saw the girl again.'

'What girl?'

'The one who was washing the plates.'

'Get up!'

I got up. I felt very strange, as if I too were dissolving. I sat on the stool. There was only the froth of soup which had spilled over where the girl's head had been.

'Where did you see her?'

'There,' I said, pointing to the froth.

'There's nothing there.'

'She was here!' I insisted.

'Go inside. Don't bother to wash the plates. Go and drink some water.'

I went in and drank some water and sat on a bench. The carpenter's hammering gave me a terrible headache. Each time he lifted the hammer in the air I felt it was coming down on my head. I went to the barfront and sat on the sand. I watched people go past. No one came into the bar. No one even looked at it. Darkness drifted slowly over the forest. The air became cooler. Birds circled the trees. Insects thronged the evening. No one noticed the bar because it was more noticeable. I felt on the edge of reality. Madame Koto's bar seemed like a strange fairyland in the real world, a fairyland that no one could see.

I began to throw stones at her signboard. And then I threw stones at the blue door and the multicoloured plastic strips of curtain. Madame Koto came out and said:

'Who is throwing stones?'

'It's the girl,' I replied.

'Where is she?'

'She ran away.'

Madame Koto gave me a wicked stare, fingered her white beads, and went back to her washing. I stayed at the front and watched the darkness flow from the forest and gradually engulf the rest of the world. In the distance an owl hooted. A bird piped continuously. The darkness awakened the sounds of the forest. As I sat at the barfront, the sand hot beneath me, I saw a man going past with a little girl. The man saw me, looked at the signboard, and came towards the bar. With him was the same little girl who had melted away. I ran into the bar and hid behind the earthenware pot. The carpenter had almost finished his day's work and was hammering the last few nails into the wood of the counter.

'What's wrong with you?' he asked, flashing an irritated glare at me.

'They are coming.'

'Who?'

The man parted the plastic curtain strips and crossed the threshold.

'Any palm-wine?' he asked.

'Sit down. The madame is coming,' said the carpenter.

The man sat. The girl was beside him. I hadn't noticed her come in.

'This place is dark,' said the man. 'Bring a lantern.'

'Take them a lantern,' ordered the carpenter.

I took the lantern from another table and put it on theirs. The girl blew it out. The place went dark. Fireflies punctuated the gloom.

'What's wrong with your head?' asked the man.

'It's that foolish girl,' I cried. 'She did it.'

'What girl?'

'The one next to you.'

The carpenter, raising his voice, said:

'I will knock your head with this hammer! Can't you see I am doing something? Go and bring matches!'

I fumbled my way out of the bar. Madame Koto was lifting the cauldron off the grate. She had tablecloths protecting her hands.

'That girl is here again with a man. He wants palm-wine and matches.'

She gave me a box of matches and said she would be bringing in the palm-wine. I went inside and lit the lantern and the girl blew it out again. Her eyes shone in the dark. They glittered like the green eyes of a cat.

'You are wicked,' I said to her.

'Me?' said the man. 'I come here to drink and a small goat like you abuses me? Who is your father?'

'Not you,' I said. 'It's that girl. Your child. She's wicked.'

I lit the match again and the man knocked me on the head. I dropped the match. It burnt on the table. The man hit me again and the girl smiled, her eyes sad, her mouth curiously tight. The match burnt out. I backed away into the dark.

'Come and light this thing!' the man said.

I heard the carpenter stumbling his way over wood and metal tools. He brought the smell of glue with him as he came towards us. He kicked a bench in the darkness and cursed.

'When I catch you,' he said, without being able to see me, 'I will crack your head!'

I ran outside and stayed near the path that had become a street. The carpenter appeared, saw me, bent down, took off his slippers, and sprinted after me. I fled towards the forest. He gave up and went back, cursing me. I stayed out till I saw the man leaving with the little girl. They went down the street in the direction of our compound.

The carpenter had finished his day's work. He sat at a bench, near the earthenware pot, and drank palm-wine. There were lanterns on every table.

'You are lucky you're not my son,' he said, sullenly.

I stayed at the door, watching him.

'You have just driven away the only customer that has come here today. Madame Koto is angry with you. The man refused to drink in the dark and left, you wicked child.'

I watched him.

'Either you come in or stay out. But don't look at me as if you are a lizard.'

I stayed out. There were stars in the sky. The moon was fading. Some of the stars moved as I watched them and I was so engrossed I didn't hear the carpenter creep up to me. He caught my neck and dragged me into the bar. Madame Koto came in with two bowls of peppersoup.

'Leave that wicked boy alone!' she told the carpenter. Then to me she said: 'I was going to give you plenty of meat but you will only get half because you drove away my customer.'

'Let me flog him,' the carpenter offered.

'Go and flog your own children,' Madame Koto replied.

The carpenter let me go. I made an ugly face at him. He went on drinking. Madame Koto gave us our respective bowls of peppersoup. I retired to a corner and sat on the floor with my back to the wall and drank the soup from a position where I could keep an eye on the carpenter. But the spoon Madame Koto had given me was too big for my mouth and I went out to get a smaller one. When I got back I found that most of my meat had gone. The carpenter was licking his fingers with great childlike relish.

'Who stole my meat?' I asked.

'The little girl,' replied the carpenter, with mischief and wickedness glinting in his eyes.

'What girl?'

'The girl.'

I stared at him a long time, trying to decide what to do. Then I went out and complained about the theft and Madame Koto gave me some more meat. I ate without taking my eyes off the carpenter. He kept winking at me. When I finished I went and washed my bowl and spoon. And when I came back in I saw a man sitting at a table near the door. He turned his head towards me. At that moment I recognised him.

'Dad!' I cried, and ran over.

He put his arm round my shoulder. I embraced him. Then I ran out to tell Madame Koto that my father was around. She brought in some palm-wine and peppersoup.

'This son of yours', she said, putting them down, 'drove away my only customer.'

'He's a bad boy,' Dad replied, with something like fondness.

He was about to pay for the drink, but Madame Koto said:

'Keep your money. This is to welcome you.'

'I see you are improving the place.'

'I'm doing my best.'

'Plenty of customers, eh?'

'They will come.'

Madame Koto fetched herself some peppersoup and wine and sat near the counter. Everyone drank and ate in silence. Then the carpenter, swaying on the bench, waving away flies, turned to Dad and said:

'So which party do you support?'

We all looked up at him. Dad made his reply.

'The Party of the Poor.'

'They are as corrupt as everyone else,' said the carpenter, banging his hand on the table.

'Still, I support them. At least they don't spit on us.'

'They are all corrupt. In my home-town they killed a man because he wouldn't support them. They too are trying to rig the elections. They have thugs who beat up people in the markets. They take bribes and they help only themselves.'

'But still I support them,' Dad said, stubbornly.

'Why? What have they done for you?'

'Nothing.'

'So why?'

'Because at least they think of the ordinary hard-working man.'

'They think of them, that's all they do.'

'No talking politics in my bar,' said Madame Koto firmly.

'You are a wise woman. Politics spoils business,' said Dad.

'They are all corrupt. They are all thieves. With the Party of the Rich everyone knows they are thieves. They don't pretend.'

'NO POLITICS!'

'But I won't vote for them.'

'They have . . .'

'NO POLITICS!'

'Money and . . .'

'NO POLITICS!'

'Power. They can help. If you support them they support you. They give you contracts. A poor man has to eat.'

Madame Koto got up and snatched away the carpenter's bowl.

'Didn't you hear me? I said NO POLITICS!'

The carpenter fell silent. Madame Koto went out. The two men resumed drinking. Dad turned to me.

'What did they teach you at school today?'

'About Mungo Park and the British Empire.'

'They are all corrupt,' said the carpenter.

Dad stayed quiet. Moths and flies circled the air of the bar. The carpenter was getting visibly drunk and he kept slurring the same phrase. Dad poured some palm-wine for me and I drank. Dad's eyes grew red. The carpenter went on slurring. Outside a bird piped an insistent melody. I got quite drunk and the carpenter fell silent, began another speech, stopped, and rested his head on the table. Soon he was snoring. Dad got drunk and began to sway gently himself.

'Very good palm-wine,' he said, loudly.

The carpenter jerked up, looked round, and went back to sleep. Dad began his own repetition.

'Politics is bad for friendship,' he said.

The carpenter didn't move. When Dad finished his palm-wine he got up, swayed, staggered over to the carpenter, and slapped him on the shoulder. The carpenter started and turned his head in every direction like a bird. His eyes were heavy-lidded.

'Friendship is bad for politics,' he said.

'They are all corrupt,' the carpenter slurred, and lay his head on the table again.

Dad staggered to the backyard.

'Madame Koto, we are going,' he announced.

'Good night.'

Dad muttered something. At the threshold he said:

'Let's go home.'

And we left the edge of reality, the fairyland that no one could see, and went home through the swaying night.

SIX

WHEN THE CARPENTER had finished the construction of the counter, the bar lost some of its fairyland quality. Madame Koto set up a chair, her plastic bowls for giving change, her basin of peppersoup, and some gourds of wine behind the counter. She was experimenting with efficiency. The carpenter was paid partly in money and partly in wine. He was already drunk when I arrived and Madame Koto was trying to get him to leave. He wouldn't budge, he kept requesting more wine. He said it was important for him to drink after he had completed a job. Madame Koto protested that he had been drunk all through the job, that the counter was bent over in one direction and that it gave an overall impression of unsteadiness.

The carpenter was untouched by the criticism. Madame Koto carried on quibbling and the carpenter went on drinking. A blue fly drowned in his palm-wine and he drank on stolidly, muttering his replies to her, complaining about how poorly he had been paid. The counter took up a lot of space. The fresh wood smelt good in the bar. There were wood shavings and nails on the floor which the carpenter refused to sweep. Madame Koto refused to give him any more wine. He asked me to fetch him water.

'I can get drunk on water too,' he said.

'Don't give him any water,' Madame Koto ordered.

She sat behind her newly built counter, her thick frame wedged between the wood and the wall, surveying everything with a proprietorial air. The carpenter dozed. She whipped the table with a broom. The carpenter got up, staggered to the backyard, and soon we heard him urinating and farting. Madame Koto rushed out, I followed, and we found him urinating on her firewood. She reached for a nearby broom, whipped him round the neck, and he ran, urinating and laughing. She pursued him all the way down the street. I went in and sat at my corner and not long afterwards she returned, sweating above her upper lip. She dropped her broom near the earthenware pot and said:

'I am going to lie down. If anyone comes, call me.'

She shuffled out. I heard her struggling with the firewood and abusing the carpenter. Then I didn't hear her any more. It was hot in the bar, but the smell of fresh-planed wood was sweet and soothing. Flies spiralled in the air. I noticed a Coca-Cola poster on the wall. It had the picture of a half-naked white woman with big breasts. Lizards ran into the bar, stopped in the middle of the floor, and saluted me, nodding. I nodded back and they sped on. I lay down on a bench and drifted off to sleep.

I woke up when a man in dirty clothes came running into the bar, holding one of his slippers in his hand. He rushed in and rushed out through the backyard door and came in again. He stood there, in a panic, looking in all directions. Then he brought out a handkerchief, wiped his face, and stared at me pleadingly.

'Where can I hide?'

'Why?'

'People are after me.'

'Why?'

'Politics.'

'Are you a politician?'

He looked confused.

'Does this compound lead to the road at the back?'

'I don't know.'

'If I give you money will you help?'

'Why?'

'Are you a dunce or something? Do you want them to kill me?'

'No.'

He started to speak again, but we heard rough voices coming from the street. Crowd voices. They were coming towards the bar. The man rubbed his hands together, his slipper between his palms, he ran one way, then the other, said 'Oh God, save me' and held my hand. I pointed to the backyard door. As a sort of payment he gave me his handkerchief, and sped out. I couldn't understand his handkerchief. It was very filthy and it didn't look like any colour on this earth. I went and threw it away in the backyard.

When I got back the rough voices were just beyond the curtain strips. Some of the people went away towards the street, squabbling and shouting as they went. Then two men, bare-chested and muscle-bound, stepped into the bar. They strode towards me. I had seen them before. One of them had come with the landlord to our room. And the other was one of the thugs that had been involved in the mindless battle along our street. He had a bandage round his head. They both towered over me. The one with the bandage had a massive and ugly pair of nostrils which swelled and contracted as he breathed. The other had large lips and small eyes.

'Where is the madame?' the bandaged one asked.

'I don't know.'

'Who are you?'

'I am a boy.'

They both stared at me with malevolent faces. Their sweat stank out the bar. They exuded an air of raw menace, their mighty chests rising and falling. Then suddenly they spread out and one of them looked under the benches and tables, while the other looked behind the counter and the doors. They came back and stood in front of me again. Then, as if they both shared one brain, they spread out a second time, one went out through the backyard door, and the other went out through the front door. They both came back in through opposite doors. They sat across from me.

'Is there any palm-wine?' the small-eyed one growled.

'No.'

'Why not?'

'The tapper hasn't brought it yet.'

'Any water?'

'No.'

'Why not?'

'The well ran dry.'

They glowered at me. The bandaged one said:

'Any peppersoup?'

'No.'

'How come?'

'The madame hasn't cooked it yet.'

The small-eyed one went to the earthenware pot, took off its lid, and peered in.

'Isn't that water?'

'Yes, but a madman pissed in it.'

'How come?'

'I don't know. The madame said he was mad.'

'Why haven't you thrown it away?'

'I can't carry it.'

He put the lid back on. He went back to his bench. Flies circled the men.

'Are you fooling us?'

'No.'

The bandaged man brought out a flick-knife from his trouser pocket. He began to cut away at the table, chipping off the wood.

'Don't do that,' I said.

'Why not?'

'The madame will be angry.'

'She won't. She is our friend. Our party likes her.'

They stayed silent for a while. One of them swotted a fly, killing it, and he flicked it off his palm, and laughed.

'I killed a fly,' he said to his companion, who nodded, but stayed silent.

Then the bandaged one looked at me with a ferocious and menacing squint and said:

'Did anyone come in here?'

'No,' I replied.

They stayed still for a while. Then, as if they had ears outside the bar, as if they had smelt something a long distance away, they both got up and ran out through the backyard door. Flies buzzed in the silence. I went to the backyard and looked around. They had gone.

Later, I heard voices. Two men were shouting, and a thinner voice was protesting its innocence. The voices got closer, louder, and then moved away, became distant. And then, from the backyard, the voices sounded again, swelled by multitudes. Many people, it seemed, were in argument and disagreement. The thin voice cried out, the noise of multitudes drowned it under. I hurried outside and saw that the two thugs had caught the man. They had dragged him through the passage and into the backyard. The thugs held the man's arms and he let them hold on to him while he meekly protested his innocence. Some people in the crowd surrounding them kept asking what the man had done. Madame Koto came out of her room, saw the thugs and the unfortunate man, and hurried back in again.

The crowd and the thugs created a frightening din. The man's voice became thinner, his protestations feebler, and his face was pathetically contorted as though he wanted the world to know that he had accepted his fate.

Then he began to plead. He pleaded with the men, begging them to leave him to go free, that he would never oppose them again, that he had been blind. Then he begged the crowd to help him. The crowd was becoming increasingly divisive about their response to his fate when the man suddenly bolted. He pushed his way through the crowd, shoving aside a mother and child, accidentally hitting a pregnant woman in the stomach with his elbow, and he ran into me with such frightened force that I fell hard on the ground and banged my head on a thick block of firewood.

'Catch him! Catch him!' the thugs shouted.

'Hold him! Hold the traitor!'

'Thief! Thief!'

They bounded after him and the small-eyed thug dived and caught the man's feet in a flying tackle. The man went down and the two thugs set on him and kicked him and slapped him around and hit him in the stomach. He collapsed on his knees and the two men went on unleashing a barrage of blows and kicks on him. He folded himself into a ball and still they went on, inventing new forms of beating, new kinds of hand-chops, knuckle-cracks, jabs and elbow attacks, enjoying their invention.

'That's enough,' Madame Koto said from the crowd, without much conviction.

The thugs ignored her. They went on beating up the man to their satisfaction. Then they dragged him up. He was weeping and trembling, his nose ran, his mouth quivered, he bled from one eye, his face was all bruised, he had cuts in six places, and the crowd merely looked on. Then someone began to plead for him. The woman spoke of mercy, kindness, God's love, Allah's compassion. The two thugs, switching methods to suit the mood of the crowd, said that the man was a vicious creature who had beaten his wife unconscious and abandoned his three children. They were starving and his wife had been in hospital for seven days. His wife, they said, was their sister. The crowd was enraged by the man's wickedness. And as the thugs dragged him away the women all knocked him on the head and rained curses on him for his cowardice and brutality.

The thugs led the man towards the forest. His clothes were torn. His head hung low. He walked with the submissiveness of a man who is soon going to die.

When the thugs and the man disappeared, the crowd dispersed, but the compound people remained. In their poor clothes, with their hunger, their pain, their faces stark with the facts of their lives, they stood outside the bar and stared at the forest as though it were about to release an ominous sign, or sound, or yield its awesome secrets.

They did not move, even when they heard the innocent cries of the man echoing through the trees.

It was Madame Koto who broke the stillness. She went to her

stack of firewood and began to prepare her fire, as if acknowledging the fact that there are few things that happen which can make it impossible for life to continue.

The women looked at her as she started the fire. I looked at all of them. Madame Koto, in her activity, seemed apart from them, different, separate from their fevers. A formation of birds, densely clustered, and consisting of a fast-changing set of geometric patterns, circled the sky, spreading their shadows on the burning earth. The compound people melted back to their rooms, to their disparate occupations.

I went inside the bar and lay on a bench. I shut my eyes. I heard Madame Koto come in. She said:

'If you misbehave the same thing will happen to you.'

'What?'

'The forest will swallow you.'

'Then I will become a tree,' I said.

'Then they will cut you down because of a road.'

'Then I will turn into the road.'

'Cars will ride on you, cows will shit on you, people will perform sacrifices on your face.'

'And I will cry at night. And then people will remember the forest.'

She was silent. I didn't open my eyes. I heard her lifting the earthenware pot, heard her pouring water out of it, heard her leaving.

The heat changed the colours in my eyes. Lying on the bench, within the shade of the bar, with birds calling outside, an immense space of peace opened inside me. It spread deep. It lowered the heat on my skin.

Soft voices sang from the bushes. I listened to the muezzin. I listened to myself faintly snoring. A strange shape, like the body of a mythical animal grown rotten on the path, burst into my mind. I sat up. My feet didn't touch the ground. I looked about me and saw a lizard staring at me as if I were about to break into song. Outside, birds piped their indecipherable melodies.

I lay down again, listening to the voices of school-children, shrill with the joy of play and encounter. I listened to the many voices in me. The bench bit into my back. I shut my eyes and, within, everything was black. A deeper shade of black unfurled within the blackness. I was drawn into a vortex. I reached out; the blackness was light, like air. And as I floated, transfixed, captive, a face – luminous with emerald brilliance, its eyes a deep diamond blue, its

219

smile that of an unhappy man who had died at the right moment – opened on to my gaze. Was he an incarnation of the great king of the spirit world? He stared at me and as I tried to look deeper into the mysteries of his face I felt myself falling into light. My eyes opened of too much brightness.

I shut them again. I heard a sudden sound. A curious terror, like arms grabbing you from out of a trusted darkness, swept over me. I didn't move. I felt no fear. Then I saw the elongated faces of spirits, with blood pouring out of their eyes. My mouth opened into a scream, and the faces changed. Then a bald head turned round and round under my gaze. On all of its sides were sorrowful eyes. It leant towards me, then bowed, disembodied; and on its scalp opened a mouth which spread into an ecstatic, elastic, smile. I woke up suddenly. I saw glimpses of wise spirits in a flash before I saw Madame Koto's rugged face. She caught my flailing hands, and said:

'Get up. Customers are here!'

And when I sat up and looked around I knew we were in the divide between past and future. A new cycle had begun, an old one was being brought to a pitch, prosperity and tragedy rang out from what I saw, and I knew that the bar would never be the same again.

It was evening. Outside, through the curtain strips, I could see birds whirling round and round in the air, as though marking, with the centre of their circle, the spot where a comrade had just fallen. The sun was an intense orange, a molten object strangely unconnected with the cooling breeze of the forest. Madame Koto's face had broken into the smile she reserved for the customers who spent the most.

There were a lot of people outside. They were elegantly dressed in bright kaftans and agbadas and safari suits. They laughed and talked in animated tones. There were many women amongst them. The strong scent of their perfumes was heavy and inescapable on the evening air.

The two thugs who had earlier led the man away stepped into the bar. They surveyed the place as if to ascertain whether it was big enough for the celebration they planned. They did not look like thugs. In spite of the bandage and the animal expression in their eyes, they looked like modern businessmen, contractors, exporters, politicians. Dressed in lace kaftans, with matching hats, they were wonderfully high-spirited. They went out, came in again and, walking towards Madame Koto with the dignity of honourable crooks, said:

'It will do. We want to celebrate here. You are our friend and supporter. Since you have been good to us, we will bring business to you.'

The man with the bandage round his forehead went out and I heard him say:

'Come in, my people. Come in.'

He led the way, walking with a lilt. The small-eyed man stood in the middle of the bar, making expansive gestures. Neither of them looked like the people they had been. I was fascinated by their transformation.

'My favourite customers, welcome!' Madame Koto said, in a voice of such extreme unctuousness that I turned to her, surprised. Her face glistened. She rubbed her palms together. The two men sat. The people outside came in, bringing their thick perfume smells, their crackling lace, their clinking bangles and trinkets and strange jewellery, and the smell of new money.

'More light!' cried one of the men.

'And plenty of your best palm-wine!' said another.

Madame Koto, who seemed to me afraid of nothing under the heavens, moved with such alacrity it appeared she was afraid of incurring their displeasure. She rushed out and got a clean cloth and wiped the benches before the women and the men sat on them. She wiped the tabletops till they shone and she opened the curtains wider by hanging the lower parts of the plastic strips on a nail. She rushed out and came back in and gave me a terrible stare and for the first time she shouted at me as if I were her servant.

'Get up, you ugly child. Get up and fetch water for my customers!'

I was too stunned to move. She grabbed me by the scruff of the neck, and tossed me out of the bar. Furious and confused, I picked up a length of firewood. I stayed out a long time. Madame Koto came out looking for me. I held the firewood high, ready to use it.

'What about the water?' she asked.

I said nothing. I held the wood harder. I withstood the metal in her eyes. She approached. I backed away into the bushes. She smiled, her breasts heaving. She got close, arms outstretched, and I lashed out, and missed, and the firewood flew out of my hands, and splinters caught in my palm. She stopped. A new expression appeared on her face. Then she said:

'Okay, okay.'

She fetched the basins of water herself. I stayed near the bushes and watched her run up and down, trying frantically to please her customers. She came out with a heavy face and re-entered with a big false smile. I went to the front and watched as more of the thugs and their friends poured into the bar. They laughed roughly and talked about money. They talked about politics and contracts and women and the elections. I peeped in and saw Madame Koto sitting behind her counter, sweating. She listened with wide-eyed attentiveness to what was being said and jumped up with an elastic smile whenever they wanted something. She seemed like a total stranger.

'Madame,' one of the men said, 'why don't you turn this place into a hotel? You will make plenty of money.'

'And why don't you get women to serve us instead of that strange child, eh?'

Madame Koto made a reply which raised laughter, but which I didn't hear. They went on drinking endless bowls of soup, endless gourds of palm-wine. I stayed out till the evening began to distribute itself across the sky. Madame Koto came looking for me and when I saw her I ran.

'Why are you running?' she asked in a gentler voice.

Then she pleaded with me to go back in and said that they were her special customers and I should behave properly towards them. She promised me some money and a generous portion of soup. Cautiously, I went back into the bar. But by then the men were quite drunk and had begun to shout and to boast. Two of the men were so drunk that they danced without music, staggering, sweating peppersoup. One of them climbed on a table and danced to the tune of his party's song. The table wobbled. He sang and stamped. The other man tried to climb a bench, but couldn't. The two thugs kept trying to get them to come down. The bandaged man went round his table and tried to grab the dancer, but he jumped from one table to another and eventually jumped so hard that he crashed right through the wood and remained entangled. No one moved to help him.

'Don't worry, Madame,' said the small-eyed thug, 'we will pay for your table.'

Madame Koto remained still behind the counter. Her lower face vibrated. I could sense her tremendous rage. But she managed a smile of incredible sincerity, and said:

'Thank you, my favourite customers.'

Two women from the group got up and helped the man out of the table. He was bleeding from the thighs and round the area of his crotch but he didn't seem to notice. He lay down on a bench next to me and fell asleep. His shoes stank. His horrible perfume mingled with peppersoup sweat. I moved two benches away from him. The others resumed their drinking and their rowdy merriment. Madame Koto watched them with a fixed smile on her huge face. She watched passively, not doing anything, even when fresh customers turned up and were driven away, shouted away, by the bandaged man and his friends.

'Go and find somewhere else to drink. This is our bar tonight,' they would say, laughing.

They went on turning people away, preventing them from so much as coming in, and all Madame Koto did was smile.

'This madame is going to be my wife!' announced the bandaged thug.

He got up, swaying, and dragged her from behind the counter and danced with her.

'That madame,' said one of the men, 'will swallow you completely.'

The others laughed. Madame Koto stopped dancing, went out, and returned with her broom.

'Run! Run-o!' came a drunken chorus.

The man who had provoked her was already outside by the time she reached him.

'Sweep away my sorrows,' crooned the bandaged man, holding her from behind.

She shook him off. He said, with eyes both feverish and earnest:

'Madame, if you marry me you will sleep on a bed of money!'

And as if to prove it he brought out a crisp packet of pound notes and proceeded to plaster note after note on her sweating forehead. She responded with amazing dexterity and, as if she were some sort of desperate magician, made the money disappear into her brassière. She danced all the while. He seemed very amused by her greed. He swayed, his eyes opening and shutting, behaving as if he hadn't noticed anything. And then quite suddenly he put away his packet of money, and danced away from Madame Koto, his face glistening with the ecstasy of power.

The darkness outside spread indoors. The flies were intense. It became quite dark. Madame Koto brought in the lanterns, lit them, and distributed them round the tables.

'Madame,' slurred the small-eyed thug, 'we will give you electricity and you will play music for us one of these days and we will all dance.'

At that moment the curtain parted and the carpenter, eyes wide, clothes dirty from another job, came into the bar.

'Go and drink somewhere else!' said one of the men.

'Why?'

'Why not?'

'Because I built this bar.'

'So what?'

'No one can tell me to get out of here.'

'Is that so?'

'Yes.'

The bandaged man, who had clearly been spoiling for some confrontation all evening, made a great show of tearing off his agbada. Then he unceremoniously jumped on the carpenter. They both fell on a bench. A lantern rocked on the table. They wrestled, rolling, on the floor. One of the lanterns fell and broke and set the table on fire. The women screamed, grabbed their handbags, and fled outside. Madame Koto got her inevitable broom and whipped the fire. Her broom began to burn. The two men went on fighting. The carpenter ripped off the thug's bandage. The thug attempted to strangle the carpenter. The companions of the bandaged man began hitting the carpenter, booting him, smashing his head with their shoes, punching his ribs. But each time they hit the carpenter, it was the bandaged man who cried out. Then, in a flurry, benches and tables came tumbling over, glasses and plates broke, calabashes were cracked open, spilled palm-wine burst into flames, and smoke filled the air. I didn't move. I heard one of the thugs screaming. His agbada had caught fire. He ran out, his garment flaming all around him, into the blue night. The curtain strips caught fire as well. Soon it seemed everything was burning. Madame Koto rushed in with the compound people, bearing buckets of water, which they poured everywhere, on the tables and walls, on the men fighting over flames and broken calabashes, over the man who lay asleep and drunk and who had earlier jumped into a table, over the curtains. Soon the fires were extinguished and the men had stopped wrestling on the floor. They were thoroughly drenched. They both got up, bits of glass and wood sticking to them, and they leant forward, groaning.

Madame Koto fetched a new broom and waded into the crowd of bodies and began lashing out, thrashing everyone with such viciousness that the commotion in the bar became incredible. She whipped the thugs and their guests, pursued them to the door, she turned and flogged the carpenter and chased him round the bar, then she attacked the compound people who had come to help, and who fled screaming that she had gone mad, she lashed me on the back and neck and I ran outside. She went on hitting out and whipping the air with her broom even when there was no one left to hit.

She emerged suddenly at the front door and her presence sent the women screaming, the men yelling. She bounded after the thugs and their friends, soundly beating the women on the back, the men round the ankles, pursuing them up the road towards the forest. For a while, we didn't see her. Then, breathing heavily, she materialised amongst us, and pounced on our astonishment, quick on her feet for one so heavy. She tore after us, managing the curious feat of being in several places at the same time, and whipping those of us who had run either north or south, west or east, crackling the air with the electric fury of her new broom, cursing everything, raising the dust and kicking up stones, whirling and swearing, chasing us into the bushes, into the backyard and down the passages. People fled everywhere. I ran into the stinking bathroom and remained there for a long time and only came out when I heard other voices tentatively emerging from their hiding-places. I crept up to the bar.

Madame Koto sat at a table. There was only one functioning lantern in the room. The place was a mess. Tables were broken and burnt, there were broken glasses and bones of chickens and crushed bowls and twisted spoons and shattered calabashes and torn clothes and spilt wine and soup everywhere. There was vomit on one table, the Coca-Cola calendar was on the floor, with peppersoup stains all over the breasts of the white woman. Benches were upside down. There were burnt pound notes on tables and patches of blood on the walls. Madame Koto sat in the soft darkness. Her breasts heaved slightly. Her face was a mask. She sat alone in her bar, surrounded by confusion and night-flies. Her hands trembled.

With her sad, hard eyes she stared straight ahead of her, not surveying her domain. She bit her lower lip. Then to my greatest amazement she began to tremble worse than ever, sitting bolt upright, her face bold, her eyes defeated. She wept, quivering, and her tears ran down her massive cheeks and dripped on the table. Then she stopped, swallowed, wiped her face with her wrapper, and began to lock up the bar for the day. She too had crossed the divide between past and future. She must have known that a new cycle had begun. She turned suddenly, saw me, became stiff, her eyes widening with the horror of being discovered in a secret moment, and then she said, somewhat harshly:

'What are you looking at?'

'Nothing.'

'Haven't you seen a grown woman cry before?'

I was silent.

'Go home!' she commanded.

I didn't move. Neither Madame Koto, nor her bar, would ever be the same again.

'Go home!' she ordered.

I went.

SEVEN

MUM WAS ALONE in the room, praying to our ancestors and to God in three different languages. She knelt by the door, her kerchief partly covering her face, rubbing her palms together fervently.

'Shut the door and come in,' she said.

I went and sat on the bed. The intensity of her prayer overwhelmed the room. I listened to her calling for strength, pleading for Dad to get a good job, for us to find prosperity and contentment. She prayed that we should not die before our time, that we should live long enough for the good harvest, and that our suffering should turn into wisdom.

When she finished she stood up and came and sat beside me on the bed. She was silent. The space around her was full of energies. She asked about Madame Koto and I told her that people thought she was going mad. Mum laughed, till I told her what had happened. There was a long silence. Then I realised that she hadn't been listening to me. Her eyes were distant.

'Did you see the door?' she asked suddenly, breaking out of her contemplation.

'Our door?'

'Yes.'

'I did.'

'Go and look again.'

I went out and looked but couldn't see anything because of the darkness. The compound people, like figures in a red dream, milled about in the backyard, moved about the passage. I came back in.

'Did you see?'

'No.'

I took the candle, cupped my palm over a side of its flame, and went out again. Our door had been crudely hacked with machetes. They had almost splintered the wood. Gashes were long rather than deep on the door. A foul-smelling substance, glistening red under the candle-light, had been smeared across the wood in a set of menacing signs. Our door had been marked. I went back in.

'Who did it?'

'It was the landlord.'

'How do you know?'

'Dad challenged his party.'

Mum was silent for a moment. I put the candle back on the table.

'Be careful of the compound people,' she warned. 'One day they are our friends and the next day they are our enemies.'

'Yes, mother.'

'I was cooking food. I came to the room. When I went back to the kitchen someone had poured water on the fire.'

We were silent.

'I am now afraid to walk the compound at night. Who knows if they are poisoning our food, eh?'

I became afraid. I held on to Mum. She patted my head gently. For a moment I could see our door being broken down at night, while we slept. I saw the great monstrous Egungun, belching white smoke from seven ears, bursting into our room and devouring us all with his bloodied mouth.

'Let's run away,' I said.

Mum laughed. Then she became serious. And for the first time I saw how the world had sharpened her features. Her cheekbones jutted out, her nose was pointed, her chin was sharp, and the two corners of her forehead stood out like the rock-shaped result of permanent bruising. Her eyes were narrowed as if they were endlessly trying to exclude most of what they saw.

'Our destiny will protect us. Don't fear anything, my son. The worst they can do is kill us.' She paused.

Her face took on the bizarre immobility of a mask. Her eyes didn't move and they seemed to stare past the window in an uncanny vacant concentration.

'I am tired of this life anyway,' she said, eventually. 'I want to die.'

Suddenly I had a vision of her death. It came and went so fast and it left me perplexed. I remembered her face when she nearly died just after my homecoming. I remembered that it was because of her bruised face that I had chosen to live, to stay, in the confines of this world, and to break my pacts with my spirit companions. One of the many promises I made before birth was that I would make her happy. I had chosen to stay, now she wanted to die. I burst out crying. I threw myself on the floor and thrashed and wept. The demon of grief seized me completely. Mum tried to hold me, and console me, and find out why I had so suddenly begun crying. She didn't know how inconsolable I was at that moment, because she didn't know the cause of my grief. She didn't know that the only thing that could make me stop was a promise from her that she would never die.

'What's wrong with you? Is it because of the door? Or the compound people? Or the landlord? Don't be afraid. We are too strong for them.'

Her words came too late. I could not separate myself from unhappiness. I became my grief. I wept in advance for all the things that would happen, the unimaginable things beyond the horizon of all the narratives of our lives. Misery filled me like water fills a deep well after a heavy downpour. I started to choke. My spirit companions drank of my grief and filled me with sweet songs to make my wretchedness more sublime. My heart stopped beating. I froze, became rigid, didn't breathe, my mouth open, eyes wide. Darkness rushed over me, a powerful wind from the forest. The darkness extinguished my consciousness.

But deep inside that darkness a counterwave, a rebellion of joy, stirred. It was a peaceful wave, breaking on the shores of my spirit. I heard soft voices singing and a very brilliant light came closer and closer to the centre of my forehead. And then suddenly, out of the centre of my forehead, an eye opened, and I saw this light to be the brightest, most beautiful thing in the world. It was terribly hot, but it did not burn. It was fearfully radiant, but it did not blind. As the light came closer, I became more afraid. Then my fear turned. The light went into the new eye and into my brain and roved around my spirit and moved in my veins and circulated in my blood and lodged itself in my heart. And my heart burned with a searing agony, as if it were being burnt to ashes within me. As I began to scream the pain reached its climax and a cool feeling of divine dew spread through me, making the reverse journey of the brilliant light, cooling its flaming passages, till it got back to the centre of my forehead, where it lingered, the feeling of a kiss for ever imprinted, a mystery and a riddle that not even the dead can answer.

EIGHT

MUM HELD THE candle in her hand. The wax dripped down on to her fragile skin. She did not flinch. She did not move. Her eyes were wide open. Her face was a rock in the dark shadows where the candle-light couldn't reach.

'One day I will tell you the story of how Death was conquered,' she said, in the voice of a mysterious priestess.

She stared at me for a long time. The candle-light created a golden aureole round the scattered fringes of her hair. The wax turned white on her fragile skin. She put down the candle and peeled off the wax. She stared beyond me. There was fear and love in her eyes. She moved her hand across the darkness and created a raft in the shadows. It was a blue darkness. Everything turned blue.

I floated on the raft and found myself on the mat. The candle had burned low on the table. There were mosquitoes and midges in the room and the window was open. The wind blew in, fluttering the candle, and it brought the smells of the world cleansed by the freshness of the night air.

Someone tapped gently on the door of my spirit. I opened the door and found the photographer outside. At first I didn't recognise him. I hadn't seen him for many days. He looked different. His face shone with health. His eyes were bright. His mood was buoyant as though he had discovered fields of hope somewhere in the night.

'It's me,' he said, a little hesitantly, 'the International Photographer.'

He came in half crouching, half bouncing. His spirit swung between fear and buoyancy. He had new cases for his equipment. On his photographic encasement was written the legend, white against the black leather: TO BECOME A MAN. Was it a question unasked, a riddle unstated, or a declaration unfinished? I had no idea. I stared at the words, mesmerised.

'Do you remember me?' he whispered, as I locked the door.

'Where have you been?'

'Round the world and back.'

'How is that?'

'Wonders will never cease.'

'Why not?'

He didn't answer my question. We listened to the sleeping world. Still whispering, he said:

'I am going to move soon. I am going to get another job soon. Is there any food? I think those thugs have stopped looking for me. The landlord wants me to move away from his house. I am hungry.'

'There is no food.'

'Why not?'

'Didn't you see the door?'

'What door?'

'Our door.'

'Of course I saw it.'

'You didn't.'

'How did I get into the room?'

'You didn't see it.'

'Why not?'

'Some people tried to break it down. Then they put something strange on it.'

'Why?'

'I don't know.'

'Who did it?'

'We don't know.'

'Wickedness will never cease.'

'What?'

'So there is no food?'

'They poured water on our fire when Mum was cooking.'

Dad turned on the bed. He grunted in his sleep. The rats began to eat. Mum chewed her mouth and fell silent.

'Why?'

'I don't know. Mum thinks they might poison us.'

'Sssshhhhhh!'

'What?'

'A spirit passing might hear you.'

'What will it do?'

'Depends.'

'On what?'

'Is there any garri?'

'Yes.'

He went to the cupboard and, quiet as a thief, dug out some garri from the basin with a bowl. He poured water in the bowl, got rid of the excess water in the passage, put salt and cubes of sugar in the garri, some more water to achieve his desired eccentric balance, and ate. The simple food satisfied him. When he finished he said:

'Show me the door.'

I took the candle outside, cupping the flame against the wind. He studied the gashes, touched the foul-smelling red stuff, smelt it, tasted it, and said:

'Blood of a wild boar.'

'How do you know?'

'I used to be a hunter.'

We went back in. He knelt in silence on the mat.

'Maybe it's because of me,' he said after a long time.

He paused.

'I will go soon. I will disappear. I will go underground.'

Another pause.

'I don't want to bring you trouble.'

The wind blew in through the window and blew out the candle. We stayed in the dark. When he spoke again his voice had changed.

'Do you know what I did today?'

'No.'

'I took photographs of women at the market being attacked by thugs. The women fought them back. I took pictures of riots against our white rulers. I took pictures of a policeman taking bribes. The policeman saw me and pursued me. I escaped.'

'How?'

'Magic.'

'How?'

'I turned invisible.'

'How?'

'I have a lot of powers.'

'Then why are you hiding?'

'Because if you have power you don't use it all the time.'

'What else can you do?'

'I can fly.'

'To where?'

'To the moon.'

'How?'

'On a flash.'

'I don't believe you.'

'Last night I flew to the moon and took pictures of its incredible face.'

'Let me see them.'

'Another time.'

'Why not now?'

'Because I have to sleep.'

'What else can you do?'

'I can change people's faces.'

'How?'

'With my camera.'

'Into what?'

'I can make them ugly or beautiful.'

'Why?'

'Because I can do it.'

'What else can you do?'

'I can drink ten bottles of ogogoro without getting drunk.'

The rats began to chew.

'Can you understand what the rats are saying?'

'No.'

'Can you talk to them?'

'No. But I can kill them.'

'Why?'

'Because they are never satisfied. They are like bad politicians and imperialists and rich people.'

'How?'

'They eat up property. They eat up everything in sight. And one day when they are very hungry they will eat us up.'

I was silent.

'When you wake up tomorrow all the rats will be gone. I will finish them off. I will use my powerful medicine and my secret charms. But they won't work if you don't sleep.'

He got up and shut the window. We lay on the mat. I tried to sleep but the rats went on chewing and the mosquitoes went on tormenting us.

'I can teach you how to fly to the moon,' he said in the dark.

'How?'

'Just think about the moon and fall asleep.'

I tried it. I fell asleep, but I did not fly to the moon, nor did I even dream about its mysterious face. And I didn't wake up early enough to tell the photographer that what he taught me didn't work.

NINE

MUM WAS SHRIEKING. Dad stood over her, a fiendish look on his face, dangling six large rats by the tail. One of them was still barely alive. It kicked feebly. Mum got out of bed.

'Where did you find those rats?'

I sat up. All around the mat, under the centre table, by the door, on top of the cupboard, near the bed, were the bristling corpses of rats. I screamed. The room was a Calvary of rats, a battleground of them. They had died in every conceivable position. There were rats near my pillow, clinging on to the mat with their bared yellow teeth. There were rats all over my cover cloth. Some had died beside me, died beneath the cloth, perished on the centre table, their long tails hanging over the edge. Some had clawed their way up the window curtain and had died at the foot of the wall, leaving long rips on the cloth. They had died in Dad's boot, their tails mistakable for his shoe-lace. They had died with their yellow eyes open, gazing at us with a solemn vacant threat of vengeance. A few of them were still struggling, still alive, and Dad put them out of their misery, crushing their heads expertly with his boots. The rats, in dying, squirted yellow and blue liquids from their mouths. Big furry rats with long thin tails writhed among the bodies of their companions, kicking with their little paws. Dad picked one up to add to his pendular collection and it made a sudden motion of rip and snag, catching Dad on the cuff of his shirt, and tearing it, and Dad slung the creature against the wall, and it left its imprint there as it collapsed to the floor, clinging on to a piece of sacking with its jagged teeth, refusing to die. Dad stood ankle-deep in the corpses of rats. I was too scared to move.

Dad came over to me, mischief on his face, and waved the six rats over me like an obscene pendulum. I ran to Mum.

'They are only rats,' she said, having obviously recovered from her own horror.

'So many!' Dad said.

'I will count them,' I said.

'But what happened to them?'

'They had bad dreams,' Dad suggested.

'What bad dreams?'

'About the landlord's party. When they heard his speech they decided to commit suicide.'

'What is suicide?' I asked.

'What happened to the rats?' Mum wondered.

'The photographer killed them.'

'How?'

'With a special moon poison. It works.'

'Works too well,' Mum said, getting out of bed.

She fetched the broom. When she moved the cupboard she gasped. The number of rats that had died there was frightening. It was impossible to imagine that we had been sharing our lives with so many rats. They had eaten the sacking, the wood of the table, had eaten their way through clothes, shoes, materials. There were crumbs of food and ratshit. Lying in a thousand different positions – tails entwined, pale bellies showing, teeth bared, snarling in their death-throes – was an unholy horde of rats.

'Don't touch anything!' Mum said.

She swept every corner. She swept beneath the bed, under the cupboard. She moved her hole-ridden sacks and basins behind the door, gasping in horror all the while. The sacks had been more or less devoured, and rats had died amongst her provisions. Mum swept them to the door and made a pile out of their corpses. I went searching for a carton. I found a big one used for the packing of chocolate drinks. The rats filled the carton. The creepy mass of them nearly made me throw up. Mum went and dumped the carton of rats on the growing rubbish heap at the back of the burnt van. Then she came back and drenched the room in disinfectant. She made us practically bathe in the stuff. Then she made us wash our hands in a concentrated solution. Then she made food, while Dad prepared for work.

While we were eating there was a knock on the door.

'Come in,' Dad said.

It was too early for visitors. We were struck by the sight of the man in ragged clothes who came in, looking around furtively, his eyes yellow, his complexion pale, his mouth bitter. He was from the landlord. He was the bearer of a message. We were informed that our rent had been increased. Apparently we were the only ones to suffer an increment in the compound. After he had delivered the message, which included an option to move out if we didn't like the new rent, and after he had gone, Dad sat in front of the table of food like a man who had been kicked in the ribs. He betrayed no pain, but sat still, his eyes a little bewildered. When he moved it was to creak his neck and his knuckles. Then he moved restlessly, fidgeting, his face contorted.

'I don't feel like eating any more,' he said after some time.

But he picked up his spoon, continued with his food, and cleaned up everything on the plate. Then he sent me to buy some ogogoro. The woman who sold it wasn't awake and Dad lost his temper when I came back without any. So I went and woke up the woman, banging on her door, and she got up and abused me while measuring out the amount Dad wanted. Dad drank half of it in one gulp. Mum cleared the table. Then she went to the backyard, singing a song from the village. In the room Dad sat and stared straight ahead.

'You see what life does to you?' he asked.

'Yes.'

'You see how wicked people can be?'

'Yes.'

'That's how they make you commit murder.'

He cracked his knuckles again. He sighed.

'Where am I going to find that kind of money every month, eh?'

'I don't know.'

He stared at me. So intensely did he stare at me I felt that I was the enemy.

'Do you see how they force a man to become an armed robber?'

'Yes.'

He sighed again. He lit a cigarette. He smoked in silence. Then, as if he had hit upon a most brilliant idea, he put out his cigarette, and put on his work-clothes. I was disappointed when he said:

'When I come back I will go and see Madame Koto.'

'She is mad,' I told him.

He stared at me in that curious fashion again.

'Maybe she can loan us some money,' he said, ignoring my piece of information.

He got into his shoes, stamped them on the ground, touched me on the head, and went out to work.

After a while Mum came in, her wrapper wet. She had been washing clothes in the backyard. Washing and thinking. Washing

237

and singing. The compound had awoken. A stray dog wandered up the passage. It was a dull morning. The sky was grey as if it might rain. The noise of metal buckets clanking at the well, the sound of water being poured, a woman raising her voice, grew on the morning air. The school-children were in their uniforms. A cock crowed repeatedly. Mum got her tray together. I was ready for school. Mum went down the street, swaying, moving a little sleepily, with one more burden added to her life. Soon she was merely a detail in the poverty of our area.

TEN

I TRIED TO sneak past Madame Koto's place but she saw me, and said very loudly:

'Are you running from me again?'

She looked different. She wore a new lace blouse, an expensive wrapper, coral beads round her neck, and copper bangles round her wrists. She wore eye-shadow, which darkened her eyes, and powder on her face, beneath which her sweat ran. The day had become hotter. It seemed impossible to avoid the sun. I was thirsty.

'Come and have some palm-wine,' she offered.

The bar had changed again. There were two almanacs of the Rich Party on the walls. It was surprisingly crowded for that time of the afternoon. There were normal, decent-looking people, as well as men with scars, women with bracelets that weighed down their arms, men with dark glasses. Arguments reverberated in the heated place. They discussed politics and scandals in loud, passionate voices. Some of them had thunderous faces, gleaming with sweat, and when they talked their mouths opened to astonishing degrees. Some of them were thin and bony, with ragged hungry beards and furtive eyes. The women had long painted fingers. They waved their hands violently when they spoke. They fanned themselves with newspapers. Their noises mingled with the incessant buzz of the flies.

There was a hammer on the counter. I thought the carpenter was around, but upon looking, I found he wasn't. There were several gourds of palm-wine on the tables, and flies jostled on their rims. The plates empty of peppersoup were also a little busy with the flies. At one corner of the room a man lay on the bench, his mouth and eyes open. He was fast asleep. A wall-gecko ran across his face and got caught in his hair and he woke up screaming. The others burst into laughter.

In the midst of all the noise sat a man with a chief's cap on his head. He sat straight, with inherited dignity, and there was a boy next to him who fanned him. He had great orange beads round his neck and wore a dazzling blue agbada. He drank as if he owned the place. He looked familiar. I looked hard at him. Then I remembered him as one of the men on the van who had been overseeing the distribution of poisoned milk. His lips were large for his face and the colour of his lower lip was a curious mixture of red and black. There was more red than black and it seemed he had been burnt there as a child. He had the eyes of a rat. He caught me staring at him.

'What are you looking at?' he asked.

The voices in the bar stopped.

'You,' I said.

'Why? Are you mad?'

'No.'

He gave me a vicious stare. One of the men in the bar got up, came over, and cracked me on the head.

'You are mad,' he said.

I spat at him, but it didn't travel very far.

'Look at this bad boy,' he said, and cracked me a second time.

I spat again. It landed on my shirt. Madame Koto came into the bar. The man slapped me with two thick fingers and I shouted and rushed for the hammer on the counter. I tore at the man, who for some reason fled. Madame Koto grabbed my arms and took the hammer from me.

'Don't be a bad boy! Do you see that man there?' she said, pointing. 'He's a chief. He is going to rule our area. He will swallow you.'

The chief, satisfied with the tribute, smiled, and went on drinking. The noises resumed. Some of the people commented on my behaviour and lamented the way children no longer respected their elders and blamed it all on the white man's way of life which was spoiling the values of Africa.

Then one of the men suggested to Madame Koto that she would be better off with girls as waiters and servants than with boys. A woman amongst them said that if Madame Koto wanted some girls to work for her, and to help her serve the customers, she could arrange it.

'That ugly boy will destroy your business for you,' said the man who had knocked me twice on the head. 'Who wants to be drunk on your excellent palm-wine and see that terrible face?'

'You will die!' I said to the man.

The voices stopped. The man rose from his bench, his face quivering under the superstitious fear of a child's curse.

'Say I won't die!' he demanded.

'No!'

He came towards me. Madame Koto was counting money behind her counter. She was too engrossed to be aware of what was happening.

'Take it back!'

'No!'

He strode towards me. Only the flies made any noises.

'Flog him till he pisses on himself,' said the chief. 'That's how to train a child.'

I watched the man without moving. He raised his hand to hit me and I ran neatly between his legs and everyone laughed. I stopped and made faces at the chief and the painted women. When the man dashed at me, enraged by the trick, I fled out of the bar and went on fleeing and didn't stop till I was in the forest. I looked back. The man was panting. He gave up and turned back. I went deeper into the forest and sat on the mighty tree that had been cut down. I looked over the great pit from which they had been dredging sand to build the roads of the world.

And then I wandered. I wandered for a long time in the forest. The earth gave off a potent aroma and in the heat the palm trees released alcoholic fumes deep in their trunks which I breathed in with the smell of their barks and their wine-sap evaporating into the quivering air. I listened to the curlews in the groves of wild pine trees. Intoxicated with the alcoholic fumes of sun on earth I broke through a remote section of the forest, where sunbirds clustered in baobab branches, and I emerged in another reality, a strange world, a path which had completed its transition into a road. The surface of the road was uneven with bumps. The tarmac melted under the sun and my soles turned black. The smell of melting tarmac was heady and I saw the mirage of a trailer, quivering in its frightening speed, coursing down the road towards me. The mirage shot right through the road construction machines that stood at the intersection. It ground its way over the women who sold iced water and oranges, over the beggars and the workers and shacks within which the eternal arguments about pay and strikes raged. And then the great mirage of the trailer went on, plunging forward, right into the forest and I did not see it any more.

I came to another half-constructed road. Workers stood around the hulks of machinery, abusing those who were working. They waved sticks with words written on them. I gathered that those who cursed had been sacked. They shouted slogans at the white engineers. I did not see any white engineers. It might have been the sun. I passed them and when I looked back I saw figures setting upon the protesting workers. The sun was remorseless. Shadows were deep. Where the sun was brightest, objects were blackest. Antagonists and protesters twisted in an extraordinary dance and all I could make out were the confusing shapes of glistening bodies moving in and out of visibility. The lights made everything unreal.

Birds cawed overhead, flying around in widening circles. I re-entered the forest. The sun's rays were sharp like glass. The blue shadows of green trees blinded me for a moment. The shade was cooling and the air smelt of fine aromatic herbs and bark. Patterns of light and colours danced on the forest floor. Flowers which I didn't see scented the dense and tender breeze. I listened to the fluted sound of birds, the murmurings of a distant stream, the wind in the somnolent trees, and the pervasive concert of insects. And then, suddenly, that part of the forest was over.

I had emerged into another world. All around, in the future present, a mirage of houses was being built, paths and roads crossed and surrounded the forest in tightening circles, unpainted churches and the whitewashed walls of mosques sprang up where the forest was thickest. The worshippers in the unpainted churches wore white cassocks and prayed to the ringing of bells all afternoon. The world of trees and wild bushes was being thinned. I heard the ghostly wood-cutters axing down the titanic irokos, the giant baobabs, the rubber trees and obeches. There were birds' nests on the earth and the eggs within them were smashed, had fallen out, had mingled with the leaves and the dust, the little birds within the cracked eggs half-formed and dried up, dying as they were emerging into a hard, miraculous world. Ants swarmed all over them.

At intervals I passed people who were sitting behind trees. When I looked back they were no longer there. Nude women appeared and vanished before my gaze. The smell of earth, leaves, sun, and the merest hint of dried excrement overpowered my senses. I wandered deeper into the world of trees, amongst the solitude of acacias and needle-pines, and saw people clearing the bushes, uprooting tree stumps, raking great clusters of climbers and dried mistletoes into heaps. I saw old bicycles resting on trees. I saw men and women burning the bushes, the clusters of climbers and vines, and there must have been ecstatic herbs amongst what was being burnt for the smoke yielded up voluminous aromas of sage and rosemary, dried leaves and densities of green and yellow fumes and all manner of secret potencies and powerful crackling smells into the air.

And the smoke and the smells were dense everywhere and it was impossible not to breathe them in and the mysteries of burning plants in the deep forest charged my head and I went around stumbling into trees, tripping over roots, walking up against the ochre palaces that were anthills, or wandering round in circles, or watching bicycles riding around among the trees without riders, or noticing women pedalling the air without anything beneath them. Anthills which I had passed followed me. I became certain that the whole forest was moving.

The trees were running away from human habitation. My eyes became charged too and I saw people with serene bronze masks emerging from trees. I saw a bird with a man's hairy legs flying clumsily over the branches of the rain-tree. An antelope with the face of a chaste woman stopped and stared at me and when I moved it disappeared among the luxuriant bushes. An old man emerged from the anthill that had been following me. He had a white beard and green bejewelled eyes and a face that was both a hundred years old and childlike. His hands were up in the air, his neck slightly bent, as if he were carrying the heaviest riddle in the world. He seemed to follow me wherever I went. He had a staff which was the flowering branch of an orange tree and he hobbled slowly and came after me with inscrutable persistence. When I became aware of how intent he was I ran, but no matter how fast I fled he remained the same distance from me. I became confused and afraid. I tripped over a skull and hurt my ankle and couldn't move. I waited. I heard no footsteps, but the old man kept on at me, neither catching up with me, nor retreating. He remained at the same distance, bearing the great weight of an invisible enigma on his head.

The forest was full of mirages from which I could not escape. I dragged myself along on the ground. The man kept on coming. I grew so scared that after a while I turned and dragged myself towards the old man to find out what he wanted. I became frustrated at the slowness of my pace. When I got to the skull, I picked it up, and threw it at him. He vanished and a wind blew hard through the trees and the voluminous air was full of leaves whirling and fruits and seeds falling. I dragged myself on till I came to a palm tree. There was a tapper's gourd at its root and I was thirsty and drank of the new wine. It added to my intoxication. A black wind circled my head. A strange sound came from the centre of the tapper's gourd. Trying to escape it, I hobbled towards the houses on the rim of the forest. But they too were a mirage.

Then I came to a place in the trees where it was raining. I couldn't understand it. There was sun and wind everywhere else, but at this spot it rained and water ran down the leaves of the cicadas and banana plants. I was afraid of the rain. Beyond the curious downpour I could see a man, lights flashing at his feet, in front of a well near the houses. It was the old man. He seemed to be staring at me. For the first time I noticed that he had hooves for feet. Golden hooves. I turned in the opposite direction and hobbled away painfully. Then I got tired and didn't care what happened to me any more.

I rested against a tree and shut my eyes. After a while I heard a low continuous song. I opened my eyes and saw a tortoise moving past me. I watched it for a long time and it moved so slowly that I fell asleep. When I woke up I felt better, but my feet still hurt. I pushed on and found myself at the same place where the bushes were being burnt, where the potent fumes made the forest itself fall into dreaming. There was no one around. In the bright white smoke I saw spirits turning into air, spirits of plants and herbs and things I didn't yet know about; I saw their brightness of blues and yellows, shapes of sad faces, legs brilliant with oil becoming soot, golden eyes melting into vibrant space. I did not linger; I went on and when I recognised the place ahead, dimly at first, something fell on me and the black wind descended on my soul. It was the sunbirds that awakened me.

What had fallen on me? I looked around. Beams of sunlight converged on my face. There were branches and leaves and burst fruits on the floor. Strange stones warmed my soles. Not far from me, like a skull sliced in half and blacked with tar, was a mask that looked frightening from the side, but which was contorted in an ecstatic laughter at the front. It had eyes both daunting and mischievous. Its mouth was big. Its nose was small and delicate. It was the face of one of those paradoxical spirits that move amongst men and trees, carved by an artist who has the gift to see such things and the wisdom to survive them. When I picked up the mask a white bird flew out of the bushes, startling me with the wild clapping of its wings and its piercing cry. I dropped the mask. Then I picked it up and wore it over my face and looked out from its eyes and

244

something blurred the sun and the forest became as night.

When I looked out through the mask I saw a different world. There were beings everywhere in the darkness and the spirits were each of them a sun. They radiated a brilliant copper illumination hard to the eyes. I saw a tiger with silver wings and the teeth of a bull. I saw dogs with tails of snakes and bronze paws. I saw cats with the legs of women, midgets with bright red bumps on their heads. The trees were houses. There was music everywhere, and dancing and celebration rose from the earth. And then birds with bright yellow and blue feathers, eyes that were like diamonds, and with ugly scavenging faces, flew at me and kept pecking at the mask. I took it off and the world turned and the trees seemed to be falling on me and it took a while before things came back to normal. I held on to the mask and went on hobbling, looking for a way out of the forest.

And as I went I saw the golden hooves of the old man again. I hid behind a tree. The weight he was carrying seemed to be getting unbearably heavier. He stopped as he walked, but he showed no pain. If he saw me, he pretended he hadn't. When he went past I wore the mask and looked at him. He was completely invisible. He was not there. I could not see him at all through the eyes of the mask. But, sitting in the air above his invisible space, floating on the wind, serene in the midst of a great emerald light covering that other world, was a beautiful young boy whose slender body somehow suggested the passionate weight of a lion. The boy stared at me with simple eyes that conferred on me an unspoken benediction. I took off the mask and saw the old man re-entering the anthill. I put it on again and was amazed to see not an anthill but a grand palace with beryl colonnades and jade green verandahs, parapets of gold, mistletoe clinging to the fierce yellow walls, with sculptures in dazzling marble all around. Into this palace of turquoise mirrors the boy-king of purest innocence disappeared, with a smile like that of a god. And then darkness fell over everything again.

The wind sounded strange. My wonder turned to bewilderment. When I took off the mask the darkness was the same. Patches of light came over the wind. I had begun to lose my sense of reality, confused by the mask. I sped on, my feet in agony. I went on for a long time, turning round and round, my sense of direction askew. After a while, when some light filtered through the leaves, when confusion was really beginning to twist my brain, I suddenly broke out into the clearing.

It was the clearing where I used to play and where I had buried Madame Koto's fetish. The curious thing was that there was something different about the clearing. It was both exactly as I remembered it and different. For some reason the place felt shaded even when there were no trees around. I stared about the clearing, trying to isolate what was different about it. I couldn't. So I wore the mask and looked and saw that what was a clearing was in fact a village of spirits. In the middle of the village was a great iroko tree, golden and brown, with phosphorescent leaves and moon-white birds in the branches, twittering out the sweetest essences of music. There were rose-bushes in the radiant square. I saw skyscrapers and flying machines and fountains, ruins covered in snails and flowering climbers, grave-stelae, orchards, and the monument of a black sphinx at the gate of the village. Luminous pilgrims, celebrants in yellow cassocks, made processions in honour of the mysteries of strange gods. I took off the mask, my head turning, the world spinning, my eyes flaming. I sat down on the ground and rested.

Darkness had grown over the forest. The noises of insects and birds had diminished. The wind, scented with leaves, had become cooler. Gradually the trees, the clearing, the open spaces, became obscure. Ordinary things became riddles. In the obscurity of things I saw what was different about the clearing. Something was standing there. A tree had grown there. It had grown in the spot where I had buried Madame Koto's fetish. It was an odd tree and in the dark it seemed like an animal asleep on its feet. It was shaped exactly like a bull without horns. It was a stout muscular tree, without leaves. It seemed comfortable to sit on, to play on, and I wanted to see the darkening world from the height of its back. I tried to climb on, but couldn't take the mask with me; so I wore the mask and tied it round my head with climbers. With the mask on my face, with the darkness all around, and spirits everywhere in the darkness, I got on the back of the tree. All the moon-white birds seemed to be in the branches of my hair.

From the back of the tree I saw a completely different world to what I had been seeing. I saw a different reality. For a moment I expected to see birds twittering in my eyes, spirits dancing around me, luminous and dazzling. But when I looked out the spirits vanished, the white birds had somehow flown away, the village was not there. Instead I heard the earth trembling at the fearsome approach of a demonic being. A white wind circled my head. I was confused by the new world. The earth shuddered. The tree moved beneath me. And when I looked out through the mask, I saw before me in that new spirit world a creature ugly and magnificent like a prehistoric dragon, with the body of an elephant, and the face of a warthog. It towered before me. It was more graceful and less heavy than an elephant, but its tread was more resounding. Its face was incredibly ugly. A devourer of humans, of lost souls, of spirits, of all things wonderful, this creature opened its dreadful mouth and roared. Beneath me the tree began to change. Suddenly it seemed the tree was no longer a thing of wood. It became a thing of quivering flesh. The wood rippled slowly into flesh, transforming beneath me.

The monstrous creature drew closer and its foul breath knocked my consciousness around. I couldn't bear to look at it any more and I desperately wanted to take the mask off so I wouldn't have to see anything. I tore off the vegetable string, but the mask stayed on, stuck to my face. I tried to tear it off again, but it was like stripping the skin off my own face. And then the transformation of the wood into flesh became complete and I was suddenly blasted by the earth-shaking bellow of a wild animal beneath me. I was overpowered with the odour of its animal virility. Tossing and shivering, shaking its head, and bellowing again as if the sound in some way made its transformation more permanent, I realised that I had made a terrible mistake, and that I was riding on the back of a wild animal, awoken from a fetishistic sleep.

The monstrous creature swiped at me. In that confused moment, without caring, I ripped the mask off my face, obliterating its existence from my eyes. My face felt somewhat raw. I no longer saw the prehistoric monster, but the beast beneath me obviously did. It turned this way and that, wrenching each foot from the earth as if it were uprooting itself, and when all its feet were free it was still for a moment, drawing a deep breath. Its body expanded, bristling. I tried to get down. The beast backed off, giving a vicious snort as if it had burst open a channel through centuries of bad dreams. Then it began with an awkward canter, picked up speed and jumped about the place, tossing its head, attacking the invisible monster. Its hooves crushed the mask into pieces. It charged towards a thick cluster of bushes at such speed that I was thrown off and it was lucky I landed on grass and vegetation or I would certainly have broken my neck. I heard the wild beast returning, snorting, pounding the earth. I jumped to my feet, as if from a feverish torrent of

247

nightmares. Completely forgetting my hurting ankles, I ran out of the forest, and fled like a child being whipped to Madame Koto's bar.

ELEVEN

I DIDN'T GO in right away, but wandered in the fore-
court of the bar watching the night spread its power over the sky. I
stayed outside for a while, planting my secrets in the silence of my
beginnings. Night was falling and, all over, the shadows were short
and blurred. Lamps came on in the houses. I could make them out
through the leaves and bushes. A gust of wind, like the sighing of a
great animal, blew over from the forest. The wind brought the night
closer. It also seemed to sweep the last lights of the day to the farthest
reaches of the earth. One section of the sky was grey and deep blue, the
other was sad and red. The pain returned to my ankle. I sat outside a
long time, waiting for the world to quieten around me. My spirit took
a long time to settle. I breathed in the wind from the moon.

The bar was silent. Then I heard someone chuckling. And then
the person began to talk. I listened. It became clear that the person
was alone, talking to themselves. The pain left my ankle for a moment
and I went, limping, into the bar. Parting the curtains, I stood in
darkness. The bar was empty. There was a single lamp shining
behind the counter. I made out the form of a head bent over, of a
person rapt in a secret ritual. I went over noiselessly, limping, the
pain returning and receding in waves. The clientele had gone and the
silence of the bar was unnatural at that hour. I tiptoed to the counter
and saw Madame Koto counting money. She was so engrossed in the
counting that she didn't notice my entry. Her face shone and sweat
ran down from her hairline, down her cheeks and ears, down her
neck, into her great yellow blouse. She would count a bundle of
notes and then laugh. It was a strange kind of laughter. It sounded
like vengeance. I didn't want to speak suddenly and frighten her and
yet I found her concentration fascinating and could not take my eyes
off her. She counted her money over and over again as if she had just
woken from the nightmare of poverty. She counted her fingers, the
sums were clearly giving her problems. Then the wind blew hard

outside, fluttering the curtain, and flickering the illumination of her lamp. She looked up, saw me, her eyes widening. Suddenly, she screamed. She jumped and threw her hands up and her money went flying everywhere, the coins clattering on the floor. I said:

'It's me, Azaro.'

She stopped and for a long moment peered at me. Then her face darkened and she sped round the counter and grabbed me by the neck and slapped me on the head.

'Why did you stand there like a thief?'

'I am not a thief.'

'So why did you stand there?'

'Nothing.'

'Why did you stand there eyeing my money?'

'I wasn't eyeing your money.'

'Where have you been?'

'In the bush.'

'Doing what?'

'Playing.'

'With whom?'

'Myself.'

'With thieves?'

'I don't know any thieves.'

She let me go. She hurried round the counter and picked up all her money and tied it in a bundle at one end of her wrapper.

'The next time you do that I will have a cutlass.'

I said nothing. She found her theme.

'Things are going to start to change, you hear? You think this bar will stay like this for ever? You think I am going to be doing everything alone? No! Soon I am going to get some young girls to serve for me. I am going to get one or two men to carry heavy things and run messages. You are too much trouble. You don't respect the customers. You create trouble for me. What do you do here anyway, eh? You just come in here and sleep and drink all my peppersoup for nothing. You are useless, you hear?'

I stayed silent, but I got up and went and sat at a bench near the front door. It was the farthest I could go from her while still being in the bar. I sat in the darkness, she stayed in the light. And because the lamp was on a stool below the counter her face, bright in patches, looked big and ugly. For the first time I began to dislike her. From where she stood her eyes seemed oddly deranged, somewhat crossed. It was only a trick of the light, but that didn't stop it from feeding my growing distrust of her. She had changed completely from the person I used to know. Her big frame which had seemed to me full of warmth now seemed to me full of wickedness. I didn't know why she had changed.

She sat down. Her eyes were bright with a hungry new ferocity. She stared at me in the darkness and I knew she couldn't see me clearly.

'You think because I sit here all day long, because I cook peppersoup and wash plates and clean the tables and smile to my customers, you think because I do all these things that I don't have plans of my own, eh? You think I don't want to build a house, to drive a car, you think I don't want servants, you think I don't want money and power, eh? I want respect. I am not going to run a bar for ever. As you see me – now I am here, tomorrow I am gone. You think I want to live in this dirty area with no electricity, no toilets, no drinking water? If you think so you are mad! You are a small boy and you don't know anything. Your people are not serious. You can sit in a corner like a chicken and look at me, but when the time comes you will remember what I am saying.'

I didn't understand a word of what she said. I understood the expression on her face. When she had finished her speech her mouth was curled in contempt, as if she had profoundly demeaned herself by talking to me at all. She made a noise of derision. She got up, took the lantern with her, and went out to the backyard. The darkness in the bar became complete. I heard something moving near the earthenware pot. I heard something scurrying up the walls. The wind rustled the curtain and blew through the bar and flapped the edges of the almanacs. The night, descending with the wind, brought the smells of stale palm-wine, dead flies, cobwebs, wood, kerosine, and old food. And above all these was the smell of the night itself, like the aroma of the earth just before a storm.

In the darkness things merged into one another. The tables were like crouching animals. Benches were like human beings sleeping on air. A solid wind blew the curtains. A more concrete darkness came into the bar. It was a man. He had a cigarette. Before I smelt its smoke, I smelt dried mud, the sweat of exhaustion, and frustration, and heard the creaks distributed over his body as he moved.

'Father!' I said.

He lit a match. His eyes were not bright and his face was tired.

'What are you doing there, sitting in the darkness?'

'Nothing.'

The match went out and he fumbled along the benches and sat next to me. He smelt of overwork, sadness, and ash. He put an arm round me and the smell of his armpit overwhelmed me.

'What are you doing here?' he whispered.

'Nothing,' I whispered back.

We continued in low tones.

'Where is Madame Koto?'

'In the backyard.'

'What is she doing?'

'I don't know. But she was counting her money.'

'Counting her money?'

'Yes.'

'How much?'

'I don't know. A lot. Bundles.'

'Bundles of money?'

'Yes.'

'Did she give you any?'

'No.'

'You think if I try to borrow from her she will give me?'

'No.'

'Why not?'

'She has become wicked.'

'How come?'

'I don't know.'

'So why are you sitting here?'

'She's getting some girls and men to become servants.'

'Is that so?'

'Yes.'

Outside, the wind sighed. Dad scratched his bristles. Madame Koto came in through the backyard door.

'Who is there?' she asked gruffly.

'Me,' I said.

'I know. But who else is there?'

Dad was silent.

'Don't you have a voice?'

'It's me,' Dad said.

'Who is "me"?' came Madame Koto, in a louder voice.

'Azaro's father.'

There was another silence.

'Oh, Azaro's father,' Madame Koto said eventually, in an un-enthusiastic tone. 'So how are you, eh? Let me go and get a lamp. You want some palm-wine? I will get you some.'

She didn't move. We were silent. And then suddenly I could see her. I saw her clearly framed in a dull yellow light. The light billowed gently around her as if her skin were on fire. And then I saw her become two. The yellow light remained. But her heavier form went out of the bar. I heard her outside; but the light, billowing slowly, changing colour, sometimes gently and sometimes violently, remained where she had been standing.

'Can you see it, Dad?'

'See what?'

'That light.'

'What light?'

'The yellow light.'

'Where?'

Madame Koto came back into the bar bearing a lantern in front of her. The light of the lantern dispersed the yellow billowing light. Madame Koto came over to us. She put the lantern on the table and stared at us as if we were complete strangers.

'So how is business?' Dad asked politely.

'We are managing,' she replied. 'Your son will tell you.'

She stared at me suspiciously. Then she put the gourd of wine on the table. The bump formed by the bundle of money in her wrapper was gone. She went out again and returned with two yellow plastic cups. The cups were new to me.

'Thank you, Madame,' Dad said somewhat energetically. 'May God enable you to prosper and give you health and happiness.'

The theatricality of his prayer took us aback.

'Amen,' Madame Koto intoned, eyeing us suspiciously.

She went and sat behind her counter, a formidable figure, a solid mass of vigilance.

Dad poured palm-wine for us both. He lit a cigarette and smoked. I drank and Dad fidgeted. I became aware that Dad couldn't quite bring himself to ask Madame Koto for money. He sat beside me, wracked by dignity. Humiliation showed on his face. He drank the palm-wine as if it were a kind of necessary poison.

We stayed like that till noises sounded from the street. The noises approached: men singing, beating rhythms on glass, chanting drunkenly. Madame Koto's face brightened. With eager eyes, she got up and hurried out and put lanterns on the tables. Then a man with a scar on his forehead burst into the bar and, arms wide apart, cried:

'We are here!'

The rest of them came in, noisily chanting Madame Koto's name. One of them had a walking stick. Madame Koto came to welcome them and showed them their benches and wiped the long table and generally fussed over them. They sat, singing and chanting, till they saw us in the corner. Then they became silent.

Madame Koto, coming in with drinks and bowls, noticed their silence. She tried to cheer them up and kept looking at us as though wanting us to leave. The men drank silently. Then the man with the scar on his forehead called Madame Koto over and they talked in whispers. He kept looking over at us during the pauses. It became clear that they were silent because of our presence. Madame Koto, after the whispering between them was over, nodded, started to come over to us, changed her mind, and went and stood by the counter. I suddenly felt I was in the midst of a secret society. Madame Koto, in a gentler voice, said:

'Azaro, it's time for you to go and sleep.'

'Yes, what is a small boy doing up at this time anyway?' asked one of the men.

'That's how children are spoilt,' said another.

'Then they become thieves and steal from their fathers.'

Dad was steadily getting drunk. I could feel him clenching and unclenching his fists. He worked his jaws, creaked, fidgeted and, after the last of the men had spoken, rising late to the challenge, he said:

'He's my son! And he is not a thief!'

There was a long silence. Madame Koto went and sat behind her counter and hid her face in the shadows. One of the men laughed. It was a high-pitched laughter that would have sounded more appropriate if it had come from a horse. His laughter was cut short when the man with the scar said:

'We don't want any trouble.'

'Then why abuse my son?'

'All we want is to hold a meeting here and we don't want the boy around.'

'The boy goes when I go.'

Madame Koto came round the counter.

'I want no trouble in my bar,' she announced.

She began putting the benches face-down on the empty tables. When she had finished she went outside.

'If you don't want trouble then both of you should go.'

'No!' Dad shouted, downing a cup of palm-wine and slamming it on the table.

The men were silent.

'Which party do you support?' one of them asked, in a reasonable tone of voice.

'None of your business.'

'It is our business.'

'Well, I don't support your party.'

'Why not?'

'Because it is a party of thieves.'

One of the men immediately shouted for Madame Koto. She came in, hands on her hips.

'What?'

'Tell this man and his son to go.'

'I want no trouble.'

'Well you have to choose between them and us. If you don't tell him to go we will take our custom somewhere else.'

'I don't want trouble. If you want to hold your meeting, hold it. They will go. Everything can be done peacefully.'

'We want to hold our meeting now.'

Madame Koto looked at them and then at us.

'Because you people have money you think you can prevent a poor man from drinking, eh?' Dad said, spluttering.

'Yes, we can.'

'Okay, come and do it. Let me see you.'

'Are you challenging us?'

'Yes.'

Three of the men stood up at once. They were huge. Each of them was a colossus. They came round and towered over our table. I held Dad's arm.

'You want to fight in here and scatter the madame's bar?' Dad asked coolly.

He was actually sweating and his voice quivered slightly.

'Come outside then,' one of the colossi said.

'First I have to finish my palm-wine. I don't fight till I am drunk.'

'You are a drunkard!'

Dad drank slowly, deliberately. His arm trembled and I could feel the bench vibrating beneath me. The men hung over us, waiting patiently. Madame Koto did not speak, did not move. The other

255

men went on drinking at their table. Dad poured out the last drop of palm-wine into the yellow plastic cup.

'Dregs,' he said. 'You are dregs! Now I am ready.'

He stood up and cracked his knuckles. The men were unimpressed. They went outside.

'Go home!' Dad commanded me. 'I will deal with these goats alone.'

His eyes were bold and bloodshot. He went to the door and stood between the curtain strips. He spat outside.

'Come on!'

I stood up. Dad went out without a backward glance. I followed. I couldn't see the three men. As soon as we were outside the door was shut quickly and bolted. Dad looked for the men and couldn't find them. I helped him look. The bushes moved in the wind. An owl hooted deep in the forest. I went to the backyard and found the back door also bolted.

'They are cowards,' Dad said.

We heard them inside the bar, laughing and shouting. Their revelry increased and, because they spoke in alien tongues, I couldn't make out what they were saying. Dad stood around, undecided. Then they fell silent in the bar. They talked in whispers.

'Let's go home,' Dad said, leading the way.

I trailed behind him, my ankle hurting again. He strode down the street. I hobbled. He didn't look back once.

TWELVE

WHEN WE GOT home Mum was still discovering more dead rats. The room stank of their deaths. Mum had swept them into a corner and was ransacking the place. Some of them had died baring their teeth.

'That photographer's poison has killed more than fifty-two rats,' Mum said as we came in, 'and I can smell more.'

Dad sat in his three-legged chair and with unusual solemnity lit a cigarette. His hands were still trembling.

'I nearly fought some giants,' he said.

'We should move away from this area,' Mum replied somewhat absent-mindedly.

'I would have killed them.'

'Let's go. An evil thing will happen to us if we don't move away.'

'Nothing evil will happen to us. I won't let them drive us away.'

'How are we going to pay the new rent?'

'We will manage.'

'I smell an evil thing.'

'It's the rats.'

'I dreamt I saw you by the roadside.'

'Doing what?'

'Lying down. You didn't move. There was blood on your head. I talked to you, my husband, and you wouldn't answer. I tried to carry you, but you were heavy as a lorry. I went to get help and when I came back you had vanished.'

Dad was silent. I could hear him trying to find a way into the dream. Then he noticed me.

'Go to sleep, Azaro. You shouldn't listen when grown-ups are talking.'

I got the mat, cleared the centre table out of the way, spread the mat, and lay down. Dad smoked with greater intensity. Mum said:

'We will have to cut down the food if we are going to afford the rent.'

'Don't cut down the food.'

'We will have to sleep on empty stomachs. Starting from tonight.'

'Nonsense!' Dad said, trying to control his temper. 'Serve our food. Now!'

I shut my eyes. The mention of food made me very hungry. Mum was silent. Then I heard her among the plates. I heard the plates on the table and smelt the good cooking, the stew and the fried plantain. I opened my eyes. There was a big bowl of eba and a bowl of watery soup, with a modest quantity of meat. We ate silently, avoiding one another's eyes. After eating Dad lit another cigarette. Mum went out to wash the plates and bring in the clothes that had dried on the lines. I lay down. Mum returned and we stayed up in silence, not looking at one another, for a long time. Then Mum sighed and stretched out on the bed and faced the wall. Soon she was asleep. The candle burned low. Dad sat unmoving, his eyes hard. The candle went out.

'Tell me a story, Dad,' I said.

He stayed quiet and I thought he had vanished. Then he too sighed. He moved. The chair creaked. Outside, a dog barked. An owl hooted. A bird cawed like a hyena. The wind stirred and faintly rattled the broken window.

'Once upon a time,' Dad began suddenly, 'there was a giant whom they called the King of the Road. His legs were longer than the tallest tree and his head was mightier than great rocks. He could see an ant. When he drank, a stream would empty. When he pissed, a bad well would appear. He used to be one of the terrible monsters of the Forest and there were many like him, competing for strange things to eat. When the Forest started to get smaller because of Man, when the giant couldn't find enough animals to eat, he changed from the forest to the roads that men travel.'

Dad paused. Then he continued.

'The King of the Road had a huge stomach and nothing he ate satisfied him. So he was always hungry. Anyone who wanted to travel on the road had to leave him a sacrifice or he would not allow them to pass. Sometimes he would even eat them up. He had the power to be in a hundred places at the same time. He never slept because of his hunger. When anyone set out in the morning he was always there, waiting for his sacrifice. Anyone who forgot the monster's existence sooner or later got eaten up.

'For a long time people gave him sacrifices and he allowed them to travel on the roads. The people did not grumble because they found him there when they came into the world. No one knew if he had a wife or not. No one even knew whether he was a man or a woman. He had no children. People believed that he had lived for thousands of years and that nothing could kill him and that he could never die. And so human beings, because they were afraid of him, fed him for a long time. And because of him, and partly because of other things, a famine started in the world. There was no water. The streams dried up. The wells became poisonous. The crops wouldn't grow. Animals became lean. And people began to die of hunger. And because they were dying of hunger they stopped giving sacrifices to the King of the Road. He became angry and attacked people's houses and caused a lot of people to perish while travelling and he ate the living as well as the corpses of those who had died of hunger.

'It got to a point where all the people in the world couldn't bear it any more and they gathered together to decide what they should do to the King of the Road. Some people said they should find a way to kill him. But others said that they should first go and reason with him. Those who wanted to reason won the vote. So they sent out a delegation of people.

'They set out early one morning. They had a great mound of sacrifices which they carried in several bags and carts, bush animals, corn, yams, cassava, rice, kola-nuts, enough food in fact to feed a whole village. It was a great sacrifice. They travelled for a long time. They kept expecting the King of the Road to appear, but he didn't. They waited for many more days. And when he didn't appear they thought that he had somehow vanished or died and they began to celebrate and after their celebration they hurried back to the gathering with the great sacrifice. When they had forgotten about him, on their way back, while they were telling stories, the King of the Road appeared to them. He was very lean. He could barely talk. He was dying of hunger. He caught them and asked if they had any sacrifice for him. His voice was weak and he was thirsty because he had not drunk enough water for a long time. The people showed him what they had brought. He ate it all in one mouthful. He asked for more. He groaned and rolled and complained that what they had brought was so small it had made his hunger worse. The people said that was all they had. So the King of the Road ate the delegation.'

Dad paused.

'Get me some water,' he said after a while. 'This story is making me thirsty.'

259

Dad had been performing the story in the dark. I quickly fetched him some water. He drank. He breathed a sigh of pleasure. He continued.

'The rest of the world waited for the return of the people they had sent. They waited for seven years. Then they sent another delegation. The same thing happened. Then they decided to kill the King of the Road.'

Dad paused again and lit another cigarette.

'All the chiefs and princes and kings and queens in the world sent out messages to their people asking them to gather all the poison they could find. They gathered all the poisons and piled them up and transported them to where the great meeting was held. While the different people travelled with the poison some of it spilled over and that is why some plants can kill and why there are places in the forest where nothing ever grows.

'They gathered all the poisons from all the four corners of the earth and made a mighty dish with them. In the dish there were hundreds of fishes, roasted bush meat, yams, and cassava. The cooks made sure that the dish was tasty. The food was so much that it took more than one hundred people to carry all of it. They travelled for a long time till the King of the Road, who was by now sick with hunger, caught them. He asked what they had brought for him as sacrifice and complained bitterly about how the first two delegations were happy when they thought he was dead and about what he did to them. The leader of the delegation showed him the wonderful food they had brought him and said that they wished him long life. But the King of the Road was so angry with human beings for starving him that he ate half the number of people who went on that journey. Then he sat down and devoured the great dish.

'He ate all of it and his eyes began to swell because it made him even hungrier than he was before. The more he ate, the hungrier he became. So he ate the rest of the delegation. Only one person escaped. And that person was our great-great-great-grandfather. He knew the secret of making himself invisible. He was the one who came back and told the world what had happened after the King of the Road had eaten up the entire delegation.

'What happened was that, after his unsatisfactory meal, the King of the Road lay down to rest. And then suddenly his stomach started to hurt him and he became so terribly hungry that he ate everything in sight. He ate the trees, the bushes, the rocks, the sand, and he even tried to eat the earth. Then the strangest thing happened. He began to eat himself. He ate his legs, and his hands, and his shoulders, and his back, and his neck, and he ate his head. He ate himself till only his stomach remained. That night a terrible rain fell and the rain melted the stomach of the King of the Road. Our great-great-great-grandfather said that it rained for seven days and when it stopped raining the stomach had disappeared, but he could hear the King of the Road growling from under the ground. What had happened was that the King of the Road had become part of all the roads in this world. He is still hungry, and he will always be hungry. That is why there are so many accidents in the world.

'And to this day some people still put a small amount of food on the road before they travel, so that the King of the Road will eat their sacrifice and let them travel safely. But some of our wise people say that there are other reasons. Some say people make sacrifices to the road to remember that the monster is still there and that he can rise at any time and start to eat up human beings again. Others say that it is a form of prayer that his type should never come back again to terrify our lives. That is why a small boy like you must be very careful how you wander about in this world.'

When he finished the story Dad stayed silent for a long time. I didn't move. Then suddenly he got up and went to bed. I couldn't sleep. I kept seeing vivid colours, kept seeing intimations of the King of the Road, lying in state, eternally hungry, beneath the streets and beaten tracks and highways of the world. I stayed tossing, my mind very active and awake, till I noticed for the first time the silence of the room, the absence of the rats. Dad must have noticed the same thing for he said:

'Go and throw out some dead rats for the road to eat.'

I was scared, but I swept out under the cupboard and found two more corpses of rats. I brushed them into a dust pan, hurried out, and threw them into the mouth of the darkness. As I hurried back in I fancied that I saw the King of the Road eating the dead rats and enjoying them. When I got back in Dad was already snoring.

I was floating in the dark, on a wind perfumed with incense. I was staring into the simple eyes of the boy-king who had the smile of a god. I heard the wind tapping on our door. It tapped a code which I understood. I lit a candle. It was the photographer. He was dressed in a brilliant blue agbada. He wasn't crouching. He seemed to have lost his fear. He was not as buoyant as the last time I saw him, but he looked healthier. He came in and took off his agbada top and I

saw he had a silver-plated cross round his neck. He sat on the mat,
cross-legged.

'I am leaving tomorrow morning,' he said.

'Where are you going to go?'

'I am going to travel all the roads of the world.'

'And do what?'

'Take photographs of the interesting things I see.'

'Be careful of the King.'

'The King will die.'

'The King never dies.'

'How do you know?'

'Dad said so.'

'I am not afraid of the King.'

'The King is worse than thugs, you know. He is always hungry.'

'What King?'

'The King of the Road.'

He looked puzzled.

'Okay,' he said finally, 'I will be careful.'

There was a moment's silence.

'Where have you been?'

'Hiding.'

'Where?'

'In my camera.'

'How?'

'Travelling on the back of the silver light.'

'Doing what?'

'Visiting other continents. Flying round the universe. Seeing what
men and women do. Taking photographs.'

'What will happen to your glass thing?'

'I will leave it.'

'So you won't display your pictures any more?'

'Not here in this street. But I will display them to the whole world.'

'How?'

'By magic.'

'How?'

'You ask too many questions.'

I fell silent.

'Your poison killed all the rats,' I said.

'I told you it was good.'

'Will you give me some?'

'Why?'

'In case the rats come back to wage war on us.'

He thought about it.

'I will leave some for your mother.'

We were silent again. Then he asked if there was any food. I soaked some garri for him, which he ate with dried fish. Then I noticed a bowl of fried plantain and stew which Mum had put aside and I gave it to him. After he had eaten he opened the case of his camera and brought out a bundle of fine-smelling pictures. He looked through them and gave them to me. There were pictures of a fishing festival, of people on the Day of Masquerades. The Egunguns were bizarre, fantastic, and big; some were very ugly; others were beautiful like those maidens of the sea who wear an eternal smile of riddles; in some of the pictures the men had whips and were lashing at one another. There were images of a great riot. Students and wild men and angry women were throwing stones at vans. There were others of market women running, of white people sitting on an expanse of luxurious beaches, under big umbrellas, with black men serving them drinks; pictures of a child on a crying mother's back; of a house burning; of a funeral; of a party, with people dancing, women's skirts lifted, baring lovely thighs. And then I came upon the strangest photograph of them all, which the photographer said he had got from another planet. It was of a man hanging by his neck from a tree. I couldn't see the rope that he hung from. A white bird was settling on his head and was in a blurred attitude of landing when the photograph was taken. The man's face was strange, almost familiar. His eyes were bursting open, they were wide open, as if he had seen too much; his mouth was twisted, his legs were crossed and crooked.

'What happened to him?'

'They hanged him.'

'Is he dead?'

'Yes.'

'What happened?'

'They hanged him.'

'Who?'

'Across the seas.'

'The seas hanged him?'

'No. Another continent.'

'A continent hanged him?'

'No.'

'What?'

'They.'

'Who?'

He paused. I was confused.

'Some white people.'

I didn't understand. He took the picture from me and put it back amongst the others.

'Why?'

'You're too young to hear all this.'

I became more interested.

'Why?'

'Why what?'

'Why did they hang him?'

He was silent. I thought for a moment.

'Is it because of the white bird?'

'What white bird? Oh, that one. No.'

'Why?'

He was silent again. Then he said:

'Because they don't like piano music.'

I could see he wanted to change the subject. He put the pictures back in the case. His eyes were different. His voice had changed when he said:

'Eight of the people I took pictures of are now dead. When I look at the pictures of dead people something sings in my head. Like mad birds. I shouldn't be talking to you like this. You are a small boy.'

He stretched out on the mat. That was when I noticed that he smelt of a sweet perfume, a curious incense. I asked him about it.

'For protection,' he said. 'Protection from my enemies.'

'I smelt it before you knocked on the door,' I said.

He smiled. He seemed pleased with his charm's efficacy. He lay very quiet and after a while I thought he was asleep. I wanted to hear him talk.

'Tell me a story,' I said.

'Blow out the candle and sleep.'

'Tell me a story first and then I will sleep.'

'If I tell you a story you won't be able to sleep.'

'Why not?'

He got up and blew out the candle. The room was quiet. I could hear him breathing.

'It's a hard life,' he said.

'That's what the rats used to say.'

'What do rats know about life,' he said.

'Why is it hard?' I asked.

He was quiet.

'Go to sleep.'

'Why?'

'If you wait till the sunbird starts to sing you won't be able to sleep.'

'Will you come and visit us?'

'Every day.'

I knew he was lying. That was when I knew we wouldn't be seeing him for a long time. It even occurred to me that we might never see him again. But his lie made me less anxious. I was going to ask him to promise that he would come and see us often, but he started grinding his teeth. I lay awake hoping that he would suddenly resume talking, the way he did when he was drunk. He did start to talk, but he was talking in his sleep, and I couldn't make out what fantastical things he was saying. Then he turned, and he kicked, and his teeth-grinding lessened, and his speech quietened. He had convinced me. I would miss him.

In the morning he was gone. I felt sad he wasn't there. He had taken pictures of everyone except himself. And after a while I forgot what he looked like. I remembered him only as a glass cabinet and a flashing camera. The only name I had for him was Photographer. He left a written message to Dad to say he was leaving and to thank us for our help. Dad was pleased with the letter and on some happy nights we sat up and talked about many things and many people, but we were fondest of the photographer. And it was because of our fondness that I was sure that some day we would see him again.

Book Four

ONE

MADAME KOTO GREW distant. Her frame became bigger. Her voice became arrogant. She wore a lot of bangles and necklaces and seemed weighed down by the sheer quantity of decoration she carried on her body. She walked slowly, like one who has recently acquired power. Her face had taken on a new seriousness, and her eyes were harder than ever. I didn't go to Madame Koto's bar so much any more.

Dad spoke badly of her, though at first he did not prevent me going to sit in her bar. I would sit there amongst the flies which increased with the customers. When the thugs came in I would slip out and wander. Afterwards I would play in front of our house.

On some afternoons, after the first visitation of the thugs, it seemed that nothing ever happened in the world. In the mornings Mum went hawking. On some evenings she returned early. She often had a vacant look on her face, as though the market had disappeared.

In the afternoons the heat was humid. The shadows were sharp as knives. And the air was still. The boiling air made even the birdcalls sound like something heard in a stifling dream. The sweat of those afternoons became vapours in the brain. It became possible to sleep with eyes wide open. It was so hot that sleepwalking seemed natural. Time did not move at all.

I would sit on the platform in front of our house and watch the rubbish along the roadside reduced to crust by the flies and the sun. A flock of egrets, flying past overhead, always made the children jump up and down in the street, singing:

> 'Leke Leke
> Give me one
> White finger.'

The children would flap their fingers, palms-down, to the flight of the birds. When the birds had gone, white dots in golden-furnace sky, the children would look at their fingernails and find one or two of them miraculously speckled with whiteness.

Time moved slower than the hot air. In the distance, from the forest, came the unending crack of axes on trees. The sound became as familiar as the woodpeckers or the drumming of rain on cocoyam leaves. The noise of machines also became familiar, drilling an insistent beat on the sleep-inducing afternoons.

Sometimes it seemed that the world had stopped moving and the sun would never set. Sometimes it seemed that the brightness of the sun burned people out of reality. I sat one afternoon thinking about the photographer when I saw a boy running down the street, his shorts tattered, his shirt flapping, and he was chasing the metal rim of a bicycle wheel. Three men were behind him, also running. But as he passed the van a terrible light, like the momentous flash of a giant camera, appeared in the sky, blinding me with its brilliance, and I saw the boy's shadow vanish. I shut my eyes. Luminous colours, like the flames of alcohol, danced in my eyelids. I opened my eyes and saw the metal rim rolling along by itself. The boy had become his own shadow. The three men ran past the metal rim. The boy's shadow melted and the rim rolled over and fell near the gutter. I screamed. A dog barked. I hurried over and picked up the bicycle rim and went to the burnt van and looked all around and I couldn't find the boy anywhere. I asked the traders at their stalls if they had seen the boy and they replied that they hadn't seen anything unusual. I threw the rim on to the back of the burnt van, now bulging with rubbish, and sat in front of our compound, puzzled, annoyed.

That evening I heard that an old man who lived near us had been staring at a lizard, while drinking ogogoro in the afternoon heat, when a flaming-yellow angel flew past his face and blinded him. I did not believe the story.

TWO

THEN ONE AFTERNOON time moved and something happened in the world. I had been sleeping on the cement platform and when I woke the photographer's glass cabinet was gone. Someone had set fire to the rubbish on the back of the burnt van. The rubbish crackled with flames, the smoke was black and awful, and through the afternoon the street stank of smouldering rubber and burning rats.

It was impossible to escape the thick smoke, which formed a haze on the hot unmoving air, and it was impossible to avoid the pungency of the smells, which were harsh on the lining of the throat. So I began to wander. There was music and dancing at Madame Koto's bar. The place was packed with complete strangers. Madame Koto was singing joyfully above the loud voices and the vigorous revelry. The bar stank of cheap perfume and sweat and spilt palm-wine and trapped heat. The benches and tables had been moved. Paper handkerchiefs were soggy on the floor. Bones and cigarette stubs were all over the place. I looked for Madame Koto but all I saw were men in bright hats, women in phoney lace, waving white handkerchiefs in the air, dancing and stamping to high-life music. The men, covered in sweat, so that it seemed they had just emerged from steaming rivers, had bits of foam at the sides of their mouths. The armpits and the backs of the women's dresses were wet. I couldn't see where the music was coming from.

It seemed that I had walked into the wrong bar, had stepped into another reality on the edge of the forest. On the floor there were eaten bits of chicken and squashed jollof rice on paper plates. The walls were full of almanacs with severe faces, bearded faces, mildly squinted eyes, pictures which suggested terrible ritual societies and secret cabals. There were odd-looking calendars with goats in transformations into human beings, fishes with heads of birds, birds with the bodies of women. Sometimes the dancing got so frenzied that a couple, crushed against the walls, would bring down some of the calendars, and would themselves sink to the ground.

Everyone danced in a curious heat. A woman grabbed my hands. I noticed a female midget near the counter, staring at me. A man danced on my toes. I looked up and the midget was gone. It was very hot. I poured sweat. The woman made me dance with her. She drew me to her and my face pressed against her groin and an intoxicating smell staggered me like a new kind of dangerous wine. The woman held my face to her and danced slowly to the music while I suffocated in an old fever that sent a radiant fire bounding through my blood. The woman laughed and pushed me away and drew me to her again with a curious passion and I felt myself lifting from the ground, feet still on the ground, head swirling, a spasm seizing me, and still lifting, till I was almost flying, someone squirted palm-wine on my face, and I collapsed amongst the dancing feet in an excruciating pleasure. The woman made me get up. The world swayed; my eyes became a little drowsy; the woman turned me round, and laughed again, and danced with me, shaking her hips. The palm-wine ran down my face, down my neck, joined with the stickiness of my sweat, and mingled with the pleasurable weakness in my legs. The music and the flies buzzed around my face. Then a thick-set man, who had come between me and the woman, took one look down at me, and very loudly, so that no one could possibly miss it, said:

'Watch your women-o! There's a small boy here who wants to fuck!'

The women burst out laughing. Their large hungry eyes sought me out. I fled into the crowd and hid my embarrassment behind the counter.

That was when I located the source of the music. On the counter was an evil-looking instrument with a metal funnel that would have delighted the imagination of wizards. There was a disc which kept turning, a handle cranked round by a spirit, a long piece of metal with a needle on the whirling disc, and music coming out of the funnel without anyone singing into it. It seemed a perfect instrument for the celebration of the dead, for the dances of light spirits and fine witches. I fled for a second time, fled from the inhuman thing, and fell backwards, tripping. A woman in a red gown caught me.

The twang of an unnatural instrument raged through my head. Someone gave me a cup of palm-wine. I gulped it down. They filled my cup and I drank it all again. The woman who had caught me had a face crinkled in rolls of fat. Foams of sweat clung to her hairline. The music was full of hunger, yearnings, and the woman danced as if she were praying to a new god of the good life. Her eyes were dark with shadows, her lips red as blood, and she had white coral beads round her neck. Her face was crowded with laughter. She twirled me in an odd dance. Another man caught me, and twirled me on. I became dizzy. Flies did somersaults in my eyes. I became lost in the curious jungle of the crowd, lost in the midst of giants.

The bar seemed to keep expanding. The density of bodies got worse. I was a little comforted when I saw the woman in the red gown again. She was dancing with a fat man who seemed to have power. He thrust himself towards her, crushing her groin in the sensual yearning heat of the music. Then I saw through her changed appearance. When I stopped being deceived by her hair – which was different, as though a god had refashioned it in her sleep – and when I saw through all the make-up, and managed to brush past the distractions of her strong perfume, I was amazed to find that I was staring at Madame Koto. She was amused at my astonishment. She gave me a blue plastic cup of palm-wine. A dead fly floated on its froth. I blew the fly away, and drank. The bar gyrated.

'Madame Koto!' I cried.

She burst out laughing. The man she was dancing with swept her away into the music of celebration, into the tight-jammed bodies.

Then the bar took on a sinister light. I saw its other sides, felt its secret moods. The men and women seemed like better versions of the spirits who used to come here, and who had tried to steal me away. They had a greater mastery of the secrets of human disguise. I heard their metallic voices and the laughter of their perfumes, and underneath all the dancing and the energy was the invasion of a rancid smell. The wind blew in and the smell got worse as if it were blowing from a marsh where animals had died.

Then I noticed the women. They had convincing veined hands, their complexions were different on different parts of their bodies, their eyes were hungry, and most of them were lean. They seemed to be enjoying themselves, but their mouths, curled as if in constant repugnance, spoke to me of an infernal unhappiness which I couldn't understand. And, like some of the men, when they laughed their tongues were freckled, or like parchment. Some of their skins glistened as if with scales. I tried to escape from the bar, but couldn't find a way out of the crowding. I drank more wine. Bodies, banging against one another, grew more heated. I could see a man's hand under a table searching between a woman's legs.

Someone hit me on the head as I was staring at the hand.

I turned and saw the midget woman. She was short, with thick thighs, a heavy body, big breasts, and the beautiful and sad face of a twelve-year-old whose mother has just died. She held my hand and led me deeper into the bar, behind the counter, where the instrument sang. She made me sit down with her on a mat of chicken feathers. The midget woman had an unbelievably young face, all made up, and her eyes were the shape of lovely almonds. Then, holding my arm, she spoke to me in a wonderful voice. She made a passionate speech to me saying that she would take me with her and that she would love me for ever. Her eyes became sad. She said that she was certain that I no longer remembered her. My eyeballs began to burn. The music stopped. She was silent, and she lowered her face till the music started again. Then she began pulling my arm, pestering me with words I couldn't understand. I tried to get up, but she held me down. I tried to break into a sudden run, but she grabbed the back of my shorts with muscular arms and pulled me back and dragged me close to her. A heady smell, like charmed perfume and a secret sweating, came from her and dulled my brain. And then, with her face close to mine, her lips full like a woman's, her face small like a girl's, she drew even closer to me and whispered something which I didn't hear. She awaited my reply. I stared at her with incomprehension. Then she repeated what she had said.

'Will you marry me?'

I blinked.

'No,' I replied.

She smiled. Her lips widened, as if they were made of elastic material. Then she threw her head back and startled me with the sudden force of her ironic laughter. Her tongue too was freckled. Instead of teeth she had coral beads. I screamed. She began to weep. I bolted, crashing against the counter, producing an ugly sound from the instrument. I scurried around, saw the door, dashed for it, banged into the red form of Madame Koto, and just about made it outside.

Under the open sky, I stopped to catch my breath. My heart beat fast. My legs were quivering. I was still breathing heavily when I caught a glimpse of Madame Koto coming after me. I ran on; she pursued me in her red gown. She was barefoot and she ran so hard that her hair fell off. Underneath I saw her real hair, patchy in places, and dishevelled. It scared me. She made a determined effort and caught me just before I got to the street. She dragged me back to the bar, laughing and berating me affectionately.

'You keep running away from me,' she said.

274

She had two fresh cuts on her face. They were new scarifications. They were black as if ash had recently been used to stop the bleeding. Her face was different because of the marks.

'You let my wig fall off my head,' she muttered, as she stooped and picked it up.

When we got to the door she pushed me in, blocked the way, and wore her wig. She looked instantly younger.

'This is a party,' she said. 'Go and enjoy yourself. Go and pour drinks for people.'

Then she shut the backyard door behind her. It was rowdier inside. It seemed more people had joined the celebrations. I didn't know which way to turn, for I was crowded on all sides. The noise was louder. I wanted to avoid the midget woman. I looked around for her. She was no longer behind the counter. I pushed my way to all corners of the bar, but I couldn't find her anywhere. I wanted to spot her before she spotted me, so that I could run. I went and stayed near the counter, and planned my escape.

The men danced tightly with the women. Everyone sweated profusely. The women twisted and thrust their hips at the men. Madame Koto reappeared. She wore a different attire, a striped black and white skirt, a yellow blouse. She seemed to have a faint glimmer of gold on her hair. It was a mystery. She fanned herself with a newspaper. Some of the men had taken off their shirts, revealing muscular bodies with long scars. One of the women began yelling. No one paid her any attention. The men were quite drunk. They swayed, instead of dancing, with bloodshot eyes.

One of the women was practically cross-eyed with drunkenness. A man grabbed her round the waist and squeezed her buttocks. She wriggled excitedly. The man proceeded to grind his hips against hers as if he didn't want the slightest space between them. The woman's breasts were wet against her blouse.

Outside, the wind blew hard. The music inside spoke of release from suffering. A ghost appeared amongst the celebrants. The wind blew, the strips of curtain were fanned apart, and a yellow bird flew into the heated space of the bar. Suddenly there was commotion everywhere. The bird flew into the ceiling, rebounded against the wall, fell back dazed, and landed on the woman's hair. The woman screamed. The bird tried to fly away but its claws were caught. Screaming in mortal terror, the woman touched her hair, felt the quivering bird, didn't understand what it was, threw her head forward and shrieked as though a demon had entered her brain.

275

Her terror spread through the bar and people scattered all over the place. They had seen the bird struggling in her hair, and had taken it for a bad sign. Then the woman stopped shrieking. Her eyes were wide open.

'Help me!' she cried.

No one helped her. Madame Koto stood near the door, her hands at her breasts, an exclamatory expression on her face. The woman shook her head, letting out a high-pitched scream which must have scared the poor bird more than anything else, for it beat its wings so vigorously that its feathers came flying off. In a last desperate resort, the woman took off her wig, thrashed it in the air, and sent the bird sailing through the bar. It hit a wall, flew, and dropped in the middle of the dance floor, twitching. There was a moment's pause. People started to rush forward when the bird recovered, took off into the ceiling, bounced down, flew about the tight space, crashed against the counter, and fell first on the trumpet-like loudspeaker of the instrument, and then on the turning disc. The music ground to a feathered halt.

'It's landed on the gramophone!' someone cried.

The bird was still. I knew that this was my moment to escape. Madame Koto rushed to the gramophone, snatched up the bird, held it tight, and hurried out of the bar through the backyard door. The ghost followed her. The celebrants let out a new cry, a quivering cheer, as though the sign after all had been favourable.

I went out after Madame Koto. She was not in the backyard. I went to her room and pressed my ears against her door. From within I discerned a fever of chanting, a bell ringing, the beating of a gong, a soft voice soaring. The bird had become part of her mythology. I left off listening and made my way past the bar. The music had stopped, the voices were silenced. After a while Madame Koto re-emerged. She spoke briefly. The men departed, in a crowd, talking in hushed tones, as of a wondrous event. They had the gramophone with them. They kept looking backwards. The women stayed behind.

THREE

FOR A WHILE I wandered up and down the street, not sure of where to go. The smell of burning rats was still pungent in the air, so I followed the edge of the forest and explored the paths that had completed their transformation into streets. After a long period of wandering I burst into a world I had no idea existed before. The forest there had been conquered. There were stumps of trees, bleeding sap, all around. Workers in yellow helmets milled up and down the place. There were wooden poles jutting from the earth and wires were stretched in the air and trailed in cables on the ground. Children were gathered, watching an unfolding drama. I asked them what was happening and they said the men were connecting electricity. They pointed to the pylons in the wide open spaces. They pointed to the tents. I didn't know what they were talking about so I watched in amazement.

There were tents and lorries all over the area. In one of the tents swung an illuminated bulb. One of the boys stole into the tent with the sole purpose of blowing out the light. Before he could succeed a worker came in, saw him, and chased him out. We waited for the man to do something wonderful with the illumination of the bulb. But instead of doing anything he shut the entrance of the tent. We waited for something unusual to happen. We held our breaths. The tent entrance flapped open. And while we were looking, we saw the man come out again. His colour had changed. We could not believe our eyes. He was now a curious cream colour with blotches of pink. We stared at him in complete astonishment. His hair was like straw, like bright tassels of corn. He walked unsteadily. He wore dark sunglasses, but his eyes were visible beneath them. He wore wide-bottom shorts, a wide-brimmed hat, and a billowing white shirt. And then to crown our astonishment the man whom we thought had changed colour emerged from the tent. We suspected a devilish multiplication had taken place. We ran away, screaming. And came back.

We stared at the white man, expecting him to fly, or to jump, or to somersault. Instead he gave bad-tempered orders in an unfamiliar language. When he spoke the workers jumped and obeyed as if his orders came from the wind. And when he sat down on a folding chair one of the workers brought an umbrella and held it over him. A lizard stopped in front of him, nodding. It stared at him for a long time. In a quick movement, he stamped on the lizard's head and ordered one of the workers to throw its corpse away. We watched him, expecting him to lose his colour, or to dissolve in that blistering air. Another lizard came and nodded in front of him and scuttled round him twice. He stared at us. We stared at him. When he ordered the workers to drive us away, and when they pursued us with sticks and whipped us on the back, I conceived a terrible dislike for that white man. We watched him from a distance. The shade from the umbrella thinned and the sun, burning relentlessly, was unkind to him. I disliked him so much that I spoke to the wind and not long afterwards the air stirred, took on force, made the distant treetops bow, raised dust, and blew away the umbrella from the worker's hand.

The flies pestered him, circling his nose. Red ants formed an army round his chair. Soon he was stamping and scratching his foot. We laughed and he suspected us of some prank and he gave money to some of the workers and pointed at us and they came in our direction, abandoning the cables for a moment, and we scattered and ran, for we were convinced that if we were caught and taken back to the white man he would eat us up. I fled home through the forest and for the rest of that day remained in the safety of our familiar street.

FOUR

WHEN MUM CAME back from hawking that evening I told her about the white man. A light of interest flickered in her eyes. But it died when she said:

'The thugs came again today. Election time is near.'

What I had seen was greater than my empathy at that moment.

'How can a man become two? How can a black man turn white?' Mum asked, with weary interest.

'By magic.'

'What magic?'

Then I told her about the illuminated bulb and the cables and electricity, about how the white man had killed a lizard and how he wanted to catch us and take us away.

'What were you doing there?' she asked.

I didn't say anything. She looked lean and worried. She complained of a headache. She lay on the bed and I noticed that she had a wound that was bleeding just above her ankle. Her blood was unnaturally dark. The wound was beginning to fester. I told her about it, but she didn't stir. The flies tried to settle on it and I drove them away. She opened her eyes and, in a rough voice, said:

'Go and play!'

I lingered at the door. The flies settled on her wound. I watched her foot twitch. She lifted up her head and was about to shout something when I hurried out of the room.

In the street, people were fighting. They fought round the van. The sun turned red. The people who were fighting moved away in opposite directions, shouting threats. The evening darkened. Birds circled in the air. Dust and smoke, like a thin veil, hung in the sky. The wind roamed our street, blowing the rubbish along, and sweeping away the smell of incinerated rats and burnt rubber. Slowly, the stars began to appear.

We waited all night for Dad to return. It seemed our lives kept turning on the same axis of anguish. When Mum had slept enough she dressed her wound with the ash of bitterwood. She showed no signs of pain. She made food, cleaned the room, and counted her money in a tin-can. She calculated her profits without any light in the room. When she finished she began to repair our clothes, sewing on buttons, patching holes in Dad's trousers. She stayed silent and worked with abnormal concentration, her forehead wrinkled, like someone using one action to focus on the pain of waiting. When she had darned Dad's trousers, she began on mine. She tore off the back pockets of my shorts to patch the holes in between the legs. She gave my shirts many different buttons. She would not speak. The light got very dim in the room and I shut the windows to encourage her to use a candle. But she went on working in the absence of light. When she finished, she sighed. She put the clothes on the line in the room. The line was weighted down with a profusion of threadbare towels, old shirts, trousers, wrappers, and sundry rags. It looked ready to snap at any moment. Mum sat down. She was motionless. Then she said:

'Polish your father's boots.'

What she really meant was: 'What has happened to your father?' I searched for his boots and polished them in the dark. Then I put them in a corner and went to wash my hands. When I got back Mum wasn't in the room. I found her sitting on the cement platform at the compound-front. She was waving away the midges and the flying ants and slapping at the mosquitoes that invaded her body. It was night already and the sky was of the deepest blue. The air was cool and it tasted of rain. In the distance, towards the centre of the city, a white light kept flashing towards the sky. Some of the compound people joined us outside and made small talk.

'Is it true', one of them said, 'that Madame Koto now has prostitutes in her bar?'

'That's what I heard.'

'And that she has joined the party?'

'Not just that.'

'What else?'

'They have promised her contracts.'

'For what?'

'For their celebrations and meetings.'

'We will be looking at her and she will become rich.'

'She is rich already.'

'How do you know?'

'People say she is going to buy a car?'

'A car?'

'And get electricity?'

'Electricity?'

'And she paid cash for bales of lace.'

'Bales of lace?'

'To do what?'

'To sew dresses for party people.'

'How did she manage?'

'She knows what she wants.'

'My friend, we all know what we want, but how many of us ever get it?'

'That's true.'

'She must have used witchcraft.'

'Or juju.'

'Or joined a secret society.'

'Or all three.'

'Plus more.'

They fell silent. They contemplated the night, their condition, and the whole area sunken in poverty. One of them sighed.

'Why is life like this, eh?'

'I don't know.'

'Some people have too much and their dogs eat better food than we do, while we suffer and keep quiet until the day we die.'

'And even if we don't keep quiet who will listen to us, eh?'

'God,' one of them said.

The rest of them were silent. The wind blew over us, bringing dust, discarded newspapers, and the certainty of rain.

'One day, by a quiet miracle, God will erase the wicked from the face of the earth.'

'God's time is the best.'

'I wish God's time and our time would sometimes agree.'

'God knows best.'

'That's what my brother kept saying two months before he died.'

'My friend,' one of them said with sudden passion, 'our time will come.'

They fell silent again. Mum moved, started to say something, but stayed quiet. Then she got up, took me by the hand, and we walked down the raw street, towards the main road. She made it seem like an innocent walk, but I could feel the strength of her anxiety.

All around us voices were raised in laughter and in pain. We passed a patch of bushes behind which resonated the singing and the dancing of the new church. They sang with a frightening vigour, with terrifying hope, great need, great sorrow. They made me feel that any minute the world would end. The singing from the church made me afraid of life. We passed them and could hear them long afterwards. Further on, behind a grove of trees, the earth throbbed with more chanting, dancing, singing. But this was different. The chanting was deeper, the dancing more virile, making the earth itself acknowledge the beating on its doors, and the singing was full of secrets and dread-making voices. They sounded like the celebration of an old pain, an ancient suffering that has refused to leave, an old affliction renewed at night. They were the worshippers at the shrine of suffering and we listened to their cries for the secrets of transforming anguish into power. We could hear the incantations, the money-creating howls, the invoked names of destiny-altering deities, gods of vengeance, gods of wealth, womb-opening gods. They too made me afraid of life. They too had come from the hunger, the wretchedness, of our condition. Mum didn't seem to notice them. Her face was ridden with anxiety, her bright eyes searched the street-corners, the barfronts, hoping to see Dad. After we had walked a while, and when the wind lifted the edges of her wrapper, I asked her to tell me a story about white people. She said nothing at first. And then she said:

'I will tell you a story another time.'

We were silent. It seemed she changed her mind.

'When white people first came to our land,' she said, as if she were talking to the wind, 'we had already gone to the moon and all the great stars. In the olden days they used to come and learn from us. My father used to tell me that we taught them how to count. We taught them about the stars. We gave them some of our gods. We shared our knowledge with them. We welcomed them. But they forgot all this. They forgot many things. They forgot that we are all brothers and sisters and that black people are the ancestors of the human race. The second time they came they brought guns. They took our lands, burned our gods, and they carried away many of our people to become slaves across the sea. They are greedy. They want to own the whole world and conquer the sun. Some of them believe they have killed God. Some of them worship machines. They are misusing the powers God gave all of us. They are not all bad. Learn from them, but love the world.'

I was surprised with what Mum said. I was struck by the gentleness of her voice when she spoke next.

'Do you know what my mother said to me in a dream?'

'No.'

'She said there is a reason why the world is round. Beauty will rule the world. Justice will rule the world. That's what she said.'

We went on in silence. I wanted to ask her a lot of questions, but suddenly her mood changed, her intensity increased, and she hurried on, her ears cocked, the wind blowing us on, the night closing round us in the mysteries of its darkness. And then I, too, heard a voice crying out in the distance. It could have come from the thatch houses, the zinc huts, the mud bungalows, the tin-can houses, or from the enigmatic doors of the earth. Mum stopped at a crossing of paths. The wind was hard and the night howled. The whole area seemed to exhale an odour of struggle and death. Dogs fought near a well. And from the darkness, out of one of the obscure paths, emerged a figure in a dazzling white smock, bearing a lantern above her. The brightness of gems was in her eyes, her hair was utterly dishevelled, and if it weren't for her smock I would have taken her for a sort of divine madwoman.

'Repent! Repent!' she cried. 'The light is our life, and our life is in God! The world is full of evil. Repent! Or in your darkness you will be driven out.'

We listened to her piercing voice.

'Stay awake, you weak ones, guard your souls, for evils from Babylon have come to snatch your lives away! Repent! Ask for light and your sleep will be transformed!'

She roused the wind and parted the darkness with her voice and soon we could only see the light of her lantern. And not long afterwards, emerging from the same path, staggering like one who has been a cripple but has now found some strength in his legs, was the figure of a man. He swore and cursed. At once, without even seeing his face, Mum ran over and embraced him. It was Dad. His hair was matted with mud. He wobbled, but insisted on not being helped. His clothes were torn, his chest glistened, his eyes were deranged, and he smelt of blood and drink.

'Thank that woman for me,' he muttered. 'She saved my life. They were going to kill me but she appeared and they thought she was an angel and they ran away screaming.'

We turned, but where there had been the light of the woman's lantern there was only darkness. We could only hear her voice, speaking of a perplexing era to come, sounding from the distance. Her voice quivered on the night air, confusing her precise location. She could have been rattling the doors to our ears from a hundred different places in the living wound of our area.

'If you can't thank her today, thank her tomorrow,' Dad said, in agony.

Against Dad's wishes, Mum held him under the arms and helped him walk. I heard her gasp.

'You are bleeding.'

'They were going to cut my throat. This is just a small wound. Azaro, my son, they were going to kill your father. Because I won't vote for them . . .'

His voice failed him. I held on to his other arm. The darkness filled with people. The night had broadcast our sorrow; the people knew what had happened. The faces, hungry and sweating, peered at us, following us, a long way down the street. They showered encouragements and strengthening proverbs on us. Mum thanked them. One of the women burst out crying. Dad hobbled on, his face screwed into a mask. The wind blew against us. Women sang in our footsteps. When we got home, Mum thanked them again, and they retreated back into the night, and left us to our unhappiness. The rest of the world was asleep.

Mum boiled water and dressed Dad's wounds and pressed his bruises. He told us his story. It was a familiar one. He had been accosted by some men. They were drunk. They asked who he was voting for. He said no one. They set upon him, took his money, were about to do something worse when the woman appeared. They fled. When he finished the story we sat in silence. Mum served food. For the first time in a long while Dad didn't sit up smoking and thinking into the night, rocking on his three-legged chair. He slept promptly after he had eaten.

He woke up the next morning complaining of stomach pains. The sheets had fastened to his wounds, which had bled at night. Mum had to apply warm water. The dried surface of his wounds came off on the sheets. His pain was reopened. He went to work as usual.

FIVE

I REMEMBER THE day distinctly when, on my way back from school, great crashing noises exploded over the forest, as if all the trees had simultaneously fallen. For a moment everything changed. The sky came close to the earth. The air became charged, sharp, and unbreathable. I could not move. Then the air darkened, the noise exploded again, and a bright light flashed over everything. The sky split open. And the path became a clearing.

The world was still, as if it had momentarily become a picture, as if God were The Great Photographer. The clearing turned into a new world. Out of the flash came the sharp outlines of spirits rising into the air with weary heads. And then they fell down and bounced and floated over the stillness of the world. The spirits passed me, passed through me, their eyes like diamonds. And when the next explosion came, followed by another blinding flash, the spirits were obliterated. The heaviness of the air settled, the clouds opened, and the first torrential drenching of the land began.

The clouds dissolved into rain. Water flooded the earth. Suddenly, as if released from a spell, the photographic immobility of everything burst into commotion. The wind cracked the branches of trees. The people raised a great cry. Everyone began to run. Some dashed to clear their clothes from lines. Some ran for cover. And many ran for their buckets, hurrying to put them under the eaves, to collect the purest and most radiant water of the season. The rain released the children from the tedium of the long hot afternoons. They raised a different cry. They ran out naked, bellies protruding, screaming joyfully as the bright water soaked them, foamed their hair, and made their skin shine.

Water was blown into rooms. Mothers cried out for that window to be shut or that door to be locked. Birds and insects vanished. The water, rushing down runnels to the lower regions and the half-dug gutters, soaking fast into the ground and rising quickly above the land, released forever in my memory the mysterious aroma of a new season, of leaves and rustic herbs, wild bark and vegetation, the secret essences of a goddess rising from the earth.

The wind cleared the air of our area's desolation. Caught between the desire to throw off my clothes and run naked into the first rain of the year, or to avoid having my clothes soaked, my books wet, I waited too long. The rain lashed me and I merely stood and watched as the water rose up past my ankles and earthworms crawled up my feet. I brushed them off. It rained with such insistence. The wind whipped the water on my neck so hard that each drop felt like a stone. I feared the heavens would unleash so much water that the earth would become an ocean.

During the harmattan we always forget the rainy season. That's why it rains so viciously on the first day, reminding us with a vengeance of its existence. It poured down so hard that sometimes I couldn't see. I shut my eyes and walked blindly and even then the rain lashed my eyelids. I pushed on at an angle to the path. The downpour was a persistent weight. The force of the wind knocked me sideways and blew me off the ground. The road became slippery. The earth turned fast into mud. When I could see, the street seemed to have vanished. The forest was distorted. The houses quivered.

And then terrible wonders unfolded. Lights flashed three times in a frightening succession. Two birds fell from the branches of a tree, wings vainly fluttering. I heard sheets of zinc crumpling and twisting, heard nails complaining, wood splitting, and then saw the entire rooftop of a house wrenched away and blown across the floodtide in the air. Children howled. Women wailed. It could have been the end of the world. I saw a mud hut disintegrate and turn into clumps. The roof lowered and people came running out. Two doors away a solid bungalow wall collapsed. The roof tilted sideways. Inside was a confusion of household objects and clothes scattered everywhere. At the mouth of our street a house was being carried away on the water, as if its foundations were made of cork. The road became what it used to be, a stream of primeval mud, a river. I waded in the origins of the road till I came to the red bungalow of the old man who was said to have been blinded by an angel. He sat outside in the rain, partly covered in a white shroud. He had a pipe in his mouth. He was staring through the rain, at the watery street, in ferocious concentration. Fascinated by his intensity, by the wavy image of him in the rain, his feet deep in murky waters, his red trousers soaked through, his green eyes clotted, I went closer.

Suddenly he pointed at me, his finger gnarled and wrinkled, like an old thin pepper. And in the voice of nightmares, he said:

'You boy, come here, come and help an old man.'

'To do what?' I asked.

'To see!'

As he pointed at me, his hand quivering, rain pouring from his eyes, changing their colour to purple, a chill climbed my neck, and terror rooted me to the shifting ground. The old man, raging, shouted in a quivering voice that he could see. He got up and took a few quaking footsteps towards me, his face ugly with joy, the white shroud falling from his shoulders. He got quite close to me, but a light flashed, shaking the earth, breaking the old man's spell. I saw him stop, frozen in his gesture. I saw his face collapse, saw his eyes turn back to green. Then he began ranting and cursing the blindness that had come back to him; and with a wind rising against me, awakening goose-pimples all over my body, I shook off my trance and backed away. But the old man tottered after me and fell face down in the mud, and stayed there. I was too scared to do anything, and no one either moved towards him or saw him. I ran in the first direction that my feet carried me.

When I stopped I found myself panting against the wall of an unfinished house. Millipedes and slugs and little snails climbed up the wall. They were knocked down by the wind. Undeterred, they climbed up again. I heard the old man's voice in the rain and I hurried on down the path of origins. The earth kept slipping me. I fell into a ditch. Mud-water got into my eyes and covered my body. When I eventually found solid ground I stood up and looked around and saw a sepia universe full of the swaying statues of giants. There were shrines everywhere and God spoke in the bright wind and the giants spoke back in whispers.

I cried out for help and no one heard. As I stumbled around, walking into nettles, sliding to the ground, bumping into tree-trunks, I realised that I was both lost and blind. I washed out my eyes with rain-water and when some of the mud cleared I found myself at one of the Road Construction sites. The freshly laid tarmac had been swept away. Bushes floated on the water. Road-workers' tents had been blown everywhere and all those who were building the road intended to connect the highway had fled for cover and were nowhere to be seen.

Further on I saw thatch eaves over banana plants. I came to another site of devastation. It was the place where the men had been

287

laying out electric cables. The tents were gone. I saw an umbrella on the branches of a tree. Something had happened. There was smoke in the air. Bushes were blackened. Charred bits of tarpaulin clung to the stumps of trees. The wooden poles were burnt. Workers stood around the cables, staring at them, expecting something dramatic to happen.

The rain and wind forced me on to the forest edge, to the pit where they dredged up sand. The white man stood there with his foot on the log. He wore a thick yellow raincoat and black boots. He was looking through a pair of binoculars at something on the other side of the pit. Suddenly the path turned into a ditch. The earth moved. Floodwaters from the forest poured underneath us. I clung to a stump. The white man shouted, his binoculars flew into the air, and I saw him slide away from view. He slid down slowly into the pit, as a stream of water washed him away. The log moved. The earth gave way in clumps and covered him as he disappeared. I didn't hear his cry. The log rolled over, and a moment's flash completed the hallucination. I began to shout. Workers rushed out of the forest. They rushed down the side of the pit to try and find him. They dug up his helmet, his binoculars, his eyeglasses, a boot, some of his papers, but his body was not found. The pit was half-filled with water. Three workers volunteered to dive in and search for him. They never returned. The pit that had helped create the road had swallowed all of them.

I drifted in the chaos of grief and wind and rain and wavy patterns in the air and I came to a half-familiar fairy-land where a signboard was face-down on the earth. The door was open. Water poured in and drenched the tables and chairs. The place was empty. And then I saw the elephantine figure of an ancient mother, sitting on a bench, with a disconsolate expression on her water-logged face. She caught me before I fell, and she carried me off to her room.

SIX

SHE MADE ME bathe. She fed me steaming peppersoup. She rubbed a grainy ointment all over me and massaged me with her rough fingers. She pulled out the edges of her green mosquito net and made me lie down on the great bed of her body-smells. She smiled at me beyond the netting, her face veiled in green. Then, slowly, she receded till only her smile remained, faintly sinister in the green darkness of my mind.

When I woke up it was raining steadily. Water leaked in through the window and ceiling. The rain distorted my eyes, twisted the sheets of my memory. I was startled by my new surroundings. There were cobwebs on the massive mosquito net. I got out and sat on the edge of the bed. The room stank of freshcut wood, feathers of wild birds, camphor, aromatic plants, and an abundance of garments. There were clothes on every nail and line. There were garments everywhere, cascades of fine lace, white blouses, expensive wrappers with gold-threaded borders, massive skirts, headties, dyed cloths, and gowns that had volume enough for many bedspreads.

White sheets screened off a corner of the room. Outside, the rain drummed on the cocoyam leaves. The screen shimmered with images. All over the room there were disembodied noises, cockroaches in flight, birds flapping their broken wings. Something tapped away, measuring the heartbeat of the rain. Something breathed out an air of mahogany and breathed in silence. I resisted the urge to look behind the screen.

The mysterious smells of rain on earth and plants blew in through cracks in the window. The rain made everything alien. Its persistence altered my vision. After a while it seemed to me that beyond the screen lay a bazaar of mysteries, a subcontinent of the forbidden. I got up and tried to draw aside the white sheet. It was heavy. A cloud of dust wafted from its fabric. Shadows moved in the room. On a wall the form of an enormous sunflower changed into the shape of a bull. Mosquitoes whined. A spider drew itself up on an invisible web. I decided to crawl under the screen. It seemed I was crawling under an impenetrable foliage of whiteness. Dust rose to my face. Cockroaches scuttled at my advance. Newborn rats broke into frightened motion. Ants scattered across my arms as I went into the labyrinths of a stranger's secret life.

When I emerged on the other side I noticed the kaoline-painted floor. Its whiteness stuck to me and wouldn't come off. An earthenware bowl was near the wall. In the bowl were cowries, lobes of kola-nuts, a sprouting bulb of onion, feathers of a yellow bird, ancient coins, a razor, and the teeth of a jaguar. Three bottles stood next to the bowl. In one was pure ogogoro. In another roots marinated in a yellow liquid. In the third were little beings with red eyes in brown water. There was an upturned turtle near the third bottle, its underside painted red, its feet kicking. The turtle made noises. I turned it over. It began to crawl away. I caught it, was surprised how heavy it was, and I turned it on its back again. The turtle stopped making noises. Then I sensed the emanations of an enormous feminine presence and became aware, for the first time, that someone was staring at me from the musty darkness of the chamber.

I could feel the intense gaze of an ancient mother who had been turned into wood. She knew who I was. Her eyes were pitiless in their scrutiny. She knew my destiny in advance. She sat in her cobwebbed niche, a mighty statue in mahogany, powerful with the aroma of fertility. Her large breasts exuded a shameless libidinous potency. A saffron-coloured cloth had been worn round her gentle pregnancy. Behind her dark glasses, she seemed to regard everything with equal serenity. She gave off an air of contradictory dreams. I was mesmerised by the musk of her half-divinity.

I could hear her heart beating. It sounded like an erratic clock. There was a transistor radio near her seat. On the wall behind her was a blue mirror. Just above her head, on a little shelf, was a clock that had stopped working. On a nail, behind her head, was an iron gong and a bell. At her feet were a pair of red shoes. She gave off the accumulated odours of libations, animal blood, kaoline, the irrepressible hopes of strangers, and a yellow impassivity. White beads rested on her lap. The clock made a sudden clicking noise, and I started. She watched me intently. Under her gaze, serenity and intensity were the same thing.

The clock was still. I saw the yellow bird in the shadows behind the ancient mother. It was bound and its feathers kept twitching, its eyes shining in the niche. I became aware of the cobwebs on my face. A fly droned behind me. Then it flew round and settled on the nose of the pregnant goddess. The clock made another noise, startling the fly. The turtle kicked. The bird fretted. I looked at myself in the blue mirror and couldn't see my face. I became afraid. At that moment the ancient mother in wood spoke to me.

She spoke to me through all the objects, through the defiant noises of the upturned turtle, the bird beating against its captivity, the complaints of the fly. The clock began ticking. A lizard scuttled over my foot, and I jumped. When I recovered I found myself pressed against the wall, my heart pounding. Then I noticed that everything in the corner was alive. The bowl moved towards me. The mirror banged itself against the wall, reflecting nothing. I sensed the wall moving, disintegrating beneath my touch. Things crawled in the air. I saw a snail on the wall. I moved away and nearly stepped on the turtle. It was on its feet, behind the bowl. I noticed that there were snails all over the white screen. They were big enough to eat. I staggered against a bucket. Then I realised that there were snails all over the ancient mother, on the face of the mirror, on the edges of the bucket. I didn't know where to turn. My head expanded with the goddess who was speaking to me through the snails and objects in her chamber.

How could I find my way out of the maze of these dreaming objects which were all obstacles before me? How could I escape from the mystery of the head of a snake, its sloughed skin on a newspaper? How could I escape the stones blackened with the tar of new roads, or the single finger pointing at me in a jar of transparent liquid? The goddess in wood spoke to me through all these things, but most of all she spoke to me with her eyes. I didn't understand her speech. Without thinking, like someone wandering around in a stranger's dream, I climbed the body of the goddess and took off her glasses. In the deep hollow of her sockets she had eyes of red stone, precious stones the exact colour of blood. My breathing seized. Her eyes fixed on me with such heat that I hurriedly put her glasses back on. Sweat broke out all over me. I found myself caught in a strange immobility. Then to my greatest horror, she moved – as if she were about to crush me into her pregnancy. I jumped down from her great body and fought my way through the tangle of cloth, screaming.

I sat on the bed. My journey into the secret world changed things

I saw in the room. What I had previously thought of as tumbles of clothes became wigs, shawls, undergarments, coloured headties, batik materials. Dull almanacs of secret societies hung on the walls. Snails inched along the walls, leaving a clean wet trail. In a cupboard there were men's clothes, a black walking stick, and five umbrellas. Above the cupboard was the legend, printed in gothic lettering: GOD'S TIME IS THE BEST. High up on the wall was the image of a crucified Christ and beneath it another legend: THE EVIL THAT MEN DO. There were faded prints of Madame Koto and a man on the walls. The man had only three fingers on one hand. He had a lively face and sad eyes. It was an old picture, browned by sun and time. How could I escape that labyrinth of objects? I went to the bed, lay down under the green netting, and slept in the feverish dreams of the room.

SEVEN

WHEN I AWOKE I felt as if my memory had been wiped clean. The room had changed. Intense shadows brooded on the walls. Futures not yet visible crowded the spaces. Powers not yet active crowded the air. My eyes filled with the shapes of captors, the albumen of unbounded monsters, genies in murky bottles, homunculi in the nests of bats. Unformed beings were everywhere; trapped ghosts and masquerades in unwilling shapes of terror lurked in that forest of shadows. The rain had stopped falling. The wind whipped the zinc roof. I tiptoed out of the room and shut the door behind me. I felt different. I felt as if a wind from the future was blowing through me.

The passage was empty. At the backyard someone had attempted to start a fire with wet wood. The smoke was terrible. Evening had fallen with the rain. The sky was grey. The backyard was full of puddles. With each step I took towards Madame Koto's bar I felt our lives were changing.

There were no lights in the bar. When I went in I thought the place was empty. I moved noiselessly to my place beside the earthenware pot. The front door was partially open. Flies buzzed and I could hear the wall-geckos scuttling between the tables. As I sat I distinguished the outlines of women in the darkness. They sat still, their heads facing the front door. After a while they began to speak.

'When are they bringing our electricity, eh?'

'How should I know?'

'Madame Koto has been talking about it for a long time.'

'She has become a politician.'

'Only promises.'

'And talk.'

'They will bring it.'

'And this bar will shine.'

'And one day it will turn into a hotel.'

293

'But when will they bring the light?'
'One day.'
'One day I will build my own hotel.'
'How? Will you steal the money?'
'Politics will give it to me.'
'Will you fuck politics?'
'Isn't that what you too are doing?'
'Not only me.'
'Who else?'
'Madame Koto.'
'Don't mention her name. Her ears are everywhere.'
'I hear that she is pregnant.'
'For who?'
'How will I know? Was I there when they did it?'
'It's possible.'
'Anything is possible nowadays.'
'Who told you she's pregnant?'
'Yes, how do you know?'
'People talk.'
'People always talk.'
'I don't believe them.'
'People talk too much.'
'Rumour is a cheap prostitute.'
'So what are you?'
'I am not cheap.'
'You're cheaper than shit.'
'What about you, eh? The men say your anus smells.'
'Your cunt smells.'
'Even chicken can fuck you.'
'Rat fuck you.'
'Dog fuck you.'
'Shut up.'
'You too shut up.'
'Pig fuck your mother.'
'Goat fuck your mother and produce you.'
'Shut up!'
'Why do you keep telling everyone to shut up?'
'You too shut up!'
They fell silent for a while. The wind blew the front door against the outside wall, straining its hinges. Then the women started up again, abusing one another in blistering phrases, their

voices sharper than glass. One of them lit up a cigarette. There was a lull in their bored quarrels during which the wind moaned in the trees. Then, all over the area, the crickets started their trilling. During the silence Madame Koto came in through the back door, a lantern in her hand. She looked massive, as if she had somehow bloated in the dark. Her face shone. Outside I could see a palm-wine tapper, his bicycle encircled with climbing ropes; kegs of wine, tied together, dangled from his carrier.

'No light?' Madame Koto asked.

She came over to me and shone the lantern in my eyes.

'So you're up, eh?'

'Yes, thank you.'

'Feel better, eh?'

'Yes.'

'Why did you touch the bucket of snails?'

'I didn't.'

'Liar! Do you know how long it took me to find them. And many of them are still hiding. Why do you cause me so much trouble, eh? Did they send you into this world to punish me?'

'I don't know.'

'And you have been searching every corner of my room.'

'No.'

'What did you find?'

'Nothing.'

'What did you see?'

'Nothing.'

She stared at me for a while. The women hadn't moved. Their faces remained angled towards the door. Then one of them looked at me.

'When did you come in?'

'I don't know.'

'You better start going,' Madame Koto said.

I stayed still. She went behind the counter. One of the women got up, went out, and came back in with three lanterns. She put them on different tables.

'When are they bring your electricity?'

'Don't ask me questions,' Madame Koto said.

She came round the counter, went out, and I heard her haggling with the tapper. They reached an agreement. The tapper made a raucous joke. I heard him wheeling his bicycle away, leaving a rusted cranking sound in his wake. Madame Koto came into the bar with three kegs. Flies followed her. Wine spilt on the floor. The women didn't move. When she dropped the kegs near me she planted her fists on her hips and roundly berated the women for their lassitude. They jumped up and made themselves busy, arranging benches, washing cups and plates. Madame Koto went out again. As soon as she was gone the women resumed their places and their motionless expectancy. Then the wind blew a man to the front door. He stood outside, visible behind the strips of curtain. He came in and looked round and two of the women rushed to him and led him to a seat. It was Dad. The women sat opposite him. I went over and he touched me on the head, and said nothing. His face was gaunt, his bristles were growing wild, and there was a vacant stare in his eyes. I knew something was going to happen.

'Let's go home,' I said.

'Why? I've only just arrived. It's been a devil's day. Fetch me some palm-wine. Where is Madame Koto?'

'Gone out.'

One of the women brought him palm-wine and waited for him to pay. He waved her off.

'I don't know you,' she said. 'So pay now if you don't want any trouble.'

Dad stared at her as if he might hit her.

'He's my father,' I said.

'So what?'

Dad, very reluctantly, paid. I sat beside him.

'One day,' he said, 'trouble is going to blow up in this area.'

One of the women sucked her teeth. Another one spat.

'Spit all you like,' Dad said. 'Your trouble still remains.'

The women left him. He hung his head and drank slowly. The women began to talk about the forthcoming rally. They built such a picture of this political rally that it sounded like a fantastic bazaar to be held at the end of the world. They talked of cows that were going to be slaughtered, goats that would be roasted on spits, great musicians that would perform, cars of all kinds that would be seen, and they invoked visions of money thrown out to the people from bags, of thousands of people converging from all over the world to be fed, to be shown the miracles of power, and the promises of a new future.

'Rubbish!' Dad said, sucking his teeth.

The women were at first silenced. Then, in a gravelly voice, one of them said:

'It's people like you who eat rubbish!'

Dad finished off his palm-wine in one long slurp and then he belched. He stared intently at one of the women and the woman glared back at him. The wind blew the curtain strips into a frenzy. We all looked at the door as if expecting an unusual personage to step in from the rain. Dad went on staring right through the woman, through the walls, and the vacant concentration in his eyes frightened me. The lamp nearest the door fluttered and went out. Then Dad gave a chilling laugh that began the faintest tremor of a fever in me. He went on laughing, with an unmoving face like a mask in the darkness, and his laughter seemed to affect the wind. Something shook the rooftop. I heard the curious wailing of cats from the forest. The wind roamed the bar like a disembodied spirit looking for somewhere to sit. When Dad stopped laughing the room seemed darker and the wind had stilled. We were all edgy in the long spaces of an undefined expectancy.

'Let's go home,' I said, a shiver passing through me.

'Shut up,' Dad said, eyes still vacant.

One of the women stood up and sat down again. Another one got up and, rolling her buttocks, went and stood at the door. In the faint light I could see a scar at the back of her neck. She stood there for a long while, trembling. The rain started again, slowly drizzling. Dad poured himself more palm-wine. Another lamp went out. The eyes of the women were bright in the darkness. The wind started; I heard it howl as it gathered mass amongst the trees. A terrible spirit stirred in its movement. Gusts of air rattled the zinc roof, I heard the trees protesting, the wind blew on the croaking of frogs. The woman at the door turned and, shaking every inch of movable flesh on her body, came towards us and went round a table and sat heavily. She sighed.

'No customers tonight,' she said.

There was a moment's silence. I looked at the door. The curtain strips parted, as if giving way to a great form, and a three-headed spirit came into the bar. Each of its heads was a different shape. One was red with blue eyes, the other was yellow with red eyes, and the third was blue with yellow eyes. The spirit had about ten eyes in all. It came into the bar, stayed at the door, each head looking in different directions, smoke issuing from the yellow eyes. Then it moved slowly and awkwardly into the room. I watched it in fascination, feeling a terrible fever rising to my brain. The spirit came and stood in front of me. Then, from across the table it elongated all

297

three heads towards me and stared at me with its ten eyes. The fever got to my brain and an awful noise like an incessant drill started at the top of my skull. The spirit stared at me for a long time. I could not move. The colours of its eyes began to hurt me, began to burn out my sight. Then a voice in my skull said:

'Shut your eyes.'

I shut them and could still see. The heads of the spirit swayed and then were retracted. Then the spirit, walking through the table as if it didn't exist, went and sat between the women. Two of its heads, in opposite directions, stared at the women's faces. The one in the middle, the yellow head with red eyes, stayed fixed on me. One of the women coughed. Another one sneezed. A third stood up and sat down again. Dad burped.

'Something stinks in here,' said the woman who had just sneezed.

'I feel sick,' said another.

'I want to vomit.'

'I can't move.'

'And no customers.'

'No customers, no money.'

'No electricity.'

'Stupid rain.'

'Bad wind.'

'And Madame Koto has vanished.'

'Where has she gone?'

'How would I know?'

They fell silent. The wind was still, as if the land had finally given birth. One of the women brought out some snuff and sniffed it violently. And then, for a long moment, she gripped the table, her head swaying, her mouth poised and wide open. The spirit's blue head was in front of her. Then, suddenly, she gave the most devastating sneeze, which fairly rocked the spirit's head. The head drew back, startled. The other heads widened their eyes and the one on the farthest side began to sway and toss about. Its eyes became very big. And then it burst forth with a mighty sneeze which practically threw me against the wall.

'What is wrong with you?' Dad said.

'Nothing.'

'A woman sneezes and it blows you away? Are you not a man?'

Then I began sneezing. Dad hit me on the head. Another of the women took up the sneezing. Dad joined in. Soon we were all infected with uncontrollable sneezing. We sneezed for such a

298

long time and with such intensity, that it seemed we would lose our heads altogether. The woman who began it sprayed her mucus everywhere and sneezed out the last lamp. Dad dislodged snot into his cup of palm-wine and then knocked the cup over. We were all contorted in paroxysms, when the wind, roaming the bar, took our sneezing away, and in its place left five rowdy men who laughed at us. We didn't realise we had stopped sneezing till one of them said:

'Is this how you welcome customers?'

Then the women, wiping their noses, struggling amongst themselves, falling over one another, rushed to the men and led them to a table.

'More wine!' Dad said.

No one paid any attention. The spirit's central head turned to Dad as if he had suddenly materialised.

'And more light!' he added.

One of the women got up and lit the lamps. The spirit was reduced in visibility.

'Just because you have customers doesn't mean you shouldn't serve me,' Dad said in a bad-tempered voice.

'Shut up,' said one of the men.

Dad gave the man his vacant, intent stare. The men stared back at him. Dad looked away, sank back into himself, and became silent. The woman lighting the lamps came over.

'You want another bottle of palm-wine?'

Dad didn't speak, nor did he look up. He seemed to have wholly retreated into himself. The woman repeated the question. Dad still didn't say anything. He hung his head.

'Leave that useless man alone,' said one of the men.

'If he doesn't want to answer you, let him swallow his saliva,' said another.

Dad looked up and looked down again. A man sneezed. The spirit moved one of its heads and looked at him. The woman placed a fist on her hip. Then she went to the backyard, came back with a bottle of palm-wine, and slammed it on the table. Dad poured himself some wine. The woman went and sat with one of the free men. They began talking amongst themselves. The spirit got up and sat next to the man who had sneezed. Dad finished the cup of wine in one swallow and then, with his face set, his eyes charged, he looked up. He surveyed the men. Then he stared at the man who had sneezed. At first I thought he was staring at the spirit. The man he stared at did not notice.

'What are you looking at?' the woman with the man asked.

'None of your business.'

The man looked up and caught Dad's ferocious stare.

'Let's go,' I said. 'The rain has stopped.'

There was silence. Then Dad stuck out his hand and pointed a wavering finger, like a man making an astonishing accusation. I looked to see who he was pointing at. The central head of the spirit looked surprised and its eyes flashed different colours.

'You coward!' Dad shouted, standing up, pointing quite unmistakably at the man who had sneezed, and who had an ominous scar near his left eye.

'Who are you calling a coward?' the man asked, rising.

'You! It was you and your friends who attacked me the other night. You are a coward!'

'You are mad!' the man cried. 'You are a thief! Your father was a coward!'

'If you are so brave,' Dad said in a thundering voice, 'why don't you fight me yourself, alone, now!'

Another silence. Then the women began to curse Dad, calling him a troublemaker. They tried to restrain the man, their hands clutching his shoulders, trying to get him to sit down. The man shrugged violently and brushed away their hands. Dad was still standing, trembling, his finger pointed, his jaws working. A woman screamed. Another one sneezed. My eyes were wide open. I couldn't see the spirit for a while. The man came round the table. The women tried to restrain him. He threw them off. The wind started. The man strode to the centre of the bar and made a great show of taking off his voluminous garment. He was taking it off for a long time. It got stuck round his neck, entangled with the beads and amulets. Another woman screamed. Dad poured himself another glass of palm-wine, downed it, got up and went round our table. He helped the man to remove his voluminous garment. The wind started and seemed strong enough to blow the bar away. I felt the floor tremble. When the man had taken off his great garment he fumed and cursed and then started taking off his shirt. It took a while. Dad went out to urinate. When he got back the man was bare-chested, except for the amulets round his neck. Scar-marks, like weird brandings, ran down his chest and converged at his navel. His followers had by this time surrounded Dad. It was frightening to see how collected and calm Dad was. I began to cry.

'We don't know you,' one of the women said, amid shrieks. 'We don't know you and you come here with your ugly son and spoil our business and cause trouble.'

Her face was quite wild, her eyes twisted, her fingernails like red claws.

Dad ignored her.

'So what do you want to do?' the man asked, fingering his amulet. 'Do you know this thing I have here, eh? If you touch me you will fall down seven times and then . . .'

Suddenly – it seemed like a flash of lightning was lost in the bar – Dad had hit him in the face. It happened very fast. The next moment the bar door was wide open and the man had disappeared. We heard him groaning outside in the dark. The lightning vanished back into Dad's fist. Then the woman with the red fingernails pounced on him from behind. She howled like a deranged cat, scratched Dad's neck, and tried to claw out his eyes. Dad knocked her away and she fell on a table. The man she was with rushed over and jumped on Dad and they rolled outside. I heard them struggling to get up. The woman who had been knocked over saw me, came over, and gave me a resounding slap. The spirit reappeared in the bar. I ran outside. The woman followed. I ran into one of the men. He pushed me away and I fell on Madame Koto's signboard that was on the soggy ground. It was still drizzling. I could see that the two men were fighting Dad. One of them held him from behind, and the other hit him from the front. Dad jerked forward and downwards and tossed the man behind him over his shoulder. Then he flattened the one in front with a crackling punch to the nose. Both stretched out in a messy heap on the mud. Dad, satisfied, smiled at me. The woman jumped on him and pulled his hair and clung to him with her nails. Dad found it difficult to shake her off. And by the time he had managed to do so the other men inside had come out.

'Let's run,' I said.

The men surrounded Dad. The two that had fallen began to stir. I tried to beat them down with a stick, but it did no good. The men, five in all, tightened the circle round Dad. Shrieking in unnatural voices, the women urged them on, urged them to kill Dad, to rub his face in the mud, force him to eat dirt. One man attempted to punch Dad in the face, missed, and tripped. Another one lunged at Dad and brought him down. Soon the whole lot of them fell on the two bodies on the floor and formed a writhing heap. The fight became confused. Everyone seemed to be hitting everyone else. Then, out of the wriggling mud-covered mass of bodies, emerged

301

the yellow head of the spirit. It looked fairly confused. Then the spirit disentangled itself altogether from the fray and wobbled towards me and stuck its yellow head close to my face, so that I couldn't escape its flaming red eyes. The voice in my head, again, said:

'Shut your eyes.'

I did and could still see. The spirit blinked rapidly and the brightness of its eyes hurt me. The men had rolled off the heap. Dad lashed at them wildly, swinging granite punches. Then he ran to the backyard and returned soon afterwards with a terrifying piece of wood. I opened my eyes. The piece of wood had several long nails sticking through it. I shouted. The spirit, ten eyes widened, leant its central head closer to me, and said:

'They told me to bring you with me.'

'Who?'

'Your friends.'

'What friends?'

'In the spirit world. Your companions.'

Dad lashed out with the piece of wood.

'You had a pact with them. Before you were born. Remember?'

The men scattered as Dad wielded his ugly weapon.

'Hold him!' one of the men cried.

'You hold him,' said another.

Dad pursued them. They fled. He pursued the woman. She ran, screaming, towards the forest.

'They said I must bring you,' the spirit said again.

'I won't come.'

The other women in the bar were now outside. One of the men picked up a long branch. Dad tore after him with a murderous expression on his face. The man dropped the branch and ran.

'Cowards!' Dad shouted, triumphantly.

He kept tearing after the men and they kept fleeing. Then he went into the bar. The women scattered as he approached. He re-emerged with a calabash of palm-wine belonging to his adversaries. He drank steadily while keeping an eye on the men.

'So you won't come?' the spirit asked me.

'No.'

'What about your promises?'

'What promises?'

'They will be angry.'

'So what?'

'Don't say I didn't warn you,' the spirit said.

'About what?'

'Remember that I have only three heads. After I have failed, your companions will send the spirit with four heads.'

One of the women jumped on Dad while he was gulping down the last of the palm-wine. Then they all jumped on him and they called the men to come and finish him off. Dad struggled. The calabash broke. A woman cried out. The men approached cautiously.

'And after that they will send the spirit with five heads.'

Dad shook off the women. They fell from him. One of them managed to snatch away his feared weapon of nails and ran off with it.

'And when it gets to the turn of the seven-headed spirit nothing will be able to save you.'

The men approached Dad more confidently. The women began to throw stones at him.

'And if you somehow escape from the seven-headed spirit your companions will come themselves.'

They stoned Dad and caught him on the head. He stoned them back. But the men joined in and soon stones flew at him from many places in the darkness.

'Prostitutes! Yam-breasted women of hell!' Dad bellowed.

They began to stone me too. Dad picked up Madame Koto's fallen signboard and used it as a shield. We edged backwards into the bar. When we were inside we locked the front door. The spirit came in through the shut door and pestered me to follow him. Dad piled up benches to keep the door securely shut. The spirit followed me everywhere, reminded me of promises that were not his business, pleading, threatening, with a head in front of me all the time, and another head talking always into my ear. The thugs stoned the door. I heard them run round to the back. Dad blew out all the lights. The men didn't have the courage to come into the darkness. The spirit, luminous, its eyes blazing, wandered around in the darkness as if it had lost its sense of direction. Dad cursed. He said he was bleeding. The mosquitoes fed on us. We tried to remain still. I had no idea what would happen next. The spirit, slightly crazy, wandered about the bar, and went outside through one of the walls. Thunder boomed above. The spirit came rushing back in. Lightning cracked. The spirit, confused, staggered and turned in all directions. The rain began falling again. We heard someone creeping in through the back door. Dad threw something. A man screamed and ran out. There was a long silence. Then we heard the loud voice of Madame

Koto at the front. She banged on the door. The thugs bolted to the backyard. The prostitutes rushed into the bar and lit the lamps and hurriedly ordered the place and took the benches away from behind the front door. The spirit came and sat next to me. The prostitutes opened the door and made excuses for it being shut, saying something about the ferocity of the rain, and Madame Koto, drenched, her face thunderous with rage, stepped into the bar. She shook herself like a great feathered bird and sent sprays of water everywhere. Dad sat still, blood dripping from his forehead on to the table. The spirit's blue head watched the blood with radiant fascination. Madame Koto stared at us. She said nothing. It was clear she was making up her mind about us in some way. She went slowly up the bar. The spirit got up and followed her. The prostitutes cowered against the walls, faces pressed into the shadows. Dad stood up and said:

'Madame Koto!'

She stopped walking. Water dripped from the bottom of her wrapper. The spirit went right through her. She shivered.

'Madame Koto, your friends nearly killed me two days ago. I saw them here today. They fought me and stoned me. Your women stoned me as well. What are you going to do about it?'

She said nothing. She went on towards the counter. She walked through the spirit.

'You are a wicked woman, a witch,' Dad said in an even tone of voice. 'And, because you don't care about human beings terrible things will happen to you. Me and my son will never set foot here again.'

Madame Koto turned to look at Dad. She seemed surprised, but not curious, at the verbal attack. She looked at me. Her eyes could have turned me to wood. I think she became our enemy from that moment. She carried on walking. She disappeared into the backyard. Dad finished his drink, took me by the hand, and led me outside.

The thugs were gone. The rain poured on us and we didn't notice. The forest was one watery darkness. The street had become a pond. The gutters overflowed. As we went the solid earth turned to mud and we waded through the slush that reached up to my knees. Dad said nothing. The steady falling of the rain silenced all human voices. The sky was very dark. As we neared home Dad said, chuckling:

'We showed them pepper, didn't we?'

'Yes.'

'That's how to be a man.'

'How?'

'When people fight you, toughen up, study them, wait for the right time, and then fight them back. Fight them like a madman, like a wizard. Then they will respect you.'

I was shivering now. My teeth chattered. Dad strode on ahead of me. The rain ran down my back.

When we got home there was a candle lit, there was the smell of a new pot of soup, the room had been cleaned, it was warm, the door was open, but Mum wasn't in. Dad changed into his towel and went and had a bath. When he came back I went and had one. By the time I got back Mum was sitting on the bed. On the table was a great bowl of steaming peppersoup. Mum looked fresh but lean. She had powder on her face and her eyes were bright. When I came in, my little towel wrapped round my waist, Mum smiled.

'So you and your father have been fighting everybody, eh?'

I went over and sat on her lap.

'Did they stone you too?'

'Yes, but I dodged.'

Dad laughed. Mum rubbed oil over me. I combed my hair, and dressed. I fell asleep in Mum's arms. Then I woke up suddenly. The light was different. There was a mosquito coil burning.

'Have some peppersoup,' Mum said.

I was now on the bed. I got up and finished what was left of the soup. It was hot and it made my mouth and head come alive. My eyes burned. Dad was on his three-legged chair.

'I saw a spirit today,' I said.

They both sat up.

'What spirit?'

'With three heads.'

'Where?'

'In Madame Koto's bar.'

'When?'

'When we were fighting.'

Dad looked at me dubiously. Then slowly he sat back.

'What was it like?'

'It had three heads.'

'What did it say?'

'That I should follow it.'

'Where?'

'Where I came from.'

They both fell silent. Dad shut his eyes, rocked skilfully on the chair, and then he opened one eye and regarded me.

'It's time for you to sleep.'

I said nothing.

'So they would have killed me and all you would have told people is that you saw a spirit, eh?'

'No,' I said.

'Go to sleep.'

I began to spread my mat.

'Sleep on the bed.'

I climbed on to the bed. Mum cleared the table and spread the mat.

'If a spirit calls you,' Mum said, 'don't go, you hear? Think of us. Think of your father who suffers every day to feed us. And think of me who carried you in my womb for more than nine months and who walks all the streets because of you.'

'Yes, think of us,' Dad added.

I nodded.

'And', Dad said, sternly, 'from now on Madame Koto is our enemy. Azaro, if I see you go there again, I will flog you and put pepper in your eyes, you hear?'

'Yes, Dad.'

'She is a witch, a wicked woman. That's why she has no children.'

'But she is pregnant,' I said.

'How do you know?'

'Someone said so.'

'Shut up. And don't listen to what people say. Is she pregnant for you?'

'No.'

'Then shut up and don't answer me back when I'm talking to you.'

'Yes, Dad.'

I turned away from him and faced the wall so as not to see his frightening expression. Besides I feared that if I looked at him it might make him angry and he might pounce on me. He muttered and cursed for a while. He abused the thugs, the party, his job, the colonialists, the landlord, and the rain. His temper, feeding on itself, grew worse. He abused Madame Koto and wondered aloud whether he should burn down her bar. At that point Mum put out the candle. I heard her shifting on the mat. Dad went on cursing in the dark.

EIGHT

ONE MOMENT I was in the room and the next moment I found myself wandering the night roads. I had no idea how I had gotten outside. I walked on the dissolving streets and among the terrestrial bushes. The air was full of riddles. I walked through books and months and forgotten histories. I was following a beautiful woman with a blue head. She moved in cadenzas of golden light. She floated on the wind of a royal serenity. Superimposed on distant plangency of Mum praying in the dark, the woman turned and beckoned me. I followed her smile and listened to the fugal birds. She drew my spirit on to fountains of light and lilac music and abiku variations. The air was faintly scented with resinous smoke and incense, flavoured with the fruit of guavas and cherries and crushed pineapples. I walked behind the woman for a long time, walking to the tunes of alto voices beneath cypress trees. I heard someone call my name from a heavier world, but I went on walking. Beyond the hair of the beautiful woman there was a landscape with luminous flying-machines, gardens brilliant with passion-flowers and cana-lilies.

My name sounded heavier. The woman urged me on. Her face, gentle in the light of a dreaming nebula, promised the ecstasies of a secret homeland, a world of holidays. A rough, familiar hand touched me on the shoulder.

'Where are you going, Azaro?'

It was Mum.

'That woman told me to follow her.'

'What woman?'

I pointed at the woman whose smile was forever in bloom, whose hair was blue, and who was disappearing amongst the pomegranate trees and the chorale of roses. Her head became a solitary cloud.

'There is no one there,' Mum said.

'Yes there is.'

'I'm taking you home.'

I said nothing. She lifted me on to her shoulder. I could still see the head of the woman. I could still hear the voices in passionate gardens, could still hear their sunflower cantatas. I saw delicious girls dancing tarantellas in fields of comets. The woman's head turned to give me a last smile before she vanished altogether in a Milky Way of music. The air became void of riddles. I heard the last notes of a flute adagio floating across a lake of green mirrors. Mum took me home over the mud and wreckage of the street, over the mild deluge, under an arpeggio of watery stars. She was silent. I smelt the gutters and the rude plaster of the corroded houses. Then all I was left with was a world drowning in poverty, a mother-of-pearl moon, and the long darkness before dawn.

Book Five

ONE

THE RAIN GOD was merciless for two weeks. It rained so much that the sky seemed to have become as inexhaustible with water as the seas. At night water leaked through our ceiling, which we soon discovered was full of holes. Mum had to sacrifice her basins and pots used for cooking to catch the water that dripped down. In our room there were so many containers that it became almost impossible to move about. Some of them were near the bed, some in the middle of the room, some on the cupboard. We had to move the clothes-line and Dad's boots. One night as I slept the rain dripped on my head: it seemed the rain was corrosive and ate through new places in the zinc roof. I had to move my mat. Sometimes it rained so much that the containers filled up and overflowed, and the floor covered in water. The first time that happened I woke up thinking I had wet the mat. My amazement bordered on horror when I thought I had pissed so much in my sleep. I got up and quietly tried to clean the urine. Mum woke up. I felt ashamed. Then, I realised the trick the rain god was playing on me.

The rain swept down so badly that I could no longer sleep on the floor and had to share the single bed with my parents. When more holes opened above us we had to keep moving the bed round the room. It got so awful that we couldn't find a place that wasn't leaking. We ended up settling for having the water drip on our feet. Dad complained to the landlord, but he merely threatened to increase the rent further if he fixed the roof. We couldn't afford the rent as it stood so we had no choice but to settle for being soaked through at night.

Sometimes in the morning we would wake up and find slugs, worms, and millipedes crawling about the room. Little snails appeared on our walls. In the containers we found tiny fishes. Dad was convinced that an enemy was trying to poison us. He became suspicious of the whole compound and warned me not to take anyone's food or play with their children. We became quite lonely.

The rains made the days short. I was ill a lot of the time. At first Mum went hawking with polythene over her basin of provisions. But as the weather got worse she stayed at home and she made very little money. Dad returned in the evenings covered in mud, his clothes stinking, his eyes mad. He developed livid cuts and boils all over his body. His feet became raw and twisted. It was a rough time for load-carriers.

Our street turned into one big stream. Water flooded into our rooms from the gutters. Sometimes it rained so much the compound began to stink because of the water that flowed past the pail latrine. During that time children fell ill, and many people caught strange diseases and had to be rushed home to their villages for special herbal treatments. Those who could afford it built little cement dams in front of their rooms to stop the bad waters going in. The rest of us sat helpless in our rooms and watched the water rise. I was cold most of the time. When Mum got back from her restricted hawking she would bathe and change clothes and sit on the bed, huddled up, her teeth chattering. With the steady drone of rain around us, there was little to say. The noise of the falling rain penetrated our bones, our silences, and our dreams. Dad's face took on a watery quality. Sometimes when Mum came back from hawking, with earthworms clinging to her ankles, and rain pouring down her face, I couldn't be sure whether she was weeping or not.

I continued to attend school in the mornings. My exercise books got soaked, the ink ran, and I was flogged all the time. Our improvised school-building, of mud and cement, roofless and low-walled, crumbled in the rain. Plants grew wild in our classrooms. Snakes slithered in to our hygiene lessons. And when the rain got too much we held our classes under the eaves of nearby buildings.

On my way back from school one day it was raining heavily. I passed Madame Koto's bar. A lot of cars were parked outside. Through the curtains I made out women with red lips and painted faces, men in bright clothes. I didn't see Madame Koto. As I passed the bar there was a flash in the sky. It broke over me, and I ran. I fled towards the forest, but the wind was strong. It lifted me up and flung me to the ground. I got up, stunned. At that moment I heard a terrible groan. Then a tree fell in slow motion, as if in a dream, and collapsed on several other trees. Branches and leaves blocked off the road behind me. I ran towards the lightning flash. I ran on water. Stones chafed the soles of my feet. The rain whipped my face. Feeling that I couldn't go much further, my lungs bursting, I ran under the eaves of a house near us. It was only when I was there, shivering, temporarily free from the violence of the weather, that I realised I had run right into the territory of the old man who had been blinded by a passing angel.

He too was on the verandah, sitting in a chair, his face turned towards me, his eyes green and half-dissolved. He was smoking a pipe. He wore a hat. When I saw him I was scared. I was about to run out and brave the lightning, when he said:

'Don't go, boy.'

His voice was both gentle and frightening in the rain.

'Why not?' I asked, trembling.

He knocked his pipe against the chair, and gave me a sinister smile. His eyes moved oddly.

'Because', he said, 'if you don't listen to me, and if you go, you will drown in a pit. Snakes will crawl into your mouth.'

The wind sprayed my face.

'Come here,' he said.

'Why?'

'I want to see with your eyes.'

I wanted to run.

'Don't move!' he commanded.

I froze. My limbs were numb. I was rooted. I couldn't move. The old man laughed. His teeth were more or less brown and his mouth was like a wound.

'COME HERE!' he commanded again.

I stayed still. The wind rose again and hurled a fine spray of rain at us. After a while, I felt myself moving. Something in me moved. I resisted. But the wind was stronger. The blind old man laughed as I struggled. I discovered that the wind had divided me, had separated me from myself. I felt an inner self floating towards the blind old man. Or was it that the blind old man was floating into me, invading my consciousness? I wasn't sure.

The wind stopped. The rain fell in silence. Everything went dark. I tried to blink, but couldn't. As if I had woken into a nightmare, thick green substances passed over my eyes. They settled. Gradually, my eyes cleared. When I looked out at the world again, what I saw made me scream. Everything was upside-down. The world was small. Trees were like slow-moving giants. The rain was a perpetual nightfall, and night a perpetual rain. The earth was full of craters.

313

It kept moving as if it were a monster fretting in sleep. The spaces between things were populated with the most horrifying spirits I have ever seen. They had wounds all over them which dripped pus. When they talked green spit poured from their mouths. I screamed. My eyes caught fire. Then the smile of the boy-king appeared to me and vanished, cooling my sight. I heard shrieking witches confessing their evils. The monster that was the earth opened its gaping mouth and out sprang a big yellow animal with blazing ruby eyes and long claws. It leapt into my eyes, and I fell back. A savage wind blew in my head. My eyes heated up again, and I thought they would combust. Then blackness came over me.

When I opened my eyes I found myself still standing. The rain poured on my face. Behind me the blind old man had fallen off his chair. He clawed the air with his crooked fingers. His pipe was on the ground. His hat was in the rain. And in the hat, brilliant against the brown felt, was a big white cat. It was a beautiful cat with gnomic eyes. When I moved the cat leapt. In an instant, it disappeared. The blind old man called for help. A door opened. Two women came out. They saw the old man twisting on the wet ground, his mouth open, choking. They saw me standing there. They made strange connections between us. They shouted. I fled out into the malevolent weather. They did not follow.

The rain hurt my skin, but I ran without stopping. As I ran, I saw a future history in advance, compacted into a moment. I saw an unfinished house crumble under the force of the rain. And then all that was left were metal rods sticking out of the watery earth. It happened so fast I was convinced I was still seeing the world through the blind old man's eyes.

When I got home Mum was at the door, baling water out of the room with a plastic bowl. All the holes were leaking like open taps. The bed was thoroughly wet, the clothes dripped. There were pots and buckets everywhere.

'Help me empty the pans,' Mum said as if I had been there all along.

I dropped my school bag. Still wet, I began to empty the buckets and pots. I put them back in their places.

'I'm cold,' I said.

'Empty the pans.'

'I'm going to be ill.'

She went on baling water out of the room, into the passage.

'If you don't fall ill I will give you a big piece of fried fish. And if you empty the pots and help me dry the room, I will tell you a story.'

'What story?'

'About rain and the rain god.'

I emptied the pans with greater enthusiasm. Our co-tenants looked out at us from their windows. The rain showed no sign of abating. When I finished emptying the pots I got a rag and helped Mum dry the floor. Night fell over the rain. When the floor was as dry as we could make it, we washed our hands. Mum went out to prepare our dinner. I stayed in, overcome by a chill. I listened to the wind. I lay on the bed and covered myself with a wet blanket. As I slept I heard the momentous growlings of the rain god. When he flashed his eyes, there was a sharp light everywhere. Sometimes it was like a dazzling bottle hurled against a black wall.

The room was warm with the smell of food. A lit candle was on the table. Giant shadows moved fast on the walls. I sat up. Dad was punching the air, ducking, bobbing and weaving, hitting out at his shadow. I watched him till he noticed me. He said:

'Your father is going to become a world champion.'

'Of what?'

'I'm going to be a boxer.'

He sounded very pleased about something. He went on hitting out, grappling with the air, in-fighting, blocking. The rain had become gentle. Mum was looking better, her hair was neat, her face glowed a little. Dad boxed round her.

'Your father has gone mad,' she said.

'Why?'

'He is training to be a boxer.'

We both watched him attacking the mosquitoes and the flying ants. He was sweating and his face was screwed up in absurd concentration.

'You see how poor we are,' Mum said. 'How are we going to feed a boxer, eh?'

Dad suddenly stopped, as if he had been struck in the stomach. Then he slowly collapsed to the floor and lay there, pretending to have been knocked out. Mum laughed. A light flashed past in one of my eyes, as if I had a camera in my brain. For a moment everything was still. The walls dissolved, the room vanished, and in the relative space of that time we moved to somewhere else.

'We are now on the moon,' I said.

'Isn't food ready?' Dad asked, getting up and dusting his trousers.

Mum passed the food and we ate in silence. Dad had a tremendous appetite and he ate the poor food with clear relish. After we had finished Dad lit a cigarette while me and Mum cleared the table. Dad smoked on his chair, dragging deeply and exhaling in long sighs. Mum sat down with her basin and began counting her money.

'This rainy season is going to make us poor,' she said.

'Soon there'll be a break,' Dad said.

Then I remembered the story Mum promised to tell me. I asked her about it and she smiled, but went on with her calculations, using all her fingers. Suddenly Dad shivered, his shoulders trembled. He got up swiftly, put on his boots, and went out.

'What happened?' I asked.

'Your father felt something.'

'What?'

'A message, a warning.'

'How?'

'In his body.'

I fell silent. An inexplicable dread came over me. I could hear the world breathing. Mum stopped counting her money, put the basin away, and sent me to buy a small measure of ogogoro.

Outside it was dark. The rain had stopped falling but the air was wet. Water gleamed from every surface. The passage was covered in puddles. The compound was silent, as if the rain had extinguished all the sounds. The buildings were still in a way I had never noticed before. The walls were wet through and water dripped down from the rooftops. At the compound-front I heard water gurgling in the gutters. There was no one around. The trees weaved in the dark sky and I could only hear them as leaves breathing. I shivered and crossed the street. The burnt van seemed to have reduced in size. Glass splinters on the ground were the only reminder of the photographer's cabinet. I knocked on the ogogoro-seller's door. It was a while before she opened.

'Yes?'

Her serious face, with long scarifications, frightened me. I asked for the measure. She took my bottle and went back into the room, leaving me in the wet passage. I could hear the family talking within. After a while the woman came out, her face still grim. She had a dollop of eba in one hand. In the room behind her I could see her five children and her husband, seated in a circle on the floor, eating from the same bowls. She gave me the bottle and my change. I left the compound, which stank of dried fish and urine, and went to the front. I was thinking about the photographer when I saw a man go behind the burnt van. I thought it was Dad. When I got there I encountered a perfect stranger urinating on the door of the van. His urine steamed.

'What are you looking at?'

'Nothing.'

'Get away from here, you badly trained child.'

'I am not badly trained.'

'Shut up,'

'No.'

'What?' he shouted.

Then he cursed.

'You made me piss on myself.'

I laughed and backed away.

'Who is your father, eh?' he asked angrily.

I turned and started to leave when I heard him curse again. When I looked I saw that he was coming after me, urinating. I broke into a run.

'God punish you, useless child!' he cried.

'God punish you too,' I said.

He pursued me. I ran. The ogogoro spilled. I went and hid in a bush and crawled round till I got to the backyard of a house. I could still hear the man shouting abuses at the new generation of children. His drunken voice faded into the darkness, occasionally emerging louder.

'Stupid children,' he said. 'Looking at my prick. As if his father doesn't have one.'

When his voice had gone far enough I crept out of my hiding-place. The wind rose again and whistled in my ears. A cat shrieked and leapt out from the darkness near me. I jumped in fright. Blood pounded in the side of my face. Then I heard gentle voices calling me in the dark. I went towards the street. The voices moved. They began calling me from the bushes nearest the front window of a bungalow. When I heard the voices I was afraid. The wind dropped. When I answered the voices they changed and began singing my name in twisted melodies. I challenged the voices to come out, to show their faces. I was of the opinion that they were not spirits but children mocking me in the darkness. I got angry and threw bits of wood and balls of wet paper at them. But to my surprise they threw stones at me. One of them got me on the shoulder. So I put

317

down the ogogoro bottle and threw stones back at them, swearing and cursing. I got so involved with throwing stones, angry at not hitting them, at not hearing them cry out, that I didn't notice when the voices stopped. The next thing I heard was the breaking of glass. I had shattered a window. A light came on in the room. I heard a key turn in a lock. The curtain parted and the blind old man, holding a lantern, face pressed against the broken window, looked out at me with malignant concentration. His eyes became flames. He shouted for help. It was only when I realised that it was the house where the blind old man lived that I picked up the bottle and ran home.

'Where have you been?' Mum asked, when I came in.

'Nowhere.'

'You have sand on you. Sand and mud. You have poured ogogoro on yourself. You stink of it. What have you been doing?'

'Nothing.'

She got up and came over to me, menacingly. Her face changed.

'You have been drinking the ogogoro, eh?'

'No, no,' I said, helplessly.

She reached out, swifter than the wind, and caught me. She hit me on the head. She lifted up her foot, took off a slipper, and lashed me on the back.

'You are still a child and yet you are drinking ogogoro, eh?'

'No.'

'Stealing ogogoro, eh?'

'No!'

'Hiding in the bush and drinking, eh?' she shouted.

Each statement was accompanied by the cracking of the slipper on my back. I tore away and ran to the door, opened it, and saw Dad standing there, like a stranger. He didn't move. Mum put down the slipper and sat on the bed. Dad came in, shut the door, and said:

'An evil wind is blowing in my head.'

He didn't sit on his chair, but stood at the window. Then he said:

'How long will a man have to struggle?'

There was a moment's silence. My back was singing with the lashes. I wanted to cry out, but Dad's mood made it impossible.

'There is some ogogoro on the table,' said Mum.

With vacant eyes, like someone who had woken up from a deep sleep into a strange land, Dad picked up the bottle and went to the door. Mum covered her head with a headtie. Dad made profuse libations, using up half the drink. He prayed to his ancestors to save us from poverty, from hunger, from trouble. He asked for guidance and signs of what to do. Then he poured ogogoro for us all and downed his in one. He shut his eyes.

'Something strange is going to happen,' he said wearily, 'and I don't know what it is.'

Dad stayed still, his eyes shut. Now and again he tossed his head backwards.

'An evil wind keeps a man poor,' he said.

Me and Mum watched him intently. He stayed silent for a very long time. Mum began clearing the room. The place stank of ogogoro and rain. I prepared my mat, and lay down, when crude knocks sounded on the door. I thought of the photographer. I opened the door and saw a man, a woman, and the blind old man.

'That's him!' one of them said.

Instantly I tried to shut the door, but the man wedged it with a big foot, and pushed his way in.

'Who is it?' asked Dad.

'I don't know,' I said, running to hide behind him.

The three apparitions came into the room. A terrified look appeared on Mum's face. The old man – blind, chewing his mouth – waved his cane in the air. The other man held on to the old man's arm. The woman stood in the middle of the room, hands aggressively on hips. The blind old man, cocking his head, moved his face in one direction and then another. Green liquid leaked out of his eyes. He waved the cane again and knocked the candle over. Mum picked it up and stuck it back on the saucer on the table. The blind old man's cane hit her on the bottom and Mum straightened and the cane fell from the blind man's hand. The woman picked it up and put it back in his grasping fingers. Then she said, in an angry voice:

'Your son broke our window.'

'I didn't,' I said.

'Shut up,' said Dad.

'He broke the old man's window with stones.'

'You should discipline your son,' the man said.

'Flog him,' added the woman.

Then the blind man, moving forward, stumbling, arms stretched, confused by the unfamiliar room, working his mouth, said:

'Where is the boy? Bring him here.'

I went and hid beneath the bed.

'We want you to pay for the window,' the woman said.

'Glass is expensive.'

'Bring him here, let me hold him,' came the blind old man in a cracked, unnatural voice.

'How do you know it was my son who broke the window?' asked Dad.

'The old man saw him,' said the woman, changing her stance.

There was silence.

'The blind old man?' asked Dad, a little incredulously.

'Yes.'

Another silence.

'How did he see?'

'He saw your son stoning the window.'

'How?'

'What kind of question is dat?'

'I said how?'

'The old man can see when he wants to.'

I looked out furtively from behind the bed. The blind old man was now completely still, his hands frozen in the air, his head cocked, his eyes moving strangely. Then, to my utmost horror, the old man pointed his cane in my direction. Everyone turned towards me. The blind old man, caught in a sinister fever, began stammering. Weird noises issued from his mouth. Then, suddenly, he broke free from the man who was acting as his eyes. He came forward, pushed past Mum's knees, and tripped against the table, felling the candle, plunging the room into darkness. He crashed on the bed and fought his way up. Dad lit a match. The old man, arms flailing, a terrible, guttural, ancient howl pouring from him, charged towards Dad like a mad animal. For some reason Dad was scared, and he fell off the chair. With uncanny resolution, the old man moved towards me, eyes wide open, green tears streaming down his face. Then he stopped. Dad lit the candle. With another howl, the old man pounced at me. I ducked. He fell behind the bed. The woman and the man rushed to pick him up. When he was standing again, he made another demented cry, threw their arms off him, like an enraged beast, and stalked me again. Mum screamed. The blind old man tracked me round the room. I kept running in circles, round the centre table. I was completely horrified at the thought of being clutched by the old man. Then suddenly he was silent. He became very still. He was like someone serenely fighting to get out of a dream. The room changed. The lights became tinged with red. Then to my amazement I saw that the old man had two heads. One had good eyes and a gruesome smile of power. The other remained normal.

'Come here, you abiku child, you stubborn spirit-child. You think you are powerful, eh? I am more powerful than you,' the old man said, in a resonant, young man's voice.

'Leave my son alone,' Mum said before letting out a deafening high-pitched shriek.

The old man stopped in his tracks.

'We will pay for the window,' Dad said, in a voice of conciliation.

The two heads of the old man became one. Then, as if released from a spell, the woman said:

'Of course you will pay.'

The other man came forward and held the old man. The woman gave him back his cane. The old man slumped curiously, his shoulders dropped, his back hunched, his head cocked. He became passive and frail. His bones rattled. He stumbled and muttered. A macabre agedness came over him, as if his uncanny exertions had dried up his life. Without another word all three of them left the room.

Holding our breaths, we watched them leave. When they had gone Mum got up and locked the door. Then she turned on me.

'Why did you break their window, eh? Do you want to kill us? Don't you see how poor we are, eh? Have you no pity on your father? Do you know how much glass costs, eh?'

'I didn't break it.'

'Who did?'

'The spirits.'

'What spirits?'

'How can spirits break a window?' Dad wondered.

'I don't know.'

'You use these spirits as an excuse every time you do something bad, eh?'

'No.'

'You're lying.'

'I'm not,' I screamed.

I began to cry.

'You're lying.'

'I'm not. It was the spirits. They stoned me and so I stoned them back.'

'Why did they stone you?'

'I don't know.'

'So you went and broke the window because the spirits stoned you, eh?'

I was silent.

'Do you see what a dangerous son you are? You will kill us, you know. You will kill us with your troubles. Look at what you've done. You let that blind old man come into our room. Do you know what powers he has? Did you see the way he behaved? If he had caught you, only God knows what would have happened.'

Mum got so worked up in her fear that she came over and grabbed my ears. She held them tight between her fingers and thumbs. She twisted them till I thought she was going to wrench my ears from my head. I howled. My cry seemed to enrage her further, for she pulled and twisted my ears harder and pinched them and then she swiped me across the head. She hit me so hard I went flying across the room. I collapsed against the wall and slid down to the floor. I sat still, eyeing Mum with a vengeful solemnity.

'Don't look at your mother like that!' Dad said.

I lowered my eyes and cried silently, tears dripping on to my thighs. I stayed like that even when Mum put out the candle. I stayed sitting against the wall when they went to sleep. I didn't move from my position even when they snored and turned on the bed. It did not matter whether they saw my protest or not. I was determined to stay like that to the end of time.

And then it was morning. I found myself stretched out on the mat, a cloth covering me. Tear-tracks were stiff on my face. I woke up happy. It was only after Mum gave me some bread and set out hawking that I remembered I was supposed to be angry with everyone.

TWO

IT WAS IN the evening, after Dad came back with the carpenter and a pane of glass, that I got the full force of his anger. I was in the room when he returned from work. He came in, put down the glass, changed his clothes, and went out. He didn't say a word. I followed him at a distance. He went with the carpenter to the old man's house. It was the same carpenter who had built Madame Koto's counter.

The blind old man sat outside on the verandah, with a cat in his lap, and a pipe in his mouth. He wore the same hat I had seen him in. Dad said nothing to him. He showed the carpenter the window. With a hammer the carpenter broke the jagged edges of the glass left standing in the window frame. The noise startled the cat, which jumped away from the old man's lap. When the glass fell into the room it brought protestations from the woman. She complained and insisted that the carpenter sweep the room. The carpenter said he wouldn't, and dropped his tools. The other man came out. Other people from the compound came out as well. The man began to push the carpenter around. Dad stepped in. The man pushed Dad around as well. I could see Dad struggling to contain his anger. The shouting and arguing attracted a crowd. Soon even Madame Koto came to see what was happening and when she saw Dad she tried to calm everything down but only succeeded in drawing a spate of abuse from him. She slunk away, cursing Dad and men in general.

The argument about sweeping the room raged for a while. Then the old man shouted that they should allow the carpenter to continue with his work.

'Do you people want mosquitoes to kill me in my old age!' he said.

The quarrels were instantly resolved. The woman allowed the carpenter to continue on the condition that he made the glass fall outside. The carpenter, however, only resumed work after Dad had appeased his anger with bottles of beer and some kola-nuts. The old man nodded as the carpenter put the glass back into the wooden frame. Then, as if to complete the pleasure he derived from listening to the carpenter work, the old man called for his accordion. While the carpenter fixed the glass and dextrously hammered away at the little nails to keep the pane in place, the blind old man played the ugliest music I have ever heard. The music made the carpenter miss a nail and hammer his thumb. The music made me slightly nauseous. Dad obviously hated it. He kept frowning at the blind old man, who played happily, his pipe in his mouth. Dad retreated to the far end of the housefront. The carpenter, anxious to flee from the noxious sound of the music, worked swiftly. The old man soon got tired of the accordion. Not long afterwards the carpenter finished, the pane sat in the window. The woman complained that the glass wobbled in its frame, but the carpenter ignored her and packed his tools. Dad swept the glass into a dustpan and threw the rubbish to the back of the van. As he and the carpenter left, the old man said:

'The next time that son of yours troubles me I will teach him a lesson he will never forget.'

Dad said nothing. He went home with the carpenter, and bought him another beer. The carpenter drank happily. They talked about Madame Koto. They didn't talk about politics. I watched them from the door.

'Come in, or go and play!' Dad said.

I went in.

The carpenter, slightly drunk, offered to fix Dad's chair.

'No, I like it like this,' Dad said philosophically. 'It reminds me that whatever we sit on will one day make us fall.'

The carpenter laughed, finished his beer, haggled about his payment, received his money in a grumbling spirit, and left.

It was when Mum returned exhausted from hawking, her face a mask of dust and shadows, that Dad suddenly pounced on me. He whipped out his belt from his trousers, locked the door, tore the shirt off my back, and flogged me mercilessly. He lashed me as I ran, wincing, round the room. He thrashed me with the full energies and muscles of his great furious body. His flogging filled me with lightning flashes of pain. Every part of me burned with rawness. He had a savage expression on his face. The belt cracked like a horsewhip. I jumped and danced in fiendish contortions. He belted my feet, my neck, my back, my legs, my hands. He chastised me the way a master boxer beats an inferior sparring partner, with rage and methodical application. As he did so, he said:

'You are a stubborn child, I am a stubborn father. If you want to return to the world of spirits, return! But if you want to stay, then be a good son!'

I gave up running round the room and collapsed in a heap near the door. I no longer felt the pain. Not once did I cry out. He wanted evidence that his punishment was being felt. I didn't give him that satisfaction. His anger increased. And so after a long time, when I was no longer sure whether he was still punishing me or whether I was merely dreaming the pain, he stopped, gave up, held his arm, and sat on his chair. I lay on the floor. Mum came and lifted me to the bed.

'Don't give him any food tonight!' Dad thundered, getting up.

That evening I watched them eating. Later, Mum relented and gave me some food in secret, but I refused it. Dad slept peacefully that night, snoring like a bully. The next day I refused to go to school. I refused to play. I refused to eat. And I stayed in bed, growing in stature, full of vengeance. That was how I went into a curious state of being. I began to feed on my hunger. I fed well and had a mighty appetite. I dipped into myself and found other worlds waiting. I chose a world and lingered. There were no spirits there. It was a world of wraiths. A world of famine, famishment, and drought. I dwelt amongst them for a long time. Mum would sometimes wake me up. Dad grumbled incessantly about the amount of money it cost to feed me. He ranted about the cost of glass, the humiliations I had made him suffer in secret and in public, about the agony of his work and how I made his dreams wither because I was such a bad son. I stopped listening to him. I withdrew from the world of feelings, sentiments, sympathies. I refused to eat the next night. My mouth became dry. I lost energy and felt myself becoming light. I felt a terrible ecstasy growing in me. I smelt the world of holidays, the world of spirits. I saw the fields of music, the fountains of delights. My head filled with air. My face shrank. My eyes expanded. I listened to the music of famine.

On the third day of refusing to eat, I began to leave the world. Everything became distant. I willed myself away, wanting to leave, singing the song of departures that only my spirit companions can render with the peculiar beauty of flutes over desolate mountains. Mum's face was far away. The distance between us grew. Dad's face, large and severe, no longer frightened me. His assumption that the severity of his features gave him power over anything made him look a little comical. I punished him by retreating from the world. I tortured them both by listening with fullness of heart to the unsung melodies of spirit companions. My stomach, feeding on the diet of the other world, on the air of famine, grew bigger. I drank in the evils of history. I drank in the food of suffering that gathers in the space just above the air we breathe, just within range of all that we see. And then I heard Mother weeping. I refused to be moved. I sank into the essential indifferent serenity of the spirit-child's soul – the serenity that accepts extremes of experience calmly because the spirit-child is at home with death. I did not sleep for three days. I did not eat. Mum wept. She seemed a long way off, in a remote part of the earth. I ranged deeper into that other world.

On the fourth day, the amnesia of hunger began to spread its curious ecstasy over my paradoxical soul. Then I found the three-headed spirit sitting beside me. He had never left. He had been waiting patiently. He could always count on the unintended callousness of human beings, their lovelessness, their forgetfulness of the basic things of existence. For a while, the three-headed spirit stayed silent. Dad was on his chair, polishing his boots. He looked at me furtively. I felt the frailty of parents, how powerless they really are. And because Dad said nothing to me, because he made no attempts to reach me, made no gestures towards me, did nothing to appease me, did not even attempt a smile at me, I listened to what the three-headed spirit was saying.

'Your parents are treating you atrociously,' he said. 'Come with me. Your companions are desperate to embrace you. There is a truly wonderful feast awaiting your homecoming. They yearn for your lovely presence. You will be treated like a prince, which is what you are. Human beings don't care. They don't know how to love. They don't know what love is. Look at them. You are dying and all they do is polish their boots. Do they love you? No!'

I paid attention to the words of the spirit. And his words led me into a blue terrain beyond the hungers of the flesh. Sunbirds sang from branches. The trees were golden. I travelled on the wind of amnesia till we came to a mighty green road.

'This road has no end,' said the three-headed spirit.

'Where does it lead?' I asked.

'Everywhere. It leads to the world of human beings and to the world of spirits. It leads to heaven and hell. It leads to worlds that we don't even know about.'

We travelled the road. All the trees around could move and had their own form of speech. Every tree had a distinct personality and character. Some of the trees were quite evil and the bizarre forms of witches and wizards were perched on their branches, eyeing us with special interest. As we travelled on I saw a bird with Madame Koto's face. It circled over us three times and flew on ahead. The road sloped downwards. The deeper we went the more vivid the colours of that world became. There were colours I never knew existed, colours so dazzling, so full of health and radiance, colours that blurred all distinctions between brightness and darkness, that seemed to occupy the highest octaves of new dreams, that I travelled in a state of perpetual astonishment. The world kept changing. The road began to move. It behaved like a river, and it flowed against the direction of our journey. Travelling suddenly became very difficult. My feet hurt, I was excruciatingly hungry, and with each step I felt like giving up. I had thought the journey to the other world would be an effortless one.

'Are we travelling this road to the end?'

'Yes,' the spirit said, walking as if distance meant nothing.

'But you said the road has no end.'

'That's true,' said the spirit.

'How can it be true?'

'From a certain point of view the universe seems to be composed of paradoxes. But everything resolves. That is the function of contradiction.'

'I don't understand.'

'When you can see everything from every imaginable point of view you might begin to understand.'

'Can you?'

'No.'

Dad got up from his chair and stood over me. His breathing manifested itself as a heavy wind in the world in which I was travelling. The wind blew me on. I felt very light. Every time my exhaustion threatened to wash over me completely, this wind lifted me up in the air. The spirit caught me and dragged me down to the ground.

'Don't fly away,' the spirit said. 'If you fly away I don't know where you will land. There are many strange things here that devour the traveller. There are many spirit-eaters and monsters of the inter-spaces. Keep to the solid ground.'

Dad coughed, and I tripped over a green bump on the road. We travelled on. Then we came to the beginnings of an orange-coloured valley. The colours of the valley also kept changing. One moment it was blue, the next it was silver, but when I first saw it the valley was orange. Trees with each fruit as a human head populated the roadsides and the high grounds of the valley. I recognised some of the faces. The fruits fell, the faces dropped to the ground, the sun melted them, they became precious waters which flowed to the roots of the trees, and new faces appeared as beautiful fruits on the branches. The process of falling and regrowing seemed very quick and I saw several faces die and be reborn in moments between a single footstep.

The valley was essentially populated with strange beings. Instead of faces they had masks that became more beautiful the longer you looked at them. Maybe their masks were their faces. They had houses all along the sides of the valley. They also had their palaces and centres of culture below, under the earth. Their acropoles, along with their fabulous cemeteries, were in the air. In the valley they were all hard at work.

'What are they doing?' I asked.

Dad crouched low, his face close to mine. He touched me, and I shivered.

'They are building a road.'

'Why?'

Dad held my hands. I felt cold and began to tremble. He breathed in my face and the wind almost knocked my head away and I kept being flung up into the spaces and the spirit finally had to hold me down by my hair.

'They have been building that road for two thousand years.'

'But they haven't gone far at all.'

'I know. They have only built two feet of the road.'

'But they are working so hard.'

'What has that got to do with it?'

'All they seem to be doing is building the road.'

'Absolutely.'

'But why are they building it?'

Dad touched my face and his hands burnt me. He shook me. I felt my bones rattle. My head rocked violently. He churned the emptiness of my stomach, and stirred the fury of my famishment. He stared deep into my eyes. Some of the inhabitants of the valley stopped working and turned their masked faces towards us. Dad threw me back on the bed, got up, and left the room. The people resumed working.

'Because they had a most wonderful dream.'

'What dream?'

Dad slammed the door shut when he left the room. The force of its slamming shook me all over.

'They had been living for eternity as faces on the great tree. They got tired of eternity. They were the ones that the sun didn't melt into precious water. They became beings, people in masks. One day their prophet told them that there were worlds and worlds of people high up. The prophet spoke of a particular people. A great people who did not know their own greatness. The prophet called that world Heaven and said they should build a great road so that they could visit those people, and that those people could visit them. In this way they would complete one another and fulfil an important destiny in the universe.'

'Why did the prophet call that other world Heaven?'

'Because his people are the dead.'

'How can the dead have prophets?'

'There are many ways to be dead. Besides, the dead are not what you think.'

'Carry on with what you were sáying.'

'About what?'

'About why the prophet called the other world Heaven.'

'Yes, because the prophet's people are the dead. Heaven means different things to different people. They wanted to live, to be more alive. They wanted to know the essence of pain, they wanted to suffer, to feel, to love, to hate, to be greater than hate, and to be imperfect in order to always have something to strive towards, which is beauty. They wanted also to know wonder and to live miracles. Death is too perfect.'

'So why has it taken them so long to build so little?'

'Their prophet said many things which they never understood. One of the things their prophet said was that the road cannot be finished.'

'Why not?'

'What their prophet meant was that the moment it is finished all of them will perish.'

'Why?'

'I suppose they will have nothing to do, nothing to dream for, and no need for a future. They will perish of completeness, of boredom. The road is their soul, the soul of their history. That is why, when they have built a long section of it, or forgotten the words of their prophet and begun to think they have completed it, landquakes happen, lightning strikes, invisible volcanoes erupt, rivers descend on them, hurricanes tear up their earth, the road goes mad and twists and destroys itself, or the people become distorted in spirit and start to turn the road into other things, or the workers go insane, the people start wars, revolts cripple everything and a thousand things distract them and wreck what they have built and a new generation comes along and begins again from the wreckage.'

I looked at the road with new eyes. It was short and marvellous. It was a work of art, a shrine almost, beautiful beyond description, created out of the most precious substances in the world, out of amethysts and chrysoberyl, inlaid with carnelian, brilliant with patterned turquoise.

'Why is it so beautiful?'

'Because each new generation begins with nothing and with everything. They know all the earlier mistakes. They may not know that they know, but they do. They know the early plans, the original intentions, the earliest dreams. Each generation has to reconnect the origins for themselves. They tend to become a little wiser, but don't go very far. It is possible that they now travel slower, and will make bigger, better mistakes. That is how they are as a people. They have an infinity of hope and an eternity of struggles. Nothing can destroy them except themselves and they will never finish the road that is their soul and they do not know it.'

'So why don't you tell them?'

'Because they have the great curse of forgetfulness. They are deaf to the things they need to know the most.'

'Can I tell them?'

The spirit stared hard at me, and continued travelling. We went down into the valley. When we got to the lowest point the colour of the place transformed from orange to deepest red. The sun was blue. Constellations were visible in the sky, each star a different colour, luminous and pulsing. The redness of the place came from the lights converging on the substances of the valley. The redness hurt me all over and then it changed, astonishingly, to a ravishing golden hue, pierced with a shimmering of crimson lights. The valley was a place of marvellous reality. We went amongst the inhabitants working in the valley, creating their road. As they worked, striking their tools against the earth, against metal, compressing and distilling the gemlike substances with which they made their road, they produced wonderful music. The music came entirely from their tools, from their work. When we were amongst the inhabitants of that golden valley I experienced a rare serenity. The people could not speak; they had no need of speech. Lights came out of the holes of their eyes. The lights were understood. They clustered round us and led us to their houses. We stayed amongst them and rested. We were treated like honoured guests, like people whose coming had been prophesied in oracles and riddles. We were given food, which the spirit told me not to eat, but which he ate with great relish, feeding all three heads, while I became more wraith-like with hunger. My growling stomach alarmed our hosts. They held feasts in honour of our presence which lasted several days. They had clearly misunderstood the prophecies concerning our arrival, if it was us they meant, for towards the end of the feasting Mum came into the room and wept over me. Her tears became a rainfall which wiped away the most recent labours of the people. Dad came in and shouted at me and his anger resulted in thunder and rainstorms and hurricanes. The people began to look upon us as harbingers of disaster, bringers of misfortune. They were so disgusted that they began to make plans to sacrifice us on altars of gold in the names of those most revered prophets whom they had consistently misunderstood.

'It's time to leave,' the spirit said.

Mum wept over me, pleading with me in simple words of love, and I was a little moved. It rained so heavily that the houses of the valley got flooded. A river, roaring and delighted with the prospect of fresh destruction, descended on the land, smashed the houses, felled the trees, which instantly regrew, and destroyed sections of the enchanting road. The spirit grabbed me and led me over the wreckage. The acropolis had become a place of ruins. Time had accelerated over the land. Heliotropes and hibiscus, wall-flowers and cana-lilies grew wild in the once flourishing sites of the enact-ment of their Mysteries. Their city stank of dead lands. The people were in deep mourning, not for the children and families that had been killed in the flood, but for the destruction of parts of their road. Their wailing sounded everywhere. The sun was now a pure white. The sky was black. The stars were drunk with the brilliance of their own indescribable colours. The road of two thousand years had been laid waste and the people bewailed their fate and some of them committed suicide at the loss of a way and their bodies were burnt at the root of evil trees. The warriors began to search for us everywhere, believing that only our deaths could in some way restore the potency of their ancient dream, the power of their way.

As the spirit led us through secret tunnels of water, up into the land, a group of warriors attacked us. They stoned us, shot arrows at us, and fired guns at us. We fled. I was wounded in the stomach. The wound bled into my hunger. I shouted at them, saying:

'Why are you attacking us? It's not our fault . . .'

'Shut up!' the spirit said.

I ignored him.

'. . . Your road will never be finished anyway!' I cried.

I had barely completed the statement, which was drowned out by all the noise and wailing around, when a most ominous roll of thunder gathered.

'You are a fool!' the spirit said.

'Why?'

The thunder broke over our heads and lightning cleaved the land and in front of us a monstrous chasm burst open on that strange earth. On the other side of the chasm our own road continued. The chasm was the lowest point of our journey.

'Because,' said the spirit, 'you have annoyed their god.'

'How?'

'Their god didn't want them to understand what the prophet said.'

'Then why did their god allow the prophet to say it?'

'Because it is true.'

'You mean their god doesn't want them to know the truth?'

'Yes and no. They will know what they need to know when they need to know it. Only gods know the truth. Only all of the gods united into one God can know all of the truth. The people will have to become gods, and they are not ready, and will not be ready for thousands and thousands of years. Besides, it is bad to have too many gods in the universe. And so the people know as much as they need. When they need more, seek more, they will find more. Do you think it is good to know all the truth when you are just beginning to build a great road?'

'No.'

The spirit was silent.

'I don't think they heard me anyway. There was a lot of noise around.'

'Don't worry about that. The people are deaf to the truth. It is their god you have angered. Our journey will become a bit more perilous, that's all.'

It was my turn to be silent. All around houses collapsed of their own enigmatic will. The road howled. The land contorted in the agony of a bad dream. The people were bewildered. Wondrous flowers burst out of the barren places, sprouted out of the wreckage. The blood of the dead bloomed into silver-coloured trees. Red geraniums, like spontaneous flames, leapt into being on the golden edges of the valley. Roses flowered in the air. The acropolis smelled of death and beauty, the aroma of beauty conquering decay. The weeping inhabitants didn't notice the transformation taking place under the alcoholic potency of the air.

'How are we going to cross this chasm?'

'It was your fault.'

'I am sorry.'

'We are going to have to cross it. Your companions are desperately waiting for your arrival.'

'How are we going to cross it though?'

The spirit said nothing. Thunder growled in the distance. The lights changed over everything and the golden hue deepened till it became a kind of radiant darkness.

'I am going to have to tie you to my back, because I still cannot trust you.'

'Why can't you trust me?'

'I'm still not sure you want to return to your companions.'

Before I could protest the spirit caught me, pinned me to the ground with its weight of a mountain, and tied me up with silver cords. At the same moment Mum came into the room, lowered her face to mine, and embraced me tight. The spirit tied me to its back.

'You've become so light anyway that you will be no problem in the flying.'

Mum talked to me in the deepest hours of the darkening golden hue. Her embrace tightened. The spirit stood poised over the chasm.

'Are you ready?'

'No,' I said.

Mum pressed her warm face to mine and lifted me up. The spirit leapt into the chasm. The silver cord kept me steady. My feet dangled. My hands were free. A powerful wind rushed through my mind. My hunger enveloped me in its void. Something inside me expanded with terror. The spirit flew over, fighting the white wind, dipping into the chasm. There was a terrifying whiteness at the bottom of the abyss. I screamed. The whiteness was a force that seemed to pull us down. Suddenly, I couldn't see. The wind felt like rocks hurled at us. The abyss was full of lurking terrors, monsters, prodigies, black illumination, white cries and incantatory noises that never ceased speaking with the wind's frightening voice. With a supreme effort, the spirit lifted us higher, into a roseate sky. Mum held me aloft and carried me to the bed. She hovered with me in the air for a while, speaking good words to me in the voice of the sky. The spirit said:

'Don't be afraid.'

I wasn't any more. Mum's voice was in my soul. The spirit hovered over the green road and as we landed I heard a great noise behind us, a bolt of thunder, the clapping of mighty godlike hands. Mum laid me gently on the bed. The silver cords binding me to the spirit were loosened. They vanished. When I got up and looked back I saw that the chasm had gone and the valley of gold had disappeared.

'They have reappeared somewhere else,' the spirit said.

The spirit pushed on and I followed reluctantly. The road swept upwards. There were no trees around. I heard the susurration of rivers.

'Up at the top of the road is where all the rivers of this world meet,' the spirit informed me.

'What happens there?'

Mum touched my face. Her fingers smelt of rosemary.

'When we get there I will tell you.'

Mum left the room and I travelled lightly. I found it difficult going up the long road.

'I'm hungry.'

'Don't eat anything,' the spirit said. Taking my cue, he produced some food from the air, and ate happily. 'If you eat anything you won't arrive and you won't be able to return. You'll be stuck here in the dreaded interspaces.'

We travelled up the road for a long time. I grew weary, but the spirit wouldn't let me rest. We came to a swamp full of crocodiles and snakes. The swamp kept bubbling. Yellow gases wafted up from the surface. And then the bird with Madame Koto's face alighted on the bank. A snake slithered towards the bird. There was a sudden noise, and the bird took off. To my horror a yellow hand emerged from the swamp, shot up in the air, and caught the bird with a terrible precision. The hand withdrew swiftly into the swamp and the bird vanished under.

Further on I saw a lizard with the blind old man's face. It was playing an accordion at the roadside. I chased it.

'Come back!' the spirit ordered.

I ignored the spirit and pursued the lizard, which scuttled into an aquamarine undergrowth. I tore after it into the undergrowth. The lizard ran on. I stamped on its tail. The tail came off. The lizard stopped for a moment, mystified. Then I pounced on its head with a stone, but the lizard escaped me and dropped its tiny accordion, which I squashed completely with the stone, producing a little din of angry music. I was still searching furiously for the lizard, to smash it utterly, for I was sure it would have some sort of effect on the blind old man, when the spirit came and dragged me away.

We went on climbing the road. Soon its gentle green surface gave way to green rocks and stones. They were sharp underfoot and they hurt with each step. Then the stones and rocks became a fine spread of bright green glass which cut into me. I bled all the way up the endless road. Behind me the redness glittered on the green, and the blood evaporated, and its mist coloured the air.

'You need to lose all your blood before you arrive,' said the spirit.

When I thought I could no longer bear the pain underfoot and the hunger, when the roadsides became littered with dried corpses, skeletons of babies, skulls chattering rhymed verse, the road changed into a green stream. It was carpeted with thickly matted weeds. We walked on the carpet of stream-weeds.

'Soon we will get to the great river,' said the spirit. 'Be grateful. When we cross the river there is no turning back. Your companions and the whole of the spirit world and the goddess of the spirit-rivers will have a wonderful banquet awaiting you, because you are their prodigal friend.'

We travelled on. I dragged behind, my stomach flaming, my soles wounded, and my blood no longer red but blue, like ink, inscribing my barely decipherable history on the matted weeds. The spirit marched on in front, occasionally looking back to make sure I was still following. Then the stream became a plateau of cotton-wool, or was it mist, or was it clouds? I heard wailing all around. The spirit, after a while, yelled:

'Look! I see the river-bank!'

I did not share its exultation. We approached the river-bank. The river was an expanse so smooth, so unruffled, it seemed impossible that it was composed of water. It seemed like nothing, emptiness, air. Near the bank, on what should have been the water, there was a dug-out canoe. Next to the canoe was a figure, head covered in a black hood, whom I assumed to be the ferryman of the dead.

When we got near the bank I saw no birds. No breezes wafted

over the river. There was no spray, no mist. Nothing stirred on its blinding expanse. There were no sounds of any sort, not even the gentlest ripple of water could be heard. As we neared the canoe the figure stood up. Over the expanse of unnatural water, still and frightening, an infinity of silver, the figure's reflections were multiplied. It was only when I looked at the river properly that I realised it was a vast, undisturbed mirror. The canoe stood on a haze of light, without troubling the mirror's surface. The lights of that world, converging on its shimmering surface, made me utterly transparent, as if I had disappeared from reality, become a ghost. For a moment my eyes, suffused with light and silver, were blinded. Then Dad came back into the room with the moon in his eyes.

He hovered over me.

'My son,' he said, gently, 'there is a wonderful wind blowing in my mind. I drank the moon tonight. The stars are playing on a flute. The air is sweet with the music of an invisible genius. Love is crying in my flesh, singing strange songs. The rain is full of flowers and their scent makes me tremble as if I am becoming a real man. I see great happiness in our future. I see joy. I see you walking out of the sun. I see gold in your eyes. Your flesh glitters with the dust of diamonds. I see your mother as the most beautiful woman in the world.'

And then he was silent.

I wanted him to carry on speaking. His words offered me water and food and new breathing. But he stayed silent and his quiet breath did not stir the slightest wind on the face of the great mirror.

And then, to my utter astonishment, Dad knelt by the bed. He rested his head on the pillow and the smell of alcohol floated on his quiet breathing. When he moved his head, turning the moon in his eyes away from me, as if he were ashamed of revealing something that would free him, the figure by the canoe turned towards us and lifted off its black hood. Standing there, crowned in black light, was a naked young woman, with an old woman's face. Her eyes were harder, and glinted brighter, than diamonds.

'Where is the ferryman?' asked the spirit imperiously.

The spirit's voice reverberated, becoming sharper each time, over the horizon of mirrors. The woman did not reply. She took a step towards us and for the first time I noticed that she had the feet of a lioness. Her eyes were those of a tiger. The spirit went forward, attempted to brush her aside, to reach the canoe. Lightning flashed from their contact. The light was so dazzling that for a while all I saw were two small moons revolving in a glass of clear alcohol.

Dad was saying:

'I see us dancing on lovely beaches. The water-maiden sings for us. I see the days of our misery turn over and become bright. My son, my only son, your mother has never ceased being a young woman rich with hopes, and me a young man. We are poor. We have little to give you, but our love. You came out of our deepest joy. We prayed for you. We wanted you. And when you were born you had a mysterious smile on your face. The years passed and we watched the smile grow smaller, but its mystery remains. Don't you feel for us? Every moment that my head is bursting with loads at the garage, my soul is brimming with good dreams for you. In this life you have seen how sweet even sorrow can be. Our life appears to be a sad music. So how can you come and then leave us? Do you know our misery? Do you know how you make even that bearable? They say you are an abiku child, that you care nothing for your parents, that you are cold, and that you have eyes only for that special spirit who is a beautiful young girl with golden bangles and copper anklets. But I do not believe them. You have wept for us and watered the tree of love. We have suffered for you. Suffering is our home. We did not make this strange bed that we have to sleep on. But this world is real. I have bled in it. So have you. Your mother has bled in it even more than we have. There are beautiful young girls here with soft tender voices and eyes that God made with moonlight. Must I sing to you all night, for seven days, and sacrifice two white hens, and two dizzying bottles of ogogoro, before you hear me? And even now your mother is wandering about in the night, crying to the wind and the road and the hidden angels, looking for a way to reach you. Does this life not move you? When you play in the streets and see the children die, and hear the mothers weep, and hear the old ones sing of each miraculous birth, is your heart untouched? We have sorrow here. But we also have celebration. We know the special joys. We have sorrow, but it is the sister of love, and the mother of music. I have seen you dance, my son. And if you will not listen to my song, I will not sing any more.'

Again he fell silent.

I tried to move, to indicate to him that I had been listening, that tears flowed in my soul, but he made a sudden movement which alarmed me. I heard a loud noise in advance. I looked for his eyes. I saw only the spirit crouching, swaying violently, a weapon in its hands, attacking the woman. They fought one another through all their reflections. The spirit struck the woman and a great din, steel on steel, crashed all around me. The spirit went on striking her till golden blood flowed from her wounds. She made no attempt to defend herself. The golden blood flowed down her and resolved itself into a dazzling protective shield. Then she drew a weapon from her body, and waved it in the air. Suddenly I saw both of them mirrored to eternity. They were everywhere and each reflection was real. And then, as if behind a glass window illuminated at night, I slowly made out Dad's face. He watched me with calm eyes, while the spirit fought the woman. They fought on the river of glass, fought on the canoe, fought in the sky. And Dad spoke gently in my ears, as if I were a flower.

'We are the miracles that God made to taste the bitter fruits of time. We are precious, and one day our suffering will turn into wonders of the earth. The sky is not our enemy. There are things that burn me now which turn golden when I am happy. Do you not see the mystery of our pain? That we bear poverty, are able to sing and dream sweet things, and that we never curse the air when it is warm, or the fruit when it tastes so good, or the lights that bounce gently on the waters. We bless things even in our pain. We bless them in silence. That is why our music is sweet. It makes the air remember. There are secret miracles at work, my son, that only time will bring forth. I too have heard the dead singing. They tell me that this life is good. They tell me to live it gently, with fire, and always with hope, my son. There is wonder here and there is surprise in everything that you cannot see. The ocean is full of songs. The sky is not our enemy. Destiny is our friend.'

Kneeling by the bed, he sang wonderful tunes into my ears. He told me stories in songs about our ancestors who had left their original land and made a strange place their home; about grandfather who fought a great spirit of the forest for seven days and was made the Priest of the Shrine of Roads; about gods who divided the universe between the land of spirits, the land of humans, and the infinite regions of heavenly beings, and who gave in all realms a special homeland for the brave.

Then abruptly he stopped speaking. The lights changed. Time contorted. Weapons created great sparks over my face. Dad held a knife over me. I heard the cry of a white bird. The old woman, waving her weapon, golden in the brightness of mirrors, swung at the spirit, and severed one of its heads. The spirit let out a horrifying cry, utterly human. The woman slashed off its second head. Feathers

338

fell in frenzy over me. The blood of the spirit spattered my face and momentarily blinded me. And when I looked again I saw Dad tower over me, a white hen in one hand, a knife of menacing sharpness in the other. Mum stood with her back to the window, surrounded by nine blue candles, and a configuration of cowries. Dad held the white hen firmly, wings and feet and head. Blood dripped down his arms. There was another figure in the room, whose shadow expanded the spaces, filled it with the aroma of wild village shrines, and the solemnity of rock-faced priests. He danced about the room with a mighty fan of eagle feathers that threatened to set the room into flight. His dancing, fervent and insane, with red amulets and cowries cackling round his neck, became the whirling torment of the twice-beheaded spirit.

The weapon of the old woman with the feet of a lioness had become golden-red. One of the heads of the spirit had rolled on to the river of mirrors and its eyes stared at the eternity of reflections in a bad-tempered astonishment. The spirit, turning round and round, howling, spinning, confused, made for the dug-out canoe. He suddenly jumped in, pushed the canoe out on the mirror, and began to row on the lights. The old woman went towards him, striding on silver, weapon raised. Dad's knife, full of reflections, was lifted above me, as if I were to be the sacrificial victim of my own birth. I screamed. The knife in Dad's hand descended swiftly, slashed the air twice. The herbalist released a piercing cry. The old woman struck the spirit at the same moment, with a mighty swipe of her weapon. Dad slashed the chicken's throat. The old woman severed the spirit's last head. The spirit fought vainly in the canoe as the chicken twitched. Its blood dripped on my forehead. The herbalist fell silent. The spirit's head, landing on silver, looked around, saw itself separated from its body, and let out its final scream of horror, cracking the surface of the river. The mirrors shattered. It became dark. Splinters and reflections caught in my eyes.

THREE

MUM WAS SITTING beside me, stroking my eyelids. Dad sat on his chair, his forehead creased, stubbles of beard on his chin. There was a full bottle of whisky on the table. There was the smell of superb cooking in the air. I opened my eyes wide and said:

'Where is the road?'

Dad immediately rushed at me and kept my eyes open with his fingers. Mum poured a black liquid into my eyes. The liquid hurt when I shut my eyes. But when they were wide open they did not hurt. I stared wide-eyed at everything. The herbalist was gone. His shadow and the flight of his eagle feathers remained. Mum made me drink bitter herbs. Dad made razor incisions on my chest and shoulders and forehead and pressed stinging potions on the cuts. I cried out for food. They paid no attention. I tried returning to my journey but couldn't shut my eyes. Mum fed me water, and pap, and orange juice. Dad, lingering in the shadow of the herbalist, looked as if he hadn't slept all his life. Mum was so gaunt, and bony, and beautiful in her sorrow, so radiant at seeing me alive, that I wept for them both. Dad burst into song. Mum stroked my temples. I hadn't eaten for two weeks. The doctors had pronounced me dead. But I had never really left the world of the living.

FOUR

I WAS FED gradually; from pap, they moved me on to heavier food. Mum spent much love creating for me the most ravishing dishes. I wondered where they got the money for delicious soups of goat-meat and stockfish, the peppersoup full of new yams, the vegetable dishes, the stews with aromatic peppers and bright-red lobsters. I had become very lean and insubstantial, too weak to move. Walking was painful, my soles hurt, my eyes developed odd irritations. Each night the liquid they poured into my eyes made my sleep shallow. I slept the way rabbits do, with eyes open, to fool antagonists. Dad stayed up most nights, alternating with Mum, watching over me. Candles burned into the dawns.

The herbalist came again on another visit. He performed rituals and treated me with the deepest suspicion. He told Dad and Mum to be kinder to me, to not shout, not beat, not restrict me, to not quarrel amongst themselves, and he hinted at the prospect of performing the ceremonies that would cut off my access to the world of spirits. He said something about the importance of retrieving my spirit tokens which he believed I had hidden in secret places. He spoke to them at night, while they thought I was asleep. I immediately thought of him as an enemy. He collected his exorbitant fee and when he left he took his sentient shadows away.

And so for a long time they spoke to me gently, and treated me kindly, as if I were a newborn child. When I ate the choice dishes Mum prepared both sat opposite and watched me, smiling. Mum's eyes became bright with joy and, curiously, with pride. Dad watched me as if I were a strange and surprising animal. They kept pleading with me to eat more than I wanted. They bought me soft drinks and Dad shared his whisky with me. If they had enormous difficulties earning money, if Dad had suffered untold humiliations, unspeakable torments borrowing the money or carrying loads, if Mum walked the entire city selling her provisions, crying out in

341

dust-dried streets, her voice hoarse, they did not show it. Somehow my return had assumed great importance. I felt bad that I may have increased their suffering. I tried to please them, to run errands, wash plates, stay in, attend school. But they seemed more anxious to please me and they took offence if I tried to do anything. During that time Dad swept the room, fetched water from the well, came back from work always with a cheerful spirit, was delicate and kind to Mum, and would hug her often, and would sit on his chair, smoking and singing bright ancestral songs.

It seemed that our lives would know a new dawn, take on new colours of sweetness, and that in the warm spirit our miseries would be transformed into something miraculous and tangible like the birds of heaven. The world was new to me, everything was fresh. It was the earliest days of creation. I marvelled at cobwebs and cockroaches. I couldn't stop staring at people's faces and their eyes. The fact that human beings talked, laughed, wept, sweated, sang, without some visible thing which made all the animation possible, the fact that they were alive in their bodies, contained this thing called life in their flesh, seemed incredible to me. I watched babies with open-mouthed wonder. I couldn't get over the fact that we can look out of our eyes, out of our inner worlds at people, but that people, looking at us couldn't see into our eyes, our thoughts, our inner worlds. How transparent one feels, but how opaque: it mystified me. Even the act of motion, human beings walking on two legs, balancing on them, surprised me. With eyes wide open from a new fear of sleep, I looked at the world, I tried to see all that was in it, I embraced all things into my life. I hugged the alarming mystery of reality, and grew stronger.

Everything felt strange to me. Everything felt as if it were both floating away and being reborn for ever. Even our neighbours who had grudges against us came one evening to pay us a visit. They brought gifts of sweets, drinks, and lengths of new cloth. They brought their children to play with me. They drank and talked merrily with Mum and Dad, as if there had never been great animosities between us. Their faces were all vaguely familiar. I felt I had been away a long time. During that period names were a mystery to me and I pronounced their different nicknames or public names over and over again as if for the first time. I played, it seemed to me, in slow motion, with the children, touching them tenderly.

Our neighbours spoke warmly to me. As they spoke I watched their faces. My heart heaved for them all. Like a stranger, I saw the suffering on their faces, the years of misery and suspicion, their extreme sensitivity to slights, the vigour of their reactions, the energy of their appetites, their boundless enthusiasm and hope. Their faces, solid and thickly masked with time, seemed fragile to me. Everywhere terror looked out at them. Years of frustration had turned their eyes into instruments which looked out at the world with a peculiar, unforgiving, sharpness; often, even, with meanness. And yet, there they were, with privation before them, hunger behind them, paying us a visit to welcome me back from being dead.

FIVE

DAD BOUGHT THEM drinks. Mum served them food. They all talked in subdued tones as if in the presence of a corpse. It was from them that I learnt of some of the things that had been happening during the time that I had been away.

There had been a break in the rainy season. Houses had been flooded and whole families had been forced to move. Streets had become streams. Improvised graveyards had become so waterlogged that coffins had been seen floating past houses, or beached in front of the abodes of certain minor politicians. Electric cables had been brought down by the force of wind and rain and, some people added, by the forces against progress. Fishes had been found in wells. A snake had slid into a house and killed a woman. People said the snake had been sent by an enemy. I heard stories of politicians, who were members of secret societies, who tried to hold back the rain because of the grand rally which they had to keep postponing. I heard that Madame Koto had joined them. I also heard that one day she had slipped on the muddy ground, had taken a nasty fall, and had to be rushed to a powerful herbalist. That was how the talk went, from the most ordinary events to the most singular, from the man who had raved under a tremendous downpour, swearing that he saw red eagles with flowers in their mouths, to the woman who was said to have given birth to a big white egg.

They spoke of strange things and omens, of the blind old man who had woken up one night screaming that a giant lizard was pursuing him and that it had smashed his accordion. They spoke of omens in the movements of giant constellations. A star had fallen into the Atlantic. Another star had burst into being over our area. Birds of gold had been seen at night. Sweet songs had been heard by women in the dark, songs wandering down the empty street. People dreamed of statues that walked, bringing gifts to the area; they dreamed of birds and butterflies, of hybrid animals, of antelopes

344

with jewelled necklaces, of beggars who were princesses, of a rain of gold dust, of the land suffocating with plenitude while the majority starved, of a cornucopia two decades long with darkness to follow, of miracles on hungry roads, of the wise man who would emerge from nowhere to rule and transform the future agonies of the land. They even talked of widespread rumours, confirmed on two continents, about one of our most important politicians who had been sighted on the moon. Listening to them instilled in me an absolute awe of the world. I was lightning-struck by life. When they left, my brain fairly combusted with the realities they had conjured in low voices. A brilliant aura linked Mum and Dad that night. They glowed with an almost spectral radiance. I felt exhausted and restless. I wanted to see the world again. Mum sang. Dad said:

'Birth brings glory.'

I slept on the bed that night. Mum and Dad slept on the mat. Later I heard them moving and whispering, moving and shaking the floor, as if they were in a hurry to fill the world with glories.

SECTION TWO

Book Six

ONE

I BECAME STRONGER. I ventured out into the street. It dawned on me that I had been granted a greater freedom, so long as I stayed alive. When I went out to play it seemed that something had altered the world. Bushes and strange plants had grown wild everywhere. The rain had beaten holes in the ground. Streets were unpassable for mud. Trees had fallen across paths and roads. Electric cables dangled in the air. I tried to wander – my feet had begun to itch – but water blocked off my attempts. The rain too had made the world smaller. In the forest the ground was thick with mud and yellow leaves and sacrificial offerings. I wandered about in the devastation of our area. It wasn't much fun. The rain had completely joined whole streets to the marshland. All the streets in our area were once part of a river. As always, the river god was claiming back his terrain.

And so with nowhere to go I was forced to be content with the distractions our street offered. As I had to avoid two places along our street I found them both quite magnetic. I climbed a tree, sat on a branch like an awkward bird, and watched both houses. Children were playing outside the blind old man's bungalow. He was not around. His chair was on the verandah, soaked with rain. His window had been broken and the room seemed empty. Madame Koto's bar was different. The barfront was covered in water and weeds. Planks on stones led to the bar. Her signboard was askew. The curtain strips had thinned and I could just about see in. Electric cables had been connected to her roof from a pole on the street. She was the only one who had this privilege. A few cars arrived at the barfront and blasted their horns. A great number of women came out of the bar, chattering and laughing. Dancing to strains of music, they filed across the planks. Madame Koto, her stomach bigger than ever, her right foot bandaged, came out and waved to them. The cars drove the women away.

Madame Koto paused at the door, and surveyed the world. Her white beads sat proudly round her neck. Soon her eyes fixed in my direction. She stared at me for a long time. Then, to my amazement, she started coming towards me. I tried to get down from the tree, but the branch caught the back of my shorts. I resigned myself to what she would do. Rolling the fat of her body with each measured step, avoiding the treacherous puddles and mudholes without seeming to do so, she strode up to me. She was massive. The sheer weight of wrappers gave her a queer grandeur. There was an impressive new exhaustion on her face. She stood beneath the tree, fixing me with a stare, and said:

'Azaro, what are you doing?'

'Nothing.'

'Do you think you are a bird?'

'No.'

'Why were you staring at me just now?'

'I wasn't.'

'Come down!'

'No.'

She glared at me. Then, suddenly, she said:

'What were you doing in my dreams?'

'Nothing.'

She made an attempt to catch hold of my feet, but I withdrew them. She jumped, landed badly, hurt her foot, and gave up trying to get me to come down. She said:

'If I catch you in my dreams again I will eat you up.'

Then she hobbled back to her bar. When she had disappeared behind the curtain strips her women came out and stared at me and made abusive signs. When they got bored with watching me I got down from the tree and went home.

Dad had returned early from work. He was bare-chested and sweating. He had attached a bag full of rags to the wall and was punching it. He looked at me, sweat pouring down his face, and said:

'My son, your father is practising.'

'For what?'

'To be world champion.'

He went on hitting the bundle, making the walls tremble, each punch vibrating the foundations of the house, grunts escaping from his mouth. He went on punching the bundle till a neighbour banged on the door.

'What are you trying to do, eh?' he shouted. 'You want to break down the wall? Go and join the army instead of disturbing people!'

Dad stopped punching the bundle and began shadow-boxing. Each especially solid punch at the air was accompanied by the names of real or imagined enemies and a string of abuses. He jumped about, ducked, jabbed, threw upper cuts, feinted, and bobbed. Foam appeared on the sweat of his chest. He grew tired. He went and had a bath. When he came back I began to serve his food. He stopped me. He served the food himself. We ate together.

When we finished I went off to wash the plates. Dad sat in his chair, smoking. He was restless when I returned. I watched him silently. He looked at me every so often and smiled. Not long afterwards the landlord turned up. He didn't knock. He pushed his way in, left the door wide open, and addressed his complaints to the whole compound.

'They tell me you have been breaking down the walls! If you damage anything in my house thunder will destroy you. And you better start getting ready to move away. I am tired of your trouble!'

He stormed away. Dad carried on smoking. He hadn't moved. When the landlord left Dad got up, shut the door, and went back to his chair. We didn't say anything till Mum returned.

TWO

WE HAD NO idea how serious Dad was with his boxing. He began to train dementedly. Sometimes he would wake up at night and bob and counter-punch, hit and jab, swing punches and lash out at imaginary adversaries. In the mornings, before he chewed on his chewing stick, before he ate, he would work out all around the room. He would wake me up with his footwork and laboured breathing. I would look up from the mat and see his giant feet jumping around my head, his elbows protecting his face. He punched at the clothes-line, till the line snapped. He punched at flies and jabbed at mosquitoes. He specialised in fighting his own shadow as if it were his most hated antagonist. He would get me to stand on the bed and hold a folded towel for him. He would punch it from all angles. His movements became crab-like, and he developed the oddest upper cuts. The more he became involved in boxing, the more he ate. His appetite got so large that Mum pleaded with him to stop. We couldn't afford the money, she said. Dad ignored her. We cut down on what we ate so he could build his body. He didn't know that we did.

It got worse. Dad took to sparring with the air on his way to work. On his way back he did the same thing, shuffling, performing fancy footwork, executing kink jabs, throwing combinations. We began to think something terrible was happening to him.

'Poverty is driving him mad,' Mum said.

People began to look at us as if we were freaks. The room became too small for Dad to practise in. He had by then punched practically everything in sight. He had made my mat threadbare by standing it against the wall and thumping it. He had punched holes in the mattress. He burst the bottom of one of Mum's basins. He stopped listening to anything anyone said. He became so engrossed in his obsession. We couldn't understand it. But it was when he took to boxing on the verandah that we abandoned all attempts to comprehend what had seized hold of his brain. Something had changed in him. His eyes became cool, serene, fierce, and narrowed, all at once. He seemed to look at people as if they were transparent, insubstantial. His knuckles became big and raw from bashing the backyard walls. One day I stumbled on him in the backyard. He had a cloth round his fists and he was hitting the wall with all his strength. He went on hitting till the white cloth was covered with his blood. Then he stopped.

'To be a man is not a small thing,' he would say to me.

His shadow-boxing, however, began to attract attention. When he punched walls in the backyard the women would appear round the well, on the slightest pretext. Fetching water without using it suddenly became fashionable with the married and unmarried women. He didn't mind performing to the crowd of women and children. But he got dissatisfied with the backyard because the water spilt on the floor made it difficult to do his footwork. One day he slipped and fell. The women laughed. The next evening he shadow-boxed down the passage. And that night, when he thought the world was asleep, he resumed training in the compound-front.

On those nights Dad had the best sparring partners. He fought the wind, the midges, and the mosquitoes that rose from their millions of larvae all over the swamp of the road. I would wake at night and be aware immediately that he wasn't in the room. It was the absence of his restless energy. I would rise, tiptoe out of the room, and go to the housefront. Like a hero of the night, alone, invincible, and always battling, Dad boxed all over the grounds. He always fought several imaginary foes, as if the whole world were against him. He fought these foes unceasingly and he always knocked them out. When they had hit the floor he would throw up his arms triumphantly. For me, then, he was the king of the ghetto nights. I would watch him for a long time. The night became safer for me. And while he trained I would wander our road. When he was around the night turned everything familiar into another country, another world. What a new place the night made the ghetto! The houses were still. There were no lights anywhere. The forest was a mass of darkness, a deep blue darkness, deeper than the surrounding night. The houses, the trees, the bushes, made of our road a curious mountain range. The houses were humped like sleeping monsters in the dark. Isolated trees were a cluster of giants with wild hair, sleeping on their feet. And the road was no longer a road but the original river. Majestically it unfolded itself in the darkness, one step at a time. It was when I wandered the road at night that I first became aware that sometimes I disappeared.

353

At first it frightened me. I would be walking along, never able to see far, and then I would pass into the darkness. I would begin to look for myself. I became a dark ghost. The wind passed through me. But when I kicked a stone, or tripped, or when a light shone on me, I would become miraculously reconstituted. I would hurry back to our housefront, where Dad was still training, unaware of my presence.

He seemed so solid on those nights. The darkness became his cloak and friend. His eyes burned bright. He talked to the wind and his voice was powerful; it had weight, it was the voice of a new man. When he had finished his training he would skip and shuffle about in fascinating footworks, calling himself Black Tyger. The name began to fit. I never saw him so radiant and so strong as when he practised at night. And it was through his night training that his name began to spread. When he shadow-boxed he began to attract strange kinds of attention. I was watching him one night, with mosquitoes swarming all over me, when I saw a single light come down the road and stop not far from him. The light was by itself. It was smaller than a matchlight, but it stayed there and watched Dad box with the darkness. As time passed the number of lights that watched him increased. One day I counted three of them.

'Dad, there are three lights watching you,' I said.

'What?'

He was startled to hear my voice. I guess it was the first time he realised that I was there.

'What lights?'

I showed them to him, but he couldn't see them.

'It's your eyes,' he said, and went on with his boxing.

The lights watched him till he finished. They didn't move. The wind had no effect on them whatsoever. When we went in I looked back. They were still there.

On another night Dad was training with a peculiar ferocity when I saw a bright yellow pair of eyes come from over the swamp. It stopped not far from Dad and watched his moves. Dad ducked, shuffled sideways, switched from an anchor punch to a right cross, from an upper cut to a hook punch and ended with a jab. I saw the eyes following him. The eyes studied him as he changed from orthodox to southpaw stances. I went over to the yellow pair of eyes and found nothing there. I went back to where I had been sitting and the eyes reappeared. They stayed watching Dad till he finished for the night. We left, I stole back, and the eyes were gone.

354

An unusual thing happened the next night that I stayed up watching Dad. The lights turned up, one by one, as if they had a meeting, as if they were forming an earthly constellation. Then the yellow eyes came over from the swamp. And when Dad was taking a short break after the night's first session, a huge man stepped out of the darkness. He was too big for me not to have heard his footsteps. It seemed he had stepped out of nowhere, out of a different space. I couldn't see his eyes.

'Who are you?' he asked Dad.

Dad sized him up.

'My name is Black Tyger,' Dad said, fearlessly.

'Good.'

'And who are you?' Dad asked in return.

The man chuckled.

'They used to call me Yellow Jaguar,' the man replied.

'Good.'

'So you will fight me?'

'Yes,' Dad said.

The man chuckled again.

'Your fame is beginning to travel. But I will put an end to it.'

'Don't talk too much,' Dad said, taking up a southpaw stance.

It worried me that I couldn't see the man's eyes. The two men circled one another. Dad lashed out at him and the man grunted. Dad hit him again on the face and this time Dad cried out.

'You're like wood!' Dad said.

'Now you're talking,' the man said, and struck Dad in the face.

Dad fell, rolled over, and landed in a puddle. The man waited for him. I still couldn't see his face. Dad got up slowly, his head hanging. Suddenly he rushed the man. The three lights dispersed at the assault. Then I noticed that many other lights of different colours had appeared. The two men fell in another puddle. They picked themselves up. Dad hit the man with all his might. The man grunted again and Dad cried out.

'You're like a tree!'

The man launched a barrage of punches at Dad. And I saw Dad ducking, parrying, shuffling, blocking with his elbows, bobbing and weaving, but he didn't give way, or give ground. Then Dad, planting his feet solidly, let out a continuous animal cry, a wounded cry, and unleashed an onslaught of wild blows. He rained them down on the man. He released a veritable hurricane of combinations, of swinging punches, wild hooks, vicious crosses, crackling upper cuts. I saw

355

the man rush backwards, I saw his head lower, his arms helpless. Dad didn't stop his cry till he had beaten the man into the swamp. My spirits lifted with pride. And then the darkness, seeming to rise thicker from the swamp, covered them both. There was silence. I waited. I heard nothing. I saw nothing. Then after a while I heard feet tramping through mud. Dad emerged and slouched towards me.

'Where is the man?' I asked.

'I don't know,' Dad said, his voice heavy with exhaustion. 'He disappeared in the swamp.'

And then I heard someone kicking in the mud. Then a mighty voice, speaking with the power of the darkness, rose and said:

'I have just started!'

And the man, all thunder and density, came rushing back into the fight. As he pounded towards Dad, emerging from the darkness, two things struck me about him: he was covered completely in mud, and his eyes burned yellow. He descended on Dad like a whirlwind, a mistral, a tornado. He shattered Dad's defences. He anticipated Dad's every movement. And he knocked Dad about the place, cutting him down with swift punches and combinations, merciless blows, blinding and accurate counter-punches. Dad fell under the savage assault like a puppet. The man had become a ferocious energy, an unnatural force of nature, a storm. Like the five fingers of lightning over the forest, he appeared everywhere at the same time.

'Your eyes are too bright!' cried Dad.

And then I realised that the yellow pair of eyes had joined on to the man.

'I am a mad Jaguar!' the man boasted, and poured a frightening torrent of blows on Dad.

The man went on beating Dad, pulverising him, crushing him with an avalanche of ceaseless punches. I could see Dad falling around in exhaustion and bewilderment. There was a terrified and cowardly look in his eyes. Blood poured down the sides of his nose and the corners of his eyes. Dad was taking a cruel beating but he didn't turn around and run. He took the blows. He absorbed them. He withstood them. He soaked them into his body and spirit. I heard the wrenching of his neck. I heard the rattle of his teeth whenever the man's knuckles connected with them. I heard the grinding crunch of fists on bone. Dad cried out and groaned. And then he cowered. With his fists barely held up, Dad bent low, as if he were grovelling. The man towered over him, his yellow eyes steaming in the darkness. And then Dad crouched. He made the movements of a trapped wild animal. Then, slowly, he moved this way and that, swaying, hands in front of him like a praying mantis. Then I saw how Dad was transforming. He was going back to simple things. He was going back to water, to the earth, to the road, to soft things. He shuffled. He became fluid. He moved like a large cat. Sliding backwards, he entered into the midst of the gathered arabesque of lights. I felt a great strange energy rising from him. He was drawing it from the night, and the air, the road, his friends. The man closed in on him and Dad went on dancing backwards, shuffling, floating on his agonies, into the darkness. The lights followed him. And when his back hit the body of the burnt, rusting van, Dad stopped. He had nowhere else to go. Then suddenly, and I don't know why, and it may be one of those riddles of the Living that only the Living understand, suddenly, I cried out. My voice, sounding a moment after I had uttered the words, floated on the wind. My voice sounded too thin and frail for what it helped unleash.

'Black Tyger, USE YOUR POWER!' I cried.

And Dad, dead on cue, utterly surprised the man with the unrestrained and desperate fury of his own counter-attack. Dad rose miraculously in stature. And with all the concentrated rage and insanity of those who have a single moment in which to choose between living and dying, Dad broke the chains of his exhaustion and thundered such blows on the man as would annihilate an entire race of giants. I don't know if it was the sheer monstrous accumulation of all the blows and punches, the howitzer combinations, or if it was just one that connected with the right place, but suddenly, amidst the blur of Dad's madness, the man let out a terrified howl. He staggered backwards. Dad followed him, baffled, arms raised. Then the man stood straight and still, his bright yellow eyes askew. The wind sighed above his head. The yellow eyes dimmed. Then they shut. When his eyes closed it became darker all around, as if a mysterious lamp had been blown out. Then like a tree that had waited a long time after its death to fall, the man keeled over slowly. And when he hit the earth with an unnatural thud, the strangest thing happened. The man disappeared. Into the earth. Into the darkness. I have no way of telling. Steam, tinged with yellow, like low-burning sulphur, rose from the wet earth. The gathered lights had all gone. The night was silent. And then a hyena laughed in the forest. We looked for the man in the dark, but couldn't find him. Dad was mystified, crushed with exhaustion.

'What happened?' I asked.

357

'I don't know,' he whispered.

We waited. The wind moaned over the sleeping ghetto. Branches creaked. We felt around on the earth and then I came upon a hole. Dad went in and fetched a match. It wasn't a hole, but the full imprint of a grown man on the ground, as if he had fallen a long way. Dad was covered in mud and blood. His mouth had been beaten out of shape and his lips had grown monstrous in a short space of time. His nose was all cut up and the swellings on his forehead frightened me. Blood drooled from the cut near his eyes and from the corner of his mouth.

I began to feel cold.

'What was his name again?' Dad asked, blowing out the match.

'Yellow Jaguar,' I said.

Dad gripped me in a sudden horrifying realisation.

'Yellow Jaguar used to be a famous boxer in this area,' he said, lowering his voice fearfully.

'What happened to him?'

'He died three years ago.'

A shiver ran through my bones. I heard the wind draw a breath. Dad had beaten a boxer from the spirit world. He trembled. Then he held on to me, as if for support. I could feel him quaking.

'It's cold,' I said.

'Let's go in,' he said, hurriedly.

Then he lifted me up, ran back into the compound, and into our room. He locked the door. He sat on his chair. In the darkness we listened to Mum sleeping on the bed. Dad lit a cigarette. He smoked, his eyes blazing. I could smell the mud, the sweat, the fight, the excitement, the terror, and the blood on him. I could smell the fists of Yellow Jaguar on his spirit. I could smell Dad's rebirth in advance. Sulphur stank on his breath. It was a mystery. When he finished his cigarette he went and had a wash. He came back and swiftly got into bed. I heard him tossing, turning, and creaking his body all night. He couldn't sleep for thinking about the dead boxer. And neither could I.

THREE

DAD STAYED AT home for six days after the fight. His bruises got very big, his eyes swelled to extraordinarily bulbous proportions, and his lower lip grew larger than a misshapen mango. He wasn't ill, but he wasn't well either. He lingered in a curious state of shock, between agony and amnesia. He was silent the whole time and his eyes were vacant. Occasionally he would give me a concussive smile, an idiotic wink. We had to feed him pap, as if he were the biggest newborn baby in the world. He slept for long hours, day and night. He slept like a baby. He grinned like one every now and then. He howled like one. And he sometimes even betrayed the curious stare of genius that only babies and certain madmen have. For a time he lost control of his limbs and he jerked constantly on the bed. He drooled and farted indiscriminately. He made funny faces and twiddled his great big fingers like a horrible buffoon. I expected his wounds and bruises to reveal the full extent of the beating he had taken. But the bruises proved short-lived, the swellings were not alarming, the growth of his bulbous eyes ceased, and his wounds didn't bleed after a while. The true extent of the beating was not visible and that is what worried me. I watched him kicking on the bed like a beetle or an upturned cockroach, as if he had found a new freedom to be an insect, to enter into other states of being not permitted to adults. He would be morose for hours and then suddenly delirious and idiotic. Our poor relations came to see us. They had heard what transformations had come over him, but no one could find an explanation for his condition, nor understand what had happened. All they could offer were the usual litany of stories about the hundreds of strange cases they had picked up over the years of consoling themselves on the miseries of others. We kept the business of Dad's having fought a dead man to ourselves. During those three days the house was crowded with visitors and well-wishers. Dad's cart-pulling, load-carrying colleagues came and they brought gifts and sat around, drinking in silence. Even the landlord came to

359

see us briefly. He hoped, he said, that Dad had learned his lesson, and that when he recovered he would give up destroying his walls. He brought no gifts and didn't even notice Dad's condition, or the mood of the house. Everyone else felt it. Visitors were silenced by Dad's deliriums and baby-talks, his flatulence, and vacancy, his inability to recognise people, his fits of playfulness. He seemed very tragic in his grotesque condition of an adult trapped in the consciousness of a child. The mood in the room was sad. It was as if an elephant was dying. No one wanted to see how monstrously comical Dad was in his condition. If I had said that a fully grown man, bearded and big-chested, married and with a son, was being born as certain huge animals are born, I would probably have been chastised by all the grown-ups around.

On the day that Dad's bruises began to take on strange colours, Madame Koto paid us a visit. She too had heard of Dad's condition. When she entered the room everyone fell silent. This also included those who didn't even know who she was. She sat on Dad's three-legged chair. She looked at everyone and everyone avoided looking at her. She had changed. Her face had become big and a little ugly. Her foot had swollen and was wrapped in filthy bandages. There was a patch of rough darkened skin on her face which made her expressions sinister. She had become more severe, more remote, more powerful. Her perfume filled the room and her expensive clothes illuminated everyone's poverty. Her stomach was bigger. Her eyes were fierce and disdainful. Outside the room there were two men who had come with her. They looked like thugs, paid protectors. Mum invited them in and they stood in the doorway, blocking most of the light. One of them held a bundle under his arm.

For a long moment Madame Koto did not speak. Then, jabbing Dad on the shoulder with her stubby fingers, she asked:

'What happened to you?'

Dad stared at her without recognition. She jabbed him again. He made insect-noises. She turned to me. Then she looked round the room. She drew up straight on the chair.

'So nobody wants to talk to me, eh?' she said, suddenly. 'What wrong have I done anybody that you all keep quiet when I come in, eh? Have I stolen your money? Did I burn down your houses? Am I your landlord?'

There was a pause. Then:

'You too proud,' someone ventured.

'And you support *that* party,' said another.

There was another pause. No one said anything. The silence waited for her reaction. It didn't have to wait very long.

'You are all jealous!' she said. 'And none of you can touch me.'

She stood up. She began to gesticulate, waving her arms about, but Dad made noises from the bed. Madame Koto restrained herself. She rearranged her wrapper, a clear sign that she had put up with enough and was now leaving. She made her exit address to Dad.

'I heard you were ill and I came to see you. We are all human beings. We are neighbours. Your son helped me. I brought some gifts for you. I have no quarrel with you. This earth is too small for people to forget that we are all human beings. As for these other people who keep quiet whenever I come into the room, they will see what I am made of, they will find out what I am.'

She took the bundle roughly from her protector and put it on the table.

'I pray you should be strong soon,' she said, and left the room.

Mum went out with her. I heard them talking in the passage. The people gathered in the room were uneasy. Dad made faces at them. There was a long silence. Dad went on making strange faces, his blue bruises and his green wounds concentrating his expression into a distillate of indecipherable mockery. He was actually in great pain. One of the gathered visitors, speaking for the others, said it was time to go. But they didn't move. Mum and Madame Koto stayed talking in the passage for a while. The gathered visitors stayed a while too. In silence. When Mum returned, her face bright, the gathering dispersed, one by one, leaving their modest gifts behind.

On the sixth day, when Dad had shown a few vague signs of improvement, the blind old man came to pay his respects. He wore a bright yellow shirt, a red hat with feathers in the felt, and blue sunglasses. He was led in by a younger man. He sat on Dad's chair. He had brought his instrument.

'When I heard that you were ill, I brought my accordion so I could play for you,' he said in his weird voice.

Dad groaned. Mum served him ogogoro and the blind old man made a libation and drank the alcohol down as if it were a soft drink and began to play the accordion with astonishing vigour. Now and again he would swing his blind eyes in my direction, as if he were demanding applause. He played blissfully, happily. He played the most dreadful music that could possibly be imagined by the most fiendish mind of man. He deafened us with the sheer fabulous ugliness of his music. He made our flesh crawl and bristle with his noise. Mum's face began to twitch. I kept jerking. A strange smell, as of a rotting corpse, or of a great animal in the throes of death, rose from the music, and occupied the room. It was incredible. Dad twisted and contorted on the bed as if the cruelty of the music were causing him greater agony than all the unearthly blows of the celebrated Yellow Jaguar. Mum opened the door and window to let the music out. The foul air of the compound came in. Dad began to sit up on the bed, struggling, kicking, fighting to get out of the womb of the vile music, as if he were trapped in a space too small for his spirit or his frame which was accelerating in growth. Fighting to get up, he groaned, almost weeping because the music hurt him so much. The blind old man turned to me again and intensified the full ugly power of the music. Dad was struck still, unable to move, frozen by his own efforts. Then suddenly the old man stopped playing. Dad slumped back down. The old man said:

'How many times is a man reborn in one life?'

He chuckled, looked at me, and carried on playing with un-restrained zest. Then someone came in through the door, bringing ghosts and memories and a magic, fleeting smile. I looked up. A flash dazzled me. It was the photographer. He had just taken a picture. He hurried over to Dad's bedside. He made a quick speech about his best wishes and hopes for recovery. Dad did not recognise him. The photographer didn't let it bother him. He took Dad's hand and shook it. Dad made faces. The photographer took another picture. The flash hurt Dad and he groaned. The photographer, with an air of mystery, said:

'They don't know I am here. So I'm going.'

He touched me on the head, fondled my hair, put on his hat, and crept out into the compound as if everyone were after him.

'When people keep running, something keeps pursuing them,' the blind old man said, in his sepulchral voice.

The old man started to play again. Dad was so irritated that, to our amazement, he got out of bed and saw the blind old man to the door.

On the seventh day Dad rose miraculously from his condition. It was as if he had snapped out of a trance. The colours of his bruises had become fairly normal. His face was still disfigured, his eyes still swollen and angry, his wounds livid, but something in him had mended. His recovery surprised all of us. I woke up to find him jumping and shadow-boxing again. He looked lean but his eyes glowed. It seemed as if his illness and his escape into the world of infancy had given him fresh energies and accelerated his healing. He went to work, but came back early. He slept for a while, boxing in his dreams. When he woke up he made me tell him about his epic battle with Yellow Jaguar. He made me tell it several times. He didn't seem to be able to remember most of what had happened. He spoke of the fight as something that he had dreamt, and the illness as the only thing that had been real.

Mum returned late and told us of the preparations for the great rally. She said women were earning a lot of money cooking for the event and that Madame Koto had offered her a job. She asked Dad if she should accept.

'People will think you are a prostitute,' Dad said.

'But what about the money?'

'We don't need their stinking money.'

Mum sulked for the rest of the night. It didn't bother Dad because all he wanted to do was talk about his fight with Yellow Jaguar. He grew so obsessive about the fight that all through the next day he talked about it, made me repeat my account of how he had crouched low, and moved into the dark, how he had launched his counter-attack. The only thing that spoiled it for him was that there had been no one else apart from me who had witnessed the strange battle.

'Are you sure no one else saw it?'

'Yes.'

'Nobody woke up?'

'No.'

Dad grunted in agony. It seemed to hurt him a little to have performed such a heroic feat unwitnessed.

'So no one saw it?'

'No.'

'Not even a woman?'

'No.'

'No other children, no one passed along the street, no traders?'

'No.'

'So no one else saw me beat him?'

'No one.'

'Not even a dog, a cat?'

'Not even a dog or cat.'

'No strangers?'

'No. Except three lights.'

'What three lights?'

'Three lights,' I said.

He hit me on the head.

'Then other lights came and joined them.'

He hit me again. I shut up. Dad was so impressed by his performance that he badly wanted to boast about it. He knew no one would believe him. But that, in the end, didn't matter because after Dad got well he developed interesting powers and a kind of madness.

'Maybe you have to overcome things first in the spirit world, before you can do it in this world, eh?' he would say to the wind.

He went around, demented and restless, as if a jaguar had somehow got trapped in his brain. An unbearable energy bristled in him. Whenever he came near me I felt him shivering like a great animal startled by its own ferocity.

FOUR

AND SO DAD resumed training. He woke us up with his exercises. He went off to work, and came back early. In the evenings, after he had slept, he would practise at the housefront. The neighbours, who stayed outside drinking and talking because of the heat in their rooms, watched him. Most evenings they brought out their chairs and stools and made themselves comfortable in anticipation of Dad's arrival. When enough people had gathered he would bound out of the room.

'Black Tyger!' the people would cheer.

Then shamelessly he would begin to shadow-box and make grunting noises. His activity drew so much interest that street hawkers, prostrate from a whole day's wandering, would stop to watch him. Sellers of oranges, boiled eggs, bread, roasted groundnuts, would crouch and stare at him. Some of them did quite well for themselves, selling their wares to the compound people. Some of them, seated on the sand, their basins of goods beside them, would eventually stretch out and fall asleep while Dad trained. Mallams and children on errands, old women on visits and charm-sellers, all stopped to watch for no other reason than that a crowd had formed around him.

Meanwhile, Dad jumped about, throwing combinations to the four winds.

'Is this a new thing?' one of them would ask.

'Yes.'

'Is that so?'

'Yes.'

'A new thing, eh?'

'Completely new.'

'So who is he?'

'They call him Black Tyger.'

'Is that so?'

'Yes.'

The shop-owners and street traders around did excellent business on account of Dad. They all did good business, except Mum, who was unaware of the interest Dad was generating, and who at that moment was probably pounding the dust of the great ghetto wastes, selling nothing but a box of matches for the whole evening. While Mum wended her long way back home the street traders sold drinks and sweets, cigarettes and mosquito coils, kola-nuts and chewing gums, cheap sunglasses and kerosine lamps. They wove Dad's antics into their sales cries; meanwhile, Dad sparred with the air and dust and shattered bricks with his fist. He developed such a reputation from fooling around at the housefront that everyone became afraid of him. His fame spread on the wings of their fear.

I would wander round our area and pass bars and drinking houses and hear people talking about Black Tyger. I heard his name mentioned in the wind. Women talked about him in dark places. People argued about how he rated in comparison with current boxing heroes and decided in Dad's favour, because he was unknown, because he belonged to the ghetto, and because he was not afraid to show the range of his styles to the people. When I told Dad about all this his obsession grew. We became very poor because of his obsession. We ate very little and he ate a lot, because his increased powers needed it. His appetite grew legendary, like that of the elephant. After he had trained for the evening, bathed, drank bottled malt and stout, he would settle down to eat. He ate ravenously. We would stare at him in horror as he swallowed mighty balls of eba.

'There was once a man,' Mum would say to me, 'who choked on eba. They had to cut open his throat to get it out.'

'That man was not Black Tyger,' Dad would say, in between one gulp and another.

Not only did he swallow such death-defying dollops of eba, he ate gargantuan quantities as well. He ate as if his body were some sort of abyss. And he ate fast, as if he were attacking the food, ranging counter-gulps and eating-combinations on the massive portion. He ate so much that Mum became very lean indeed and I lost appetite for food. Dad did all our eating for us. And at the end of every meal he always complained about how the eba was never enough and how he could have done with more stew. He never spoke of the taste of the cooking. My stomach began to expand.

What made all this worse was that he brought back less money from work. He spent all his time thinking about boxing. He would travel long distances to see a free or a cheap boxing match. He would disappear for hours. Then he began to spend less money on food. For one thing, he drank more. After he had eaten he would go out and visit a round of bars and everywhere, on account of his new-found fame, people bought him drinks. He would come home drunk. The more he trained, the more he drank. And the more he drank, the madder he became, the more restless. He could spend an hour creaking his joints, freeing his body of trapped energies and frustrated dreams of greatness.

He began to scare us. In the evenings, when I knew he was coming back from drinking, I would take to wandering the streets. But in the late afternoons, when he trained outside, I was always in the crowd watching him improvise and conjure new movements into being. People began, however, to comment on my swelling stomach. While keenly watching him exercise, two men said:

'His son starves.'

'His wife is lean.'

'Have you noticed that as he gets stronger . . .'

'His son gets thinner.'

'While his power increases . . .'

'His wife's presence decreases.'

'While he learns new tricks . . .'

'His son's legs become like sticks.'

The pair of them laughed. A deeper voice in the crowd said:

'He eats up all their food.'

A woman said:

'Something has entered his head.'

The pair of wits began again:

'Big man . . .'

'With no shame.'

'Big muscles . . .'

'With no brain.'

They laughed drunkenly. Hearing all this didn't make me too happy and after some time I temporarily stopped watching Dad train. I played alone in the street while people watched him perform his new feats. He had now taken to breaking planks with his fists, smashing bottles on his head, lifting several people on his arms, and bending metal rods round his elbows.

I was sitting alone, away from the crowd, watching the street, when a sharp flash of blue cracked me between the eyes. I heard

the blind old man cry out. I didn't understand. A dog barked. The
sky was clear. I watched the street and then suddenly I saw the metal
rim of a bicycle wheel rolling along by itself. I froze. The metal
rim, rolling along, dispersed flashes of lights with each revolution.
I waited. I looked around. The street was empty, but the metal rim
rolled towards the burnt van. I heard a noise. I blinked. And when
I looked again I saw a shadow, and then the shadow became a boy.
He wore white shorts and a blue shirt and he was driving the hoop
along, round and round the burnt van. Where had he come from?
I was amazed. He seemed to have appeared from nowhere. I was
furious. And then, just as suddenly, he disappeared. I got up and went
to the van. The metal hoop was on the ground. I looked round the
van and saw nothing. I was about to leave when a shadow blocking
out the sun from my face made me turn round. Standing on the top
of the van, like a child-conqueror surveying his newly won lands,
was the boy who had been burnt out of reality during the blistering
afternoons of the harmattan and who had now materialised in the
break of the rainy season. He was watching Dad practise from his
height.

'Are you the boy who vanished?' I asked.

'No.'

'Did you turn into your own shadow?'

'No.'

He answered my questions, barely giving me a glance.

'Come down!' I said.

'Why?'

'You are not allowed to play on the van.'

'Why not?'

Disconcerted by his serenity, I clambered up the van and tried
to push him down. We began to fight. I hit him in the face and
he hit me back. I hit him again and he grabbed me round the waist
and we wrestled. He tripped me, I fell, and he fell on me, knocking
the wind out of my chest. Soon we were on solid ground. I kicked
him, he caught my foot, and threw me down. I jumped back up
and lashed out in all directions, with the sort of blind ferocity
that Dad sometimes had, and one of my punches made contact.
His nose sprouted blood. He was untroubled by the bleeding
and he unleashed a volley of blows on me, cracking the side
of my face, and we wrestled again, and fell, and we got up,
and hit one another blindly and soon several adult hands tore
us away from one another. Like two wild fighting cocks separated

in a bloody battle, we kicked and raged in the air, cursing and swearing.

On another day, when Dad was training, I saw the boy standing on the top of the van again. I went over.

'Come down from there!' I said.

'No.'

I clambered up again. He didn't move.

'My father', he said, 'has given me something special.'

'For what?'

'If you touch me . . .'

'Yes . . .'

'And I hit you . . .'

'Yes . . .'

'You will fall down seven times and then die.'

'Who is your father?' I asked him.

'My father is a great cobbler and carpenter,' he replied.

'My father', I said, 'is Black Tyger.'

And then I hit him in the face. He hit me back. Nothing happened. I began to laugh.

'Why are you laughing?'

'Because of the stupid thing your father gave you.'

He didn't say anything. After a while he got down from the van and went and played nearer the crowd watching Dad. I stayed on the van for some time. It wasn't much fun and I got bored and I noticed that people were staring at me. I got down and went to look for the boy. At first he didn't want to talk to me. Then I told him again that the man shadow-boxing was my father. His face lit up in transferred admiration.

'What's your name?'

'Ade. What's yours?'

I told him. We shook hands. His father was a cobbler and carpenter and a fierce supporter of the political party on the side of the poor. He was also something of a medicine man and counted many feared thugs as family friends. I was somewhat impressed.

He took me to their house. They lived in our area, in one small room. Their family was large; his father had two wives and ten children. I don't know how they all managed in that room. His mother was buck-toothed and small and ferocious. She was the eldest wife. His father had great scarifications, noble and impressive like the statues of ancient warriors; he was tall and his spirit was rather terrifying. His teeth were kola-nut-stained and

369

his eyes bloodshot, and he beat his children a lot, in the name of the sternest and most corrective discipline. His voice had a chilling, piercing quality. I didn't like him much.

Ade took me to his father's workshop and showed me the tools of his trade – his hammers and tongs, his chisels and boxes of heavy nails, his long work-bench and tables crowded with a mountainous tumble of shoes and handbags, the place smelling of glue and rusted nails and old metal and raw earth and ancient wine spilled on fresh-planed wood. The shadows gave off the aroma of cobwebs and the intense sleep of cockchafers, of fetishes twisting on rafters. The ceiling was dark with a fastness of ancient cobwebs, and lengths of leather hung from the ceiling. The workshop was an exciting place and it seemed I had found an entirely new universe in which to explore and play. We tried on the different shoes, with their incredible variety of sizes and shapes. We hid behind the cabinet. We banged nails into fresh-planed wood. We glued bits of abandoned leather together, trying to create new shoes instantly. We were totally absorbed in our play when his father came in suddenly. He saw us playing, saw the laughter on our faces, and brought out the long whip he kept on a nail behind the door. He thrashed us on the backs and we ran out screaming. I decided not to go there again.

I tried to get Ade to wander the streets with me, but he never went far. He was scared of his parents. If they called him and he didn't answer he got whipped for it later. I told him to run away from home and to come and stay with us, but he was afraid. He said his father would thrash him and put pepper on the wounds. He showed me his back and I saw the old whip marks along with numerous razor incisions for the herbal treatments he received. I felt sad for him. And because of him I didn't go wandering for a while. I tried to take him to Madame Koto's place, but he wouldn't go there either. His father had told him that she was a witch who supported their political enemies.

We were playing in the forest one day when we came upon Madame Koto. She lay on the earth, at the root of the legendary iroko tree, her white beads like a jewelled snake in her hand. When she heard us coming she jumped up and dusted herself. She looked very embarrassed.

'Who's your friend?' she asked, blinking.

'Ade,' I said.

She gave him a curious intense scrutiny. Ade said he was going home. He wandered off and waited a short distance away, watching us furtively. Madame Koto turned her disquieting gaze on me. She studied my stomach. The merest hint of compassion crossed her face.

'So you don't like my bar any more, eh?'

'No.'

She smiled.

'Are you hungry?'

'No.'

'How is your father?'

'No.'

She stared at me. Then she unwound her wrapper and untied the big knot at the end. I had never seen so much money in my life. She had a thick wad of pound notes at her wrapper end that could easily have choked a horse. She unwrapped several notes and gave them to me. At first, looking over at Ade, I refused. But she pressed them on me, shutting my fingers tightly.

'If your mother asks, tell her you found them in the forest, eh?'

'No.'

'Don't tell her I gave them to you, you understand?'

'Yes.'

She touched me gently on the head. For the first time I saw that she had changed. She was now wholly enveloped in an invisible aura of power, a force-field of dread. Her stomach was really big and she seemed very wide. There was a heaviness about her that made her look as if weariness had moved into her face as a permanent condition. Even her shadow weighed me down. Her eyes were distant. They couldn't come near human beings any more. They had the same quality that the eyes of lions have. Her face was round and fresh and she seemed very well.

'I am not happy,' she said, suddenly.

'Why not?'

She gave me a puzzled look, as if she were surprised that I had spoken. Then she smiled, and turned, and shuffled down the forest paths with the grace that most human beings seldom have. The midges trailed her.

Ade didn't speak to me for days because Madame Koto had given me money. And when I gave the money to Mum it caused an upheaval in the house. It turned out to be much more money than I had imagined. She made me sit on the bed and spent hours subjecting me to the most rigorous questions about where I had found the money. She feared that it belonged to some trader, to ritualists who could infuse syllabic curses into their possessions, or some powerful figure who might hunt us out and punish us. But it was her suspicion that I had stolen it which annoyed me so much that I burst into angry weeping. Dad sat in his chair, rocking himself, smoking. Mum insisted that I take her to the spot where I had discovered the windfall. I told her I didn't remember, that I had stumbled upon it as if I were in a dream, and that it was on the ground near some bushes.

'Are you sure it wasn't spirits who gave it to you, eh?' Mum said with more than a hint of mockery.

'Yes,' I said.

Then Dad broke out of his imperturbability and threatened to beat me if I didn't tell the truth. I went on lying. He got so impatient that he slapped me on the face. I stared hard at him. My body suddenly became serene. Then he held me to his chest and swayed and said:

'Forgive me, my son. I did not mean it. But we are not thieves in our family. We are royalty. We are poor, but we are honest.'

Then he asked me again where I had stumbled upon such an amount of money. Still I went on lying. They gave up trying to get any sense out of me. They had been at it for hours and night had fallen. They decided they wouldn't touch the money for a week and if they didn't hear anything from anybody they would consider it a gift from heaven. Dad, in a mood of celebration, sent me to buy a big bottle of ogogoro. When I got back he spent another hour praying to our ancestors and to the inscrutable deities. Then he and Mum spent the rest of the night discussing what they would do with the money. Dad wanted to buy all the paraphernalia he needed for boxing. Mum wanted to open a shop of provisions and a boutique. They argued bitterly all night and I fell asleep to the sound of their raging acrimony. When I woke up in the morning they were still boiling with discord. They were both foul-tempered. For three days they went on like that. Another four days passed and they still hadn't reached an agreement and they quarrelled the whole time, dredging up old memories about a hundred unforgiven matters relating to money. During that time Dad used some of the windfall to buy drinks, entertain friends, and to buy a pair of canvas shoes and a second-hand pair of boxing gloves. As it turned out there was more than enough to get Mum a completely fresh stock of provisions for her trade, to buy us all some new clothes, to pay our rent, and to feed us happily for more than a good month.

372

FIVE

THE DAY OF the great political rally, which had been much talked about and much postponed, drew nearer. The most extraordinary things were happening in Madame Koto's bar. The first unusual thing was that cables connected to her rooftop now brought electricity. Illiterate crowds gathered in front of the bar to see this new wonder. They saw the cables, the wires, the pylons in the distance, but they did not see the famed electricity. Those who went into the bar, out of curiosity, came out mystified. They couldn't understand how you could have a light brighter than lamps, sealed in glass. They couldn't understand how you couldn't light your cigarette on the glowing bulbs. And worse than all that, it was baffling for them to not be able to see the cause of the illumination.

Madame Koto, much too shrewd not to make the most of everyone's bewilderment, increased the price of her palm-wine and peppersoup. Then, for a while, she began to charge a modest entry fee for merely being able to enjoy the unique facilities. She was after all the only person along our street and in our area who had the distinction of electricity. She was so taken in by this distinction that she had her signboard amended to highlight the fact.

The next thing was that people heard very loud music blaring but saw no musicians performing. After that came stories of strange parties, of women running naked into the forest, of people who got so drunk they bathed in palm-wine, of party members giving away large quantities of money to the women whose dancing pleased. There were lush rumours of the things the men and the women did together, screaming into the electrified nights. In the midst of all this Madame Koto grew bigger and fatter till she couldn't get in through the back door. The door had to be broken down and widened. We saw her in fantastic dresses of silk and lace, edged with turquoise filigree, white gowns, and yellow hats, waving a fan of blue feathers, with expensive bangles of silver and gold weighing her arms, and necklaces of pearl and jade round her neck. When she walked all her jewellery clattered on her, announcing her eminence in advance. She painted her finger-nails red. Her eyelashes became more defined. She wore lipstick. She wore high-heeled shoes and moved with an increasingly pronounced limp, walking stick always in hand. She began to resemble a great old chief from ancient times, a reincarnation of splendour and power and clannish might.

Cars began to converge at her place. The lights burned till deep into the night and always from the street I could hear them talking, planning heatedly, and could see their shapes through the strips of curtain. Rumours, always stale, began to circulate that she had joined the most terrifying cults in the land, that she had been accepted in organisations that usually never allow women, that she performed rituals in the forest. I heard of bizarre sacrifices, goats being slaughtered at night, of people dressed in white habits danc-ing round her house, heard of cries that pierced the ghetto air, of drumming and thunderous chants, but the strangest thing I heard of was the forthcoming birth of the four-headed Masquerade. No one knew what it was.

People came to believe that Madame Koto had exceeded herself in witchcraft. People glared at her hatefully when she went past. They said she wore the hair of animals and human beings on her head. The rumours got so wild that it was hinted that her cult made sacrifices of human beings and that she ate children. They said she had been drinking human blood to lengthen her life and that she was more than a hundred years old. They said the teeth in her mouth were not hers, that her eyes belonged to a jackal, and that her foot was getting rotten because it belonged to someone who was trying to dance in their grave. She became, in the collective eyes of the people, a fabulous and monstrous creation. It did not matter that some people insisted that it was her political enemies who put out all these stories. The stories distorted our perception of her reality for ever. Slowly, they took her life over, made themselves real, and made her opaque in our eyes.

In spite of what people said, however, she prospered, while the rest of us suffered. She opened another bar in another section of the city. She divided her time between both. She opened a mighty stall in the big market where she sold garri, lace materials, and jewellery. She had many servants. Conflicting stories, however, did reach us about her wealth. Some said she wasn't very rich, that she had too many people to support. Others maintained that she had so much money she could feed the entire ghetto for five years. I heard that she spent endless days counting her profits, that when she went to the bank she needed an armed truck. Then we began to hear of how mean she was, that one of her servants needed money for treating a liver condition and she wouldn't give him so much as a farthing. On the other hand, we heard that she had given a lot of money to a woman she didn't even know, whose child would have died from food poisoning if it hadn't been for Madame Koto's timely intervention. It began to seem as if there were many Madame Kotos in existence.

And then one day as I was playing with Ade we saw several people gathered outside her barfront. They all stood in the mud. They all wore white smocks and had ostentatious Bibles. Their leader had the biggest Bible of them all. It looked like an instrument of vengeance. He had wild hair and the rough, scraggy beard of a self-anointed prophet. He was barefoot. If it hadn't been for the authority with which he held the wooden crozier, he could well have been mistaken for a complete madman. A large cross dangled from his neck. The whole group of them, whipped up to paroxysms of denunciation by their leader, constituted the representatives of one of the most influential new churches springing up in the city. The group consisted of prophets of varying ranks and they danced with righteous fervour and prayed with fearful certainty in front of the bar. They evoked visions of fire and brimstone, sulphur and torment and damnations. They prayed as if they were purging the land of a monstrous and incarnate evil. They sprinkled holy water over the ground and threw holy grains of sand towards the bar. They stayed for a long time, singing with brio and might, in lusty voices, in perfect rousing harmony, chanting and stamping in the mud. Their presence stopped people going to the bar. The women in the bar would occasionally peep out between curtain strips and the leader of the group, the chief prophet, foaming at the mouth, would point a crooked finger at the women and the singing would reach new proportions of intensity. They carried on till nightfall and completely succeeded in imprisoning Madame Koto and her women within the bar, souring their business for the day.

The following evening they returned, bringing a larger congregation. We saw them chanting and beating their church drums along the street. It seemed they had an entire orchestra with them. Brass sections pierced the air with their clash and roll, the trumpets blasted the wind, and the deep voices of the prophets leading the way to the battle against evil woke the street from its mid-season slumber. As the procession approached Madame Koto's bar the world joined them. They became a great flood of human beings, a surging mass of spectators, like an army of divine vengeance. They sang different songs all at once. They arrived at Madame Koto's bar and found it shuttered. They sang, played their music, chanted, and stomped. They bellowed and belted out their holy tunes till they were hoarse. Those who had expected something to happen were disappointed. The only thing that happened was that the frustration made factions of the crowd begin to quarrel. Fighting broke out between musical sections, between prophets of differing denominations, between contending visionaries. The head priest was leading a song of exorcism, his staff and Bible high in the air, when the fighting encircled him. He found himself torn between quelling his unruly flock and launching his bitter attack against the scourge of Madame Koto's electricity. He managed to deliver, in the midst of all the chaos, a tremendous philippic on the apocalypse of science. The shouting grew wilder amongst his congregation. A man was hurled to the mud. Another man was being strangled with the folds of his smock. Soon everyone seemed to be fighting everyone else.

'The DEVIL has come into our midst!' the head priest cried.

No one listened.

'Let us stand as one to drive out this ABOMINATION!'

No one heard.

'THEY WILL START WITH ELECTRICITY AND THEN THEY WILL BURN UP THE EARTH!' he thundered.

No one cared. And then the most extraordinary thing happened. The sky was rent asunder. The air lit up as if an unbearably radiant being was going to descend from the heavens. The light in the sky, flickering brightly, stayed for a long moment. Everyone fell silent and froze in the presence of the unknown annunciation. A terrible enchantment hung over us like a single flashing sword. The wind flowed in silence.

'GOD HAS ANSWERED OUR CRY!' said the head priest.

The sky darkened and lowered. The air became full of presence. The wind was still. I smelt, in that moment, all the known and unknown herbal essences of the forest. The world swam in aromas.

'HALLELU . . . HALLELUYA!' cried the head priest.

His congregation picked up the cry, lifted it up to the heavens, and fell silent, waiting.

Then in the deepest reaches of the sky something cracked. It broke loose altogether. Then it rolled down the unnumbered vaults of the heavens, gathering momentum and great wondrous volumes of sound as it neared us. Then it exploded over our heads and before we could recover from the incredible drama of the universe the sky opened and yielded a river of rain upon us.

The congregation scattered everywhere. The commotion was far-cical and wild. People screamed, children howled, mothers yelled. Only the head priest stood firm. Soon the entire crowd, the valiant brass sections and the rousing wind ensemble, fled their many ways, lashed by the torrential rain. I watched them fleeing as if from a burning house. The head priest called to them, denounced them, urged them to have courage and to be steadfast in crisis. He waved his staff and Bible in the air, and thunder cracked above him. But he did not move. He did not give ground. He went on praying with great fervour. He cursed the abomination that was Madame Koto and referred to her as the GREAT WHORE OF THE APOCALYPSE, and he danced and sang alone, while the rain mercilessly drenched him.

He soon became a ridiculous sight. He resembled a monstrous drenched chicken. He shivered as he prayed. His smock clung obscenely to his buttocks. As his passion waned, gradually extin-guished by the indifferent rain, he trembled more. Everyone watched him from the cover of rooftops and eaves. Trapped in his solitary defiance, his Bible dripping a second flood, his beard a sad sunken ship upon the waters, his voice disappearing in the din of cosmic events, he had no choice but to continue with his absurd posture. He chanted, shaking at the knees. And as he chanted, railing against prostitutes, science, theories of evolution, the enshrinement of reason against God, and evil women of Babylon, a procession of cars drove down the street. They parked around him. The car doors opened. Men and women in fine attire spilled out. They all had umbrellas. Madame Koto was among them. She wore a massive and dazzling black silk dress, with white shoes and a white scarf, her arms and neck glittering with jewellery. The splendid guests passed the head priest and if they heard his ravings they betrayed no signs of it. The bar door was opened, and they all went in. Only Madame Koto came back to give the head priest her umbrella. Shamelessly, he took it. She limped back to her bar, walking stick in one hand, while the head priest resumed his imprecations and denunciations of her. It was at this point that people began to jeer him. When the

377

evening fell, and the darkness spread, the head priest was a wreck of a soaked man. Under the cover of darkness, shivering, his voice hoarse, he left Madame Koto's barfront and made his miserable way down the street. Much later we learned that he had led his congregation against Madame Koto mainly at the instigation of the party supported by the poor. There was also talk of possible charitable contributions to church funds. We were disappointed by their methods.

SIX

AND THEN, TO crown our amazement, the news
reached us that Madame Koto had bought herself a car. We couldn't
believe it. No one along our street and practically no one in the area
owned such a thing as a car. People owned bicycles and were proud of
them. One or two men owned scooters and were accorded the respect
reserved only for elders and chieftains. But it most certainly was news
for a woman in the area to own a car. We clung to our disbelief till we
saw the bright blue little car, with the affectionate face of an enlarged
metallic tortoise. It was parked in front of her bar. We still clung to
our disbelief even when we saw her hopeless attempts at driving it,
which resulted in running over an old woman's stall. She promptly
had the stall rebuilt and gave the woman more money than she had
possessed in the first place. We watched her learning to drive the car.
She was much too massive for such a small vehicle and at the steering
wheel she looked as if the car was her shell and she merely the third
eye of the tortoise. The fact that the car was too small for her was the
only consolation that people had. But we were still amazed.

With a man sitting next to her she learned to drive along our
street. With a determined, half-crazed look on her face, her shoulders
hunched as if her weight somehow helped the car to move forward,
she zigzagged down our street. She couldn't keep the car straight.
When she was seen coming a voice would cry out, saying:

'Hide your children! Hide yourselves! The mad tortoise is coming!'

Then we would see her vehicle, swaying from side to side,
scattering goats and fowls, and causing innocent bystanders to flee
into the most unlikely places. Her persistence never paid off. Even
when she could manage to get the car to travel straight, she was so
fraught, working up such a fury wrenching the gears around that the
engine would make fearsome coughing noises.

'The tortoise is hungry,' people would say.

Then we heard that she had difficulties with the car because of her bad foot. Whenever she applied the brake she did it so abruptly that the man teaching her had his head banged against the dashboard. And because she couldn't drive it, she left the car for her driver to take on errands.

It didn't really matter that it was a small car, or that she couldn't drive it properly. What mattered was that yet again she had been a pioneer, doing something no one else had done. People became convinced that if she wanted she could fly over the ghetto on the back of a calabash.

When the day arrived for Madame Koto to wash her new car, many people came to celebrate the ritual with her. Our landlord was present. People brought their bicycles and scooters. Many came on foot. There were old men whom we had never seen before. And there were a lot of powerful strange women with eyes that registered no emotion. We saw chiefs, thugs, and there were even herbalists, witch-doctors and their acolytes. They gathered in the bar and drank. They talked loudly. Eventually everyone was summoned for the washing. They formed a circle round the vehicle. The great herbalist amongst them was a stern man with a face so battered and eyes so daunting that even mirrors would recoil and crack at his glance. He uttered profound incantations and prayed for the car.

'This car', he said, after much mystification, 'will drive even to the moon and come back safely.'

The people nodded.

'This car will bring you prosperity, plenty of money. Nothing will touch it. Any other car that runs into it will be destroyed, but nothing will happen to your car. This is what we call superior magic. Even if you fall asleep while driving this car you will be safe. Anyone that steals it will immediately have an accident and die. Anyone that wishes evil on the car will die!'

The people assented. Madame Koto, her walking stick in one hand, nodded vigorously. At this point, everyone was more or less drunk.

'If people want to be jealous of you, let them be jealous. Jealousy is free. People can eat it and grow fat on it if they want. But anyone who thinks evil of you, may this car run them over in their sleep. This car will hunt out your enemies, pursue their bad spirits, grind them into the road. Your car will drive over fire and be safe. It will drive into the ocean and be safe. It has its friends in the spirit world. Its friends there, a car just like this one, will hunt down your enemies.

They will not be safe from you. A bomb will fall on this car and it will be safe. I have opened the road for this car. It will travel all roads. It will arrive safely at all destinations. This is what I say.'

The people cheered. Some laughed. The herbalist sprinkled his complex potions and his corrosive liquids on the car. He emptied half a bottle of precious ogogoro on the bonnet. And after the ritual washing was complete, after the old people present, the powerful ones, the chiefs, and the cultists, had made their libations, the gathering got down to the momentous business of getting drunk. They drank solidly. They argued to drink better and they drank to argue better. More people joined them. The prostitutes served palm-wine, peppersoup, fried bushmeat and grilled rabbits. The blind old man turned up and threw himself into the serious drinking and got involved in a heated discussion with a chief. The gathering got rowdy. It was to be expected, it was even desired. But suddenly an uproar broke out. No one knew how it started. Birds wheeled overhead and alighted on the roof of the car. The sky darkened. The great herbalist, looking uglier than ever before because of his drunkenness, began to utter the most controversial statements. Then he said something which brought on complete silence.

'This car will be a coffin!' he suddenly announced. 'I have just seen it.'

The people stared at him in utter bewilderment. A strange wind seemed to blow over his head. His eyes became crossed. His twisted mouth gave his utterance the weight of destiny.

'Unless you perform the proper sacrifice this car will be a coffin! I have to speak the truth when I see it or I will die,' the herbalist carried on.

The mood of the gathering changed instantly. The old men and women hobbled home with unusual alacrity, disturbed by the mention of the dreaded word. The chiefs and high-level party members got into their cars. The young men and women retired into the bar. Only the prostitutes, our landlord, the blind old man, who carried on his argument with the air as if nothing had happened, and Madame Koto remained.

'But if you give me one of these women,' the herbalist said, lunging at one of the prostitutes, and missing, 'then I will drive the coffin away from the car.'

He stood, swaying, his eyes bleary and focused on the forest. The birds took off from the car top. The wind fairly howled and whistled along the electric cables. Then the herbalist gathered his potions and staggered past the car and up the street, towards us. When he neared me and Ade as we sat perched on a branch the herbalist, foaming, drunk, his eyes distorted, said to us:

'Very soon one of you will die!'

Then he went on towards the forest.

We jumped down and followed him. He stopped to urinate against a tree. His urine was yellowish. When he finished he staggered on, gesticulating, waving his arms, shouting:

'All these trees will die,' he said, bitterly, 'because nobody loves them any more!'

And then flinging his arms about he turned and faced us and said, pointing a charm-ridden finger at me:

'You, spirit-child, if you don't take your friend away from here now – I will turn both of you into snakes.'

We turned and fled. As we ran we heard him wailing in the forest, his voice echoing amongst the trees, rebounding from the absorbent earth. We heard his drunken lamentation, as he cried:

'Too many roads! Things are CHANGING TOO FAST! No new WILL. COWARDICE everywhere! SELFISHNESS is EATING UP the WORLD. THEY ARE DESTROYING AFRICA! They are DESTROYING the WORLD and the HOME and the SHRINES and the GODS! THEY are DESTROYING LOVE TOO.'

We heard his insane laughter, lacerating the air. He continued with his cries, in a different voice.

'WHO CAN DREAM A GOOD ROAD AND THEN LIVE TO TRAVEL ON IT? Who can GIVE BIRTH TO HIMSELF and then BE HIS OWN FATHER AND MOTHER? Who can LIVE IN THE FUTURE and LIVE IN THE PRESENT and not GO MAD? Who can LIVE AMONG SPIRITS AND among MEN WITHOUT DYING? WHO can EAT AND SLEEP WITH HIS OWN DESTINY AND still KNOW THE HAPPINESS OF A BEAUTIFUL THING?'

The same laughter rang out.

'THOSE ARE RIDDLES FOR THE TREES!' we heard him shout, from a long way off.

Then we didn't hear his voice again.

When we got to the barfront Madame Koto sat outside, on a cane chair. Her women surrounded her. We watched them for a while. They sat without moving. They sat in complete silence. They were all staring at the car.

SEVEN

DAD'S PUBLIC PERFORMANCES had to take on spectacular dimensions. During the period in which Madame Koto got electricity, and bought her car, people lost interest in his training. They were more interested in the car. In the evenings people went to Madame Koto's bar and hung around the vehicle, touching it, marvelling. One night I even dreamt that she drove the car to the moon and couldn't come back. When her servant drove up and down our street, bringing supplies of palm-wine and food, people stopped what they were doing to renew their wonder at the machine. Children always ran behind the vehicle, cheering.

Madame Koto graduated from palm-wine to beer. There was more money in beer and breweries had begun to be established in the city. Sometimes, after the evening's supplies of beer had been delivered, she would invite the children of the area for a ride in the car. It increased her pleasure in her own possession and she considered the free ride as an act of charity. Ade refused to have anything to do with the car. His father had warned him that it was the work of the devil. She gave me a ride once, and I never forgot it. She sat at the back. I sat at the front. I couldn't see the road. It seemed to me that we were driving on the wind. She stopped to give people lifts. When I was the only one left she told the driver to increase the speed. The driver relished it and drove at such nightmare speed that I was certain we were flying to the moon. When I begged the driver to slow down, because I felt nauseous, Madame Koto said:

'Faster! Faster!'

And the driver drove like a madman, pressing on somewhat vengefully at frightening speed. I didn't understand the source of the vengeance. Madame Koto's face was radiant, her eyes widened, and her massive frame became luminous from the sheer pleasure and the power of acceleration as much as from my own horror. But then the speed and my fear made me throw up. I threw up on the driver and

383

Madame Koto ordered the car to be stopped and gave the driver the sign to bundle me out. The driver did just that. After he had cleaned my vomit off him, using sand and rags, he gave me savage looks. The looks didn't do anything to me so he sidled over, pretended to touch my head in a gesture of forgiveness, but gave me such a cracking with his bony knuckles that I was too dazed to notice them drive off. I walked the long distance home and I never accepted a ride in the car again.

When I got home late that evening, Dad was training as if he had gone insane. No one watched him except a boy, two chickens, a goat, and the blind old man. That night, furious at the fickleness of the world's tastes, angry that people were now bored with his antics, Dad began to rave and storm about the road, issuing challenges to the entire planet. He boasted that he could fight three people at once. No one took up his challenge. Then he insisted that he could beat five men. It was only when he increased the number to ten that people stepped forward from the darkness.

I was exhausted that night. I sat on the cement platform and watched as seven men moved in on Dad. They were load-carriers and part-time bodyguards. I had often seen them among the crowds that studied Dad as he trained. Dad unceremoniously knocked one of them flat out with an upper cut to the jaw. After the man fell he didn't move. The six other men crowded round him. Dad jumped about, charging himself with recitations of his fighting names, his secret names, the names he had given his spirit. Two of the men rushed in. One of them caught Dad on the head with a roundhouse punch, poorly executed. Dad laughed derisively and executed the very same punch. The man fell brutally. Dad pursued a third man, changed direction, and smashed a fourth man in the solar plexus, then put him out of the fight with a rather cruel-looking left cross. Three men lay on the ground, motionless. The other four fled as with one mind. Dad didn't follow them. The blind old man clapped for Dad and the boy called out his fighting name. When they came and led the blind old man away we heard the strains of his accordion in the darkness as he went. We were surprised that it sounded rather pleasant.

EIGHT

WE WOKE UP to find the world staring at us with new respect. It had gone round the globe and even to the world of spirits that Dad had beaten seven men in a fight. Dad, who had become something of an impresario, didn't train in public for three days. He explained the curious principle to me:

'When people don't believe you can do something and you do it, they begin to respect you. That is the time to disappear. The longer they respect you, the better. Then you keep your secret. Their interest grows. Time passes. They get tired of you. They get bored waiting for you. Then they don't believe in you any more. That's when you really begin to show them.'

I had no idea what he was talking about. Instead of training at the housefront, he now took to jogging down the street.

'Black Tyger!' the people would call.

He wouldn't respond. He would jog into the distance, and wouldn't be seen till nightfall. He would jog to the housefront, shadow-box for a few moments in public, and then disappear into our room. The interest in him grew. His name travelled. His legend sprouted into being. Whenever I got back from school there were always some men around making enquiries about Dad. They wanted to know where he trained, who his coach was, and what party he belonged to. In the evenings crowds gathered round our housefront. People who had heard of Dad's prowess came from the far reaches of distant ghettos, from remote places. They hung around, staring at the house. The neighbours came out early, with their little centre tables and chairs and drinks. Street traders, hawkers, beer-sellers, traders in iced water and snuff, gathered round in anticipation. When Dad got back from work they chanted his name and urged him to train for all to see. He responded by demonstrating some punches, some footwork, and then he would vanish into our room. He didn't oblige them. He refused to satisfy their fickle dictates. The crowd grew restless, then bored, then disenchanted, then they disbanded. Then the word began to go round that Dad hadn't beaten seven people at all, that in fact he hadn't ever fought anybody, and that he was now too scared to train in public.

When Dad heard about these rumours, he smiled mysteriously. He went on jogging off towards the forest, to a place no one knew.

NINE

IT WAS AROUND this time that the political season
started up anew. Suddenly one morning we heard amplified voices
again. The voices urged us to join the Party of the Rich. The voices
told us that they were going to stage the greatest political rally in
the world and that the most famous musicians in Africa would be
performing on the day and that there would be gifts for children,
prizes for women, and jobs for men. Later in the day we saw the vans
driving past slowly, making their extravagant announcements. They
had more thugs and bodyguards with them. Big party flags draped the
vans and men distributed leaflets. When they first appeared I thought
there would be trouble in the area. I thought houses would burn and
party vans be destroyed and thugs roasted. I thought people would
remember how the very same party had poisoned them with bad milk
and had unleashed their rage upon our nights. But people had forgotten, and those that hadn't merely shrugged and said that it was all such
a long time ago, that things were too complicated for such memories,
and besides the party had new leaders.

Dad missed the dramatic return of politics to our lives. He kept
going off to train somewhere in secret. When he got back the street
would be littered with pamphlets, which no one read. He took very
little interest in what was growing in the world about us. When we
told him about the vans, he blinked.

'What vans?'

'The politicians' vans.'

'Oh, politicians,' he would say, his eyes returning to their vacant
contemplation.

When Mum asked him where he had been, the same thing
would happen.

'Been?'

'Yes, where have you been?'

'Oh, training.'

'Where?'

'Where what?'

'Where have you been training?'

'Oh, somewhere.'

'Tell me.'

'What?'

'Where?'

'Why?'

'Have you been training with another woman?'

'Woman?'

'Yes, woman.'

'What woman?'

Mum would give up. It became quite exasperating asking Dad questions. He ate as much as ever, and stayed silent most of the time. His being took on a new intensity. Mum tried to start one or two quarrels, but Dad, deepening in impenetrability, refused to be drawn into any arguments. It was a while before we realised that a new power was enveloping him. He was becoming a different man. His eyes were harder, like flint or precious stones that can make their mark on metal. He was more withdrawn, as if belonging to a different constellation. His face had become more abstract and mask-like and, curiously, gentler.

One day he said to me:

'I am beginning to see things for the first time. This world is not what it seems. There are mysterious forces everywhere. We are living in a world of riddles.'

I listened intently. He stopped. Then he looked at me, as if pleading with me to believe what he was about to say.

'I was training yesterday when this old man carrying something invisible on his head came to me. He asked me for money. I gave him all I had. He gave it back to me and said that I was lucky.'

'Why?'

'He said if I hadn't given him any money I would have died in my next fight.'

'So what did you do?'

'At first I didn't believe him. He knew I didn't. Then he pointed to the sky. There were two birds in the air, fighting one another, making strange noises. Then many other birds flew towards them in the sky. One of the birds fell. Slowly. I ran and caught it before it touched the ground. The bird melted suddenly in my hands, like ice into water. But in this case it melted into blood. I tried to clean the blood off, but it wouldn't clean. The old man came up to me and spat in my hand. The blood disappeared. The old man pointed again. I looked but I saw nothing. When I looked round the old man had gone. I saw him in the distance and I ran after him and no matter how hard I ran I couldn't shorten the distance between us. I gave up. I didn't train any more that night. Don't tell your mother what I just told you, you understand?'

I nodded. After that he withdrew into his cavernous silence. I too became silent. His story had infected me. Mum found us both unbearable and began to pick quarrels and blame me for things I hadn't done. But I didn't say anything. Me and Dad stayed silent the whole night.

TEN

I BECAME VERY curious about Dad's secret place of training. The next day I waited for him to jog there, so I could follow him. I waited, but he stayed in, sleeping. He was tired. I woke him up and reminded him of his training, but he turned over and went on sleeping. I went outside, stayed close to our compound, and kept watching for him while I played. The air was full of noises. The politicians' vans rode up and down, blaring their party music, making their interminable announcements and promises. It became quite confusing to hear both parties virtually promise the same things. The Party of the Rich talked of prosperity for all, good roads, electricity, and free education. They called the opposition thieves, tribalists, and bandits. At their rally, they said, everyone would be fed, all questions would be answered.

That evening the van of the Party for the Poor also paraded our street. They too blared music and made identical claims. They distributed leaflets and made their promises in four languages. When the two vans, each packed with armed bodyguards, passed one another, they competed with the amount of noise they could generate. They insulted one another in their contest of loudspeakers; and the heated blare of their music clashing created such a jangle in the air that the road crowded with spectators who expected a tremendous combustion. The two vans clashed twice that evening. We kept expecting some sort of war to break out, but both parties seemed restrained by the healthy respect they had developed for one another. The truth was that the time hadn't yet arrived.

Madame Koto's car was seen in the service of the Party of the Rich. She wasn't in the vehicle. Which was probably why the driver took to showing off. When the driver saw us in the middle of the road he would come speeding at us as if he intended to run us over. We would all flee. Only Ade would remain where he was, unafraid, almost daring the driver to kill him. And always the driver stopped very close to Ade, a big grin on his face. The driver developed this taste for frightening us with the car. When we saw that he didn't run Ade over, the rest of us didn't move either when he threatened us. Terror always seized me though, when the car screeched to a halt and I could smell the engine oil smouldering and could see the driver smiling. Ade, always defiant, never smiled back. He would stop what he was doing, and go home. He was a lonely kid.

When the driver took to showing off with the car, blasting the horn, shouting insults at goats and chickens and passers-by, the people began to dislike Madame Koto very intensely. But it wasn't her fault that her driver gave lifts to girls and splashed mud on hard-working folk and, whenever he saw the chance, drove at us in his macabre idea of a joke.

Three days after Dad's encounter at his secret training ground, there was an unusual gathering of people along the road. There were more vans than normal. They made so much noise with their music and loudspeakers that children cried and the rest of us were deafened. We no longer heard what they said. They obliterated their own messages with their noises. That day some men came to make enquiries about Dad. They hung around, waiting for him to return. One of the vans, packed full of party stalwarts, had stopped across the road and had set up a permanent blare of discordant music and meaningless exhortations. They spoke in many languages, in such vigorous voices, that the loudspeaker made complete nonsense of their utterances. Everyone was on edge that day. The hot spells of the seasonal break were quite infernal, the air was humid, and the noise grated on our teeth. There was a feeling that something unpleasant was going to happen.

When Dad got back from work the men converged on him and asked him questions. He didn't answer them and he brushed them aside and went into the room. He was catatonic with overwork, his eyes dazed, and his silence was like the mood of an ancient grudge. I fetched him water, he bathed. We placed food before him, and he ate his usual huge quantities. And then he slept. He slept through till the evening. The men outside still waited. Then they left. The van stayed parked and occasionally one of the men would keep up a running commentary on who would win the forthcoming elections. They played their music very loudly. It was not the sort of music we liked. It could only have been the awfulness of the music, its loudness, which angered Dad; for, an hour before his usual waking time, we saw him with a towel round his neck, storming towards the van, his chest bare.

When Dad got to the van the men who had been waiting for him reappeared. They surrounded him. Dad went to the driver's door and shouted something. The music got louder. Dad shouted again. I saw him reach for the steering wheel. Suddenly the music underwent a vicious scratching transformation, and then went dead.

'Trouble has arrived!' someone said in the new silence.

For a long moment nothing happened. One of the men grabbed Dad round the neck and he lashed out. The man stood still, back against the van, eyes frozen. None of the others moved. Dad stormed back to the house. The man he had struck fell down slowly.

The party stalwarts, the bodyguards, and the thugs came pouring down from the back of the van. They were all mighty men, with muscles of solid teak. Their faces were fierce and some of them carried clubs. The last thug to come down was the mightiest of them all. He wore a tracksuit and as he emerged he took off his top. I had never seen anyone so cramped and crowded with muscles. His eyes blazed and he was rugged and handsome and his face twitched as if an implacable agony was lodged in his brain. The others cleared the way for him. He was obviously their leader. The others ran round him in a kind of obeisance and they pointed to our house. The chief thug gave our compound the contemptuous glance it probably deserved and slowly, with the great dignity of one for whom victory has always been certain, he strode towards our housefront. Crowds trailed behind him. Children cheered. The inhabitants of the street hissed and cursed. The music was resumed on the loudspeaker and someone sang proverbial variations on the theme of the trouble that people bring upon themselves.

By the time the chief thug reached our housefront the crowd had formed the perimeter of a ringside. The compound people had brought out their chairs and drinks and sat where they had a clear view of the centre. And then from behind the crowd a voice started to chant Dad's name.

'Black Tyger! Black Tyger!'

The chant was picked up and grew in momentum, till everyone was calling for Dad, stamping their feet rhythmically.

'SHUT UP!' the chief thug barked suddenly.

A hush fell over everyone.

'Who is this Black Tyger? Is he not afraid of death? Why did

he insult my men and spoil our music? Tell him to come out –
NOW!'

The crowd resumed chanting.

'SHUT UP!' barked the chief thug again.

He strode around the human ringside, baring his chest, inflating
his stature.

'Do you know who I am?'

'No!' replied the crowd.

'They call me . . .'

'Yeeeessssss?' came the crowd.

'THE GREEN LEOPARD!'

'Is that so?' sighed the crowd.

Then there was silence. His name alone was a myth of terror.
He was a legendary personage, the most feared fighter and terroriser in many of the ghettos. He used to be an armed robber, was
nearly a world champion boxer, and spent years sowing dread in a
thousand streets, making the nights horrifying for women and men
alike. His name was always spoken in low tones, for fear that he
might materialise behind you, and up till that day no one had seen
what he looked like; they had only heard the myth of his terror.

Dad didn't show his face. The world began to think him a
coward. The crowd grew restless. The legendary Green Leopard,
who had, it was said, given up his days of armed robbery, stalked
the human ringside proudly. They said he was now a proper party
man, rehabilitated into the mould of bouncer, bodyguard, and can-
vasser of votes. He was actually the great bully of the ghetto, and
he strode about the place, chest pushed out, arms bouncing at his
side.

In the meantime they had wheeled out the blind old man. He
fretted excitedly in his chair. He had brought his accordion. He
wore a red hat and startled us with his green glasses.

'Ah, so there is going to be a fight?' he said in his graveyard
voice, laughing, and fretting in his chair like a large cockroach.

'Ah, a fight, eh? Good, Fisticuffs! Excellent. When I was a young
man . . .' and he pressed strains of music from his accordion.

The beer-sellers, the trinket merchants, the stall-owners, the hawkers of dried fish and roast ground-nuts circled amongst the crowd
selling things. Drinks were bought in great numbers. Ade found
me and we kept close together and waited. Madame Koto, with her
swelling foot, and her black walking stick, pushed to the front of
the spectators. We heard her servant blasting the car horn up and

393

down the street. The blind old man had fallen into an argument with someone about who would win. They made a bet. Then the fever of betting caught everyone and the fat man who owned the betting-shop up the street went round collecting odds on Dad. Most people favoured Green Leopard. Dad had stayed inside too long and the feelings of the people had turned against him. Sami, the betting-shop owner, realised while collecting the bets that he needed a bucket for all the money. He bought a bucket. Then he sent for his brothers. Six of them came, with machetes and dane guns, and surrounded the bucket. Then Sami went and spoke to the Green Leopard. He gave Sami a terrible stare and then said, very loudly:

'If I don't destroy that Black Chicken in two minutes I will give him one hundred pounds!'

The spectators went wild with cheering.

'GREEN LEOPARD!' they chanted.

And still Dad didn't emerge. I got worried. I went into the compound to see what was happening.

ELEVEN

THE ROOM WAS DARK. Mum sat on Dad's chair mending his shirt. Dad lay on the bed, snoring. I woke him up and told him what was going on outside.

'Don't go,' Mum said.

When Dad heard about the hundred pounds his face brightened.

'So they are ready?' he asked.

I nodded vigorously.

'And there are a lot of people?'

'The whole area. Even Madame Koto is there.'

He smiled. Then, filtering through the walls of the compound, we heard them chant the chief thug's name.

'Who is that?'

'The crowd. They are hailing the man.'

'What man?'

'Green Leopard.'

Dad got up. His alacrity betrayed the fact that he was clearly aware of his opponent's reputation. He began to shadow-box. He stretched his muscles. He limbered up. He was soon sweating. The chanting outside grew louder. He went through his pockets, brought out some pound notes, and gave them to me to go and bet on his behalf.

'Don't lose it,' he said. 'It's the last money in the house.'

Mum had a miserable and helpless look on her face, as if she were going to be sick for a long time.

'So you are going to fight him?' I asked.

'Don't,' Mum said.

'And beat him', Dad said, 'in ten minutes.'

'That's what the man said he would do to you,' I informed him.

'Wonderful,' Dad replied, absent-mindedly.

I left the room. At the housefront the spectators had multiplied.

395

There were faces everywhere. Hungry faces. And now they were hungry for spectacle.

It was a bright evening. The heat alone was enough to make everyone feverish. I went and placed Dad's bet with Sami. The odds against Dad were high and Sami smiled as he took Dad's money.

When Dad emerged from the compound I understood why the odds were so high against him. Dad looked puny compared to the Green Leopard. Dad's appearance drew cries of derision. He came out and jumped around, snorting, shadow-boxing. Green Leopard regarded him with an expression of purest scorn and, in a powerful voice, asked:

'What is your weight?'

'I have no weight,' Dad replied.

The crowd broke into laughter.

'The man has no weight,' they said.

I felt sorry for Dad. I started to go over to pull him away from the ring when Ade held me back.

'My father gave me this strong spell,' he said, waving a dead frog in my face. 'Throw it into the ring,' he added, giving it to me.

I aimed at Green Leopard's head, and threw the dead frog. And missed. It landed on the head of one of his followers, who turned, saw the mischief on our faces, and pursued us. We ran to the burnt van, circled it twice, ducked under a stall, and dashed to the forest. He went back to the spectators. We followed cautiously. When we got to the crowd, and wriggled our way to the front, the two men had begun warming up. Music from the party van was strident over the loudspeaker. Green Leopard had limbered up and worked himself into a great sweat. He was a veritable Titan. He seemed to have been carved directly from the core of a granite mountain. His muscles glistened in the evening sun as if he had bathed in oil. Dad looked lean and tough, but nowhere near as mighty as I had imagined before I had anyone to compare him with. I feared for him and began to feel quite sick.

'So you have no weight, eh?' Green Leopard asked, dancing around heavily, aiming a few trial punches at Dad's head from a short distance.

'No,' Dad said, hopping like a mudskipper, moving like a crab, a defensive animal, 'but I will beat you and disgrace your philosophy.'

Green Leopard laughed contemptuously again and Dad struck

him full in the face with a lightning jab. Green Leopard's head rocked backwards. His laughter stiffened into a mask of pain. Blood appeared on his mouth. He was completely surprised by the speed of Dad's jab. The crowd gasped. The loudspeaker fell silent. For a moment the wind howled over our hungry heads. The blind old man fidgeted excitedly on his chair and broke the silence with a few strains from his ancient instrument.

'The first blow has been struck!' he said.

Then the Green Leopard mounted a ferocious attack of punches on Dad, swinging wildly, using his elbows, throwing crosses and hooks, shouting. Women in the crowd screamed. Dad disappeared under the fury of punches and was sent reeling into the crowd. The people pushed aside for him and as he got up a few hands propelled him back into the fray. One of the people who had pushed him was our landlord.

'The first attack!' cried the blind old man.

I hated him intensely.

'Have you got another frog?' I asked Ade.

'No. But I've got this.'

He brought out a catapult. I snatched it from him, found a little stone, loaded the catapult, and fired a shot at the blind old man's face. I hit his red hat instead. Someone conked me. The old man squealed. The crowd gasped again. Dad had been sent flying with a barrage of crude, heavy-handed blows. The thugs helped him up and, smirking, shoved him back into the fight.

'Successful attack number two!' the blind old man announced, and hid his face.

I searched for another stone. Someone snatched the catapult from me. The crowd yelled. I saw Green Leopard staggering backwards. Dad pounced on him and unleashed a cascade, an avalanche of punches so fast his hands seemed like a machine. Dad's speed was marvellous, his hands were a blur, and the Green Leopard was sent sprawling on his buttocks. His followers started to move. But Green Leopard picked himself up. The blind old man winced in his chair.

'Finish him off!' I cried.

My voice disappeared in the noise and murmurings of the spectators. Dad waited for his opponent to get up. He began to dance, to perform his fancy footwork. He skipped, he even pranced a little. He looked very defined. His power had all of a sudden grown. His skin shone. And there was a look on his face I had never seen before. It was the look of a man at home with the great hinterlands and energies of his spirit. There was no fear on his face. He seemed both serene and insane at the same time.

'No weight! No weight!' he cried. 'But I am the Black Tyger of this forest.'

Green Leopard rushed him. But Dad wasn't there. So deftly had he jumped out of harm's way. He stood behind Green Leopard. He waited for the famed terroriser to turn round. Green Leopard was confused. He looked for Dad and couldn't seem to find him. When he turned round his face was all squashed and swollen, beaten out of shape like a tin car in a bad accident, his eyes narrow, blood streaming from an ugly cut at the corner of his nose. It seemed as if Dad's fists were made of something more unpleasant than metal. When Green Leopard turned, blinded by his swellings, Dad struck him again. And again. Then proceeded to unravel a combination of hooks, upper cuts, right and left crosses, and body punches, so savage and methodical that the crowd was breathless with amazement at the sheer nerve of the smaller man. Green Leopard looked dazed, bewildered, trapped in the higher mathematics of a thorough beating. Dad, with all of his might, smashed him on the nose. Then ended with a roundhouse punch to the ear. But the Green Leopard refused to fall.

Then suddenly the blind old man let out the strangest laughter that ever proceeded from the mouth of a living human being. Dad stopped. And turned. The blind man grinned.

'Don't look!' I cried.

It was too late. Green Leopard caught Dad with a punch of such malevolent power that I heard bones snap in his neck, I heard the base of his skull protest, and felt his entire world-view undergo several revolutions. Dad was sent flying and went crashing into the blind old man. The old man and Dad disappeared into the bodies and the feet of spectators. Green Leopard rushed him, lashing out at the spectators in his way. He suddenly became uncontrollably mad. He threw people about. He tossed women and children out of his path. He unloaded vicious hooks at shadows and faces. He spat blood on people and cursed and grabbed the blind old man and hurled him into the scattering crowd as if he were a mere dummy. He grabbed the wheelchair, and brutally smashed it to the floor, then he caught Dad by the neck, jerked him up, and proceeded to trounce him with maniacal viciousness. There was wailing and pandemonium everywhere. The fight had lost its rules. It had gone crazy. Green Leopard had swung off into an orbit of purest insanity. He raged, pounding Dad's body, as if his brain had become flooded with the ecstatic liquids of tyranny. He finished his barbaric attack with a punch to the stomach that should have indented it for ever and again Dad disappeared into the crowd. When he reappeared I couldn't recognise him. His face was swollen beyond description, bloodied, mashed, and pulped; his nose was cut; blood spurted from underneath an eye; a cut had widened on his forehead; and his mouth was so monstrous it resembled an obscene fruit. Blindly, he flailed about in the crowd, his arms everywhere, his legs wobbly. He kept staggering, but he didn't fall.

'Dad!' I screamed with all the power of my lungs.

He stopped, turned, looked around with eyes that couldn't seem to focus. Then he vanished. I thought he had fallen. I ran there. The crowd had swarmed the place I had last seen him. We looked for him among the feet of people, among the fallen. He wasn't anywhere. Green Leopard stood in the middle of the ring, his arms outstretched as if he had won an important championship fight, his face pouring with blood and a mess of gore.

'Where is the man with no weight?' he asked.

The crowd replied:

'He has run away!'

'Tell him to run far. Because when I catch him I will . . .'

Suddenly Dad reappeared. He stepped out from the spectators, a ghastly, horrifying sight, an apparition covered in rubbish. From the waist downwards he was pouring with mud and slime. For some reason he had gone into the swamp. He was an ugly sight. He was beyond caring, his eyes were not afraid of dying, he was no longer a defensive animal, and his eyes burned as if he had the sun in them. He had gone back to some primeval condition. He stepped into the ring and said:

'What will you do?'

'Kill you,' Green Leopard said.

'First you have to find me.'

'That's easy.'

'Then promise me that your followers will not interfere.'

Green Leopard looked confident and puzzled at the same time. Then he spoke to his followers rapidly in the only language they would thoroughly understand. His followers protested, but he spoke angrily, berating them, and they nodded reluctantly.

Madame Koto kissed her teeth and said:

'Men are mad! I am not going to stand here and watch people kill themselves.'

She pushed her way out of the crowd. I heard her calling her driver.

'Women!' the blind old man said.

Dad went into the ring. He didn't dance, or do anything fanciful. He stood, fists guarding his face, ready. Green Leopard danced towards him, swaggering almost, confident, arms at his side. His followers began to chant his name.

'Green Leopard!'

'Master boxer!'

'Destroy the Tyger!'

'Eat up his fame!'

The music started again from the loudspeaker. The blind old man squeezed additional discord from his accordion. I found a hardened lump of eba on the floor and threw it and this time I didn't miss. I caught him flush on the mouth. He looked blindly around. He stopped playing his instrument. Then I heard him say:

'Take me away from here. The spirits have started attacking me in broad daylight.'

The woman who had brought him wheeled him off. When he had gone the mood of the fight swung into a new hemisphere. The Green Leopard lunged in, wading, arms swinging in a curious half-hearted attack on Dad. He was half-hearted, it seemed, because Dad looked finished anyway, he looked wobbly on his feet, a defeated man whom a few ordinary punches would destroy. And that's why we were all so surprised. Suddenly, from seeming so weak, Dad became rock-like, and charged. He let out a manic scream. Energy, concentrated, glowed from him in an instant. His fists, released from their immobility, shot out in a series of fast, short punches, raining down from a hundred different angles. The punches were blistering, mud from Dad's fists flew everywhere, and the entire action lasted a short time but the speed of the attack seemed to elongate the moment. It was mesmerising. Dad didn't rush into an attack. He didn't move forward. He punched from the spot where he stood, as if he were in an invisible, invulnerable circle of power. A short burst of this close-range fighting ended with an upper cut that travelled from Dad's solidly planted feet and all the mud of his rage. It connected with Green Leopard's jaw, drawing a great sigh from the crowd. The day darkened. A cloud passed over the face of the sun. Birds wheeled overhead. The music from the loudspeaker was full of victory and celebration. Green Leopard stood, arms out, as if he had gone deaf, or as if he had been shot from behind. His eyes were blank, his mouth open. A cloud of dust flew up as the great boxer collapsed slowly to the floor. It was like a dream. Dad was on one knee, within his invisible circle. The crowd was silent, stunned by its unbelief.

I let out a cry of joy. Green Leopard's followers rushed to pick up their man. But he was out cold and didn't so much as twitch. His mouth flopped open and his body was limp as if he had totally given up on reality. The crowd, profoundly disappointed, spat abuses at Green Leopard and his followers. They showered curses on his reputation. They damned his fame and booed his reputation and they began to leave in utter disgust at the money they had lost betting on a man who was much weaker than his legend had suggested. Green Leopard's followers lifted up the prostrate form of their chief protector, master boxer, terroriser of ghettos, the orchestrator of their myths of invincibility. They looked overcome with shame. The music died out and a funereal silence reigned. They carried the horizontal form of their legend, they lifted him high as if he were dead, as if he were a corpse, and they took him to the van. Hurriedly, they bundled him in. Hurriedly, they drove away. Green Leopard did not honour his bet. They left with their philosophy in disgrace. The pamphlets they had distributed, which were scattered about the street, flew all about as the van sped off over them.

No one rushed to congratulate Dad except me and Ade. The crowd were curiously unforgiving of his surprising victory. We jumped around Dad and he lifted us up and carried us in the air and our thin voices rang out his name and sang out his achievement so that the earth and the wind and the sky would bear witness to it even when the spectators didn't. The crowd scattered in shame at having backed the wrong man, in shame for having judged things by appearances, and in bad temper because they didn't know how to achieve the swift turnaround in appreciation. We were not bothered. Dad's victory was all the world we needed. And beaten, mashed up, his face broken, he carried us, cheering, towards the room. Then Ade remembered our bets.

'Sami has run away with our money!' I cried.

Dad immediately put us down and stormed to the betting-shop. We strode, proudly, behind him.

When we arrived, Sami was counting the money he had collected in his bucket. His hefty brothers sat around him in the shop, their faces glowing with money and the light from the kerosine lamp. Sami sat on a stool, his face covered with sweat, his eyes glittering. When he looked up and saw us his face darkened. Then he broke into a smile.

'Black Tyger,' he said, 'you surprised everybody. Sit down. Have a drink. We were just counting the money. Then we were coming to give you your share. So, what will you drink? This fight of yours has made me more money in one day than I have made in months.'

'So I see,' Dad said, refusing to sit.

We stood on either side of him, his minute bodyguards. There was a long silence.

'Are you going to give me my money or not?' Dad asked finally. 'Or do I have to fight everybody here as well?'

Sami smiled. There was silence. The flame crackled. Then Sami got up, went to the back room, and eventually came back with a thick bundle of notes. He gave them to Dad, who gave them to me. I counted the money. Dad nodded his satisfaction. As we turned to leave, Sami said:

'Send one of your boys the next time you are fighting.'

'Why?'

'We could make more money together.'

Dad said nothing. We left. On the way Ade said he had to go home. Dad gave him a pound note and Ade went on home, dancing down the street, singing of our triumph.

It was only when we got home that a monstrous exhaustion seized hold of Dad. As we opened the door Mum was sitting on a stool, with a candle on the table in front of her. She was in an attitude of prayer. She looked up, saw Dad, and rose. Her mouth opened wide when she saw the devastation of Dad's features. She rushed to Dad and embraced him. She began weeping. Then Dad collapsed on her. It took us an hour to carry him to the bed. He did not stir.

TWELVE

DAD SLEPT, WITHOUT waking, for two days. He was like a giant on the bed. It was a shock to see his bruised feet, the cuts on his soles, corns on his toes. His swollen face grew bigger as he slept. His mouth puffed out, red and frightening. His forehead became almost twice its normal size and the cut on his nose widened. While Dad slept, his face swelling, his eyeballs expanding, blood occasionally spurting from his numerous wounds and lacerations, Mum applied warm compresses to his bruises and treated him with herbal fluids. Mum nursed him, washed him, combed his hair, as if she were nursing a corpse she didn't want to bury. On the second day we worried about him and tried to wake him up. He turned in our direction, opened his swollen eyes, and threw a feeble punch, clobbering Mum. She went around that day with a swollen jaw and had to hide her face with a headtie. We gave up on waking him and took to watching over him, as if to ascertain that he was still alive. We would sit in the room in the evenings, three candles on the table, our faces long with anxiety. His sleeping form spread a ghostly silence in the room and made the shadows ominous. Occasionally, Dad would mutter something. We would wait and listen. But he would be gone again.

On the third day, in the evening, when the wind started to rattle our rooftops, Dad began to howl in his sleep. Then he kicked and struggled on the bed, and fell down. He jumped up, his eyes big and mad, ran around the room, kicking things over, sowing havoc with his gigantic shadow, wounding himself on sharp objects, and then he collapsed at the door while he was trying to get out. It took us another hour to drag him back to the bed. Mum lit three sticks of incense and stuck them in strategic corners of the room, to ward off evil spirits. Then that evening, as I sat in the room alone, watching Dad heave on the bed as if breath were deserting him for ever, Mum brought three women into the house. One of them was Madame Koto. They were all dressed in black. One of them, I learned later, was a powerful herbalist who had once been a witch and who had confessed in public, and who was stoned. She reappeared a year after her confession, transformed into a strong herbalist who had promised to do some good to the community. Everyone feared her and few trusted her.

When the three women came into our room I knew something very serious was happening. I stayed silently in a corner, hidden by clothes. They didn't seem to mind my presence. I stayed silently in the corner and watched them calling Dad's spirit back from the Land of the Fighting Ghosts. All through the night they called Dad's public and secret names in the strangest voices. All through the night they performed their numinous rituals, singing the saddest songs, weaving threnodies from his names, chanting incantations that altered the spaces in the room, that increased the sepia-tinted shadows, that made the cobwebs writhe and flow as if they had become black ancient liquids. The forms of night-birds took shape amongst us, fluttering swiftly over the candle-light; the room filled up with nameless presences, passing through the air of burning sacrificial herbs. The black sea-waves lashed on the dark shores of the ceiling as the women conjured a hundred forms to fight the things that prevented them reaching Dad's spirit in the remotest regions of the human hinterland. The herbalist who had been a witch sweated and performed, conjured and contorted, she changed her guises under the cover of shadows, she fought heroic battles with the spirits we couldn't see, and she fought them with her frail form, her face crushed and wrinkled like the skin of the aged tortoise which she put on the bed to help her travel faster through those realms where speed is an eternal paradox. Over the door she hung the dried heads of an antelope and a tiger, the skull of a boar and the bristling paws of a lion long dead in its prime. She sacrificed two white cocks. Their blood, mixed with strong smelling potions, was smeared on our walls. The feathers of a parrot and an eagle were burned on our floor and nearly burned down the house. The herbalist made razor incisions on Dad's shoulders and pressed ground herbs into the bleeding cuts. Dad didn't move. I watched his blood trickle down his shoulder, black with the herbs. Then deep in the night the women began to dance round the bed, shrieking. A crowd gathered outside our room. Dad began to stir. The wind seemed intent on blowing our houses away. The door was thrown open, all the candles were extinguished, and in the darkness I saw the huge white form of a swollen spirit suspended in the room. I

404

screamed and the form weaved in the air and came falling down at great speed. It fell down on Dad. When the door was shut, and the candles lit, Dad jerked up suddenly, gasping for breath, heaving, his eyes wide as if he had woken from a dream of terrors. The women rushed to him and Dad, not knowing who they were, or whether he had indeed woken up, pushed them aside, sent the herbalist collapsing on the bed, and shoved Madame Koto, who came crashing down on me. Like someone trying to escape from a nightmare he fled out of the room and was seen tearing down the road towards the forest.

The three women, Mum, and me, went after him. It was fearfully dark. The three women, faces veiled with shadows, kept changing shapes in the darkness. Madame Koto seemed to have recovered the full use of her bandaged foot. The third woman had a presence so featureless that no one noticed her even when she ran. She was like the air or like a shadow or a reflection. Her presence was important in ways I couldn't fathom. The smallest of them was the herbalist and as she ran I kept noticing that her hands flapped in her black smock. It came as a surprise, a shock from which I didn't recover for a long time, to see her lift up into the dark air, as if the wind were her ally. Then the darkness increased round her, became concentrated, like a black smock of cloud, and when the cloud cleared I saw only two women in black running, Mum beside them. The herbalist had disappeared. Then I heard the clapping of great wings in the air above me and I saw a great eagle, black, with red eyes, take off towards the forest, into the night of mysteries. When we got deep into the forest we found Dad asleep, his back resting on the trunk of a baobab tree, with the herbalist standing over his haunted form.

'We must take him back now. Before the spirits of the forest start to smell him,' she said.

We were worried about how we were going to carry Dad back. But the third woman, who seemed to have no features, and who never spoke, took his arm and pulled him up. To our amazement Dad stood up like a child, his eyes open and vacant. Mum held his other arm; they both supported him. And like a man who is neither asleep nor awake, neither dead nor alive, we led him down the forest paths. When we got home the crowd had gone. We lay Dad on the bed. He refused to sleep. He kept jerking up, saying:

'If I sleep I won't wake.'

The herbalist gave him something to drink. It seemed a very bitter drug and Dad's eyes widened as he swallowed the herbal draught. Then he got up and sat on his three-legged chair. With his eyes bulging, his mouth big, slurring his words, Dad began to speak. The three women in black sat on the floor. Mum sat on the bed. I sat in a corner and could see Dad's face, gaunt in the candle-light, his eyes like those of a man who has stared into the deepest pits of existence. At first it was difficult to hear what he was saying, but we got used to it.

'I have been having the most terrible experiences,' said Dad, staring straight ahead, as if he were talking to someone in the room that we couldn't see. 'I was sleeping and then I wasn't sleeping any more. Suddenly I found myself fighting seven spirits. They said they had been sent by Green Leopard's mother. And they wanted to kill me in my sleep so that I wouldn't wake up. I fought them for a long time. All the time you thought I was sleeping I was battling with them. They fought me viciously and kept trying to come out of my dreams to fight my wife. Eventually I defeated them. Then I tried to rest. And then a seven-headed spirit . . .'

'No!' cried the third woman.

'Yes,' said Dad. 'A seven-headed spirit armed with seven golden swords came to me and said because I killed his comrades he wants my son's life in return.'

The women screamed. Mum rushed over and held me, smothering me.

'I said NO!'

The women wailed in low monotone. Mum held me tighter. I feared she might break my neck without knowing it.

'Then the seven-headed spirit attacked me. I fought him for nine nights. I only managed to cut off one of his heads. The spirit was much too powerful for me and there was nothing I could do but run. I ran into the forest. The spirit caught me and tied me up with silver ropes and began to drag me to the Land of the Fighting Ghosts. They are ghosts who spend all their time fighting. The spirit dragged me and I never stopped resisting, but the only thing that saved me was . . .'

Dad paused. The women made sad noises, heads craned forward.

'. . . was my own father, Priest of the Shrine of Roads. He said the spirit couldn't pass any road that he has blocked. The spirit fought him. They battled it out for a long time. I didn't know my father was so powerful. He cut off two of the heads of the spirit. They both became tired. They agreed to make a truce. My father said if the spirit let me go, he would take my place. I didn't understand what he meant.'

Mum began to wail.

'Shut up, woman!' Dad said.

Mum fell silent. I heard her swallow down her tears.

'And then both of them vanished. I freed myself from the ropes. All of my energy had drained from me. An eagle perched on my head and then it turned into a woman. And then four women, three of them dressed in black, just like you,' Dad said, pointing at the three women, 'came and led me from the forest. And then I woke up.'

We all stared at him in silence.

'Pour me something strong to drink!' he demanded.

Mum poured him some ogogoro. Dad finished it in a gulp. The herbalist made Dad drink some more of her herbal draught. Then she got him to bathe in specially treated water. When Dad got back she had prepared another potion for him. He drank it in one and surprised us all by the tenderness of his ravings. He sat on his chair and began to talk about how sweet the black rocks of the moon tasted, and how he drank of the golden elixir of the sun, and of the innumerable geniuses of the future that black people would produce, and of how he saw Mum dancing naked in the forest, her hair suspended by the brilliant cobwebs that the gods had spun, and how he saw me walking backwards into a yellow river, and of a beautiful young woman he saw who called him deep into the place where dead bodies grew red flowers from their mouths. And then just as suddenly as he began, he fell silent. His mouth stayed open. His eyes were shut.

'This man has got a strong head,' the herbalist said. 'My medicine usually puts people to sleep before I count to three. Help me carry him to the bed.'

We carried him. Dad snored. After a while the three women got up. Mum talked to them about money. A small argument ensued. Mum loosened the end of her wrapper, counted out some money, and paid the herbalist and the third woman. Madame Koto said to Mum:

'We must continue that conversation of ours.'

'My husband says no,' Mum said.

'Ask him again.'

The three women left. It was the first time in three nights that we got any sleep.

THIRTEEN

WHEN DAD WOKE up the next morning he bustled with energy as if nothing had happened to him. His face was still swollen, his eyes almost invisible, his mouth puffed out, but he swore that he felt twenty years younger. He talked of grand schemes. He talked of buying enough corrugated zinc to roof the whole ghetto. He talked of buying enough cement to build houses for all the large families who lived in one room. He spoke of tarring all the roads and clearing away all the rubbish that had accumulated in the consciousness of our people. He dreamt of opening massive stores that would sell food cheaply to all the poor people. He got us worried when he began to dream of becoming a professional musician. And we started to think that Green Leopard had dislodged something in his brain when he talked of becoming a politician and bringing freedom and prosperity to the world and free education to the poor. And it was when he began to talk loudly about becoming the Head of State, seizing power from the white people that ruled us, and of all the good things he would do for the suffering people of the world, that we stopped paying too much attention to him.

Then one morning he went from room to room, knocking on doors, waking people up, and asking them if they would vote for him. Most of them slammed their doors in his face. It was unfortunate that, to humour him, one or two people said that they would. It gave him greater encouragement. He went from compound to compound. He spoke to stall-owners and provision-sellers. He queried the ground-nut hawkers and the urban shepherds and the amulet traders. He had long arguments with palm-wine tappers. He was seen in bars, at night, talking to drunkards, outlining his policies for government. A new idealism had eaten into his brain with the freshness of his recuperation. He made enquiries about the cost of zinc. He wondered aloud about how long and how wide the ghetto was. He made extensive, illiterate calculations about how much it would cost to build a house, to build schools, about the population of the poor, and how much money he would need to win an election.

He astonished us with the crankiness of his thinking. He conjured an image of a country in which he was invisible ruler and in which everyone would have the highest education, in which everyone must learn music and mathematics and at least five world languages, and in which every citizen must be completely aware of what is going on in the world, be versed in tribal, national, continental, and international events, history, poetry, and science; in which wizards, witches, herbalists and priests of secret religions would be professors at universities; in which bus drivers, cart-pullers, and market women would be lecturers, while still retaining their normal jobs; in which children would be teachers and adults pupils; in which delegations from all the poor people would have regular meetings with the Head of State; and in which there would be elections when there were more than five spontaneous riots in any given year.

Dad began to spend a lot of the money he had won in buying books. He couldn't read but he bought them. I had to read them to him. He bought books on philosophy, politics, anatomy, science, astrology, Chinese medicine. He bought the Greek and Roman classics. He became fascinated by the Bible. Books on the cabbala intrigued him. He fell in love with the stories of the *Arabian Nights*. He listened with eyes shut to the strange words of classical Spanish love poetry and retellings of the lives of Shaka the Zulu and Sundiata the Great. He insisted that I read something to him all the time. He forced me to have a double education. In the evenings he would sit on his chair, feet on the table, cigarette in his mouth, eyes misty, paper and pencil beside him, and he would make me read out loud. Occasionally he would interrupt me for an explanation. Most of what I read made no sense to me. So he bought a large dictionary which must have cost him at least ten mighty punches from the fists of the Green Leopard. Dad's bloated eye twitched when he opened it out on our table, releasing into the air of our room the aroma of words and freshwood. Like a battered but optimistic salesman, he said:

'This book explains books.'

His passion began to drive us slightly mad. The room became cluttered with books of all sizes, ugly books with pictureless covers and tiny letters as if intended only for the ants to read, large books that broke your back to carry them, books with such sloped lettering that they strained the neck, books which smelt like cobwebs and barks of medicinal trees and old sawdust after rain. Mum complained and sometimes made piles of the books and balanced her basins and cooking pots on them. Dad got furious at her disrespect and they argued bitterly. Then Dad began to contemplate the notion of compulsory military service for women. Then, looking at me, he included children. He saw himself both as invisible Head of State and as fitness master. In the mornings he took to drilling us. Whenever we annoyed him in any way he would wake us up very early and take us through exercise routines. Mum obliged at first, even when she was cooking. That was the first time I saw Mum burn an entire pot of soup. We went hungry that day. Mum became exempt from all drilling. Maybe that was when the future notion of joining the army first entered Dad's head.

He didn't go to work for days. He went around, driven by the new lights that Green Leopard had knocked into his head. He spoke to the prostitutes at length. He persisted even when they abused him, even when people began to speculate loudly about his strange alliances. Then he talked of getting a delegation of Madame Koto's prostitutes to go and protest to the Colonial Administration. For three days Mum refused to cook. And Dad, forced to eat beans cooked by hawkers, and brought down by a bout of stomach trouble, gave up the notion of the Council of Prostitutes. But he created a special place for them in his imagined country.

It didn't take Dad long to realise that he didn't know what he was talking about. When he tried to organise the men of the area to start clearing up the rubbish along the streets, he was surprised at the ferocity of their insults.

'Do you think we have nothing better to do?' they said.

Dad, never to be daunted, took to clearing the rubbish himself.

'We have to clear garbage from our street before we clear it from our minds,' he said, echoing something he had heard in one of the books.

But when he had cleared a bit of rubbish, and dumped it in the swamp, people would litter the section he had cleaned up. In one week his efforts seemed to have resulted in there being more rubbish around. The street got worse. People began to think it more natural to dump their garbage on the street. Dad quarrelled with them. Those that might have voted for him, few as they were, publicly withdrew their support. After a while they began to see the possibilities of the swamp. Dad had shown them the way. When the street became too cluttered, they emptied their garbage into the swamp. When the rains fell, the swamp grew and covered half the street.

But it was when people took to bringing their problems to him, when they asked him for money, for advice on everything from how to get their children admitted to hospital to how to get books for their youngsters, that Dad realised he couldn't be a visible or an invisible Head of State just by himself.

'A politician needs friends!' he announced one morning.

And he began to contemplate a new alliance with Madame Koto. He thought seriously of the importance of information and knowledge. First he dreamt of making me a spy. He wanted me to begin to revisit Madame Koto, to listen to the conversations in the bar, and to find out how to become a politician. We were amazed by Dad's volte-face. Mum, at first, rebuked him, called him a hypocrite and a coward. But, when she had got rid of some of her vengeance, she openly supported the plan. She clearly had in mind the possibilities of making money cooking for the great rally.

Dad's next idea was that shortly after I had re-entered Madame Koto's bar, he would begin his reappearance. His intention was to speak to her customers, to her party supporters and colleagues, learn something about how politics worked, and maybe even win some of them over to his philosophy.

'You used to hate politics,' Mum said. 'What has happened, eh?'

'I've been thinking.'

'So it took Green Leopard to start you thinking, eh?'

'Where there's politics, there's money,' Dad said.

Mum was silent.

'We can't remain poor for ever.'

'Yes, we can,' I said.

Dad gave me a vicious stare.

'In this world,' he said after a while, 'this is what happens to you every day if you have nothing.' He pointed to his swollen face, his puffed-out eyes, his bruised lips.

He paused.

'But while we are doing these things, spying on Madame Koto, finding out everything, I will continue as I was.'

We didn't understand him. The subtlety of his campaign eluded us. He didn't explain. And then, slowly, we realised that Dad's manner had changed. When he pointed at something he did so with authority, as if distinguishing objects in space for the first time. His eyes were still obscured, so we couldn't see what new lights dazzled in them. But he was no longer like a demented boxer, spoiling for a challenge to prove himself. He was slowly taking on the manner of a soldier, a commander. Me and Mum and anyone that listened to him were his team. It was a small army; and because we were a captive audience, Dad had his secret stage from which to spring. He filled our lives with a strange excitement. At the time we didn't know it.

'You,' he said, pointing at me, so that I felt myself distinguished from everything else in the universe, 'you can do what you like, but you also do what I tell you. From today listen carefully to what I say, watch carefully what I do. This life is a joke that is not really a joke. Even mosquitoes know they have to survive.'

FOURTEEN

GRADUALLY WE SAW the subtlety of his campaign. We thought he had changed. He had. But to our chagrin instead of saving the money he had made from the fight, as Mum had suggested, he immediately let it be known that he was throwing a party. He invited the compound people, Madame Koto, the blind old man, Ade's father, and the herbalist who had treated him. The word went round that the man who had conquered Green Leopard was having a party to celebrate his victory. Dad invited only a few people, but the whole world came.

It was meant to be an intimate party. Dad ordered some drinks and got Mum to fry three chickens. While Mum fried the chicken, coughing from all the smoke, Dad kept appearing and walking off with his favourite pieces. A fourth chicken had to be ordered, which I fried, because Mum said she'd had enough of the smoke. Dad confined himself to a steady consumption of beer.

'You used to drink ogogoro,' Mum said.

'Life gets better,' replied Dad, opening another bottle.

When I had finished with the frying and the burning of the chicken, I was sent to go and hire some chairs. When I came back with the chair-hire man, as we called him, Dad was outside, at the housefront, sweating. He had been training again. We piled the folding chairs in front of our room and Mum, grumbling, paid the chair-hire man, who asked if he too could attend the party.

'It's a small event,' Mum said.

'Good, so I can come with my wife.'

Mum had no choice but to give her consent. At the housefront Dad had begun to stride up and down the street, bare-chested, his battered gloves on, calling himself the champion of the world, and inviting all challengers. He was quite drunk and he boasted with a fury I never knew he had. He said he could beat five Green Leopards. He said he could kill three lions with his bare hands. He announced that he could knock out ten trees and destroy a building with a single punch.

'Isn't that the man who humbled the Green Leopard?' asked Mr Chair-Hire.

'Yes.'

'Excellent. I will come and enjoy his party. I will bring all my friends.'

And he hurried off to attend to his business. Dad went on raving. He boasted with such ferocity, lashing out with such energy, and sweating so profusely, that his drunkenness soon left him and he had to keep going into the room to replenish his intoxication with bottles of beer. When he returned and resumed his furious boasting Madame Koto's car drove past. The driver slowed down to listen to him.

'As I was saying, I can destroy a house with only one punch! I can lift a car with one finger. If the car is coming at me I can put out one hand and the car will stop. I can build a road in one day!'

The driver laughed.

'I can punch a man so hard', Dad shouted, 'that all he will be able to do is laugh for the rest of his life.'

The driver took the hint and moved on. When Dad had spent himself with training and shouting, and no one took up his challenge for a battle, he went in, had a bath, and prepared for the party.

The evening came slowly. On the road I watched as the forest darkened. Flocks of white birds settled on the topmost branches of the trees. Madame Koto and her driver went past several times, carrying cartons of beer, boxes of paper plates and napkins. I watched also as the women of her bar helped with piling up hired chairs. Preparations for the great rally were underway. There was now a general fever of anticipation about the event. Those who swore they wouldn't attend it had changed their minds. Its promise of spectacle, the numbers of popular musicians appearing, the hints that money would be distributed to the crowd, the talk even of witnessing free films, made the staunchest opponents waver.

Ade's father, his two wives, and Ade himself, were the first to turn up for Dad's modest celebrations. We opened a few folding chairs for them and poured them drinks. Dad talked to Ade's father about politics. Mum talked to the wives about opening shops and trading in the market. I talked with Ade about Dad wanting to be Head of State.

414

Then the blind old man turned up with his accordion and his helper. After them came Madame Koto, her stomach massive, her face sad. And after her were the herbalist and her silent, distrustful acolytes. Behind them came the compound people, with their children. We ran out of chairs. The room was already crowded. People carried on turning up. We didn't recognise many of them. Traders, lorry-drivers, clerks, stall-owners, hawkers, bicycle-repairers, the carpenter and his colleagues. The party spilled out of the room and into the passage. By this time the room was excruciatingly stuffy and hot. Flies buzzed over the drinks and settled on our sweating brows. Someone tried to open the window, applied too much force, and practically destroyed it. The carpenter promised to fix it for free. The blind old man supplied music from his vile accordion.

Meanwhile, outside, the problem of those who turned up, uninvited, to the party grew worse. They clamoured and raised a terrible din along the passage. When I felt I was going to suffocate inside, from the sweat and the old man's music, I struggled to get out. I was shocked at the size of the crowd. Dad's modest party had been overrun by tramps whose hair was the breeding ground of lice and sprouting rubbish, and who stank; by the wretched and the hungry and the homeless, all of whom had such defiant and intense eyes that I felt they would pounce on anyone who dared ask them to leave; by the deformed, whose legs looked like the letter K, whose mouths always seemed to be dribbling, whose rickety feet were turned somewhat backwards; by weary ghetto-dwellers, people I had seen sitting outside mechanics' workshops dreaming about sea-journeys, people I had seen in the streets or at the markets, faces worn, eyes yellowish. There were handsome young men who brought their girlfriends, women of unknown histories, old men and women who looked like all the old people I had ever seen. There were people in black habits, with wizened faces, eyes bright like royal jaguars, chests and arms covered with spells and amulets. There were also people long rumoured to be witches and wizards. I could recognise them instantly by their anti-smells and by the way they didn't want anyone to touch them. They always stayed on their own. I stared at one of the wizards intently. He stared back at me. Then he began coming towards me. When I turned to run, I heard a dog barking. When I looked again the wizard had gone and a dog stood in his place. It was a white dog with green eyes.

'Kill that dog!' I shouted.

The dog had an almost human expression of bewilderment on its face. Someone threw a stone at it. I aimed a kick at its mouth. The dog fled, howling. Moments later I saw the wizard coming down the street. One of his eyes was swollen. He avoided me for the rest of the evening.

Apart from the witches and the wizards, who brought an almost sweet smell of evil to the crowd, there were thugs from both of the main parties as well as some from the lesser organisations. They had come to see what Dad looked like and to pay their respects to the man who had tamed the legendary Green Leopard. The thugs struggled to get to our room, but the crowd was too dense along the passage. So they lolled around the compound-front, flexing their muscles, expanding their chests, and chatting up the women.

Evening fell and more people poured in from all over the place. Boxers turned up in their training shorts, with their boxing gloves on, with towels round their necks. Men with guns and rounds of ammunition also turned up. They were soldiers and policemen, some of them. They strolled proudly into the gathering and chatted with the prostitutes. They, too, had heard of Dad's feat. They were all ex-ghetto men, who wore their wretched pasts proudly. They kept asking for Dad, but he was nowhere to be found. He wasn't in the room, along the passage, in the toilet, or at the compound-front.

Then as we were looking for Dad we saw a procession of beggars coming down the road. They were led by a hypnotically beautiful young girl. There were about seven or eight of them. Some of the beggars had legs that were limp and pliable as rubber. Some had twisted necks. Others had both feet behind their heads. One of them had one eye much higher up on his face than the other. Another seemed to have three eyes, but on closer inspection it turned out to be a wound like a socket with an eye missing. One was almost completely blind and could see only through pupils so scrambled up and confusing that they seemed like mashed egg yolk. It was when the girl got closer that we saw she was blind in one eye. All the beggars trailed along the ground, in filthy clothes, each with sticks and pads of cloth beneath the joints of limbs that scraped on the rough earth. Dust rose with their advance. Then to our puzzlement the beggars, looking up with the bright faces of arrivants, turned into our compound-front. The girl arranged them into a semi-circle. Then I saw that the procession of beggars were a family. The most deformed was the father. He seemed to have all their deformities. As the line went towards the youngest each member seemed to

416

have a peculiar variation of a particular deformity. It ended with the clarity of the little girl's blind eye. I couldn't stop looking at the girl. She was extremely beautiful, like a flower whose flaw is its luminous perfection. She was also curiously familiar, like the distant music heard on those afternoons when all the world is resolved into a pure dream, a music without a location, the music of one's mood and spirit, distilled by a secret affinity. I went over to the beggars and asked who they were.

'We are from a distant place,' said the girl, 'and we heard that a famous boxer was throwing a party for people who are hungry. We have always been hungry and it took us a whole day of travelling to get here.'

I immediately renewed my search for Dad. I found him in the room, surrounded by boxers, all of whom wanted to try their new techniques on him. Dad was in a frantic state. The room was overcrowded. People were screaming in terror at the spaces being crushed about them. The clothes-line had been pulled down and our clothes lay scattered on the floor and trampled on by mud-covered shoes. The window had been splintered open by one of the boxers who was practising a southpaw punch. The bed was in complete disarray with children jumping about on it. Our cupboard had been invaded by strangers who were helping themselves to our food. There was nowhere to move in the room. In a corner one of the boxers relentlessly punched the wall with his bare fists. Mum sat where all the clothes had fallen. She had a frightened expression on her face. I couldn't reach either Mum or Dad. As I fought through it I became conscious that the crowd was actively preventing my entry. I was completely encompassed by witches and wizards. One of them smiled at me and revealed her dazzling white teeth. A tall witch looked down at me. She was very pretty indeed and had an almost royal bearing. Then she got out a pair of glasses and put them on. Her eyes looked monstrous. She laughed. She put her hand on my shoulder. It brushed against my face. Her hand was so cold in that heated place that I came close to fainting with shock. The witches and wizards closed in on me. I felt myself suffocating. Their smells were so sweet, so without sweat, it made me ill. The one with the swollen eye brought out a black sack. I screamed. When I stopped screaming they weren't around me any more. I found myself surrounded instead by thugs. One of them slapped my head.

'What's wrong with you?' he said.

417

I made a new effort to get to Dad. I called to him. At the other side of the room I could hear him telling everyone to leave, that the party would be held at the housefront. No one listened. He spoke louder and said he wouldn't serve any drinks or food if people didn't leave the room. Gradually they pushed their way out. They were rowdy in the passage, muttering their disappointments. Only Madame Koto, some of the prostitutes, Ade and his family, and the blind old man remained.

'What are we going to do?' asked Dad.

'You invited them,' Mum said. 'Why are you asking us?'

'I didn't invite the whole planet!' Dad said.

'What's the problem?' Madame Koto asked.

'Not enough drinks, plates, chicken, chairs.'

'What do you have?' said the blind old man.

'Too many people.'

I went up to Dad and told him that some beggars had come to see him. I told him they'd been travelling for a whole day and were hungry.

'You mean beggars came to see me, eh?'

'Yes.'

'And they travelled for seven days?'

'One day.'

'And they are outside?'

'Yes.'

'Come and show them to me,' Dad said, staggering.

Then I realised he was very drunk. We left the room. Outside, it was crowded. Dad mingled with the soldiers, his fellow load-carriers, cart-pullers, and boxers. He became very exuberant and talked about political miracles. By the time we got to the housefront, I had lost him. A group of thugs descended on him and they got very animated about some issue. I went over to the beggars. The old man began to sing. The girl stared at me with her sad hungry eye. All around there was chaos. People were struggling for the folding chairs. Boxers began sparring. Witches and herbalists converged and heated arguments grew from their conflicting philosophies. They had furious rows about the superiorities of their powers and their way, the values of their accomplishments, the extent of their influence in the visible and invisible worlds. One of the herbalists brought out a red pouch, waved it about, and threw it on the ground. A cloud of green smoke rose in the air and hung over the gathering. Another herbalist brought out a bundle wrapped in silver foil, screamed incantations, and threw

418

the bundle in the air. The green cloud dispersed. The soldiers crowded the prostitutes. Madame Koto came out of the room and ordered one of her women to call her driver, who had been seen driving up and down the place, terrifying women, drunkenly threatening people who crossed the street, blasting his horn, and shouting insults at those who moved too slowly. The thugs crowded Madame Koto and sang her praises. Dad got on to the cement platform and attempted to make a speech. He was very drunk and he weaved about, a bottle in his hand.

'There is food for everybody!' he shouted. 'There are drinks for everybody! Madame Koto has made a generous contribution.'

Silence fell gradually over the noisy celebrants.

'Today there will be a miracle!' he announced again.

The crowd roared with anticipation.

'I am going to divide one chicken so that everyone will have their share,' he said, and left the platform.

The noise started up. Shortly afterwards Mum and Ade's mother came out and distributed small chicken pieces to the crowd. People complained. Paper cups with small quantities of beer were also passed around. The thugs grumbled that the quantity was an insult to their saliva. Arguments started up. Disagreements flared in the bad-tempered reception of the food and drink. Shop-owners around mingled in the crowd and sold bottled beer and ogogoro. The soldiers and thugs drank a great deal. Dad appeared amongst the beggars. I saw him give them a whole chicken. There was a flash. The beggars fell on the food, rushed it, dismembered the chicken, and ate like famished beasts. Then Dad, standing proudly amongst them, his eyes big, his lips swollen, a bottle in one hand, said:

'These are members of my party. This is my world constituency, the beginning of my road. Watch them. One day we will remember their hunger when we are as hungry as they are. These people are our destiny!'

No one listened to him. He went on with his political declaration, untroubled by the fact that no one listened. He criticised the people of the ghetto for not taking care of their environment, for their lazy attitude towards the world, for their almost inhuman delight in their own poverty. He urged them to lift themselves up by their thoughts.

'THINK DIFFERENTLY,' he shouted, 'AND YOU WILL CHANGE THE WORLD.'

No one heard him.

'REMEMBER HOW FREE YOU ARE,' he bellowed, 'AND

YOU WILL TRANSFORM YOUR HUNGER INTO POWER!'

One of the soldiers burst out laughing. Dad screamed at the soldiers for carrying guns, for always having weapons, and for their arrogance. Then he launched an attack on all the thugs who went around terrorising people. He abused the government, he denounced both political parties for poisoning the minds of the people. But he reserved his most furious assault for the people of the nation. He blamed them for not thinking for themselves, he lashed out at their sheep-like philosophy, their tribal mentality, their swallowing of lies, their tolerance of tyranny, their eternal silence in the face of suffering. He complained bitterly that people in the world refused to learn how to see properly and think clearly. He swore that days of fire and flood were coming when soldiers and politicians would drown in their own lies.

'He has gone completely mad!' someone said.

'No more political speeches!' someone else cried.

'Give us food!'

'Give us wine!'

'Give us music!'

'Keep the politics for yourself!'

Dad's arms flailed. He attempted to answer his hecklers, but the voices crying out for drinks, the confusion and the arguments, the fury of drunken women and noise of the soldiers among the prostitutes, drowned out his speech.

'Music!'

'Food!'

'Wine!'

Dad was confused. At that moment the blind old man, vaguely resembling a centaur, struck up on his accordion, and altered the mood of the entire party. Music, like the awful sound of wild beasts gnashing and grinding their teeth in the forests, poured from the pleats of his instrument. He played with great abandon, unleashing such discordant notes on the air that it wasn't long before a herbalist, hand wrapped in a black pouch, slapped one of the wizards. Pandemonium broke over the party, orchestrated by the soaring cruelty of the accordion's resonant ugliness. A woman screamed. A soldier accidentally fired a shot in the air. The wizard who had been slapped whirled round and round on one spot, arms outstretched, eyes wide open. A witch slapped the herbalist, whose face turned blue and then red where he had been slapped. He began to wail. The beating of mighty wings sounded over our heads. Shadows descended on us. Darkness came on silent wings, filling out the empty spaces. I saw one of the witches struggling with her garment. Her eyes turned blue. Her fingers became claws. Her face became wonderfully pretty. A chair was hurled, which landed on the thugs. The beggars attacked the soldiers. The tramps pounced on the prostitutes. A flash blinded me. I heard the blast of the car horn, piercing the night like a forlorn and angry cry. Out of the incandescent flash, human forms materialised in the darkness. Someone caught me as I fell. And when my eyes cleared I saw people fighting, chairs hurling themselves in perfect parabolas through the air, members of the political parties pouncing on one another. Bodies tumbled in bizarre entanglements, fists connected with faces, a woman scratched a man's eyes, one of the witches had fastened on to the back of a soldier and the soldier howled as if a crude pair of claws had been dug into his soul. Dad vainly tried to restore order, while the boxers and thugs blinded one another with punches.

Bottles broke on heads in the darkness. Yellow birds, like the leaves of fertile trees, scattered amongst us. Another flash startled me. And it was only when Madame Koto's car shone its garish headlights on us that I noticed the new silent presence of the photographer. And before I could shout him a greeting I became aware that something had gone wrong with the nerves of the world. We heard the whirring engine, heard the possessed cry of the driver, and saw the two arc lights of the car intently bounding towards us, pressing on, growing brighter, flooding us with confusion. Several screams rose at once. There was a moment during which I saw the illuminated face of Madame Koto's driver. He looked thoroughly drunk, his eyes were barely open, his neck was all tight with tendons, and sweat like melting wax poured down his brow. Then the car swerved. Panic showed on the driver's face as he seemed to wake up suddenly, and in his awakening he lost control. People fled, disorientated by the yellow birds. In the arc of lights I saw the forms of people leaping into the air, leaping, some of them, into invisibility; leaping, others, into new forms. Finally, the car cut through the crowd, and knocked Ade and one of the beggars sideways. Then the car smashed into the cement platform, into the wall of the compound, and its lights went dead. The engine roared, the wheels turned, churning up the soil. After the tide of shattering glass there was a long moment of silence.

Then the real confusion began. Wailing rose in the dark. Another shot was fired into the air. Dad, who didn't seem to have registered what was happening, launched into another speech, pouring scorn on all politicians who deliberately keep their people illiterate. I heard someone fall on the blind old man's accordion. People fought in the darkness everywhere. Ade began crying. Abuse fell in torrents, voices cursed Madame Koto and her doomed ambition, and in the car we heard the trapped driver screaming. The compound women fetched lanterns. The men managed to wrench open the mangled car door and bring out the twisted form of the driver. He had blood all over him. His chest had a weird gash as if he'd been shot there. Broken glass, like the wild spikes of certain plants, had lodged itself in his face. Shards of glass were everywhere, in his wounds, mingled with his blood and scattered on the seats. There was a long splinter in one of his eyes. Wailing and kicking, he was like a man who had woken into a nightmare. Green pus and all the fluids of sight and blood, poured down the sides of his face like a burst egg. They carried him and stretched him out on the cement platform. One of the herbalists, howling the secret names of arcane deities, plucked out the glass from his eye and the other herbalists prepared potions to staunch the bleeding and the flow of eye fluids. Not far from them Ade, who had been struck in the hip and had landed on his arm and wrenched it, beat and wailed on the ground. His father held him down and his mother spoke words into his ears, which made him wail louder. A witch pulled at his legs and a herbalist was twisting his bad arm. His father shouted that his son should be left alone. Behind them, the thugs of both parties fought on the mud, fought in the swamp, fought like giants in old legends. Wood broke on skulls. Chairs flew through the air. The family of beggars, led by the beautiful one-eyed girl, had begun their departure. They filed out, the girl in front. She kept looking back. She had no expression or judgement on her face. And behind her – hobbling and crawling on the earth, each with their unique deformities, twisted legs behind their necks, soft legs uselessly trailing on the ground, heads big and strange with the agony of survival – were the rest of the family of beggars. I wanted to follow them on their journeys, to be with the beautiful girl who had refined all their deformities into a single functioning eye, whose face would pursue me in dreams and loves and music.

But Mum screaming in the crowd, Dad who was caught in a barrage of accusations, Madame Koto who was surrounded by enemy thugs, and Ade who wept bitterly on the ground, held me back and kept me rooted. I watched the beggars leave, and one aspect of my destiny left with them. And as they went I heard the wind rush, laden with all our sorrows, over the branches of the trees. The wind circled our heads. I saw the forms of angels in the dark sky. The yellow birds in our midst, startled by the new horrors of the smashed car, and by the aroma of blood, beat their wings and took off into that night of lamentation. And then, without any heavenly event, the rain began to fall. The rain fell on the devastated car, on Madame Koto who wept openly, on the thugs of both parties as they clashed and wounded themselves over obscure loyalties. The rain poured on the driver, who had now passed out, on the herbalists, who didn't seem to know what to do, and on my friend, who had now become serene within his own pain. It was not the tragedy of the night that dispersed everyone. It was the rain. The thugs fought themselves right through different stratas of time. The soldiers left as a group, drunk on beer and the smell of cordite. The tramps, who had come because of the rumours of a feast, the people who had turned up to hail their new hero, the wretched and the curious, were all washed away by the gentle flood. Ade's father left with his wives, carrying my friend away on his back. The chair-hire man stormed up and down the street, cursing Dad for the destruction of his chairs. The witches and wizards simply disappeared. I didn't see them go. And the herbalists carried Madame Koto's driver away for proper treatment. As the rain became heavier, the only people left at the housefront were Dad, who was distracted and drunk; Madame Koto, whose wig gyrated in a swirling puddle and who sat on the ground covered in mud; and Mum, who stood beside the car, blood and rain-water flowing round her feet. The blind old man was led home. His mangled accordion dangled at his side, as if it were an instrument that had been destroyed by its own bad music. Immobile and obscene, the car stayed smashed against the cement wall. Nothing could be done about it for the night.

The chair-hire man pounced on Dad. And Dad had to knock him down twice. He rushed off and came back with a machete and he had to be held. Dad swore that he would pay for the chairs or repair them himself. Disconsolate and drunk with rage, the chair-hire man had to be led home by four men. Madame Koto's prostitutes came and took her away, holding her by both arms, as if she might do something dangerous. In the distance she could be heard wailing, not about the driver, but about her car.

When everyone had finally gone, Mum went silently into the room. Dad had a long bath. I stayed at the housefront while the rain went on falling, staring at the flotsam of broken chairs, shattered glass, tatters of clothes and feathers, broken bottles, and chicken bones on the road. I think most of our real troubles began that night. They began not with the devastation of voices and chairs and the car, but with the blood mingling with rain and flowing right into the mouth of the road. I heard the slaking of the road's unquenchable thirst. And blood was a new kind of libation. The road was young but its hunger was old. And its hunger had been reopened. The roads were not even flooded that night although the rain didn't cease. For a long time I couldn't see the sky. As I stood there the firm hands of the wind came from behind and lifted me up.

'Come in,' Mum said. 'This is not a night for a child to see.'

Dad was asleep on the bed. I could hear his snores over the rain and the thunder. Mum lit a candle on the table. After we ate we stayed up. Mum said nothing. Both of us stared at the candle, feeling the wind and the thunder banging on our broken window.

Book Seven

ONE

THERE ARE MANY riddles of the dead that only the living can answer. After the catastrophe of the party, Dad's philosophy began to expand in strange ways. The spirit encroachment on my life increased. In many respects, and without knowing it, Dad kept the spirits at bay with his battles in different realms. But along our road, there wasn't much anyone could do. Fighting broke out all the time. In the morning after the disastrous party, Madame Koto organised six thugs to come and push her car to the mechanic's workshop. We woke to the noise of confrontations. As the thugs pushed the car along a group of opposition thugs ambushed Madame Koto and her protectors and attacked them in retaliation for knocking over Ade.

I returned from school to hear that people were going around armed with clubs. Dad had returned early and was having an argument with the chair-hire man about the number of chairs that were destroyed. Mum also returned early because everywhere she went there were clashes between the warlords of both of the main parties. When the chair-hire man left, with some money, and a little mollified, Dad asked me to read. I read to him from Homer, while Mum vented her anger about the horrors of the celebration. The food that evening was quite tasteless. Dad didn't notice. He ate with his usual large appetite.

His face had begun to return to normal. A new fierceness had entered his eyes. After I had read to him again from Homer's *Odyssey*, Dad wondered aloud about how he was going to be able to do any good in the world if he didn't learn more about politics, and didn't infiltrate the existing organisations. It was around this time that Dad conceived the idea of using the ever-approaching rally as the platform to preach his ideas and gather voters. Then he remembered his notion of using me as a spy.

'My son is not a spy,' Mum said.

'One way or another we are all spies,' Dad asserted.

'Don't put my son in trouble.'

'But he will make a good spy.'

'Why?'

'You won't understand.'

'That's what you men say when you don't want to tell the truth.'

Dad kept quiet. Mum complained about how Dad was using me for his mad schemes, about all the money wasted on the tragic party. But Dad didn't listen. He called me and said he wanted me to resume visiting Madame Koto's bar. He said he would join me later. I didn't think he was serious. But later in the evening, as I sat outside watching the world revolve slowly with the movement of clouds, he came and reminded me of my mission. He told me that new things were happening in the world and in our area. Was I not curious? I wandered off to Madame Koto's bar.

Our road was changing. Nothing was what it seemed any more. Some of the beggars that came to Dad's unfortunate party had set up at the roadside. One of them lay on a mat in front of the blind old man's house. With his beads between his fingers, the beggar asked me for money as I went past. His eyes were hollow, his mouth was like a curse. I hurried on. The bushes along the roadside were getting wilder. A young tree had fallen between the blind old man's house and Madame Koto's bar. The wind rose suddenly and when it lessened I could smell the small things rotting in the forest. As I neared the bar, with its bright new signboard, I heard loud voices and music from within. I stayed at the barfront. I wasn't sure how I would be received. The car wasn't there. A man came out of the bar, stared at me, spat generously on the bushes, and went back in. Shortly afterwards one of the prostitutes emerged.

'What do you want?'

'Madame Koto.'

'Who sent you?'

'My father.'

'Who is that?'

'Black Tyger.'

She gave me a long stare. She went in. For a while nothing happened. The voices became louder. A fight started. Chairs tumbled over. Glasses broke. Women's voices intervened. The fight died down with subsiding abuses. Someone put a record on the phonograph and a deep octave voice, lifted by brass instruments, sang out into the evening. The wind blew. Trees bowed. A procession of beggars came down the road. They were not beggars I recognised. They stopped in front of Madame Koto's bar. Then they came towards me. There were about seven of them. Two of them had malformed legs and dragged themselves on the ground like hybrid serpents, with the cushioning aid of elbow pads. The rest of them had twisted arms, elongated necks. One of them had only one arm, another had two fingers, and another, to my horror, seemed to have three eyes. I tried to run, but I was curiously rooted. Salaaming, bringing with them all the smells of the gutters, street-corners, dustbins, rotting flesh, and damp nights, they pressed on me. Their leader was a man of indescribable age, with a face of wrenched metal, deep eyes, and a crumpled mouth. He came to me, begging for generosity, in a language which seemed to belong to another universe. He crowded me, and the others did as well, till I couldn't breathe for their smells. The youngest of the beggars laughed and it seemed that a mashed insect fell out of his mouth. I shouted. The oldest beggar grabbed me, with his two fingers, and his grip was like that of an infernal machine. Pressing his face close to mine, so that I was suspended in a moment of fainting, he said:

'Follow us.'

I kicked out and pushed the beggars away and ran into the bar. The floor was crowded with dancers. The room was full of smoke. I knocked over a bench, and collided with a dancing couple. A woman shrieked. The music stopped. And everyone, frozen in their particular motion, as if I had brought an alien enchantment, stared at me.

'What's wrong with you?' one of the prostitutes asked.

'Nothing.'

'Get out of here!' one of the men shouted.

I recognised him as just another thug. He had big shoulders and a thick neck.

'Get out!'

'No!'

'Are you mad?'

'No.'

One of the women slapped my head and I jumped on her and a hand grabbed my neck from behind and lifted me away.

'If you don't go I will throw you out,' a mighty voice said.

'I will go.'

He put me down. I waited. Then I pointed at the door. They all looked. The strips of curtain were parted. And the old beggar, salaaming, his face weirder in the red lights, came in. Behind him was the train of beggars. They brought with them all the foul, unwanted smells of the world. I went to a corner of the bar, and sat down on a bench. There was a long silence. The old beggar, looking round at everyone with fearless eyes, came towards me, bringing his entourage with him.

'I want that boy,' he said loudly, pointing at me with a crooked finger.

As he moved into the bar the darkness came with him. The darkness was a wind that blew from their crowding of the doorway. When one of the prostitutes saw the collective deformities of the beggars, she let out an anguished cry. Suddenly, with no one activating it, the music started. The bravest of the thugs yelled. The beggars brought a ferocious unbending force into the bar. They imbued everything with their smells. One of the younger beggars, who had no legs and moved on low crutches of uneven lengths, climbed up on the table where most of the clientele were gathered. For the first time I noticed that the thugs and warriors of grass-roots politics were afraid. The prostitutes retreated, holding their noses.

'They sent me to bring that boy,' the old one said, moving steadily towards me.

'Who sent you?' I asked.

All the faces in the bar turned to me. One of the beggars laughed. Another one picked up a calabash of palm-wine and drank it all. As if on cue the rest of them suddenly noticed the drinks and the plates of peppersoup on the tables and, discarding their crutches, fell on all the available food. The ones without legs propelled themselves up on powerful hands. The ones without hands leapt up and, with the expert grip of their teeth, seized the peppersoup bowls and drank. Soup ran down the sides of their mouths and on to their filthy clothes. The old beggar, standing still, his eyes burning on me, remained apart from the mêlée, his battered frame twitching, a strange smile on his lips. He stood still, and so did everyone else. The music stopped. Plates had been turned over; the beggars drank soup and ate the meat and bones from the table tops. The thugs and other clientele were transfixed. A beggar boy began to choke. Another one laughed. The old one rushed at me. When I fled amongst the prostitutes gathered at the door, it seemed I released the spell hanging over the place. Suddenly the thugs lashed out at the beggars, kicked them, threw plates at them. The beggars ate and drank as though untouched. When the wine had been emptied from the cups, the soup all consumed, the bones cracked, the marrow sucked out of them, the beggars – amazing in the virtuosity of their incomplete limbs – jumped on the thugs. The prostitutes fled outside. The thugs also panicked and ran. The old one sat down beside me. I did not move. He surveyed the chaos of bones being thrown, tables overturned, glasses breaking, and then he said:

'How many eyes do you have?'

'Three,' I replied.

He stared at me.

'How many ears?'

'One.'

'Why?'

'I hear things.' I continued. 'Voices. Words. Trees. Flowers.'

He laughed.

'They sent me to bring you.'

'Who?'

'Your friends.'

'Who are you?'

He looked around and waved his hand over the bar. The darkness cleared. He hit me on the head and I heard the cry of a cat. A dog's eyes stared into mine. Water poured over me. I did not flinch. An eagle flew in from the door and landed on the old one's head. He touched the eagle with his good hand and a black light shot into my eyes. When I opened them I saw that I was in a field. Around me snaked a green river. I looked up and saw a blue mountain. Voices called my name from the river. A cat jumped right through me. I moved. The beggar laughed. I turned, looked at him, and screamed. He had four heads. One of them was the head of a great turtle. I tried to move but he held me. Spirits, shrouded in sunflower flames, rose from the ground about me. The field shook. The river hurled its waters on the coral shores, the water turned into spray, and in the spray I saw my spirit companions, all of them holding blue mirrors over their heads. My friend, Ade, was among them. I did not get a chance to recognise the others because in a flash, in which all the lights converged in the mirrors, the spray dissolved. A loud voice disturbed the mountain. I fell, and woke to find myself lying on a bench. I sat up. It was dark. Fishes swam in the black lights of the bar. I stayed still. When I surveyed the place I noticed that there was another person in the bar. Someone brought a lantern through the door. The yellow light obliterated their form. I waited. The form put the lantern in front of me and said:

'You were lucky today.'

'How?'

'I failed, but after me comes the spirit with five heads.'

'Why?'

'To take you back.'

'Why did you fail?'

The lantern flickered. The other person in the bar, a massive figure, stirred. She lifted up her swollen face. She had the saddest eyes. They were big and lonely.

'Madame Koto!'

'Don't call my name!'

'Why not?'

She was silent. Her eyes changed. They became a little menacing.

'There are spirits in the bar.'

I looked for the form behind the lantern. The form was gone. I noticed something moving behind the lamp. I looked. Writhing, its head green, its eyes scaly, was a large lizard. I moved slowly, felt for an object on the floor, touched a stone, and struck the lizard on the head. The lamp went out. A blue wind whistled in the bar and crashed at the door. I edged my way to the backyard. Madame Koto caught me in the dark and said, in the voice of an old bull:

'Why did you bring them?'

'Who?' I cried.

'Your friends.'

'Which friends?'

'The beggars, the spirit.'

'They are not my friends.'

'They are your father's friends.'

'No.'

'He is their representative, not so?'

'I don't know.'

'He has gone mad with politics.'

'I don't know anything.'

'What did the spirit say to you?'

'I didn't hear.'

She let go of me.

'You want some peppersoup?'

'Yes,' I said.

She went out and left me in the strange darkness of her bar. I wondered about what had happened to the electricity. I began to smell the corpse of the lizard, as if it had accelerated in its decomposition. The front door opened. The curtains parted. I smelt boots, restless energy, and saw a form at the doorway, the odour of mosquito coils preceding him.

432

'Dad!' I said.

He lit a match. His face was long, his eyes bright and deep-set, a cigarette in his mouth. The match went out. He sat. I listened to him thinking. Then he laughed airily and said:

'A man can wander round the planet and still not move an inch. A man can have so much light in his mind and still not see what's right in front of him. My son, why are you sitting like that?'

I didn't know what to say. He chuckled in the dark.

'A man can carry the world and still not be able to bear the load of his own head.'

'What load?' I asked.

'Ideas, dreams, my son,' he said, a little wearily. 'Since fighting the Green Leopard the world has changed. The inside of my head is growing bigger.'

After a while, he said:

'Maybe my thoughts are beginning to smell.'

'There's a dead lizard on the table.'

'Who killed it?'

'Me.'

'Why?'

'It's a spirit.'

'How do you know?'

'The spirit spoke to me and then changed.'

'Don't kill lizards.'

'Why not?'

'They are messengers. Sometimes they are spies. My father once sent a lizard to warn me.'

'Of what?'

Dad was silent. Then he said:

'Some of our enemies were going to poison me. This was in the village. They put poison in my soup. I was about to drink when I saw this lizard shaking its head at me.'

'That's what lizards do.'

'You are a goat, my son.'

'So what happened?'

'I ignored the lizard and was about to drink the soup when the lizard ran up the wall. I watched it, fascinated. Then it fell into the soup and died.'

I thought about what Dad had said. Outside I heard loud drunken voices from the forest.

'Where is the lizard?'

'On the table.'

Dad lit a match.

'There's nothing here.'

The match went out.

'Maybe it went back to the land of the spirits.'

'Don't talk about spirits.'

The voices outside grew louder.

'Someone gave the beggars wine to drink. I've never seen beggars so drunk. They are all members of my party.'

I could hear them laughing, cursing, fighting amongst themselves.

'They see me as their leader,' Dad said. 'And I have no money to feed them. But I will build them a school. You will be one of the teachers. Is there any palm-wine? Where is Madame Koto?'

'In the backyard.'

'Go and call her.'

I went out through the back door. It was very dark and I saw the prostitutes on stools or standing around, smoking in the night. When they saw me they kissed their teeth. The thugs and other clientele had gone. I went and knocked on Madame Koto's door. After a while she opened. She had a lamp in one hand, a wig in the other. Her stomach was very big and wide, her face was swollen, as if someone had been hitting her. Weariness weighed on her eyes.

'You bad-luck boy, what do you want?'

'My father . . .'

'What father? Leave me alone. My business was doing well, then you went and brought all those beggars and drove away all my customers.'

'I didn't bring them.'

She stared at me a long time. She looked quite frightening. She gave me the lamp to hold and then put on her wig. She shut her door and went to the backyard and asked the prostitutes to go for the night. They grumbled about not being paid.

'I will pay you tomorrow, when this bad-luck boy is not here.'

One by one the prostitutes got up. Grumbling, cursing, they went out into the darkness of the housefront. Madame Koto sat on a stool. There was a large green pot on the fire-grate. Frogs croaked in the bushes. From the forest a bird piped three times and stopped. The crickets trilled. Mosquitoes bit us. After some time one of the prostitutes came back.

'What's wrong?' Madame Koto asked.

'Those beggars are drunk.'

'On my wine.'

'If we don't get rid of them our business will fail.'

'Don't talk nonsense. Go home. Come tomorrow.'

She went. We listened as the beggars called out to her. She cursed them. The beggars laughed raucously.

'Those friends of yours broke all my glasses,' Madame Koto said. 'And my plates. Abused my customers. Broke two chairs. Who will pay, eh?'

'My father wants to talk politics with you.'

'Who?'

'You.'

Madame Koto reached for a stick and began to hit me. I didn't move. She stopped.

'You and your father are mad.'

'We are not mad.'

'I'm not well,' she said, in a different voice.

'What is wrong?'

'Money. Politics. Customers. People.'

I was silent.

'What does your father want?'

'Palm-wine.'

She gave a short laugh.

'I gave all the palm-wine to the beggars.'

'Why?'

'They were causing trouble so I gave them palm-wine and they left. I told them to go far away, but they went to my frontyard.'

'They want to vote for my father,' I said.

Madame Koto stared at me.

'Your father?'

'Yes.'

She laughed again.

'Only chickens and frogs will vote for him.'

'What about mosquitoes?'

'Them too. And snails.'

'He said I should call you.'

'Where is he?'

'In the bar.'

'So he has come back to my bar after calling me a witch, eh?'

'He wants politics.'

'Go and tell him I'm coming.'

435

When I went back into the bar Dad was asleep. He slept with his head held high, as if he were in a trance. I drew close to him and listened to him grinding his teeth. Fireflies lit up the darkness. A yellow butterfly circled Dad's head. I watched the butterfly. When it landed on Dad's head I could suddenly see him clearly in the dark. A yellow light surrounded him. The light was the exact shape of Dad and it rose in the air and came down and began to wander about the bar. I watched the light. It kept changing colour. It turned red. Then golden-red. Then it moved up and down, lifting up in the air, and bouncing on the floor. It went round Dad as if looking for a way to get back in. Then the golden-red light came and sat next to me. I started to sweat. I cried out. The light changed colour. It became yellow again, then a sort of diamond-blue. When I touched Dad the butterfly lifted from his head and disappeared through the ceiling. Dad opened his eyes, saw me, and gave out a strange cry. Then he looked around as if he didn't know where he was.

'You're in Madame Koto's bar,' I said.

He stared at me, lit a match, and when he recognised me he blew it out. He drew me close to him. I could smell his frustrated energies, his mosquito-coil fragrances. He lit a cigarette and smoked quietly for a moment.

'A man can wander the whole planet and not move an inch,' he said. 'My son, I dreamt that I had set out to discover a new continent.'

'What is it called?'

'The Continent of the Hanging Man.'

'What happened?'

'When I landed with my boat I saw mountains, rivers, a desert. I wrote my name on a rock. I went into the continent. I was alone. A strange thing happened.'

'What?'

'You're too young to understand this.'

'Tell me.'

'As I went I started to dream the place into existence. I dreamt plains, forests, paths, great open spaces, spiked plants, and then I dreamt up the people. They are not like us. They are white. Bushmen. They advanced towards me. They wore strange clothes and had precious stones round their necks. To the eldest man, I said "What are you people doing here?"

'"What about you?" he asked.

'"I have just discovered this place. It is supposed to be a new continent. You're not supposed to be here."

'"We've been here since time immemorial," he replied.

'And then I dreamt them away. And then a shepherd came to me and said:

'"This continent has no name."

'"It's called the Continent of the Hanging Man."

'"That's another place," he replied.

'"So why doesn't it have a name?"

'"People do not often name their own continent. If you can't give it a name you can't stay here."

'The continent vanished. I found myself on a strange island. The people treated me roughly. They were also white. Unfriendly people. Unfriendly to me, at least. I lived among them for many years. I couldn't find my way out. I was trapped there on that small island. I found it difficult to live there. They were afraid of me because of my different colour. As for me, I began to lose weight. I had to shrink the continent in me to accommodate myself to the small island. Time passed.'

Dad took a drag from his cigarette. His eyes were bright in the darkness.

'Then what happened?'

'I began to travel again. I travelled on a road till I got to a place where the road vanished into thin air. So I had to dream a road into existence. At the end of the road I saw a mirror. I looked into the mirror and nearly died of astonishment when I saw that I had turned white.'

'How did it happen?'

'I don't know.'

'So what happened?'

'Then everything changed. I was in a big city on the island. I was a news-vendor, selling newspapers outside a train station. It was a temporary job. I had bigger plans. It was very cold. There was ice everywhere.'

'Ice?'

'Yes. Ice fell from the sky. Ice turned my hair white. Everywhere ice.'

'Then?'

'Then one day you came to buy a newspaper from me. You were a young man. When you gave me the money it burned my hand. I started to run away when you woke me up.'

We sat in silence. Dad creaked his bones for five minutes. Then he stretched. Then he banged the table and said:

'Where is the wine, eh?'

The electric light came on in the bar, driving away the shadows, rendering the objects curiously flat. Madame Koto, two bottles of beer in one hand, a bowl of peppersoup in the other, hobbled over to our table.

'Finish this and go,' she said, banging down the beer and soup.

'The Great Madame Koto, aren't you pleased to see me, eh?'

'After you called me a witch?'

'That was your palm-wine talking, not me.'

She hobbled away. Her foot had grown worse, and had been rebandaged. She went to the counter, sat behind it, and put on some music. Dad drank the soup hungrily. He gave me some meat. He opened the bottle of beer with his teeth.

'No wine?' he asked.

'I gave all the wine to your friends.'

'What friends?'

'The beggars,' I said.

'They broke my plates and glasses. Why did you have to bring them here, eh?'

'I didn't bring them.'

'Why did you invite them to your party?'

'I didn't invite them.'

Madame Koto stopped the music. Dad finished the first bottle of beer and started on the second one.

'Madame Koto, I want to talk politics with you.'

'Why?'

'Out of interest.'

'For what?'

'People.'

'Who will you vote for?'

'Myself.'

'I hear you want to start your own party, eh?'

Dad said nothing. I looked up at the posters of the political party that Madame Koto supported. I studied the pictures and almanacs of their leaders. She said:

'Don't bring me trouble. Take your beggars away. I don't want to lose my customers.'

'Beggars also vote.'

'Let them vote for you, but take them away.'

The wind blew at the door. Then we heard a curious drumming on the roof. The bulb kept swaying. Someone came in. At first I could not see them.

'Get out!' Madame Koto shouted.

Then I saw three of the beggars at the door. Two of them were legless and moved on elbow pads. The third one had a bad eye. They came into the bar and gathered round Dad's table. Dad finished off his beer.

'If you get rid of them,' Madame Koto said, 'I will forget the damage, and you and your son can come here to drink anytime you want.'

The beggars played with the empty beer bottles. Dad snatched the bottles from them and stood up.

'Let's go,' he said to me.

We went out and the three beggars, chattering, pawing Dad's trousers, followed us. Along the street other beggars were asleep. The three beggars followed us till we got to our place. Dad turned to them and waved them away. They stopped. We went on. I looked back and saw the three beggars, crouched in the darkness, staring at us with odd eyes.

TWO

THE WIND AND thunder were hard that night. We found Mum sitting on Dad's chair, a mosquito coil on the table, a tattered wig on the bed. Mum looked tired. She didn't say anything when we came in. She was rocking back and forth, while the wind blew over our roof and thunder rumbled above us. Things were changing, the room looked strange, and Mum sat there staring straight ahead as if down a long unfinished road. The candle had burned low, mosquitoes whined, a moth circled Mum as if her head were a flame, and her eyes became very bright.

'What happened?' Dad asked, sitting on the bed.

Mum was crying. She made no sound, her eyes were bright, she stared straight ahead as if into the wind, and she was crying. I went over to her and put my head on her lap and she didn't move.

'Go and buy ogogoro,' Dad said to me gruffly.

He gave me money and I hurried across the road. Some of the beggars were gathered at the mouth of our compound. They were crouched in groups. I bought the ogogoro and on my way back I saw that they were now at our housefront. They lay down on mats, under the sloping zinc eaves, eyeing me as I went past.

When I got back to the room Mum was sitting on the bed and Dad was on his three-legged chair. The smoke from the mosquito coil formed blue spirals round his head. A new candle had been lit. Dad stolidly smoked a cigarette. He snatched the ogogoro from me, poured himself a generous quantity, and drank. Mum watched him. I brought out my mat. I told Dad about the beggars.

'Next thing they will take over our room,' Mum said.

'I'm going to build a house for them,' replied Dad. 'I'm going to build them a school. Azaro will teach them how to read. You will teach them how to sell things. I will teach them how to box.'

'Who will feed them, eh?' asked Mum.

'They will work for their food,' said Dad.

Mum stretched out on the bed. She was silent for a while. Then she sat up and began to complain that her stall had been taken over at the market, that she had been hawking all day and had sold very little, that her feet were swollen, her face raw from the sun, and that the chair-hire man had come by and she had given him the little money she had.

'You must pay me back,' she said.

'I will pay you double,' Dad replied.

Mum went on about how she went hawking and was selling provisions along the main road when she saw a classmate of hers. They used to be in primary school together. Her classmate now had a car and a driver; she looked ten years younger than Mum, and she wore rich clothes. Mum sold her oranges and the woman didn't recognise her. Mum didn't sell anything else that day; she came straight home.

'This life has not been good to me,' Mum said.

'Your reward will come,' Dad said, absent-mindedly.

'I will make you happy,' I said.

Mum stared at me. Then she lay down. Soon she was asleep. The wind blew in through all the cracks in the room and made us shiver.

'Something is going to happen,' I ventured.

'Something wonderful,' Dad said, rocking his chair expertly.

The wind blew hard. The moth circled the flame. Then suddenly the candle went out. We stayed still in the darkness. The room was quiet.

'I miss hearing the rats,' Dad said.

'Why?'

'They made me think. Everything has to fight to live. Rats work very hard. If we are not careful they will inherit the earth.'

The silence grew deeper. I lay down and listened to Dad thinking. His thoughts were wide; they spun around his head, bouncing off everything in the room. His thoughts filled the place, weighed me down, and after a while I was inside his head, travelling to the beginnings: I went with him to the village, I saw his father, I saw Dad's dreams running away from him. His thoughts were hard, they bruised my head, my eyes ached, and my heart pounded fast in the stifling heat of the room. Dad sighed. Mum turned on the bed. The room became full of amethyst and sepia thoughts. Forms moved in the darkness. A green eye regarded me from just above Dad's head. The eye was still. Then it moved. It went to the door and became a steady tattoo on the wooden frame. The wind increased the sound. Dad creaked his bones. When the knocks became louder I smelt something so profoundly rancid that I sat up.

'What's wrong?' Dad asked.

'Something is trying to get into the house.'

The knocks sounded on the window. I opened it; the wind came in and blew me towards the bed. Mum sat up and went to the door. She opened it and gave a low scream. Dad was still. The smells of death, of bitterness, of old bodies, decomposing eyes, and old wounds, filled the room. Then several eyes lit up the darkness. There was laughter; and from their breath came the bad food and hunger of the world. They came into the room, surrounding us. In the darkness, a bitter wind amongst them, with the calm of strangers who have become familiar, they sat on the floor, on the bed, on my mat. We couldn't breathe for their presence. One of them went and sat at Dad's feet. She was a girl. I could smell her bitter beauty, her bad eye, her unwashed breasts. They came amongst us not like an invasion, but like people who have waited a long time to take their place among the living. They said nothing. Mum stayed at the door. All the exiled mosquitoes came in; the fireflies looking for their illumination clustered round the figures in the room. A red butterfly circled the girl's head and when it settled on her the room was faintly lit up with a ghostly orange light that made my eyes twitch.

'Who are you people?' Dad asked, in a voice devoid of fear.

There was a long silence.

'Azaro, who are they?'

The girl stretched out her hand and placed it on Dad's foot. Then she began to stroke it. She stroked his feet gently, till they too caught the orange light, and looked burnished, separated from the rest of his body in the dark.

'My feet are burning,' Dad said, 'and I feel no heat.'

'Who are you?' Mum shrieked. 'Get out, now! Get out!'

There was another silence.

'They are the beggars,' I said.

Mum caught her breath. Dad pulled his feet away and sat up straight. The orange light died in the room. I heard Dad fumbling for the box of matches. After a moment the match was lit, but not by Dad. The beggar girl held the flame up in the air so we could see. She looked so wonderful sitting there at Dad's feet. Her bad eye, in the deceptive light, had turned a curious yellow colour. Her good eye was almost blue, but it was full of the deepest sadness and silence. Her dress stank. Her face was serene like that of a spirit-child. Without taking her eyes off Mum the beggar girl lit the candle. We looked round and saw them, seated peacefully, as if at a village council meeting, on the floor, their backs against the wall, on the bed, each of them fertile in deformities, their wounds livid, the stumps of missing arms grotesque, their rubber-like legs distorted. There was one with a massive head like a great bronze sculpture eaten by time. Another had a swollen Adam's apple. Yet another had two of the most protruding and watchful eyes I have ever seen. They seemed to have been made by a perverse and drunken god.

Mum cried out and charged at the beautiful beggar girl. She seemed quite demented. She grabbed the girl by the hair and tried to pull her up. The girl didn't move, didn't utter a sound. Mum seized her arms and tried to drag her out. Mum was screaming all the time. We all seemed in a trance. We all watched her without moving. Mum tried to shift the girl, but it was as if she were struggling with an immovable force. The girl's eyes became strange. She took on a great weight, as if all her poverty and her suffering had invisibly compacted her like a dwarf star. Mum began shouting:

'Get out, all of you! Get out, you beggars! Can't you see that we too are suffering, eh? Our load is too much for us. Go! Take our food, but go!'

She stopped shouting suddenly. In the silence that followed, the curious spell was lifted. I breathed in the deep fragrances of wild flowers, of herbs beaten to the ground by rain, of clouds and old wood, of banana plants and great open spaces, of verdant breezes and musk and heliotropes in the sun. The fragrances went. Then Mum turned on Dad, pounced on him, and began hitting him uncontrollably. Dad didn't move in the chair. Soon he was bleeding from a scratch right next to his eye. Then Mum tore at his shirt and when all the buttons flew off she woke from her fever. She stopped again and went to the beggar girl. She knelt in front of her. The beggar girl began to stroke Dad's feet. Mum, weeping, said:

'I didn't mean any harm. My life is like a pit. I dig it and it stays the same. I fill it and it empties. Look at us. All of us in one room. I walk from morning till night, selling things, praying with my feet. God smiles at me and my face goes raw. Sometimes I cannot speak. My mouth is full of bad living. I was the most beautiful girl in my village and I married this madman and I feel as if I have given birth to this same child five times. I must have done someone a great wrong to suffer like this. Please, leave us. My husband is mad but he is a

443

good man. We are too poor to be wicked and even as we suffer our hearts are full of goodness. Please go, we will do something for you, but let us sleep in peace.'

A long silence grew in the wake of Mum's speech. The beggar girl stopped stroking Dad's feet. I began crying. Dad lit a cigarette. He poured himself more ogogoro. He gave some to the beggar girl. She drank. Dad downed what was left. The girl coughed.

'Did you hear me?' Mum asked.

'She's a princess,' Dad said. 'They travelled for seven days to come to my party. I did not invite them but they came. A river does not travel a new path for nothing. The road gave them a message for me. Can't you see that they are messengers?'

'What is their message?' Mum asked.

'What is your message?' I asked them.

All the beggars turned to me.

'And where is your old one?' I said, remembering my encounter in the bar.

Dad looked at me.

The beggar girl got up. The other beggars changed their postures. Then, without speaking, taking their deformities and their wounds with them, but leaving their vile smells behind, they filed out of the room. The girl was the last to leave. She stared at me intensely, then at Dad, and shut the door behind her. I heard them shuffling up to the housefront. Dogs barked in the distance. Fireflies, mosquitoes, and moths, died on the table and floor, killed, it seemed, by the smell in the room. Dad drank steadily, weaving his head round and round as if he were in a profound dream. Mum leant over, slapped her foot, straightened, and in a low voice, said:

'They brought fleas and left them to eat us. That is their gift. You are crazy, my husband.'

I had never heard Mum sound so harsh. She went and sat on the bed. Dad's wound bled freely. His eyes were intense, his jaws kept working. Then he said:

'They were once a great people. Hunger drove them from their kingdom and now the road is their only palace. I will build them a school. I will teach them to work. I will teach them music. We will all be happy.'

Mum went out, fetched some water, and disinfected the room. The disinfectant, sprinkled thickly everywhere, stung my nostrils. Mum changed the bedclothes. Dad sat there, his eyes dreamy, a rough growth of beard on his face, blood dripping down the side

444

of his face and thickening on the shoulder of his torn shirt. Then Mum came and dressed the cut and put a plaster on Dad's face. She went and lay down on the bed. Dad mumbled drunkenly for a long time. He talked about building roads for the ghetto, about housing projects that would lift up the spirit of the people, about the need for world inspiration, about sailors without ships, priests without shrines, kings without homes, boxers without opponents, food without stomachs to eat it, gods without anyone to believe in them, dreams without dreamers, ideas without anyone to make use of them, peoples without direction. He made no sense to us. The candle burned low. He got up and, still muttering, came and stretched out on the floor beside me. He had the smell of a great animal, a lean elephant, the smell of too much energy, too much hope, too much contradiction. His eyes kept rolling. He muttered incoherently and soon he was grinding his teeth. When he was deeply asleep the candle burned high, it flared, as if Dad's sleep somehow allowed it more oxygen. Mum got off the bed, asked me to move, and then she did something strange. She sat astride Dad and began to hit him. She punched his face, hit his chest, beat a manic rhythm on his stomach, kicking and hitting him with all her might, screaming in a low frightening monotone all the time, hitting him unceasingly, till her hands gave.

'I think I've broken my bones on his jaw,' she said.

Dad didn't stir. Mum glared at him as he slept with his mouth open.

'Why is it that when I am happy rats die all over the floor,' she said.

I was silent.

'Go and sleep on the bed,' she commanded me.

Then she blew out the candle and lay quietly beside Dad in the airy darkness of the room. Soon I heard her sleeping. The world turned round. The night filled the room and swept over us, filling our space with light spirits, the old forms of animals; extinct birds stood near Dad's boots, a beautiful beast with proud eyes and whose hide quivered with gold-dust stood over the sleeping forms of Mum and Dad. A tree defined itself over the bed where I lay. It was an ancient tree, its trunk was blue, the spirit sap flowed in many brilliant colours up its branches, densities of light shone from its leaves. I lay horizontal in its trunk. The darkness moved; future forms, extinct tribes, walked through our landscape. They travelled new roads. They travelled for three hundred years and arrived in our night-space. I did not have to dream. It was the first time I realised that an invisible space had entered my mind and dissolved part of the interior structure of my being. The wind of several lives blew into my eyes. The lives stretched far back and when I saw the great king of the spirit-world staring at me through the open doors of my eyes I knew that many things were calling me. It is probably because we have so many things in us that community is so important. The night was a messenger. In the morning I woke early and saw one of its messages on the floor. Mum and Dad, entwined, were still asleep. There were long tear-tracks on Mum's face. I slept again and when I woke the sun was warm, Dad's boots had gone, and Mum had left an orange for me on the table.

THREE

THE BEGGARS WHO had gotten drunk on Madame
Koto's wine had unleashed the fury of their hunger at night while
the world was changing. They had broken stalls, torn down Madame Koto's signboard, shattered windows, and had finally lodged
themselves in an unfinished house on the edge of the forest. The
inhabitants of the street had risen up against them. Madame Koto
had sent her party thugs to drive them away. I saw limbless beggars,
the one-armed, one-eyed, legless, all along the road, scattered, in disarray, bruised, and beaten. They clustered under the trees overlooking
Madame Koto's bar, armed with pathetic-looking sticks. They were a
sorry army. I didn't go into the bar. I saw her sitting outside, on a high
stool, surrounded by her prostitutes and the thugs. The beggars abused
me as I went past.

When I got home the door was locked. Ade was playing on
the broken political vehicle. He looked lean and was happy to see
me. He told me about how the van of the rich people's party had
come along and begun to bundle the beggars away. But the beggars
kept coming back. There had been much fighting. Many had been
wounded. Ade spoke hoarsely, his voice was weak. The sun was
intense that afternoon. The chickens lay silent in street corners. The
dogs were listless. We played around the van and when we heard
screams from Madame Koto's bar we hurried over and saw that the
thugs were beating up the beggars again.

In the afternoon a tall man in an immaculate white suit came
looking for Dad. He was very tall and he had sunken eyes and
his head was small. He stood under the fierce sun, resting on his
walking stick of a shadow. He complained of fleas. He went and
bought a bottle of ogogoro and stood at our housefront, drinking
patiently. He didn't speak to anyone. His face was relatively long,
and he blinked away the sweat that poured into his eyes. After a
while he stood very still and when we went over to him we found

447

he had fallen asleep standing up. We touched him, and he woke up with a start, and he went up the street, towards the main road, and disappeared.

In the evening Dad appeared with the beggars who had come to our room the other night. With the abundant energies of a man entering a new destiny, Dad led them up and down the road. He tried to organise them to clear up the rubbish, to sweep the road, to paint the stalls, to plant flowers near the gutters. Bristling with great enthusiasm, wearing his torn shirt, the plaster flapping on the side of his face, Dad went from house to house asking people to vote for him. He outlined his plans for a school, he suggested to people that they contribute to the beggars' upkeep, and everywhere he went people cursed him for bringing more trouble into their lives. The beggars cleared the rubbish from one end of the road and dumped it at the other. They crushed the flowers they tried to plant. And because Dad could not afford the price of paint sufficient to give colour to the monotonous brown of stalls and the sun-bleached reds and blues and yellows of the houses, the beggars stood around most of the time with useless paint-brushes in their hands. The beautiful beggar girl followed Dad everywhere he went. When he went to another set of beggars they fell into mischief as soon as he turned his back. They turned stalls over and didn't straighten them. They tramped around in the swamp. Near the wooden bridge they found a mattress that was overgrown with fungus and mushrooms. They beat the bugs and numerous infestations from the mattress. We watched strange forms take off into the air. The beggars intended to make the mattress a bed that they could all share. The photographer appeared, brief as a flash, and took pictures of them. He fled in such a hurry it was as if his enemies might emerge at any moment from the long shadows of evening. I didn't even get a chance to speak to him. He had become mysterious and irritating. Dad went up and down the road shouting about the poverty of our will. And while he went up and down the place shouting, the second wave of our transformation was taking place.

FOUR

THAT EVENING THERE was the most fantastic gathering at Madame Koto's bar. There were yellow vans everywhere. Curious perfumes floated over the road. A great number of cars were parked along the lanes and side streets. Music rocked all night, making the houses tremble along the road. Women were attired in matching lace, in identical handwoven materials. Their imitation gold bangles and necklaces, brooches and rings of cheap rubies, their indispensable high-heeled shoes, glittered under the lights. The women were all over the place, bursting with scandalous sexuality.

Short, powerful men with chieftains' beads round their necks and fans of eagle crests in their hands; men with big feet and white shoes; men with bulbous ancient eyes and protruding stomachs, who moved with the lumbering gait of unalterable clannish power; men who were almost giants, with thick necks and sweating thunderous brows and thighs of timber-like virility; all were there. They were the inheritors of titles and extensive acres of land.

There were children in red, whole families in matching silk materials, an old man with a parrot, herbalists, ritualists, cultists, and a short man with a white cap and a string of goats for the great sacrifice. I saw them bring in a strange-looking animal, a duiker with penetrating eyes. They all clustered in the bar.

Outside, we heard rumours that the party was being thrown to celebrate Madame Koto's attainment of new powers, the installation of electricity, the consolidation of her party connections, and to widen the sphere of her influence in this and other realms. It could be said that it was an event meant to seal her entry into the world of myths. The most bizarre rumours circulated about what had been really happening at night when we slept, and during the day when we, as always, were unaware of the changes taking place in constellations of energies and alignments. New spaces were being created while all we saw were the mundane events of thugs and canvassing

449

vans and the violence of political struggles. New spaces which we couldn't name, and couldn't imagine, but could only hint at with unfinished gestures and dark uncompleted proverbs. The rumours invested everything with a higher significance. Fabulous noises floated on the air. Ground-nut sellers, corn-roasters, fortune-tellers, tyre-menders, beer-traders, all gathered outside the bar, looking in from a respectable distance, doing business, while the bar resounded with drinking noises and laughter and the occasional piercing ritual cries.

Then to our amazement electricians and carpenters, mechanics and sundry workers arrived on the back of a lorry and connected silver cables from the electric pole to Madame Koto's bar, or so it seemed; they connected cables from the ceiling to the front where the signboard used to be; they rigged up wires and brought the wonder of multi-coloured bulbs, lighting up the night. The chair-hire man, in his element, brought fifty-six chairs. Under our astounded gaze the workers rigged up a great tarpaulin tent of red and yellow. Fire-grates, surrounded by sweating women, crackled with the oil of spit-roasted goat-meat and rams' meat and antelopes' flesh. Great quantities of beer were carried in in crates with numbers and the names of the newly famous breweries. And for the first time we saw how public music could be. The sound of fiendishly virtuoso drummers, the flaming melodies of tubas, the slippery tones of clarinets and the octaves of bass saxophones, the nasal voices of syncopating musicians, the bells and gongs, made the air vibrate and the earth quiver and the feet of the spectators outside twitch with yearning. We watched the silhouettes of dancers under the tent. The light bulbs of blue and yellow and orange, the brilliant fluorescent tubes on poles drew the midges and the moths into a frenzy of dancing, their wings beating in violent rhythms.

The inhabitants of the area, who had no hope of being invited into the party, put on their best clothes and hung around the tent, hoping to catch a glimpse of the wild celebrations, hoping still more for a chance encounter, a ticket from the outer darkness where we all watched and whispered about Madame Koto's abnormal pregnancy. They said her time was drawing near. Some people made it sound almost apocalyptic. The beggars, a good distance from us, also gathered outside the tent. The delicious aroma of goat-meat and antelopes' flesh, of bean-cakes, fried plantains and rich stews made us salivate, made us curse with greater bitterness the poverty and outer darkness to which we seemed for ever consigned.

In the midst of all this Dad tried to get the other beggars to work. They had lost interest, it seemed, in his schemes. Dad began to shout along the road. Disillusion was beginning to burst in his veins. His sadness accelerated my understanding. Only the beggar girl, guiding her father around with a stick, still followed him. Dad shouted:

'We can change the world!'

People laughed at him.

'That is why our road is hungry,' Dad hollered. 'We have no desire to change things!'

One of the men outside the tent, inhabitant of the outer darkness, said:

'Black Tyger is mad!'

Dad rounded on and chastised the man. The inhabitants of the area jumped on Dad. They were already exasperated with his antics. The beggar girl screamed. She threw stones at his assailants. One of the stones hit Dad on his wound. The inhabitants in their fury at being left out of the glittering celebrations, turned on the beggars. The beggars fought back, lost the initial battle, and fled into the tent. The thugs threw them out. The thugs and bouncers had horsewhips. After they had tossed the beggars out they stormed on us, lashing out in all directions, indiscriminately whipping the inhabitants and the beggars as if we all, finally, belonged to the same fraternity. The thugs whipped themselves into future eras. They whipped themselves into future military passions. They thrashed the women and the children alike. The wind blew us all together. They flogged us and we ran howling, scattered and confused. Under the intoxication of all the ritual chants unleashed on the unsuspecting air of the area, under the fevers of their new ascendancy, the certainty of their long future rule, and their inevitable transformation into men of power, the thugs made the air crackle with their contempt for those of us in the outer darkness, whose faces all seemed like one, and who threatened the party with nothing but chaos. And then Madame Koto came out. She saw the commotion, and screamed. She screamed for order. Her bouncers and thugs recovered their senses instantly. Madame Koto was resplendent in golden volumes of lace attire, feathers in her headgear. She had a new walking stick with a metallic lion's head. Her foot had grown large. Her stomach had swollen. Her face was bunched, antimony shimmered on her eyelids. She looked glorious. Her presence alone, already legendary, made us silent in the darkness where we had been scattered. She begged us to leave her party alone. She promised us our own celebrations, a party that she would throw to show her respect for us, and her gratitude for supporting her politics. She ordered her temporary new driver to give us drinks and left-over food. She hobbled back into the tent.

The beggars and the inhabitants alike struggled for the food and drinks. The thugs and bouncers stared at us. Then they mocked us in songs. They got drunk on their mockery. Dad swore at them and stormed back to the house, the beggar girl following him at a distance. I followed her. Dad went into the room and the girl stayed outside. The compound people whispered things about us. I couldn't hear what they said. The beggar girl turned to me with her strange eye. I didn't listen to the whispers any more.

'What is your name?' I asked her.

'Helen,' she said.

'Do you like my father?'

She said nothing for a while. Then, as I was about to move, she said:

'Maybe it's you that I like.'

I didn't understand. I went into the room. Dad was dressing up in his black French suit. He had three plasters on his face. He had daubed the dreadful Arabian perfume on him. He put on his old boots, combed his hair, and parted it. I told him about the man in white.

'A white man?' Dad asked in an excited voice.

'No,' I said.

'What did he want? Does he want to vote for me?'

'No.'

Dad stamped the boots on the floor. When he was satisfied with their occupation by his feet, he said:

'All kinds of people are interested in me. From today I keep my door open.'

'What about thieves?'

'What thieves? What can they steal, eh?'

'Mum's money.'

'Does she have money?'

'I don't know.'

'Good. We need votes. I'm going to Madame Koto's party. Dress up. Go and wash your face. You are going to be my subaltern.'

'What about the girl?'

'What girl?'

'Helen, the beggar.'

'She will be my bodyguard. All beggars are my bodyguards. I will build them a university.'

'When?'

'After you wash your face.'

I went and had a hurried wash. When I got back Dad was gone. The beggar girl was at the housefront. I led her beggars to Madame Koto's party.

FIVE

Outside the tent Dad was struggling to get in.

'I am a politician!' he said.

'We don't want politicians like you,' said one of the bouncers.

'Why not?'

'Go away. If you are a politician you won't gatecrash.'

'Did I crash your gate?' Dad replied indignantly. 'I don't have a car.'

'Just go away.'

Dad began to shout insults. He made such a fuss that the bouncer sent for the thugs. They came and bundled Dad out and dumped him near the forest. He came storming back, his jacket covered in mud, dried leaves in his hair, his plaster flapping. He went to the bouncer and knocked him out with a single roundhouse punch.

'If it's only gatecrashers you respect, then I am coming in,' Dad said.

The thugs fell on him. He threw one of them on the bonnet of a car. He winded a second with a punch to the solar plexus. He was quivering with energy; his eyes had a manic glimmer. Someone screamed. Madame Koto came out, saw what was happening, told the thugs to stop fighting, and very politely asked Dad to come into the party. I followed him. The beggar girl followed me. At the door I encountered the blind old man. He had a new instrument, a harmonica. He wore yellow glasses and a red hat.

'What do you want?' he asked me.

'To come in.'

'You can't.'

'Why not?'

'You ugly child. Show me your friends and I will eat them.'

I pushed past his wheelchair and went into the celebrations. There were actually fewer people at the event than it appeared from the outside. Or maybe they were all somewhere else, at the event behind

454

the event. The noise from the musical equipment was very loud. I saw giants and midgets. I saw a white man with silver eyelashes dancing with a woman whose abundant breasts brought flames to his face. The long tables tumbled with fruit and fried meat, rice and platters of sweet-smelling stews, vegetables and plastic cutlery. Everywhere I looked the lights affected me. Crowded spaces suddenly became empty. And in the emptiness I saw the ghost forms of white men in helmets supervising the excavation of precious stones from the rich earth. The excavation was done with spectral machines. I saw the ghost figures of young men and women, heads bowed, necks and ankles chained together, making their silent procession through the celebrations. They kept moving but stayed in the same place. Over them the celebrants danced to the music of a new era that promised Independence. The men of politics, the chiefs, with their wrappers, their agbadas, their fans, the women with lace and red shoes, the paid helpers, the praise-singers, all danced vigorously, sweating, smiling. Madame Koto wandered in agony through the celebrants, her bad foot weighing her down, her head slumped to one side like a discon-solate Masquerade, her face shining with good living. It was strange to see her grown much more beautiful as she got more swollen. An expression of profound disdain hung involuntarily on her lips. An orchestrator of fantastic events, she walked right through the forms of the enchained procession and began sneezing so hard that she twisted her neck. Her women came and led her into the inner sanctum of the bar.

Dad went around talking politics. He looked miserable in his black French suit. Everyone he talked to looked at him quizzically and took a handkerchief to their noses. The women refused to dance with him. Dad paused at a corner, nibbling a piece of goats' meat, looking confused. I wandered amongst the large parrots in cages, saw featherless chickens twitching on plates, and encountered a duiker tied to a post. It kept staring at me. Its eyes were big and changed colour and it had a white bib of beard reaching down to its haunches and it had a powerful smell and it stood still while everyone danced under the heat of the tent. I saw men dancing with political erections. Sweat and sexual potency filled the air. Dancing women generated heat-waves with the gyrations of their bottoms. At one end of the party a chained monkey kept snatching off the wigs of prostitutes. A politician was contemplating a woman's quivering buttocks when the monkey snatched the piece of fried antelope from his hands. The monkey hid. The politician looked round. He fetched himself another piece of fried meat and resumed his contemplation. The same thing happened. He left with the woman soon afterwards. Then I noticed hands crawling under the tables. The music became louder. Someone gave me something to drink. It was very strong and I drank it all and had some more. The earth quivered under the assault of music and dancing. The multicoloured bulbs swayed. Beneath the tables hands with three fingers, legs with two wide-spaced toes, wandered around without touching the ground. Buckets of food floated through the air with no one carrying them. The food vanished beneath the tables. When the music stopped a midget came to the platform and sang the praises of the eternal Party of the Rich. Then he proceeded to swallow cowrie beads and bring them out of his ears. The blind old man played on his harmonica, green liquid dripping from his eyes. The people clapped and cheered and drank to the health of the party, to its long future domination of the nation, and to Madame Koto. The music was resumed. The blind old man staggered all over the place, very drunk, guided by a woman in a blue wrapper and matching blouse. When he banged against people he would pull up stiffly and say:

'Ah, a party!'

When he staggered into women he would laugh and stick out his bony hands, searching for their breasts. The women paid him much attention. He was led to his chair. He danced there like an overturned centipede. The women kept bringing him drinks. He drank heavily, looking through his yellow spectacles at the celebrations, occasionally saying:

'Ah, Ladies of the Night!'

The parrots squawked noisily in their cages. The duiker eyed me. I stared back into its eyes of deep colours. I stared into its hypnotic eyes and felt myself being drawn into its consciousness, I felt myself filling with unease and anxiety. When that moment passed, nausea and bile rising in my throat, I found myself in a yellow forest, bounding through the emerald spangles of cobwebs. Stars fell from the night sky, plunged into the forest earth, and formed deep pits. I galloped in dreams of abundant energies through the great jungles, bristling with the freedom of the wind and four feet and the soaring spirit that disintegrates the frames of all night-runners. As I bounded along I saw the forms of serene ancestors, men and women for whom the stars were both words and gods, for whom the world and the sky and the earth were a vast language of dreams and omens. I passed the stone monoliths of the deep nights of transition, when the beings of an earlier time were creators first before they were hunters;

456

I passed the clusters of the abodes of spirits. I was the messenger of the wind. The spirits rode with me, played with the language of my speed, the riddles of my words. They looked deep into my eyes and I understood. I ran through the night forests, where all forms are mutable, where all things exchange their identities, and where everything dances in an exultation of flame and wisdom. I ran till I came to the Atlantic, silver and blue under the night of forests. Birds flew in the aquamarine sky. Feathers gyrated on to the waves. The sky was full of dense white clouds moving like invading armies of mist and ghosts over the deep serene blue and under the regenerative stars. The ghost ships of centuries arrived endlessly on the shores. I saw the flotillas, the gunwales, the spectral great ships and the dozens of rowing boats, bearing the helmeted ones, with mirrors and guns and strange texts untouched by the salt of the Atlantic. I saw the ships and the boats beach. The white ones, ghost forms on deep nights, stepped on our shores, and I heard the earth cry. The cry scared me. Deep in the duiker's eyes, I ran through the yellow forests, through deluded generations, through time. I witnessed the destruction of great shrines, the death of mighty trees that housed centuries of insurgent as well as soothing memories, sacred texts, alchemical secrets of wizards, and potent herbs. I saw the forests die. I saw the people grow smaller in being. I saw the death of their many roads and ways and philosophies. Their precious stones and rocks of atomic energies were drawn from the depths of their ancestral memories. I saw the trees retreat screaming into the blue earth. I heard the great spirits of the land and forest talking of a temporary exile. They travelled deeper into secret spaces, weaving spells of madness round their arcane abodes to prevent humans from ever despoiling their transformative retreat from the howling feet of invaders. I saw the rising of new houses. I saw new bridges span the air. The old bridges, invisible, travelled on by humans and spirits alike, remained intact and less frequented. As the freedom of space and friendship with the pied kingfisher and other birds became more limited with the new age, something died in me. I fled deep into the salt-caves of rocklands. Hunters with new instruments of death followed. When human beings and animals understood one another, we were all free. But now the hunters pursued me in the duiker's eyes. And as I escaped into the forest of thunder, whose invisible gates are sealed with seven incantations, a knock crashed on my head. A flaming star spun me round. Laughter rocketed me into a silver emptiness. I opened my eyes and found myself cradled by a female midget. Her eyes were enormous and sad. I tried to get up and shake the confusion from my head, but she held me down tightly. Eighteen eyes regarded me. Beyond the eyes I saw the duiker gazing at me intently, drugged on its captivity, gazing at me as if my freedom lay in freeing it from imminent death, from being sacrificed for the opening of the road of Madame Koto's destiny.

SIX

'OH, MY FRIEND, you've woken up!' the female midget said to me.

She wore a white dress with lace frills and imitation sequins. I had seen her before. She had a demented smile stretched tightly across her face. Her eyes were moon-like and when I looked into them the insides of my head kept shifting. The eyes of the duiker pulled me. Warm, old, magnetic, they spoke a language of mood and blood.

'I asked you to dance with me, but you refused,' the midget said, flashing her weird animated smile.

She took my hands and placed them on her big frantic breasts. They palpitated like two mighty hearts. The female midget quivered, the smile became fainter on her face. She stared at me with such frightening tenderness and longing that I broke out in a sweat. She dragged me to the dance floor, and amidst bemused laughter from the other celebrants, drew me into the pounding rhythms of the music. She held me tightly to her breasts and drenched me in the strange sexuality of her soft body and before I was aware of it I was swirling amongst the sturdy legs of adults. She turned me round, threw herself at me, shook her breasts in my face, and clasped my young bottom, and clung to me, made me dizzy, and dissolved things around me, in her torrid dance. She kept spinning me, filling my head with bizarre potencies of desire, her smile widening. She held me so tight that the blood threatened to burst drunkenly in my ears. Red lights flooded my brain and when my eyes cleared, the smells of a thousand perfumes, of wild sex on hot illicit nights, of vaginal fluids, of animal sweat, overpowered my senses. In the terrible heat of the dance I saw that, among the erotic dancers, the politicians and chiefs, the power merchants, the cultists, paid supporters, thugs and prostitutes, all moving to the beat of the new music, among them all, there were strangers to the world of the living. I saw that some of the prostitutes, who would be future brides of decadent power, had legs of goats. Some of the women, who were chimeras and sirens and broken courtesans, had legs of spiders and birds. Some of the politicians and power merchants, the chiefs and innocent-looking men, who were satyrs and minotaurs and satanists, had the cloven hoofs of bulls. Their hoofs and bony legs were deftly covered with furry skin. Fully clothed, they danced as men and women when in fact they were the dead, spirits, and animals in disguise, part-time human beings dancing to the music of ascendant power. Everything around me seemed to be changing and yielding its form. I cried out. The female midget swirled me round. Tables flew towards me. They flew through me. And I was twirling, dizzy, my being in disintegration, dancing not with a female midget but with the four-headed spirit who had been biding his time. I was falling in love with life and the four-headed spirit had chosen the best moment to dance with me, turning and twisting me through strange spaces, making me dance my way out of the world of the living. The lights turned violet. Still in a dance which I couldn't control, I found myself in a desert waste where shadows were real things, where the sand blew in the air and fixed into the shapes of fabulous glass monsters. The four-headed spirit led me in a dance through the desert, holding me in an iron grip. The harder I fought the tougher the grip became, till my arms turned blue. He danced me through the desert winds, which concealed the forms of master spirits and powerful beings who borrowed the sandstorms to cloth their nakedness; through the striated sands, over the vast desert worms, through the mirage cities in which the liquid apparitions of air concealed cities throbbing in rich bazaars and marketplaces and dens of hallucinations; he danced me through the mirage cities where tall women had breasts of glass and beautiful women had the phosphorescent tails of cats, over the wells, past the oasis where obscure figures turned silver into water, through the streets of the elite quarters where people cried out for love, past the slave alleys where innumerable souls had written their names on the walls with their flesh, along the precincts of drugged soldiers, the garrisons of slave towns, into the heart of forgotten civilisations where Pythagoras came to learn mathematics, into the sacred groves of desert gods, and the empty houses of reincarnated prophets, and the great wastes of desert stretches which were in fact populated with adventurous tribes and warring beings and people who had become their own stone carvings, through it all the four-headed spirit led me in its dance of death. I beheld the

Sphinx, with its original black face. I was plunged into sandstorms and whirlwinds, the sands howling, and I saw the invisible trees and plants, the meadows of flowers with passionate calyxes, all ghosts of the vegetation that used to be there. And I was thrust up through the burning vents of sandwhorls and I felt so hot, my head bursting with fires, my eyes full of steaming sand, and when I cried out the music of the desert gods drowned my cry. I fought to escape. I struggled, I kicked. I did not want deserts in me. And as we neared the scorching centre of the desert, where a ship in full mast waited to set sail, the four-headed spirit said:

'That ship will take us home to your companions across the oceans of sand.'

Then a new music, composed entirely of desert vowels, poured over me and filled me with anguish. I called out to the great king of the spirit world, but he didn't appear. And so I called out, with all my being, for Mum. Out of the stillness of a strange love, I saw her in a tattered wig, a pair of blue glasses on her face, bangles on her arms. She wore a bright wrapper and a blouse blinding in its whiteness. She stood over me and lifted me up. The desert burned its way into my brain, scorching my head. The calmness of cool water flowed down my face and Mum, in the gentlest voice said:

'Azaro, why are you crying?'

She held me gently. The midget had gone. The four-headed spirit had evaporated into the mysteries of dance. I couldn't see the giants any more, or the hoofs of part-time human beings, those who would wreck our hopes for two generations, or the bird-feet of strange women. Forms had lost their mutability.

'What's wrong with you?' Mum asked.

I held on to her. She wiped the tears from my face. My throat was dry. I stayed silent for a long time. Occasionally a cool wind blew in from outside. Mum gave me some iced water to drink. I drank it all and had some more. Then after a while, when I began to feel a little better, I looked up at her. She smiled.

'We watched you dancing, my son. You danced like your grandfather. And then you fell. Are you all right now?'

I didn't answer her question.

'Why are you wearing those blue glasses?' I asked her.

She laughed.

'I will tell you later. It's a good story.'

'Tell me now.'

'There's too much noise. Where is Madame Koto?'

'I don't know.'

'If you help me find her, I will tell you the story when we get home.'

I set out to search for Madame Koto. Everyone I asked said they had just seen her. The beautiful beggar girl, sitting under a table, watched me as I went up and down. I was about to ask her a question when she motioned me to be quiet. She pointed. I followed her finger with my gaze and saw that the beggars were carrying out a complicated stealing operation. They grabbed fruits and fried meat and bowls of stew and plates of rice from the tables and passed them on in a relay of hands. The food disappeared beneath the tent. Helen was their watch-woman.

'Do you want me to help?'

She waved me on.

'Can't you talk?'

She stared at me mutely and then, gently, pushed me away.

SEVEN

ONE OF THE politicians was plastering money on the sweating breasts of a woman who had danced with unbounded sensual ferocity. Dad was having a heated argument with a man in a red hat. The man kept pushing Dad away and Dad kept coming back. Mum went over to him and held his fists and soon they were dancing together. It was the first time in a while that I had seen them dance. I continued with my search for Madame Koto. In the bar the women were serving bowls of steaming peppersoup. I was given a plate and I drank hurriedly and had to have some palm-wine to extinguish the heat the pepper generated in my brain. The wine swam in my eyes. I staggered to the backyard. The duiker held me with its brilliant eyes. The eyes held me fast and I carried on walking while still looking at it and I crashed into a woman bearing a tray of food. The plates fell everywhere, the food tumbled to the ground. The beggars materialised from the night and scraped together the fallen food and vanished again. The woman swore at me. I swore back at her. She picked up a piece of firewood and chased me all over the backyard. I ran into the bushes and into the figure of Madame Koto. She started and stood very straight. Her eyes were blurred, as if she were in some sort of trance or in a moment of passionate anguish. She stank of odd perfumes, queer aromas, of flint and hyena-hides, feathers and old trees.

'What are you doing here?' she asked. 'Go to your father.'

I backed away.

'My mother is looking for you.'

'Go away!' she shouted.

I retreated. I hung around the fire-grate. I hid behind the earthenware pot that had been brought outside. I watched her. She remained still. Behind me the celebrations raged, the music shook the vegetation, loud voices cavorted in the night air. Then she came out of the bushes. She came towards me. She stretched her hands upwards in a dramatic plea, and then she sighed. I caught the green glint of the duiker's eyes. The green glint stirred something in my brain.

463

I scurried from behind the pot and hid near the duiker. Madame Koto turned to where I had been, but she saw nothing. She was still again. The moonlight touched her eyes. The duiker pawed me and drew me into itself and the wind blew a curious darkness from my consciousness and water flooded my ears and I found myself in the eyes of the magic animal, looking out for a brief moment into the reality that it saw. There were forms everywhere, the humped shapes of writhing animals, eyes floating on the wind, organic houses that behaved like carnivorous plants, flowers with worms in them, worms with flowers in them, silver cords lighting up the air. And I saw that Madame Koto was pregnant with three strange children. Two of them sat upright and the third was upside down in her womb. One of them had a little beard, the second had fully formed teeth, and the third had wicked eyes. They were all mischievous, they kicked and tugged at their cords, they were the worst type of spirit-children, and they had no intention of being born. I heard a terrible scream. Something knocked the curious darkness back into my consciousness. Madame Koto was bent over. I backed away from the duiker. Madame Koto straightened, came over to me, and said:

'Why were you staring at my stomach like that with your bad-luck eyes?'

'I wasn't staring,' I said.

She hit me again. It didn't hurt. Then she put on her moonstones, cursing and muttering about the pain in her stomach. She went to her room and soon re-emerged with a fan of peacock feathers. She walked with great dignity back into the celebrations.

The politicians pasted money on her forehead when she performed an impromptu dance; the praise-singers sang of her accomplishments; women clustered round, showering her with compliments. Mum went over and they talked and pointed at the food. Madame Koto seemed to be telling Mum who the important personalities at the event were. Mum looked lean and famished besides Madame Koto. Her wig was in a sorry state, as if it was something she had rescued from the roadside. Her blue sunglasses made her look slightly mad. And her copper bangles had turned greenish from rust and all the water that dripped in from our roof.

While they were talking the blind old man started shouting in his chair. At first no one thought anything of it. He kicked and struggled drunkenly and then he got up and staggered to the middle of the dance floor. He turned one way, then another. Then he fell on his knees and crawled around on the ground and he kept shouting:

'Thieves! Thieves!'

Madame Koto, ever the attentive host, was the first to take note of his inexplicable agitation. Waving the fan across her face, hobbling through the weaving crowd of dancers, she went to the blind old man.

'I see food floating under the table,' he said in a cracked voice.

'Where?'

'Everywhere. Since when did fried goat fly?'

Madame Koto, humouring him, tried to get him to stand up. He refused.

'You have rats under your table. I saw a big rat. It has only one eye.'

The blind old man stood up, adjusted his yellow glasses, and started to jump up and down, squealing like a demented sorcerer. Then he brought out his harmonica and played during the silence between two records. Some of the people dancing poured scorn on him.

'Take your dirty music somewhere else,' someone said.

Madame Koto was leaving when she saw a flash behind the blind old man. A bowl of peppersoup was floating above the table. She leapt in that direction suddenly, on an impulse, and hurt her foot, and fell to the ground. Her bodyguards rushed to her and helped her up. When she was standing again, she pointed, shouting:

'Get those thieves! Flog them! Bring them here! Let me teach them a lesson!'

The place erupted with her fury. She shouted, she threw plates and food on the ground. The music stopped. She weaved about the place, waving her arms, lashing her minions with her walking stick. The thugs rushed outside. Amid the general confusion Madame Koto saw the beautiful beggar girl sitting mutely under the table and ordered her to be caught. The thugs soon came back in, dragging some of the beggars into the tent. They had incriminating bowls of food in their hands. Madame Koto made them carry the bowls on their heads. The celebrants laughed. With the full vengeance of her stomach throbbing with the abiku children, with the agony of her swollen foot and twisted neck, she ordered the bodyguards to thrash the beggars. There was silence. No one moved. The strange duiker looked on with impassive eyes. The bodyguards, one by one, said they wouldn't whip the beggars. Madame Koto burst into such a rage, hobbling around with her lion-headed walking stick, lashing her bodyguards on the back, screaming at them to thrash the beggars as a public lesson. The beggars gazed at her without emotion. They were silent. Legless, one-armed, one-eyed, soft-limbed, they gazed at her with big and placid eyes. Madame Koto, still hobbling, transforming her agony into rage, began to push her employees out of the premises, out of the tent, shouting for them to leave her service, to return to the festering gutters from which she had plucked them. Then one of the prostitutes cut herself a cane in the bushes and, crying as she did so, proceeded to whip the beggars. She whipped them hard, on their backs and on their wounds, on their faces and on their bad limbs. The bodyguards changed their minds. That night a new order of manifestations appeared in our lives. As the thugs thrashed the beggars a curious dust rose from their backs, rose into the air, and when the dust touched the lights midges multiplied everywhere. The dust turned into flying insects; the insects grew in size and soon the tent and the fluorescent lights bristled with a host of green moths.

When Dad became aware of the beatings he ran over to the thugs and snatched the whips from them. They jumped on him and held him down. Madame Koto, still in agony, ordered that the beggar girl also be flogged. The prostitute whipped the girl. Helen bore the whipping and did not move or cry. She stared at Madame Koto with gentle eyes as they whipped her. The gentleness in her eyes made Madame Koto madder. Mum went to her and said:

'Tell them to stop. You don't know who that girl is.'

'She is a thief.'

'She is not a thief.'

Madame Koto bellowed something at Mum. She insulted Mum loudly, saying that Mum too was a beggar. She gave vent to such a torrent of anger and bitterness that Mum was stunned. Then Mum did something quite odd. She tore the wig off her head and threw it on the floor. She took the blue sunglasses off her face. Then she stormed out of the disrupted party uttering the direst curses. The wind blew again when the whipping of the beggar girl was resumed. It was a strident wind. Slowly the beggar girl sank to the ground under the brutality of the whipping. Dad strained furiously against the people holding him down. The duiker let out a low snarl. The beggar girl began to bleed from the mouth. Blood dripped down her lips and fell in drops on the ground. I began to weep. Someone hit me. It was the blind old man. He started playing on his harmonica to the sound of the thrashing.

'A good whipping, eh,' he said every now and again.

The wind lifted the edges of the tent. The beggar girl crouched on the floor in a foetal position. I went round the gathered resplendent celebrants. They were fanning themselves. Their faces were animated by the new spectacle. As I pushed through them I again noticed their hoofs, their goat-legs, their spidery legs, and their bristly skins. I crept towards the duiker and untied it from the pole and released it from its sacrificial captivity. A mighty wail erupted from Dad. He stood up in a great burst of manic energy and sent the men flying. The duiker bounded from the backyard into the tent. And as the wind made the tent sway, as the lights began going on and off, a frightening cry rose from the bewildered crowd. The duiker bounded amongst the dazzling array of celebrants, scattering the bird cages, overturning the tables, stamping on the food, upsetting basins of fried meat, mashing the fruits, crashing into the cage of large parrots, shattering the tables with beer on them, and sowing pandemonium. The parrot beat its wings against the limitations of the tent, the monkey escaped and fled off with its hand full of fruits, the loudspeakers fell with a crash, people trampled on one another, howling and confused, the thugs chased the duiker, trying to recapture it, Dad hurled himself at the woman whipping the beggar girl and pushed her away, Madame Koto knocked Dad on the head with the metallic end of her walking stick, the blind old man squealed in his weird sorcerer's delight, the duiker leapt out through the tent opening and the wind burst in and tilted the tent to one side, and Madame Koto ordered everyone to be calm. The parrot flew out through a gaping hole in the tent. The thugs turned on Dad, and were about to descend on him and beat him to a mash when a voice amongst the celebrants, profound with an unearthly authority, said:

'Stop!'

Everyone froze as if in an enchantment. Then slowly they turned to see who had spoken with such power. The wind calmed down. The voices had stopped. Most of the motions in the tent ceased. And then the tall man in a white suit who had been waiting for Dad stepped out from the expectant crowd.

EIGHT

'LEAVE HIM TO ME,' he said in his thin ghostly voice.
'I will thrash this Black Tyger without even staining my white suit.'

The blind old man played a strain on his instrument.

'Ah, lovely, a fight!' he said.

And before we could register what exactly was happening the man
in white struck Dad in the face and sent him reeling. Dad fell on to a
table. He didn't move for fifteen seconds. No one saw the jab that did
the damage. The celebrants, awoken from their enchantment, clapped.
The old man played a tune. The beggars shuffled and crawled out of
the tent. The beggar girl stayed crouched on the ground. Someone
poured water on Dad. He jumped up quickly, looked around, and
kept blinking.

'Where am I?' he wondered out loud.

The celebrants burst out laughing. Dad staggered around. Then
he fell. He got up again and reached for a cup of palm-wine and
drank it down. I went over to him.

'What are you doing here?' he asked severely.

'The man in white hit you.'

'A white man?'

'No. Him.' I pointed.

Dad went all over the place, drinking all the cups of wine
he could find. Then he shook his head to clear away the thick
cobwebs, howled a war cry, and rushed over to the man in white.
Before Dad could do anything the man unleashed a whiplash of a
punch. Dad crumpled into a heap. He writhed and twisted on the
ground like a lacerated worm. I rushed over to him again.

'Let's go home,' I said.

'Why?' he yelled.

'The man is beating you.'

'What man?'

I was taken aback. Dad seemed to be in an unreal land, a

mythical land. He didn't seem to know what was happening to him. His face had broken out in two monstrous purple bruises as if under the chastisement of an invisible sorcerer. I couldn't see his right eye. I never knew that a jab could inflict such punishment, such disfigurement, or such disorientation. Dad's eyes were dazed, slightly crossed, and his lips kept moving. I leant over to hear what he was saying.

'This is an excellent party,' he said weakly, slurring his words.

'Let's go.'

'I'm enjoying this dance,' he said.

'You're not dancing.'

'What am I doing then?'

'Losing a fight.'

'Fight? Black Tyger? Lose a fight? Never!'

He got up, weaved, staggered, and fell on the beggar girl. He stayed down for a while. The music started. The man in white dusted his hands. Madame Koto took an immediate interest in him and sent intermediaries to make enquiries about him. Party chiefs, power merchants and warlords, always seeking new additions to their ranks of warriors and hired protectors, sent their men to ask who he worked for and if he would enter their services. Thugs surrounded him, asking who he was, where he came from, offering a special place in their organisation. The prostitutes and the low-life courtesans also took a great interest in him. The praise-singers invented names and fabulous deeds for him. The beggar girl, bleeding from her mouth and nose, got out from under Dad. As she got up I noticed that her bad eye was open. It was yellowish and tinged with blue. She shook Dad. The celebrants jeered. Dad sat up, holding his head. When he saw the beggar girl he smiled leeringly, grabbed her, and began to embrace her. The beggar girl freed herself from his punch-drunk embrace. Dad's face had taken on the softness of an abandoned lover and any moment it seemed he would burst into a grotesque and sentimental love song.

'My wife, where are you going?' he asked of the beggar girl.

The girl got up and brushed the sand from her hair. Her back was a mess of flesh and torn cloth. Her hair fell from her head as if it were a wig dissolving back to its original constituents.

'A magician!' the blind old man said, and played his harmonica.

Dad stood up. The girl backed away. Dad followed her.

'Let's go!' I cried.

'After I'm married,' he said, wobbling.

Then he stopped, looked around, and noticed everyone staring at him with amused smiles on their faces. He noticed the man in white and looked at him as if for the first time. He looked at the green moths and the midges and the multicoloured lights and the chaos of overturned tables and trampled food and at the dimensions of the tent. Then he said:

'I thought I was dreaming.'

'You're not,' I said.

'I thought I was in the Land of the Fighting Ghosts.'

'He is a Fighting Ghost.'

'You mean I wasn't dreaming?'

'No,' I said. 'You're losing a fight.'

'You're drunk,' said the blind old man.

'Punch-drunk,' said one of the thugs.

Dad touched his face. He winced.

'So they were real blows?'

'Yes,' I said.

'Who did it?'

'The man in white.'

Suddenly, with his curious ability to reach into deep places in his spirit, a ferocious energy swirled around Dad.

'Hurry, go and call Sami, the betting-man,' Dad said, awakening. 'We will make money from this and build the beggars a school.'

I rushed out and, with Ade, went to fetch Sami. When I got back Dad had taken off his shirt, and was shadow-boxing, working up a sweat. He seemed wide awake now. Methodically, he shook his head, did some press-ups, and practised the most amazing exercises. He creaked his joints, limbered up, stretched his muscles, did his special movements, breathed deeply, swelled up, and let out howls of energy. He was very impressive. The crowd watched him disdainfully. Only the inhabitants of the area, who had now ventured into the tent in the wake of the commotion, called out his fighting name and cheered him on. The blind old man was seated on his wheelchair, his harmonica in one hand, a fried piece of antelope meat in the other. Occasionally he kicked his feet in the air and like an over-excited child would say:

'A prize fight! Very good. Where is the betting-man?'

The man in white, tall, lean, with an air of extraordinary detachment, a small head and pinpoint eyes, stood on one leg. He was very still. His eyes were positively reptilian. He was very disturbing to look at. No one looked at him for very long.

Sami arrived with his bucket and his small army of protectors.

470

He went round taking bets. The odds were against Dad. One of the politicians brought out a great wad of pound notes and said:

'I have heard too much about that Black Tyger. He is a buffoon. From today I re-name him the Black Rat.'

There were bursts of laughter and guffaws all around. Celebrants laughed themselves into contortions. The politician made the odds very low against Dad. Everyone was excited about the outcome. Sami, sweating, went from group to group, from person to person, jotting down their names and their odds and collecting their money in the bucket. Soon another bucket was needed. All the women, the prostitutes, the low-life courtesans, the casual onlookers, brought out their money. Sami sent for more protection. His entire compound turned up, armed with clubs and dane guns. When he had finished, he was drenched in sweat. He was drenched in the horror of his utter financial ruin, instant and complete liquidation, total poverty and homelessness. He went over to Dad. Pleading reverently, mopping his brow, he said:

'If you win this one you can build a university.'

'A school for beggars,' Dad said, correcting him.

'Whatever you like. Just win, you hear? Or I will be a poor man. My children will starve. My wife will go mad. All my money, all the money I could borrow, all the money I don't even have, is on this, eh. Win!'

Dad pushed him away. The fight began. Dad circled the man in white. Dad rushed him, but the man wasn't there. The blind old man, chuckling, waving a chicken bone, said:

'That is what we call magical boxing, eh.'

I loathed him. Dad went on rushing the man, throwing wide swings, wild flurries of punches which only dazed the green moths and confused the midges, but he couldn't touch the man.

'Don't you want to fight?' he asked in frustration.

The man cracked Dad with a punch so fast that it was only when the women hurled Dad back into the arena that we registered its effect. The man went on striking Dad with electric punches, his fists were so fast that it seemed he was completely still the whole time, while Dad's head kept snapping backwards, as if the air, or an invisible hand, were responsible. His nose became swollen, the bridge broke, blood spurted out. Dad tried hard not to breathe in his own blood. When he breathed it was in excruciation and fatigue. Suddenly, he seemed terrified of pain. The man would move his shoulder slightly and Dad's head would jerk backwards. The man jabbed Dad at will, with cold menacing indifference. I couldn't bear it. The man went on pounding Dad's nose, extending the territories of his bruises, discolouring and generally realigning Dad's face, altering his physiognomy, disintegrating his philosophy, dissolving his reality, dislodging his teeth, and sapping the will from his sturdy legs. Every time Dad took a punch a searing light from another planet shot through my skull. Blinded by the beating Dad was taking I went out, found Ade, and asked him to give me the lizard spell his father had made.

'It doesn't work when the opponent is wearing white,' he said.

'Get away from here!' I screamed at him, and went back in.

Dad was absorbing monstrous punishment. The blind old man kept chuckling. Whenever Dad mounted another futile attack the blind old man would make a curious sound, a dissonant croak, distracting and discouraging Dad. He did this many times. Soon the celebrants took up the dissonant croak as a sort of dampening anthem. I decided to get rid of the old man. I went out and begged Ade to come and help me. We stole back in and, very gently, wheeled the old man's chair out of the tent. In the intense excitement and concentration, no one noticed us. When we got out we wheeled him fast, shouting for people to let us through, saying that the old man was ill. He kept screaming and threatening us with curses. His frenzy only seemed to convince people that they should get out of the way.

'A wizard is carrying me off!' he hollered.

No one believed him. We wheeled him up the road, along paths, deep into the forest, and when we stopped his glasses fell from his face.

'What has happened?' he shouted.

His blind eyes were ugly in the dark. They had a curious light in them.

'I can't see!' he cried, making our flesh crawl.

As we were about to leave he caught Ade's hand and wouldn't let go. I banged him on the head with a stick and he relaxed his grip and protected his head and uttered low cries. Me and Ade fled from him, with the noise of his wail amplified by the forest.

When we got back to the tent the fight was turning. Dad had crossed the desert of his exhaustion, had found new springs and oases of energies. He was covered in sweat and bruises. His head was firmly tucked behind his fists and his shoulders hunched. He had become more rock-like, like one who was thoroughly resigned to taking punishment as a condition of survival. There was something strange about the way he accepted his beating. He didn't seem so afraid of every bone-grinding punch the man threw at him. Dad kept staggering, wobbling, under the man's methodical, scientific combinations. It was astonishing to see that the man still hadn't worked up a sweat. Dad went on wobbling, his legs watery, and I was sure he was pretending. I shouted:

'Black Tyger, dirty his suit!'

All heads turned towards me. The man in white looked in my direction. In the brief moment of his distraction, Dad worked swiftly. He caught the man's collar and with an insane howl ripped the coat. The man tried to protect the suit, but Dad abandoned all known rules of fighting and concentrated on extending the rippage. He grabbed the torn bits of the coat, he spun the man round, and with the help of a foot to the small of the back, tore the coat off the man. Then Dad pursued him and completed the rippage, snatching off bits of white cloth clinging to his arms. Beneath the coat, there was a shirt, and Dad, with terrible persistence, tore off the shirt and tie as well. Beneath the shirt and coat the man was bare-chested and hairy. He had curious tattoos on his stomach and amulets round his neck. He had a hollow chest and a deep hole of a navel. He was so hairy, and his hair was so much like that of a bush animal that the spectators gave a shocked cry when they saw how inhuman he looked. The man began to cower. Dad feinted a punch to his head, the man blocked his face with both hands, and Dad grabbed his trousers, tripped him, and tore the trousers off him. He had long thin legs, the legs of a spiderous animal. His eyes filled with fear and shame at being unmasked. People backed away, gasping in horror. Sami, the betting-shop man, sent the buckets of money home with some of his protectors. The beggar girl began to cheer. The women's mouths hung open.

The man got up, enraged. He had on the weirdest underpants. He rushed Dad and couldn't find him. He rushed again and stunned him with a flurry of solid punches. They slogged it out for ten minutes. Dad kept hitting him, but he wouldn't fall. The man caught Dad with an upper cut and rocked his head.

'Punch his chest, Black Tyger!' Ade screamed.

Dad paid no attention. His exhaustion had returned. He puffed, he weaved, his punches had no power. The man began the long arc of a fearful swinging punch when the wind blew, shaking the tent, and the lights suddenly went out. They came back on again and the man stood disorientated, hand in the air. Dad, calling on his own name, charging his own spirit, released one of the most destructive punches I've ever seen and sent the man flying right through the tent. Tables, plates, and fried meat, crashed around him. Dad stood, weaving, bobbing, waiting. We all waited for the man to get up. He didn't. The prostitutes tried to resuscitate him, but he couldn't move. They couldn't carry him either. We heard them saying something about him being too heavy. His inert form remained outside the tent, in an outer darkness. We never saw him again.

Sami rushed into the middle of the arena and declared Dad the winner of the contest. The inhabitants of the area, who had been outside looking in, surrounded Dad. The beggar girl, me, and Ade kept touching him, wiping the great flow of sweat from his body. Overcome with the horror of his victory, and with fatigue, Dad sank to the ground. We tried to revive him, but we couldn't. No one else came to help us.

While all this was happening the blind old man had found his way from the forest and back into the tent. He was raving about wizards and bony demon children. He ran one way, then another. His helpers tried to restrain him but he threw them off. His rage was frightful.

We tried to get Dad to stand up. He was out cold. The beggar girl got the other beggars to come and help. While we were trying to revive Dad the blind old man kept pursuing me round the tent. No one could control him. I ran under the tables. I threw things at him, but he pressed on, he followed me with nightmarish persistence. I ran back to Dad, tried to wake him, but the old man came at me like a demonic sleepwalker, his hands stretched out in front of him. Then suddenly he turned away from me and with the quick movement of a snake striking an unsuspecting prey, he grabbed hold of Ade and wouldn't let go.

'Ah ha, so it's you, the flying wizard!' he shouted triumphantly.

Ade screamed. I clubbed the old man. His helpers rained knocks on me. I threw bones and sticks at them. Then the old man, tightening his grip on Ade's arm said, in a screeching ugly voice:

'Let me see with your eyes!'

The strangest thing happened. Ade began to twist, to jerk, contorting in spasms. His eyes swam around their sockets till only the whites were visible. He opened his mouth, his tongue hung out, and he gasped, and made choking noises. People tried to free Ade from the old man's grip. I jumped on his back and he shouted.

'Get off my back!'

'Leave my friend alone,' I said.

'You're too heavy, you spirit-child!,' he cried.

I bounced on his back, his bones digging into me. I hooked my arms round his neck and tried to strangle him, but he kept tossing. I attempted to scratch his eyes, but he bit me and threw me off with the strength of five men and I heard his neck creak and was sent flying and when I landed amongst broken tables and the mess of fruits and bean-cakes, everything had cleared. The old man stood, swaying. Ade jerked in a weird epileptic fit. The crowd had mostly gone. Madame Koto was nowhere around. The loud-speakers had been packed away. The prostitutes sat on folding chairs, glaring at us. The old man picked up his yellow glasses and played on his harmonica. His helpers led him away. I got up. The beggars, Sami and his protectors, people from the area, and Helen lifted Dad up on their shoulders as if he were a king fallen in battle and carried him out into the night. I helped Ade up. He stood, twitching, his mouth feverish. His fit had receded and he walked as if his legs were made of rubber. As we left the devastated tent the prostitutes abused us. I heard the blind old man's dissonant harmonica in front of us in the dark. We were at the rear of the procession that bore Dad on their shoulders. He faced the stars. And, as we went the sound of the flapping tent made me look back.

The wind had risen. I realised that the party had blocked the road. The cars were leaving. The trees creaked their limbs. The anti-music of the harmonica faded into the wind, blowing eerie harmonies over the bushes. The wind's counterpoints whistled along the electric cables. The bright yellow and blue bulbs kept going on and off. Then they stayed on. Ade said, in the voice of a cat:

'Something is happening.'

The wind stopped. It swelled again. Then I saw the tent tilt sideways, and lift up in the air. It rose, it turned on its side, and the wind hurled it over the houses, its voluminous cloth flapping, its form billowing, and it blew over, turning on rooftops, and the sky cracked, two lights flashed, and rain swept down. The rain poured down, the earth swam in mud, dogs barked, the smell of burning rubber filled the air, and we heard a brief rending cry from Madame Koto's place. Then all the lights went out.

NINE

THE DARKNESS WAS full of voices. The beggars and Sami carried Dad to the house. When we got to our room Mum was in a frenzy. They laid Dad out on the bed and covered him with a white cloth. The people were gone, but I could hear them singing low heroic melodies down the street. Dad's mouth was twisted. There was a white scar down the side of his face. His eyes had disappeared beneath his bruises. His lips were like swollen flowers. He was in a far worse condition than in all of his fights put together. He didn't move. He didn't even seem to breathe. Mum kept wailing. The beggar girl lit three more candles. Sami sat on Dad's chair. The beggars sat on the floor. I made Ade lie down on my mat. Apart from Mum, everyone was silent.

Mum rushed out, boiled water, came back, and applied warm compresses to Dad's face. It never occurred to her that his bruises needed something cold. The beggar girl stroked his feet. No one else moved. After a while Mum rested. She looked round at all of us.

'Get up from my husband's chair!' she shouted at Sami.

He jumped up as if a snake had bitten him. He stood near the window. Then he came to me and whispered:

'When he has recovered, call me. I have all the money. I will get him the best herbalist.'

Then, as if he had been caught stealing, he crept out of the room.

'And all of you, go!' Mum screamed, at everyone else.

The beggars shuffled. The beggar girl got up, touched me on the head, making my flesh bristle, and led the others out of the room. They left silently. Ade lay down on the mat, his eyes swimming. Occasionally he twitched. He had a wan smile on his lips. I leant over him.

'I am going to die soon,' he said.

'Why do you say that?'

'My time has come. My friends are calling me.'

'What friends?'

'In the other world,' he said.

We were silent.

'And what are you two whispering about, eh?' Mum asked.

'Nothing.'

'What happened to him?'

'He's not well.'

'What about his father?'

'I don't know.'

'God save me,' Mum cried.

The candles went out. Mum shut the door and searched for the matches.

'This life! No rest. None. A woman suffers, a woman sweats, with no rest, no happiness. My husband, in three fights. God knows what all this is doing to his brain. This life is too much for me. I am going to hang myself one of these days,' Mum said.

'Don't do that, Mum,' I said.

'Shut up,' she said.

I was silent. Deep in me old songs began to stir. Old voices from the world of spirits. Songs of seductive purity, with music perfect like light and diamonds. Ade twitched. The floor began to shake. I could hear his bones rattling. Mum lit a candle. She sat on Dad's chair, rocking back and forth, her eyes fixed, her face unforgiving. I felt sad. Ade smiled strangely again, sinking deeper into his weird epileptic ecstasy. I leant over him.

'Trouble is always coming. Maybe it's just as well,' he said. 'Your story has just begun. Mine is ending. I want to go to my other home. Your mother is right; there is too much unnecessary suffering on this earth.'

His voice had taken on the timbre of an old man. Soon I recognised it. A snake went up my spine and I couldn't stop shivering. He went on, speaking in the cracked sepulchral voice of the blind old man.

'My time is coming. I have worn out my mother's womb and now she can't have any more children. Coming and going, I have seen the world, I have seen the future. The Koran says nothing is ever finished.'

'What will happen?' I asked him.

Quivering, biting his lips till he drew blood, he said:

'There will be the rebirth of a father. A man with seven heads

477

will take you away. You will come back. You will stay. Before that the spirits and our ancestors will hold a great meeting to discuss the future of the world. It will be one of the most important meetings ever held. Suffering is coming. There will be wars and famine. Terrible things will happen. New diseases, hunger, the rich eating up the earth, people poisoning the sky and the waters, people going mad in the name of history, the clouds will breathe fire, the spirit of things will dry up, laughter will become strange.'

He stopped. There was a long pause. Then he continued, frightening me.

'There will be changes. Coups. Soldiers everywhere. Ugliness. Blindness. And then when people least expect it a great transformation is going to take place in the world. Suffering people will know justice and beauty. A wonderful change is coming from far away and people will realise the great meaning of struggle and hope. There will be peace. Then people will forget. Then it will all start again, getting worse, getting better. Don't fear. You will always have something to struggle for, even if it is beauty or joy.'

He stopped again. And then his fever changed gear, his voice quivered, his eyes were calm.

'Our country is an abiku country. Like the spirit-child, it keeps coming and going. One day it will decide to remain. It will become strong. I won't see it.'

His voice changed, became more natural, almost gentle.

'I see the image of two thousand years. I drank in its words. It took many centuries to grow in me. I see a great musician in a land across the seas. Nine hundred years ago. The musician was me. I see a priest, I see a ruler of gentle people. The priest was me, the ruler was me. I see a wicked warrior who killed many innocent people and who delighted in bloodshed. I was him. There was once a soldier stoned to death and fed to the crocodiles in Egypt. I was that soldier.'

'You're talking nonsense,' I said.

He laughed, coughed, and went on talking. His voice got lower and lower. His mouth moved, but I couldn't hear him any more. His limbs went into spasms. I smelt burning wood. Smoke gathered round his hair. For a moment I thought his fit was burning him up. I touched him. His forehead was cold. His eyes were open, but he didn't see me. I looked up and saw that Mum had fallen asleep on Dad's chair. I lay down, shut my eyes, and sleep came to me in the form of green moths. I followed them into Mum's dreams. It came as a shock to me to find myself in her dreams. She was a young woman, fresh and beautiful, with a white bird on her shoulder. She had antimony on her face, magic charms round her neck, and a pearl on a string round her left ankle. She was wandering through a sepia-tinted village, looking for Dad. She saw him up a tree. She climbed the tree, but Dad jumped down and ran to the river. Mum came down from the tree and sang a song from her childhood, serenading Dad's spirit. She sang to Dad, asking him not to go away, begging him to return, in the name of love. The river turned a brilliant green colour and the maiden of the water, green, with sad eyes and lovely breasts, with the face of Helen the beggar girl, embraced Dad and took him down to the bottom of the river where there was an emerald palace. Eagles drank wine from silver goblets. Swans told stories beneath the great silk cotton tree. A black tiger with a prince's crown and the eyes of my grandfather roamed the city precincts, reciting verses from ancient epics, sacred texts that could alter the nature of things. The maiden took Dad to her palace and washed his feet. In the great hall the frozen figures of warriors followed Dad with their fearless eyes. Antelopes with flowers round their necks came and sat at Dad's feet. The maiden changed Dad's clothes and dressed him in rich aquamarine robes. Then a mighty lion roared from the secret chambers. All the statues in the hall began to move. The warriors woke from their enchantment and marched into the secret chambers. The statues were beautiful. Their masks were beautiful. The statues had strange human faces, some had large pricks, some had wonderfully rounded breasts with proud nipples, and many of them had the paws of the Sphinx. Masquerades danced into the hall and presented Dad with gifts. Then Dad was led outside where a car was waiting for him. Dad got into the car. Mum stood at the river-bank, preparing to jump in when I touched her. She was angry and said:

'Get out of my dream. I'm trying to draw back your father's spirit.'

I didn't know how to leave. The sun burned down on us and the white bird on Mum's shoulder flew into the water and Mum disappeared and it grew so hot that my hair became singed, the trees burst into flame, giving off a bright yellow smoke. Butterflies multiplied everywhere, they came from the sun, and they flew round my face, filling me with vertigo and as I coughed they flew into my mouth and I sat up and saw that our room was filled with smoke and when I shouted and choked Ade smiled oddly in his jerking sleep and Mum jumped up and said:

'Azaro, get up! The candle is burning our table!'

I recovered quickly and fetched water from our bucket and poured it on the table. Ade sat up and smiled at me.

'I'm well now,' he said.

Mum whipped the table with a wet rag, as if it had annoyed her. When the flame had been put out she came and sat on the bed and held my face between her hot palms and said:

'My son, what were you doing in my dream?'

I said nothing.

'Answer me,' she said.

'It wasn't your dream. It was Dad's dream.'

Mum sat up. I couldn't see her face in the darkness. Her sadness made the night quiver.

'Your father got into the car and went to the village. Your grandfather treated his wounds and soothed his spirit. Then he travelled to Ughelli to buy the perfume that would get rid of the bad smell of poverty. Then he went to the moon. Then he travelled to the land of spirits far away. Many lands. I heard his voice crying out in the sky. They refused him entry to heaven. They sent him past hell, past spirit lands where our ancestors ask one another impenetrable riddles all day long. He came to a country full of palaces, a country of dreams, where the people are invisible, where wisdom and joy are in the air. He went to the law courts of the spirit worlds. I heard him crying for answers. Then he came back and a war broke out and they shot him on the road that he had built.'

I didn't know what to say.

'So lie down and sleep. This is a strong night. I must protect your father's spirit or it will go away.'

I lay down.

'Your father is playing a flute,' Ade said in his own voice. 'It is sweet music. I didn't know he could play so well.'

Then the room was silent. Sleep stole over me and I resisted it. Mum ground her teeth on the bed, struggling with Dad. Ade began to quiver again.

'I'm going slowly,' he said.

'Shut up,' I said.

Mum was still. I heard her snoring. Sleep came to me in the form of white birds and I saw Mum fighting Dad in his dreams, trying to get him to gatecrash his body. Ade lay next to me, twitching through the night in his fits. And his spirit, swirling and turbulent with blinding energies, began to affect mine. We swirled in the sweet savage torrent of his epilepsy and travelled the red roads of the spirits and arrived at the Village of Night, where birds were laying out electric cables, where Masquerades were alchemists, where the sunbird was priest, where the moonprince was a foundling, and where the tortoise was a wandering griot who warned me at the roadside that no story could ever be finished. As dawn approached the Village disappeared and I heard the songs of my spirit companions. In flames, the great king of the spirit world flashed past my eyes. The mountain heaved. I saw a black cat at my feet and I fed it bean-cakes. Ade lay quiet beside me. His past lives had begun to conquer him. I saw that he had not told me the whole truth. I saw his other images. I saw a murderer in Rome, a poetess in Spain, a falconer among the Aztecs, a whore in Sudan, a priestess in old Kenya, a one-eyed white ship captain who believed in God and wrote beautiful hymns and who made his fortune capturing slaves in the Gold Coast. I even saw a famed samurai warrior in ancient Japan, and a mother of ten in Greece.

Then, in the middle of the night, when I was still amongst the images, a mighty cry woke us up. I looked and in the darkness I saw Dad's face. Then it vanished.

'What did he say?' Mum asked.

'I don't know.'

'You didn't hear?'

'No.'

'I did,' Ade said in the dark.

'What did he say?'

'He said: "OPEN THE DOOR."'

Mum rushed from the bed, tripped over my foot, and hit her head against something. She didn't cry out. She opened the door and went back to the bed. Mosquitoes and night-moths came in. We slept but Mum got up and woke us, saying:

'No one must sleep. We must bring back your father's spirit.'

TEN

WE SAT STILL. The wind blew in leaves. The air smelled of the forest and the sleeping ghetto. Strange dreams, floating on the wind, looking for dreamers, drifted into our room.

'Tell us a story,' I said.

Ade sat up. His limbs were peaceful.

'Tell us the story of the blue sunglasses.'

'Okay.'

We waited. Mum went and sat on Dad's chair. She rocked back and forth. I saw Dad's spirit hovering round her. Then it entered her and I heard Mum shiver. She got some ogogoro, made a prayer and a libation, and we drank. As if Dad's personality were taking her over, she lit a mosquito coil and a candle. Then she lit a cigarette. She rocked back and forth in Dad's restless manner of a great lion in a man's body. Her face serious, her features altered, she began to speak.

'One day I was selling my provisions. I went from street to street. The sun was very hot, there was no shelter in the sky or anywhere. I was tired. I began to see things. I began to complain, weeping about how hard this world is. Then I came to a crossroad. I saw a tortoise crawling out of the bushes and crossing the road and I was about to pick it up when it spoke to me.'

'What did it say?' I asked.

'On another day I was hawking things in the city when a white man came to me. He had on the blue sunglasses. It was very hot. The sun and the dust made my eyes red. The white man said: "If you tell me how to get out of Africa I will give you my sunglasses."'

'And what did you say?'

'I said, "There are many roads into Africa but only one road leads out." He said: "What road?" I said: "First tell me what the tortoise told me." He was confused. "I don't know what you are talking about," he said. So I told him that I wouldn't show him the only road out of Africa. Then he told me his story. He had been here for ten years. For seven of those years he was an important man in the government. Then all the Independence trouble started and for three years he tried to leave but kept failing. He couldn't find a way out. Every time he prepared to leave something came along and prevented him. He even got on a plane but the plane went round the world and when he got out he found himself here, in the same place.'

'So what happened?'

'So I made him buy all my provisions. Then I asked him to tell me what the tortoise said. He stopped and thought for a long time. Then a bus went past slowly. It had a motto written on its side. The white man laughed at the motto and read it out and I said that's what the tortoise told me. "What?" he asked. "All things are linked," I said. "What has the tortoise got to do with it?" he asked. I said: "If you don't know you will never find any road at all." Then he gave me the blue sunglasses and before he left he said: "The only way to get out of Africa is to get Africa out of you."'

'Then what happened?'

'On another day I was selling fish in the market. A strange Yoruba man came to me and bought all my fishes. When his hands touched them they all came alive and began to twist in my basin. I threw the fishes on the floor and they wriggled and I started to run away, but the man held my hands. "Don't you remember me?" he asked. He was a black man but he was familiar in an odd sort of way. "I gave you the blue sunglasses," he said. Then I remembered him. But it took some time, and I first had to turn and twist my mind around. He was the white man. His face and his nose and everything was exactly the same except that now he was a Yoruba man with fine marks on his face. "I met you five hundred years ago," he said. "I discovered the road." "What was it?" I asked. Then he told me his story. "When I left you," he began, "I became feverish in the head and later in a fit of fury over a small thing I killed my African servant. They arrested me. I sat in a cell. Then they released me because I was a white man. Then I began to wander about the city naked. Everyone stared at me. They were shocked to see a mad white man in Africa. Then a strange little African child took to following me around. He was my only friend. All my white colleagues had deserted me. Then one day my head cleared. Five hundred years had gone past. The only way to get out of Africa was to become an African. So I changed my thinking. I changed my ways. I got on a plane and arrived in England. I got married, had two children, and retired from government service. I was in the Secret Service. Then before I turned seventy I had a heart attack and died. They buried me in my local parish cemetery with full national honours." "So what are you doing here?" I asked him. I was afraid now. I was very scared. He said: "Time passed. I was born. I became a businessman. And I came to the market today to buy some eels and I saw you." I said: "But I only met you two weeks ago." "Time is not what you think it is," he said, smiling. Then he left. That is the end of my story.'

There was a long silence.

'Strange story,' I said.

'It's true,' Mum replied.

The wind blew the floating dreams into our room. The yellow light of the candle fluttered. The candle had burned low. I felt I was in another place, a country of white fields.

'Look!' Ade said.

The wind had blown the dawn into our room. At the door, sitting on its tail, was a black cat. We stared at the cat in silence. It stared at us.

'The world is just beginning,' Mum said.

The cat turned and went back out of the door. We all got up and followed the cat. Sitting outside our door, her wounds still livid, was Helen, the beggar girl. We stared at her in puzzlement. Then she got up and went to the housefront. We didn't follow her. When we went back into the room Dad was sitting up on the bed like Lazarus.

'KEEP THE ROAD OPEN,' he said, and fell back into sleep.

We touched him and he didn't move. Mum was happy. Ade kept smiling. Mum was happy because Dad had begun to snore. Ade kept smiling because he could hear his father's weary footsteps, as he made his long journeys, like an ancient hero searching for his son. Ade heard his father's footsteps, heard the anxious hypertensive beat of his heart, and was following him through his guilt and confusion, as he made his way to our house. But Ade also smiled because his father had been delayed getting to our place by a funeral cortège. It was not a big procession, and there were only a few mourners at that hour, all of them prostitutes, except for Madame Koto, who wore dark glasses and a black silk gown, and who was thinking about the money she could make from the fabulous political rally rather than about the prostitute whose body lay charred in the cheap wooden coffin and who had died from electrocution after the wind blew the tent away.

ELEVEN

THE FIRST THING that woke us in the morning was wailing from the road. Someone knocked on our door and when I shouted for them to come in we saw Ade's father. He was very tall, his head was bowed, and his face bore the misery of a night-long vigil.

Ade got up instantly and rubbed his eyes. They were bulbous and inflamed. He had grown paler and more beautiful overnight. His smile had gone. When he saw his father at the door he didn't move or render a traditional greeting.

'How many times can a man be reborn in one miserable life?' his father asked the room at large.

Mum was not on the bed. There was food for us on the table. She had left before we woke and her hawker's basin was not on the cupboard. Dad was still asleep on the bed, his big legs sprawled apart, his arm dangling over the side.

Ade's father looked terrifying.

'Where have you been all night, eh?' he asked his son. 'Why didn't you come home? Your mother is almost ill with worrying about you.'

A dark glow surrounded him. He came into the room. Ade retreated to the window. His father sat on the bed. I could smell the frustration and the anxieties in his night-long sweat. His spirit had the potent odours of one who has been making ritual offerings, talking to his ancestors, trying to communicate with the gods. His spirit was charged and deep. He filled the room with terror. Ade, standing at the window, seemed radiant with the glow of his father's temper. He did not appear repentant or even rebellious. He held his head firm, and his face had the impassivity of one who knew that his father could no longer dare to beat him or make him cry. There was something cruel about my friend's spirit and I understood why spirit-children are so feared. Faced always with the songs and fragrances of another world, a world beyond death, where the air is illuminated, where spirit companions know the secrets of one's desire, and can fulfil those desires, every single one of them, spirit-children do not care much for the limited things of the world. Ade did not want to stay any more, he did not like the weight of the world, the terror of the earth's time. Love and the anguish of parents touched him only faintly, for beyond their stares and threats and beatings he knew that his parents' guardianship was temporary. He always had a greater home.

I never knew how different we both were till that morning when his father began his long tirade, his complaints, all designed to make his son feel guilty. Ade, his head held lightly, with his eyes fixed on ghosts, simply left the window and went out of the room as if he were sleepwalking. His father followed him, caught between anger and despair. I followed his father. The world was old that morning. Out in the street his father caught him and lifted him up and Ade began to cry unbearably as all the murky lights from the ghetto and the filthy untarred road and the broken-down houses and the ulcerous poverty converged on him. His father tried to console him, threw him up towards the sky and caught him again. But Ade only cried more and in that sound I knew he wasn't crying because of his father's love, or his own guilt, or his mother's illness, but because the pressure of time was tightening round his neck.

TWELVE

THE SPIRIT-CHILD is an unwilling adventurer into chaos and sunlight, into the dreams of the living and the dead. Things that are not ready, not willing to be born or to become, things for which adequate preparations have not been made to sustain their momentous births, things that are not resolved, things bound up with failure and with fear of being, they all keep recurring, keep coming back, and in themselves partake of the spirit-child's condition. They keep coming and going till their time is right. History itself fully demonstrates how things of the world partake of the condition of the spirit-child.

There are many who are of this condition and do not know it. There are many nations, civilisations, ideas, half-discoveries, revolutions, loves, art forms, experiments, and historical events that are of this condition and do not know it. There are many people too. They do not all have the marks of their recurrence. Often they seem normal. Often they are perceived of as new. Often they are serene with the familiarity of death's embrace. They all carry strange gifts in their souls. They are all part-time dwellers in their own secret moonlight. They all yearn to make of themselves a beautiful sacrifice, a difficult sacrifice, to bring transformation, and to die shedding light within this life, setting the matter ready for their true beginnings to cry into being, scorched by the strange ecstasy of the will ascending to say yes to destiny and illumination.

I was a spirit-child rebelling against the spirits, wanting to live the earth's life and contradictions. Ade wanted to leave, to become a spirit again, free in the captivity of freedom. I wanted the liberty of limitations, to have to find or create new roads from this one which is so hungry, this road of our refusal to be. I was not necessarily the stronger one; it may be easier to live with the earth's boundaries than to be free in infinity.

Given the fact of the immortality of spirits, could these be the reason why I wanted to be born – these paradoxes of things, the eternal changes, the riddle of living while one is alive, the mystery of being, of births within births, death within births, births within dying, the challenge of giving birth to one's true self, to one's new spirit, till the conditions are right for the new immutable star within one's universe to come into existence; the challenge to grow and learn and love, to master one's self; the possibilities of a new pact with one's spirit; the probability that no injustice lasts for ever, no love ever dies, that no light is ever really extinguished, that no true road is ever complete, that no way is ever definitive, no truth ever final, and that there are never really any beginnings or endings? It may be that, in the land of origins, when many of us were birds, even all these reasons had nothing to do with why I wanted to live.

Anything is possible, one way or another. There are many riddles amongst us that neither the living nor the dead can answer.

SECTION THREE

Book Eight

ONE

DURING THE THREE days that Dad stayed in recuperating, the road had the first of its wave of nightmares. The
road's sleep was disturbed first by the prostitute who had been
electrocuted on the night of Madame Koto's initiation into higher
powers. They held a small funeral for her. They carried her coffin up
the road and at night we heard the wailing of some of the prostitutes.
The next day it rained and three men who were laying out cables for
the big political rally also died of electrocution. The rains were crazy
in those days. The beggars suffered the onslaught, sleeping under the
eaves of our compound-front. Every morning Helen would come to
our door. Mum left her food which she didn't touch. Every morning
Mum went out with her basin of provisions and the rain drenched
everything and she came home in the afternoons soaking wet, no
profits made, her provisions rendered useless.

Dad slept like a giant through the new season. He missed the
big trucks of the political parties as they went round the city,
making announcements over their loudspeakers. He missed their
violent confrontations, the eruptions, when they met on the same
street. He missed the beggars who stayed on our road, begging alms
round the broken vehicle. In the evenings I watched them conferring
energetically amongst themselves. They seemed to be waiting for a
sign, so palpable was their expectancy. No one gave them alms. The
inhabitants of the area never missed an opportunity to tell them to
move on. They themselves seemed anxious to move on, to travel the
roads to a new destination. It was only Helen who held them back.
She never spoke, but around her was concentrated the initiative to
set off for new places. It was odd to see them trying to continue
with Dad's attempts to make them useful. Every now and then they
would try to clear up the accumulated garbage on the road. They
tried in their clumsy way to be of help. No one appreciated it. I
passed them on the second day of Dad's sleep and I heard them arguing

in harsh voices about the endlessly postponed forthcoming rally, about the school Dad was going to build for them, and about money. When they saw me they would brighten up, and their faces would lift with hope. They would come towards me, stop, and watch my movements with hungry eyes. I took to stealing food from the house for them. Dad's sleep made us very hungry. Mum made no money. Our meals got smaller. We would eat quietly, watching Dad snoring on the bed as he devoured the air in the room, his spirit growing larger all the time, feeding on our hunger. He grew in his sleep. I watched as his feet began to dangle over the edge of the bed. I saw his chest expanding, bursting his shirt. He gained weight; and when he tossed, as if riding mythical horses in his dreams, the bed would groan. He slept deeply, darkening the room. The candles burned low while he slept. The door was kept open. Visitors would come in, talk in whispers over his sleeping form, and depart on tiptoes.

Dad was redreaming the world as he slept. He saw the scheme of things and didn't like it. He saw the world in which black people always suffered and he didn't like it. He saw a world in which human beings suffered so needlessly from Antipodes to Equator, and he didn't like it either. He saw our people drowning in poverty, in famine, drought, in divisiveness and the blood of war. He saw our people always preyed upon by other powers, manipulated by the Western world, our history and achievements rigged out of existence. He saw the rich of our country, he saw the array of our politicians, how corruptible they were, how blind to our future, how greedy they became, how deaf to the cries of the people, how stony their hearts were, how short-sighted their dreams of power. He saw the divisions in our society, the lack of unity, he saw the widening pit between those who have and those who don't, he saw it all very clearly. He saw the women of the country, of the markets and villages, always dogged by incubi and butterflies; he saw all the women, inheritors of the miracle of forbearance. He saw the hungry eating toads. He saw the wars in advance. He saw the economic boom in advance, saw its orgiastic squander, the suffering to follow, the exile to strange lands, the depleting of the people's will for transformation. He saw the emergence of tyrants who always seem to be born from the extremities of crisis. He saw their long rule and the chaos when they are overthrown. He argued in three great courts of the spirit world, calling for justice on the planet. He argued with fantastic passion and his case was sound but he was alone. He didn't see the mighty multitudes all over the world in their lonely solidarities, pleading cases in the supreme courts of spirits, pleading for justice and balance and beauty in the world, for an end to famishment and vile wars, destruction and greed. Dad was alone because he didn't see the others, the multitudes of dream-pleaders, invading all the courts of the universe, while struggling in the real hard world created by the limitations in the minds of human beings. I followed Dad sometimes in his cyclical dreams. I followed him in his escape into the great realms and spaces, the landscapes of genius, the worlds before birth, the worlds of pure dreams and signs. I followed him sometimes in his brief reunion with his own primeval spirit and totem, in his fleeting contact with glimmerings of his true destiny. I saw angels erasing some of the memories of his journeys. He travelled far and his spirit ached and as he sweated in our room, dampening the bed, it poured with rain outside and the floods rearranged the houses of the road. The rains were sporadic. Frogs and bugs and diseases roamed in our lives and children died in the mornings when the politicians on their trucks announced the dawn of our new independent destiny. Dad saw the advancing forms of chaos and fought them alone in his sleep, his body swelling with rage, and the forms overcame him and washed over his life and when he tossed and turned Mum would light a mosquito coil, a stick of incense, and a candle, and pour some ogogoro for us and would pray at the door lintels. Mum prayed in three languages. She prayed to our ancestors, she prayed to God, and she prayed to the angel of all women. Mum prayed for simple things that made me weep while the darkness flowered in our room. She prayed for food. She prayed for Dad to get well. She prayed for a good place to live. She prayed for more life and for suffering to bear lovely fruits. And she prayed for me. For three days Mum prayed on borrowed wine. The spaces in our lives grew smaller. Mum grew leaner. Her voice began to disappear. Her eyes hid from the world, retreating into the depths of her head's dreaming. Her bones became more visible. Her blouses began to slip from her shoulders. Waves of demented mist passed over her face. I would catch her staring at Dad's empty three-legged chair. Her eyes seemed to be looking over the photographs of her life. Always the strained smile of the hunger beneath the brave pride. Always the rats and cockroaches eating away at our dreams. Always the world seems to find a method to prevent her working her way out from the corners. Always the landlords increasing our rents, the thugs telling us who to vote for, the rain leaking into our sleep. Sometimes her prayers would find Dad as he roamed the spheres that restored the balances of the earth. But Dad's spirit was restless for justice and more life and genuine revolution and he kept ranging farther out into other worlds where the promises of power were made before birth. And Dad travelled the spheres, seeking the restoration of our race, and the restoration of all oppressed peoples. It was as I followed Dad that I learnt that other spheres of higher energies have their justice beyond our understanding. And our sphere too. The forces of balance are turning every day. The rain lashes the bloated and the weak, the powerful and the silenced. The wind exposes the hungry, the overfed, the ill, the dying, and those who feed on the unseen suffering of others. But the restorations are slow because our perception of time is long. Time and truth always come round; those who seem to hold sway and try to prevent the turning of justice only bring it quicker; and Dad wanted the turning now. He wanted justice now. He wanted truth now. He wanted world balance now. He raised the storms of demands in his dreams. He raised impenetrable questions. He kept asking: WHY? After eons he asked: WHAT MUST WE DO? And then he asked: HOW DO WE BRING IT ABOUT? Pressing on, he wanted to know: WHEN? Relentlessly, twisting and turning, he demanded: WHAT IS THE BEST WAY? And with a bit more serenity, not drawing back from the inevitable self-confrontation, he asked: WHAT IS THE FIRST STEP? His body grew. Flowers fell on our rooftop. My grandfather appeared to me briefly, waving me on. A child was born and didn't get to its body. Was I being reborn in my father? In his journeys Dad found that all nations are children; it shocked him that ours too was an abiku nation, a spirit-child nation, one that keeps being reborn and after each birth come blood and betrayals, and the child of our will refuses to stay till we have made propitious sacrifice and displayed our serious intent to bear the weight of a unique destiny.

Each life flows to all the spheres; and as Dad slept he lived out a whole lifetime in another continent, while we listened to the rumours of Madame Koto's meetings with powerful women in her bar, meetings in which they planned the numerous arrangements for the rally and the responsibilities of organising votes for their party. It didn't surprise us that she had recovered so quickly from the death of the prostitute. It didn't surprise us either that she had been allocated vast sums of money to organise the women from our part of the city. Her bad foot grew larger as if the road had impregnated it; her stomach bloated with its abiku trinity. She was initiated into another secret society that was famous for its manufacturing of reality. She talked about turning her bar into a hotel. She bought great plots of land. Her driver went up and down our road in her car, knocking over goats and killing chickens, multiplying her enemies.

Madame Koto grew more powerful with the rainy season. She developed a walk of imposing and languid dignity. Her fatness became her. She wore clothes that made the beggars ill. She talked of leaving the wretched area; she was scornful of everyone. We listened to her berating passers-by. She grew more powerful and she grew more beautiful as well. The rainy season swelled her frame. She incarnated all her legends into her new spirit, joined with her myths. She became all the things we whispered she was and she became more. At night, when she slept, she stole the people's energies. (She was not the only one: they were legion.) The night became her ally. While Dad ranged the spheres crying for justice, Madame Koto sucked in the powers of our area. Her dreams gave the children nightmares. Her colossal form took wings at night and flew over the city, drawing power from our sleeping bodies. She expanded over the air of our existence. Her dreams were livid rashes of parties and orgies, of squander and sprees, of corruption and disintegration, of innocent women and weak men. Her snoring altered the geography of our destinies. Slowly, while the people of the area grew weaker, more accepting, more afraid, she grew stronger. That was when I understood that conflicting forces were fighting for the future of our country in the air, at night, in our dreams, riding invisible white horses and whipping us, sapping our will while we slept.

The political parties waged their battles in the spirit spaces, beyond the realm of our earthly worries. They fought and hurled counter-mythologies at one another. Herbalists, sorcerers, wizards and witches took sides and as the trucks fought for votes in the streets they fought for supremacy in the world of spirits. They called on djinns and chimeras, succubi, incubi and apparitions; they enlisted the ghosts of old warriors and politicians and strategists; they hired expatriate spirits. The Party of the Rich drew support from the spirits of the Western world. At night, over our dreams, pacts were made, contracts drawn up in that realm of nightspace, and our futures were mortgaged, our destinies delayed. In that realm the sorcerers of party politics unleashed thunder, rain flooded those below; counter-thunder, lightning and hail were returned. On and on it went, in every village, every city of the country, and all over the continent and the whole world too. Our dreams grew smaller as they waged their wars of political supremacy. Sorcerers, taking the form of spirits and omens, whispered to us of dread. We grew more afraid. Suspicion made it easier for us to be silent. Silence made it easier for us to be more powerless. The forms of dominance grew more colossal in the nightspaces. And those of us who were poor, who had no great powers on our side, and who didn't see the power of our own hunger, a power that would frighten even the gods, found that our dreams became locked out of the freedom of the air. Our yearnings became blocked out of the realms of manifestation. The battles for our destiny raged and we could no longer fly to the moon or accompany the aeroplanes on their journeys through rarefied spaces or imagine how our lives could be different and better. So we had bad dreams about one another while Madame Koto, dressed in red, her hair covered with a white kerchief, three green umbrellas in her hand, extended her powers over the ghetto and sent her secret emissaries into our bodies. Our fantasies fed her. Many of us dreamt of her as a future spirit-bride to heads of state and presidents. She became known as the Queen of the Ghetto Night. Anyone who wanted help went to her. She received only a few callers. Because she expanded so much at night, she suffered untold agonies in her body during the day. She showed no signs of pain. But the sweat on her forehead widened her wrinkles. Her prostitutes deserted her; they couldn't forgive her for so quickly forgetting the girl's death. When they left, the emptiness of her bar and the magnetism of her new powers drew a greater flock.

One night she appeared to me in my sleep and begged me to give her some of my youth.

'Why?' I asked.

And she replied:

'I am two hundred years old and unless I get your young blood I will die soon.'

Her enormous spirit lowered over me. Her spirit was about to swallow me up completely, when a great lion roared from above, quaking the house, and driving her spirit away. Then I realised that new forces were being born to match the demands of the age. Leopards and lions of the spirit world, dragons of justice, winged tigers of truth, fierce animals of the divine, forces that swirl in the midst of inexorable hurricanes, they too restore balances and feed on the chimeras and vile intentions of the open air; and with every monstrous breath exhaled, for every blast of wind from evil wings, and for every power on the sides of those that feed on the earth's blood, a fabulous angel is born; and I saw an angel flying over our roof on the third day of Dad's sleep. It went past and the wind quietened and strange trees cracked in the forest and in the morning the rain stopped, the floods of water sank mysteriously into the secrets of the absorbent earth. Mum went up and down the streets hawking and sold off all her provisions and she kept finding pound notes floating on the dazzling waters and it seemed that the air had been cleared. But that morning I saw the first intimations; they were not intimations of a new season of calm, but of a cycle coming to an end. And how was I to know that it would be the beggars who would represent the first sign, with their expectancy, their air of people awaiting the word of a Messiah's birth, when in fact all they were waiting for was an omen to inform them that the time for their departure had arrived.

For in the evenings, as Mum prepared food, the fevers of the rally and its whispers of a long curfew were gathering. Then one evening, under the spell of incense and prayers and mosquito-coil smoke, under the holes of our roof, with the multiplied bugs on the floor, and with the room invaded by the green moths that understood the transformative properties of fire, offering themselves as willing sacrificial victims, Dad woke suddenly, he awoke powerfully, he rose from the bed as from death. His wounds had healed, his spirit had sharpened, his despair was deeper, he was a bigger man with a bigger madness. He got up and sat on his chair. And while the candles fluttered and burned brighter for the air that his sleep no longer deprived them of, Dad with his new deep sad voice began to speak to us. He spoke as if he hadn't been away. He spoke as if he hadn't made great journeys in spirit. And he spoke with the great enthusiastic innocence of a recuperating man.

'My wife and my son, listen to me. In my sleep I saw many wonderful things. Our ancestors taught me many philosophies. My father, Priest of Roads, appeared to me and said I should keep my door open. My heart must be open. My life must be open. Our road must be open. A road that is open is never hungry. Strange times are coming.'

'What about thieves?' I asked.

'Shut up, Azaro. We are protected, you hear. We are fortified against invaders and wicked people. Nothing evil will enter our lives.'

He paused, creaked his bones, and continued.

'A single thought of ours could change the universe. We human beings are small things. Life is a great thing. As I am talking now they are holding elections in heaven and under the

497

sea. We have entered a new age. We must be prepared. There are strange bombs in the world. Great powers in space are fighting to control our destiny. Machines and poisons and selfish dreams will eat us up. I entered a space ship and found myself on another planet. People who look like human beings are not human beings. Strange people are amongst us. We must be careful. Our lives are changing. Our gods are silent. Our ancestors are silent. A great something is going to come from the sky and change the face of the earth. We must take an interest in politics. We must become spies on behalf of justice. Human beings are dreaming of wiping out their fellow human beings from this earth. Rats and frogs understand their destiny. Why not man, eh? My wife, my son, where are we going? There is no rest for the soul. God is hungry for us to grow. When you look around and you see empty spaces, beware. In those spaces are cities, invisible civilisations, future histories, everything is HERE. We must look at the world with new eyes. We must look at ourselves differently. We are freer than we think. We haven't begun to live yet. The man whose light has come on in his head, in his dormant sun, can never be kept down or defeated. We can redream this world and make the dream real. Human beings are gods hidden from themselves. My son, our hunger can change the world, make it better, sweeter. People who use only their eyes do not SEE. People who use only their ears do not HEAR. It is more difficult to love than to die. It is not death that human beings are most afraid of, it is love. The heart is bigger than a mountain. One human life is deeper than the ocean. Strange fishes and sea-monsters and mighty plants live in the rock-bed of our spirits. The whole of human history is an undiscovered continent deep in our souls. There are dolphins, plants that dream, magic birds inside us. The sky is inside us. The earth is in us. The trees of the forest, the animals of the bushes, tortoises, birds, and flowers know our future. The world that we see and the world that is there are two different things. Wars are not fought on battlegrounds but in a space smaller than the head of a needle. We need a new language to talk to one another. Inside a cat there are many histories, many books. When you look into the eyes of dogs strange fishes swim in your mind. All roads lead to death, but some roads lead to things which can never be finished. Wonderful things. There are human beings who are small but if you can SEE you will notice that their spirits are ten thousand feet wide. In my dream I met a child sitting on a cloud and his spirit covered half the earth. Angels and demons are amongst us; they take many forms. They can enter us and dwell